# All That I Ask

**Also by Jane McBride Choate in Large Print:**

Badge of Love
The Courtship of Katie McGuire
Love and Lies
Love by the Book
A Match Made in Heaven
Mustang Summer
Think of Me
Trust Me
Design to Deceive
Sweet Lies and Rainbow Skies

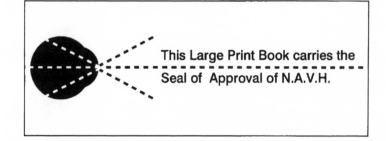

This Large Print Book carries the
Seal of Approval of N.A.V.H.

# *All That I Ask*

## Jane McBride Choate

**Thorndike Press • Waterville, Maine**

Published in 2005 by arrangement with Jane McBride Choate.

Thorndike Press® Large Print Candlelight.      LT
                                               Fic
                                               C

The tree indicium is a trademark of Thorndike Press.

The text of this Large Print edition is unabridged.
Other aspects of the book may vary from the original edition.

Set in 16 pt. Plantin by Ramona Watson.

Printed in the United States on permanent paper.

*12/05*

*Gale Gp.*
*24.95*

**Library of Congress Cataloging-in-Publication Data**

Choate, Jane McBride.
    All that I ask / by Jane McBride Choate. — Large print ed.
      p. cm. — (Thorndike Press large print candlelight)
    Originally published: New York : Avalon, 1996.
    ISBN 0-7862-8134-0 (lg. print : hc : alk. paper)
    1. Large type books.   I. Title.   II. Thorndike Press large
print Candlelight series.
PS3553.H575A79 2005
  813'.54—dc22                             2005022107

To Larry, my biggest fan

— Thanks

As the Founder/CEO of NAVH, the only national health agency solely devoted to those who, although not totally blind, have an eye disease which could lead to serious visual impairment, I am pleased to recognize Thorndike Press* as one of the leading publishers in the large print field.

Founded in 1954 in San Francisco to prepare large print textbooks for partially seeing children, NAVH became the pioneer and standard setting agency in the preparation of large type.

Today, those publishers who meet our standards carry the prestigious "Seal of Approval" indicating high quality large print. We are delighted that Thorndike Press is one of the publishers whose titles meet these standards. We are also pleased to recognize the significant contribution Thorndike Press is making in this important and growing field.

Lorraine H. Marchi, L.H.D.
Founder/CEO
NAVH

* Thorndike Press encompasses the following imprints: Thorndike, Wheeler, Walker and Large Print Press.

# Prologue

Shannon awoke to the sound of crying. A child weeping. Was there any sound more heart wrenching than a child's cries?

She hurried to Josh's bedroom, comforting, soothing.

"It's all right, sweetheart," she murmured. "I'm here."

"Mommy. I want Mommy."

Her own tears treacherously near, she forced them back and rocked her nephew back and forth. "Mommy's not here anymore. Remember how we talked about it? Mommy went to heaven."

"Is she with Grandma Howard?"

"That's right. She's with Grandma. I'll bet she's really happy to see Grandma. Remember how Mommy hurt when she was here? In heaven she won't hurt anymore."

Shannon managed to say the words calmly enough, though she winced at the inadequacy of them.

*Hurt.* A weak word to describe what Grace had gone through before death had

7

mercifully claimed her. Cancer was not a kind master. It had exacted a heavy price before allowing Grace to finally find the peace that had been denied her for so long.

Josh buried his head against Shannon's shoulder. "I wish she didn't have to die."

"I know," she said, continuing to rock him. "I know."

Her arms grew numb, her shoulders stiff, but she didn't release him even after he slipped back to sleep. She needed the warmth of contact. Despite the intense August heat, she shivered from an inner chill.

Pain did that to a person, she'd learned. Pain and fear. During the last few months of caring for Grace, Shannon had become on intimate terms with both.

The first fingers of dawn poked their way through the flimsy curtains. Knowing she had a long day ahead of her, she made her way back to her bedroom and promised herself a couple of hours of rest.

Sleep persisted in evading her, though, and she gave up the idea. What she was about to do was crazy.

*Crazy.* That was the only word for it. But she and Josh both needed a fresh start, away from the memories that surrounded them here. She'd do anything to help her nephew — including leaving their home in San Diego and traveling to another state to start a new life.

Not that she was leaving behind much. When she'd left her job, her friends had called occasionally; but with Grace and a small boy to care for, Shannon had had to refuse their invitations. Gradually, they'd stopped calling.

Her eyes filled as she remembered Grace's insistence that Shannon keep Josh with her and not let Josh's grandfather have him. Grace hadn't allowed the nurse to administer the painkillers she so desperately needed until Shannon had agreed.

At the time nothing mattered but keeping the monster of pain at bay. Shannon would have done anything, agreed to anything, if it meant easing, even for a moment, the torture Grace was enduring.

She knew her promise wasn't binding, but she wouldn't go back on it. Protecting Josh from a controlling, manipulative grandfather was the last gift she could give her sister.

# Chapter One

"You what?" Gabe Lambert shoved his hands through his hair and hoped he hadn't heard what his ears told him he had.

Loretta Foster, city council member and longtime friend, gave him a serene look. "I put an ad in papers all over the West advertising for new families."

"What makes you think anyone's gonna want to move to a blip on the map like Blessing?"

Much as he loved his hometown of Blessing, Wyoming, he had no illusions about it. Too small to attract any major business or industry, it offered few job prospects. And cultural and entertainment opportunities were practically nil.

"People'll do a lot of things for the chance to get a house free and clear."

He was running short on patience. "Loretta —"

"Just hold your horses, Gabe. I swear, you're just like your pa. Always ready to fly off the handle before you know all the facts."

"So why don't you tell me the facts."

"I got the town council to agree to donate the old Tyler place to the first family who answered my ad. The only stipulation is that they have to stay at least six months. After that, they'll be given the house free and clear." She gave a self-satisfied smile. "If this works out like I think it will, we'll repeat the process. Heaven knows we've got our share of empty houses just sitting around waiting for some kid to break into."

He couldn't deny it. In the last year over a dozen families had left Blessing and abandoned their homes, unable to sell them or even give them away. But that didn't make him like her idea any better.

Loretta gestured to the empty hardware store behind them. "Look around you, Gabe. Our town's dying. We need to attract new blood, *young* blood."

"We've got families here." He directed his gaze to two little boys scampering across the street.

"For now. But what's gonna happen when those kids start high school and there's no one here their age? Parents want their kids to have friends to grow up with. People are leaving faster than they can slap up a 'For Sale' sign."

Gabe knew she was right. Only last week

Jed Hamblin, the town pharmacist, had moved out, saying he couldn't make a living here anymore. Now the townsfolk had to drive to Laramie, sixty miles away, to have their prescriptions filled.

The month before, Blessing's only theater had closed its doors. With it went the video arcade. There was even talk that the school board was considering closing the local high school and busing the kids to one in the next town. Small things in themselves. Put together they spelled a dying town.

The end of the oil boom in the early eighties had started the downward spiral for Blessing and towns like it. The recent closure of the town's meatpacking plant was but one more nail in the coffin.

Loretta was right. He still didn't like the way she'd gone about it, though. Advertising for people to move to Blessing was a risk. You never knew who might take up the offer. Blessing still had the small-town flavor of fifty years ago, something he and many of the other residents appreciated.

Annoyance tightened his mouth. "Okay, so maybe you have a point."

"I knew you'd come around." She smiled slyly. "Who knows? She might be real pretty. You'll have a chance to find out when you help her settle in."

He'd known Loretta his whole life. She had the kindest heart of anyone in town; she was also the town's biggest busybody.

The impact of her words finally registered. "You already got somebody crazy enough to take you up on your offer?"

He'd figured he'd have a couple of weeks, maybe even a month, to talk her out of the idea. He'd convince her to see reason. Together, they'd find another way, a better way, to revitalize Blessing.

She waved a letter under his nose. "Shannon Whitney and her nephew should be arriving today. Tomorrow at the latest."

"Great. Just great."

Loretta ignored his sarcasm. "Isn't it? She sounds like a lovely woman. I told her someone would be over to help her move in. I knew you wouldn't mind."

"How'd I get to be that someone?"

She patted his arm. "Isn't it obvious? You're the sheriff and the mayor."

He'd taken the job of sheriff mainly because no one else wanted it. Now he understood why.

Fifteen years ago, he'd left Blessing with the intention of never returning. His father had died, the ranch was mortgaged to the hilt, and Gabe was tired — or so he thought — of small-town living. When push came to shove, he discovered he couldn't leave the Rocky Mountain area and headed to Denver.

Determined to make a difference, he'd entered the police academy. Ten years on the Denver police force, working his way up from patrolman to detective, opened his eyes to the world beyond Blessing. By the time he reached twenty-eight, he believed he'd seen everything there was to see. A stint on vice before moving on to homicide convinced him he'd been wrong.

What he'd left behind began to look good. He returned home, worked his rear off to get his ranch out of hock, and found what he'd been looking for in his own backyard. When the town needed a sheriff, he accepted the job.

The people of Blessing thought he'd taken the job because he missed the life of a big-city cop. Nothing could be further from the truth. The job suited him precisely because it was so different from his years in the Denver police department.

Blessing didn't rate both a sheriff and a mayor, so the town council voted to combine the two offices. The biggest crime to hit the town in recent years had occurred when some kids stole a couple of watermelons from the Paget farm. Old man Paget had fired his shotgun at the thieves. The boys were lucky they hadn't ended up with their backsides full of buckshot.

Gabe had assigned the culprits twenty hours of community service plus cleaning out Paget's barn. He figured some time spent with nature — in this case shoveling manure — was a fitting punishment. His lips tilted up at the corners as he remembered the boys' reaction to their sentence. He didn't think they'd be stealing watermelons again anytime soon.

"Besides," Loretta added persuasively, "you're her nearest neighbor."

Gabe sighed heavily. Loretta had made him an accomplice to her plans whether he liked it or not. He'd do as she'd asked because she was a friend. That didn't mean he had to like it, though.


"Will it be a real western town?" Josh demanded for the tenth time. "With horses and cowboys and everything? Like in the movies?"

Shannon smiled at her nephew's excitement and nodded. "Well, not quite like what you see in the movies. But we should see horses and cows. I don't know if there are real cowboys anymore, but there ought to be ranchers." At Josh's quizzical look, she said, "People who own large pieces of land and run cattle on them."

"Can I have a horse?"

"Horses are awfully big, honey. Too big for someone who's just six."

Too late she realized she'd said the wrong thing. At six years old, Josh was very conscious of his role as a big boy who would soon be going into first grade and stay at school all day.

"Aunt Shannon," he said with all the dignity that a six-year-old could muster, "I'm six. I'm not a little kid anymore."

"How 'bout we make a deal?"

He looked intrigued. "A deal?"

She nodded. "You give me a big kiss and I'll try to remember that you're a big boy who's going into first grade."

Giggling, he leaned across the seat and planted a smacking kiss on her cheek.

Taking her right hand from the wheel for a moment, she stuck it out. Solemnly, Josh put his hand in hers and they shook on it.

Josh settled back in his seat with a contented sigh. Shannon hunched her shoulders and then straightened them, trying to ease the dull ache that had accompanied the last six hours of driving. She wanted to put as many miles as possible between them and San Diego. But it was foolish to push herself and Josh so hard without a break.

"What would you say to a little snack?" she asked with a teasing smile.

"Ice cream?"

"After we've had something else," she promised recklessly.

With so little money in her purse, they could ill afford extravagances such as eating in a restaurant. Today was an exception, though, she told herself. A new beginning deserved some sort of celebration, however modest.

Together they looked for a place to stop and settled on a small, homey-looking café, boasting home-style cooking. They each ordered hamburgers and fries, with a chocolate malt for Josh. He munched happily.

Shannon gazed about the room, absorbed in her favorite game of making up stories to fit other people. An older couple caught her attention. Enjoying their second honeymoon, she decided.

Surreptitiously, she pulled a small pad of paper and pencil out of her purse and began to sketch them. A few deft strokes caught the serenity of the woman's face and the still young eyes of her companion. Unself-consciously, they held hands across the table, their love for each other plain for all to see.

Remembering her own parents and their deep love for each other, Shannon blinked back tears and swallowed hard. She had been twenty-five at the time of their death and long since independent. Yet, she felt the loss as keenly as though she were still a child. With Grace's death only a few years later, she would have been truly alone . . . if not for Josh.

Whatever sacrifices she'd had to make to keep him with her, they had been worth it. Josh was her sister's son, but she loved him as though he were her own.

The newspaper ad had acted as a lifeline for Shannon and Josh. "Blessing, Wyoming, needs young families. Come and enjoy the benefits of small-town living." She might have ignored that but for the added incentive of a free house and property.

Having withdrawn all her savings and sold anything of value to help with the cost of Grace's medical care, Shannon was frighteningly low on money. She'd estimated that with the little she would realize from the sale of the house, now heavily mortgaged, she and Josh would have enough to live on for the next year, perhaps even for two if they were careful.

With Josh in school this year, she might be able to find a part-time job in Blessing. Though what she might do there, she wasn't at all sure.

After taking a leave of absence from her job at an ad agency to care for Grace, she hadn't been surprised when she'd received notice after she failed to return several months later. If she had it to do all over again, she wouldn't change a thing. Caring for her sister had been the right thing to do — even if it had cost her her job.

Losing her job had made her all the more vulnerable to Josh's grandfather's attempt to gain custody. With limitless resources and the means to give Josh everything he could ever want, the old man had more than an even chance of being appointed guardian.

The last time she'd seen him had been over a year ago, when he'd blustered his way into Grace's home, threatening to take her to court. When Grace had refused to let him intimidate her, he'd offered a huge amount of money if she and Josh moved back to his home. The offer had been a thinly veiled bribe.

Shannon had been proud of the way her sister had stood up to the old man. It hadn't been easy. Gentle and sweet, Grace hadn't liked conflict, had shied away from it most of her life. But she'd fought for her son.

Shannon's lips tightened. She'd made a promise to Grace. She didn't intend to break it.

Josh's small, insistent voice cut short her musings. "Aunt Shannon," he complained, "I've been telling you, I need to go —"

"I'm sorry. Come on, we'll find it right now." She caught the eye of a smiling waitress, who directed them to the rest rooms.

On their way once more, Shannon scanned the road for signs to Blessing. Surely, it couldn't be far now. Josh had fallen asleep in the backseat, the straw from his malt still clutched in his small, plump hand.

Just as Shannon thought her arms would drop off from sheer exhaustion, she saw the sign: BLESSING — *5 miles, next exit.* A sense of exultation swept over her — they were nearly there. Her earlier tiredness gone, she noticed the passing scenery for the first time, charmed by its unspoiled beauty.

Following the directions Loretta Foster had sent her, she found the house that was to be theirs, just outside town. Her earlier delight in the landscape evaporated as she took in the ramshackle condition of the place. Broken-down fences, a porch of rotting wood, and peeling paint were the least of its problems.

The house — it was a house, wasn't it? — tilted. Or maybe the ground was tilting. Right now, she couldn't be sure. She was so tired she could barely see straight. Surely, in the morning, the house would be upright.

Her sense of humor kicked in. *Beggars can't be choosers,* she reminded herself. What had she expected to get for free? A mansion? Whatever the condition of the house, it was theirs.

She managed to half carry, half drag Josh inside, give his hands and face a swipe with a washcloth, and settle him in the trundle bed she found in the bedroom.

Nearly doubled over, she wrestled with the trunk, trying to hoist it out of the car. With her neighbor's help last night, putting it in had not been so difficult. Now, however, she simply couldn't lift it by herself. She would have to unpack part of it, she decided unwillingly, making several trips instead of one.

A deep voice, coming from behind her, startled her. "Let me help you with that."

Shannon swung around to face a tall —

he must have been well over six feet — commanding figure. She let her eyes travel upward. His eyes held her attention. In contrast to his hair, they were so dark as to seem black. Deep set, they were shadowed by a fringe of thick lashes.

He moved closer, and instinctively, she took a few steps back.

Tipping her head back to study him more closely, Shannon noticed that he was even taller than she'd first thought. He was at least six-three, maybe more, with a set of shoulders most weight lifters would kill for. Still, it wasn't only his size that caught and held her attention. It was something in his manner, a quiet strength that didn't depend upon size or muscle.

He squinted against the sun's glare, tiny lines crisscrossing the corners of his eyes, hinting at hours spent in the sun. The wind lifted his hair, drawing it across his high forehead in unruly blond waves.

Caution of a stranger warred with her need for help. The latter won.

"Thanks. I'd appreciate it."

He hoisted the trunk to his shoulder and carried it without even breaking a sweat.

He placed the trunk inside the door. Following her back outside, he gently shifted her aside when she tried to lift another box. "I'll get that." He hefted it easily, leaving her to bring two small suitcases.

With his help, they emptied the car within a few minutes.

Good manners dictated that she offer him something to drink. She opened the ice chest and tossed him a can of pop.

He flipped back the pop-top lid and took a long swallow. "Thanks."

"Have a seat."

He looked at the sagging sofa and then leaned against the wall. She couldn't blame him. The sofa looked older than the house, and that was saying something.

"Thanks for the help, Mr. . . ." She smiled, wanting to show her appreciation.

"Lambert. Gabe Lambert. Loretta Foster asked me to come over and help you move in."

Despite his words, there was no welcome in his voice. No hint of friendliness in the eyes that raked her up and down.

Her smile faded into a look of puzzlement.

Though he held out a hand, it was grudgingly offered. His grasp was light but firm, hinting at far more strength than he'd displayed.

She told herself she had no reason to feel

hurt, but his obvious dislike was hard to overlook. Especially since she had no idea why.

Her chin angled. "I don't want to keep you."

"You're not keeping me from anything that won't wait."

"But you don't want to be here."

"No."

"Can I ask why not?"

He gestured around him. "Look around you. This place needs work. A whole lot of work."

She made a production of rolling up her sleeves. "That's what I'm planning on doing."

"You said you and your nephew were alone."

She nodded.

"His parents?"

"My sister died two months ago, her husband a few years before that."

"I'm sorry." Two small words, but they said much.

Shannon noticed that the compassion in his expression transformed his features. He was even more attractive than she'd originally thought, and that was saying something. He smelled good, she thought irrelevantly, like leather and soap and something she couldn't quite identify.

The warmth dissolved as he braced a shoulder against the door frame. "Look, there're things you don't know about living here. The water pressure's unreliable. When we get a storm, we lose power. The isolation —"

"Why do I think you're trying to discourage me?"

"Maybe because I am."

That took the breath from her. She hadn't expected such honesty. Well, she couldn't fault the man for that.

"When Loretta told me a woman and her nephew were moving in, I thought it'd be someone older with a boy big enough to help out around the place."

She barely repressed a weary sigh. If he only knew just how old she felt right now, he wouldn't worry.

"I can't give up this place," she said, anticipating Gabe's next words. "I'll do what I have to," she said. "If you have a problem with that, let me know."

"No problem."

"Good."

The corners of his mouth kicked up. Her wide blue eyes and full mouth revealed exactly what she was thinking. She wasn't the least bit scared of him, a fact that pleased him on some gut level which he refused to analyze too deeply.

The lady had her own share of guts. He admired courage, even when it was misplaced. It appeared Shannon Whitney had her share and then some.

Still, he had to try to make her realize just what she'd taken on. "It needs work," he said again, as if sheer repetition could convince her to believe him. "Loretta didn't do you any favors by bringing you here. If you're smart, you'll pack up and go back home. Tomorrow. I'll help you pack up the car."

"I don't think you understand, Mr. Lambert. We have nowhere else to go. This is our home now." She stood in a gesture of dismissal and hoped her knees didn't give way. Falling flat on her face in front of this man, a man who clearly didn't believe she had what it took to make it here, had her stiffening her spine.

"You've said what you came to say. Is there anything else?" Her voice betrayed her exhaustion, and she struggled to keep it steady. Apparently, she hadn't succeeded, for his frown deepened until it bordered on a scowl.

"That's not all by a long shot. You

can't live here. You and a child alone."

"I'll do what I have to."

"Aunt Shannon!"

Josh's scream shattered the silence. Shannon raced to the bedroom. She felt Gabe behind her, as she covered the few feet to the bedroom.

In the soft light of dusk, she could make out Josh's tearstained face. She perched on the side of the bed and wrapped him in her arms, murmuring bits of nonsense to him. Gradually, his shaking subsided.

"Is he all right?" Gabe asked from the doorway.

She half turned to him. "He just had a bad dream."

"Does he get them often?"

*Only since his mother died.* "He'll be fine."

After a slight pause, Gabe nodded. "I'd better let you see to him. I'll be by tomorrow."

She followed him back to the front room. "I appreciate your help, Mr. Lambert. I apologize for taking you away from your work."

He speared his fingers through his hair. "Out here, we help each other out."

She didn't trust herself to answer that.

She followed him out to his truck, a

dusty, well-used pickup. Well, the man had a right to resent being roped into helping a stranger. Still, she couldn't help the disappointment that sluiced over her.

Loretta had painted a glowing picture of Blessing. A friendly town, she'd written, full of small-town traditions and family values. Apparently she had forgotten to inform Gabe Lambert about those traditions and values.

Shannon hurried back to Josh. Even in the muted light, she could see that the color had bleached from his face. "How're you feeling, honey?"

"All right, I guess."

She sat on the bed and lifted him onto her lap. "Remember what we talked about? Even when the bad dreams come, even when you're afraid, I'll be here. Okay?"

He nodded. "Will you stay with me till I go back to sleep?"

"Sure." She settled back and gathered him to her. Within minutes, his breathing had slowed and turned to gentle snores. The sound was oddly soothing, and she felt herself start to relax.

Long after Josh had gone back to sleep, Shannon remained awake, unable to stop thinking about Gabe, startled more by her reaction to him than by anything he'd said.

Odd that a total stranger should affect her so strongly. Resolutely, she put him out of her mind and headed outside to take a better look at what she hoped to make their home.

Dusk had settled, softening the rough edges of the Wyoming landscape with a rosy haze. She paused for a moment, absorbing the harsh beauty of the land. It wasn't an easy kind of beauty, but one that demanded a response.

The smog-free air was a welcome change from that of the city. If the vast land with the wide-open spaces was daunting, well, she'd learn to adjust.

Inside once more, she felt her smile vanish as she looked about at the shabby interior of what was now their home. Her head reeled with all that had to be done. Chipped aqua enamel on the kitchen cabinets showed glimpses of what might be lovely wood underneath. Uncovering it would require hours of tedious stripping and sanding. The oak plank floor, too, would need refinishing.

She faced a very real limitation: money — or the lack thereof, she amended wryly. Two thousand dollars was all that remained after selling everything to pay off Grace's medical bills. The small amount from her sister's life insurance had to be kept in reserve.

She and Grace had had such dreams. For a moment, she let herself reminisce.

For as long as Shannon could remember, she'd wanted to paint. Knowing her parents couldn't afford to pay for art school, she'd worked summers and saved her money. With the help of a scholarship, she managed to put herself through school. Following graduation, she found a job as a commercial artist in an ad agency, planning on saving enough to live on when she left the job to fulfill her dream of painting full time.

Grace's plans had been simpler, though no less important: marry and start a family. It was all she ever wanted, she'd told Shannon years ago. It seemed her dream had come true when she'd met and married Lee Winston.

For Grace, the dream had turned sour. Lee had died in an automobile accident when Josh was only one year old, leaving his wife and small son to fend for themselves. Having married right out of high school, Grace didn't have the skills to find a job that paid enough to support her and her son.

When her father-in-law had invited them to live with him, she'd reluctantly accepted. Too late, she'd learned that the offer came with strings attached. Lee Winston, Sr., had wanted to control her and Josh, dictating every aspect of their lives.

She'd fled from him and had been making it on her own — barely — by doing day care in her home. Things had looked good until the cancer hit. As the disease progressed, Shannon had left her job to care for Grace.

Her sister had died and so had Shannon's dream. But she'd learned something since Grace's death — she was a survivor.

Characteristically, Shannon refused to feel sorry for herself. She had spotted a good-sized garden plot — perhaps next summer she could supplement their food budget by raising some vegetables. Mentally, she added that to her list of things to do: find out what grows well here.

The first order of business would be to give the house a thorough cleaning. A minimum of unpacking, though, was all she could manage now.

Sponging off in the postage stamp–sized bathroom, she noticed the primitive plumbing and prayed it would hold out. The pipes sputtered in protest against their unaccustomed use.

Dressed in thin cotton pajamas, she slipped gratefully beneath the sheets she'd hastily put on the bed. Even the lumpy mattress felt good tonight. What a blessing that the former owner had had an old-fashioned trundle bed that she and Josh could both use. Someday, she wanted to add another bedroom. Until then, they'd have to make do with what was there.

Her body begged for sleep, but her mind refused to settle down. Even now, with over a thousand miles separating them from Grace's overbearing father-in-law, she couldn't completely squelch the fear.

Shannon understood on a rational level that she had nothing to fear. Her custody of Josh was legal and binding. But if Lee decided to take her to court to contest it, as he'd threatened to do, he could make a strong case that he was better able to care for a child — and he had the means to finance a long, drawn-out trial.

He had a battery of expensive lawyers at his disposal, lawyers who wouldn't hesitate to point out that a man in Lee Winston's position wouldn't have to scrape to make ends meet as Shannon had been doing for the last year.

When Shannon's defenses and resolve

had been at an all-time low, she'd even wondered if he could be right. How could she hope to compete with what Josh's grandfather could offer? The answer was simple. She couldn't.

Up until the last year, she'd had little experience with children. What did she really know about being a mother anyway? Grace had been too ill to tell her much. Most of the time, Shannon felt like she was making it up as she went along.

Then she'd remembered the one thing — the only thing — that truly mattered. Lee could give Josh every advantage . . . everything but love.

Lee couldn't have followed them here. She'd covered her tracks well, heading north before starting east. She'd paid cash for everything to avoid a telltale credit card trail. Her reserve of cash was dangerously low, but it couldn't be helped. She'd even changed her last name.

A creak in the floorboards startled her awake. *Stop it,* she ordered herself. She had to relax. This was their home now. She couldn't afford to let fear control her. If she did, she'd destroy any chance she and Josh had of a new beginning.

"What's that?" Josh murmured sleepily.

"Everything's all right," she said, but the

tremble in her voice belied her words. She whispered them again, this time determined to believe them herself.

# Chapter Two

Through the window of the town diner, Loretta motioned for Gabe to join her at her booth. The food was mediocre and the service slow, but the diner dished up the freshest gossip in town. For that reason, it was the most popular eating establishment in Blessing.

Sighing, he stepped inside and took the seat opposite hers. The cracked vinyl upholstery protested as he slid across it. He knew what was coming. Might as well get it over with.

"Have you seen her?" she asked without preamble.

"Good morning to you, too."

"Can it. Have you seen Shannon Whitney and her nephew?"

He nodded.

"Well? What'd you think?"

"That she has no business moving into a ramshackle house like the Tyler place."

Loretta's artificially arched eyebrows rose even higher. "You didn't tell her that, I hope."

"I told her it was no place for a woman and a child." Ignoring her glare, Gabe opened the menu, a pointless move since the diner offered only two choices for breakfast — cold cereal or bacon and eggs.

"You what?" Loretta demanded, echoing his words of a few days ago.

"I told her she'd do well to pack up and hightail it back to where she came from."

"What'd she say to that?"

"No."

The flat, uncompromising answer had Loretta grinning. "That sounds like the woman I got to know through her letters." Her grin faded. "You promised you'd help her."

"I helped her move in. I didn't say anything about helping her set herself up for failure out here. You know how isolated the Tyler place is. A city woman like that doesn't stand a chance."

"I was a city woman when George brought me here forty years ago," Loretta said. "Didn't know one end of a cow from the other."

"She doesn't stand a chance," Gabe insisted. "She's too small, too fragile, to make it out here."

A speculative look entered her eyes. "You say she's small? What color's her hair?"

"What difference does —"

"What color?"

"Dark. Almost black."

"And her eyes?"

"Blue."

"Sound like anyone familiar?"

It didn't take a rocket scientist to figure out where she was heading. He'd just described his ex-fiancée. He'd met Melissa Crossland on a trip back east to buy stock to improve the bloodline of his horses. Melissa had grown up with every advantage. The cosseted daughter of a Kentucky horse breeder, she'd expected the same kind of lifestyle she'd been accustomed to.

She hadn't made it in Wyoming. She'd lasted two months, long enough to criticize Gabe's home, ridicule everything he valued, and alienate most of his friends. Two days before the wedding was scheduled to take place, she left him a note saying she was going home to daddy.

After he'd gotten over the blow to his ego, he'd realized he'd had a lucky break. His pride had taken a worse beating than his heart.

"Shannon's not Melissa," Loretta said.

That didn't deserve an answer. Shannon's resemblance to his ex-fiancée wasn't an issue. Loretta's imagination, always active, had shifted into overdrive.

After Loretta took him to task for his bad manners, she pumped him about Shannon and her nephew. That he had little to offer served only to whet her appetite. With anyone else, he would have been annoyed. With Loretta, he felt only tender amusement, knowing that behind her curiosity lay genuine concern. Whether she knew it or not, Shannon Whitney had a champion in the older woman.

When Loretta had finished quizzing him, she scolded him once again and reminded him that Blessing needed an infusion of new blood. After extracting a promise from him to visit Shannon again, she patted his hand and told him he was a good boy.

"Loretta, someday . . ." He left the threat unfinished.

She laughed, a braying sound that never failed to elicit a smile from him. "You know you can't stay mad at me. Besides, people who diapered your bottom always think they have special privileges."

His sigh was automatic. Loretta pulled that same line every time she asked something outrageous of him. "That was over thirty-five years ago."

"Some things you never forget."

He kissed her cheek and promised to mend his fences with Shannon.

Suddenly he smiled and decided it wouldn't be a hardship at all to visit the pretty lady and her nephew.

Crossly, Shannon rubbed her eyes.

The gentle cadence of Josh's soft, steady breathing had finally lulled her to sleep last night, but when she'd succumbed to the weariness that dogged her body, nightmares had plagued her. She awoke with a start and padded out to the kitchen. Munching on an apple helped settle her nerves.

She headed back to the bedroom, pausing to look at her nephew. Her expression automatically softened. Impossibly long lashes fanned lightly freckled cheeks; one small hand gripped a much loved toy dinosaur while the other formed a dimpled fist, pushed up against his chin.

Grace had left her a precious legacy — Josh.

Careful not to wake him, Shannon stepped gingerly over the lower bed and slipped into a short robe. A quick shower — she dared not strain the capacity of the water heater with its low water pressure — and fresh clothing saw her ready for the day.

"Aunt Shannon, where are you?"

"Right here, honey," she answered, hurrying back into the bedroom. "Hey, sleepyhead. I thought you were going to be the first one up and go exploring this morning."

"Is it too late?"

"No, sweetheart, it's not late at all." She tugged on the tail of his pajama top.

An unfamiliar sound — a hollow clopping against the ground — had her racing to the porch. A tall figure sat astride the biggest horse she'd ever seen. Gabe dismounted, tethered his horse, and started toward her.

Her arms folded across her chest, she met him halfway. "Did you come to try again, Mr. Lambert?"

"Try again?"

She made an impatient gesture. "To convince us to leave."

Her voice was everything he remembered. He'd almost convinced himself that he'd imagined the husky, low tones that had caressed even as she'd argued with him last night.

He felt a quick tug at his conscience. The lady and her nephew needed help, not discouragement. "I came to apologize."

Her eyes narrowed slightly, as if she were

trying to decide whether to believe him or not. Well, he couldn't blame her for that. He'd come down pretty hard on her last night.

The small boy wandered out onto the porch. "That's a great horse, mister. Is he yours?"

"Thanks. And, yes, he is. Name's Buck." Gabe squatted down at eye level with the boy. "What's your name?"

"Josh. I'm six years old, and I go to school."

"Glad to meet you, Josh. I'm Gabe Lambert."

"How old are you, Mr. Lambert?"

Shannon intervened hastily. "Josh, that's none of our business."

"That's all right," Gabe said easily. "I'm thirty-five, Josh. A bit older than you." He stood. "Blessing has a reputation of being a friendly town. Guess I wasn't much of an advertisement for it."

"No." Her chin lifted. "You weren't."

"You don't make it easy."

"Neither do you."

For all her small size, the lady didn't back down. He liked that. He had a feeling there was a lot to like about Shannon Whitney.

She was wearing jeans again. This time

they were white, showing off long legs, slender hips, and a tiny waist. With them, she wore a denim shirt tied at the waist. The outfit was casual, yet intensely feminine.

Curls, piled on top of her head in a haphazard fashion, spilled down her neck and cheeks. Without thinking, he reached forward to tuck one behind her ear.

The contact startled him. Her eyes, soft and vulnerable, widened. He dropped his hand.

The distinctive scent of her skin and hair danced into his senses, momentarily throwing him off balance. He wanted very much to move closer for more. Recognizing the impulse as foolish, he stayed where he was.

"Can we start again?" he asked, offering his hand.

After a slight hesitation, she put her hand in his. He closed his own over it, liking the feel of it. Small but strong, like the woman herself.

"What can I do to help you get settled?"

She looked momentarily troubled. "I need to register Josh at school. I'm not sure . . ."

He nodded. "We'll take care of it. You want to do it today?"

"If we could." She gestured to Josh, who was still in his pajamas. "I'm sorry. It's going to take us a little while to get ready."

"What if I come back in a couple of hours?" He checked his watch. "Say about noon?"

"Fine. Mr. Lambert —"

"Gabe."

"Gabe. Thank you."

Her hand was warm this time when she placed it in his. He closed his own around it. Hers was slender, but she gripped his firmly.

Josh pulled at her other hand. "I'm hungry."

"We'll have breakfast in just a minute. We'll eat picnic style, okay?"

"Okay!"

Shannon felt Gabe's gaze on her and wondered what he was thinking.

"I'll leave you to your breakfast." With that, he left.

Josh looked out the window. "Look!" He pointed to the gray gelding that Gabe mounted. "Isn't he wonderful?" he asked, not making clear whether "he" referred to the horse or its rider.

"It's a beautiful horse," Shannon agreed, preferring to think that Josh's enthusiasm was directed there. "We'll probably see a lot of horses here."

"Could I have a pony? Please? I'd take good care of it."

"You know I'd get you one if I could. There just isn't a way right now." Seeing her nephew's disappointed look, she added, "Maybe if I can get a job, well, just *maybe,* we could swing a pony later on."

Josh appeared content with that, accepting Shannon's half promise with touching faith. It was dangerous letting Josh believe that she could do anything. She'd tried to point out that there were some things she couldn't do, but Josh, with a child's faith, refused to believe that.

Gabe returned at noon as he'd promised, delighting Josh with the chance to ride in a pickup truck.

Every cow they passed, grazing on the seemingly endless range, elicited a delighted response from Josh as Gabe drove to Blessing. He swung his head back and forth, so as to not miss anything.

"Look, Aunt Shannon!"

She looked out the window in time to see the V-formation of Canada geese flying overhead.

With Gabe's help, she found the elementary school and registered Josh in the first grade. He directed her to the library, where she found a stack of books on gardening. The librarian was conducting a story hour, which she invited Josh to join.

Shannon didn't like leaving him. Seeing the pleading look in his eyes, though, she gave in.

"He'll be fine," Gabe said, taking her arm and urging her from the library. "Give him a chance to meet some of the kids."

That convinced her. He gave her a guided tour of the town, which consisted of four blocks of businesses, surrounded by a few houses. Where were all the people?

"Most people live outside town, like the Tylers . . . like you," he explained, seeing her questioning look.

"Hey, Gabe, who's the pretty lady?"

"Shannon Whitney," Gabe said, a hand resting easily at the small of her back. "Meet Doc Hartman, local sawbones and county coroner."

"Glad to meet you," the doctor said. "I see you've got our sheriff showing you around. Not many people manage to drag him away from the ranch in the middle of the week."

Sheriff?

She murmured an appropriate greeting, but her mind was reeling. Gabe was sheriff? She was letting the town sheriff show her around town?

She had to get out of here. He was good at his job, she decided. She'd already told him more than she'd intended and less than he'd obviously hoped for. Well, that made them even.

"So you and your nephew have decided to settle in Blessing?" the doctor asked. "Must be a change from the big city."

"A change, yes," she agreed shortly.

Her smile felt stiff, her words stilted, as the men tried to include her in the conversation. Her discomfort must have been more obvious than she'd realized for Gabe cut the chat short, made their excuses to the doctor, and headed back to the library.

In her agitation, she hurried, until she was slightly ahead of him. She could feel his stare directed at her back, his gaze as hot as the prairie sun, which burned with such intensity.

"Something wrong?" he asked when he caught up with her.

"What could be wrong?"

"That's what I'm trying to figure out."

Gabe had taken them home after that. The easy conversation on the trip to town was conspicuously missing. Despite Josh's cheerful chatter, tension radiated between

Gabe and herself. It was in the questions unasked, the answers not given. She tried to ignore it, to feign unawareness that her odd behavior was at the root of it.

Her thanks for his help had been crisp, brief to the point of rudeness. He'd raised his brows at her clipped tone but had said nothing.

Her conscience had given her a hard time after that. The man had gone out of his way to introduce her around town and help her register Josh at school, and all she had done was repay him with a snub. She knew he was puzzled at her behavior. He had every right to be annoyed with her.

She'd done her best to avoid Sheriff Lambert after that. It wasn't difficult. She didn't have much call to go into town, and he seemed to have taken the hint that she could manage on her own.

Well, that was all right with her. As long as she was trying to keep a low profile, she couldn't afford the luxury of a friend, especially one who wore a badge.

Excitement over his first day of school catapulted Josh out of bed at 5:30 a.m. Though she longed for a few more hours of sleep, Shannon rose, too, knowing that beneath his enthusiasm lay a few butterflies. She had her own butterflies fluttering about in her stomach, each bearing Josh's name.

*He'll do fine,* she told herself repeatedly. *I won't take him to school.* He needed to meet the other children on his own terms and in his own way. An old mother hen clucking about wouldn't help him make the right start.

A lump formed in Shannon's throat. A fierce love welled up within her, making her want to hold her nephew close, to know he was safe and secure. After Grace's death, over-protectiveness came all too easily, and she had to fight against smothering Josh.

Shannon approved Josh's choice of clothes, then started to the kitchen to prepare an extra-special breakfast.

Waffles, sausages, and eggs greeted Josh and he smiled broadly. "Are they your super-duper waffles?"

"Are there any other kind?"

Though Josh made a good try, he could finish only a part of the food. "I feel a little funny here." He touched his stomach.

"I know. I feel a little funny, too. But it'll go away."

"Promise?"

"Promise."

Before Shannon was ready, the school bus arrived, its honk almost lost in the din of high-pitched voices. Shannon kissed Josh one last time, then waved him off.

She tried not to think about how small he looked and fastened her attention instead on his eager smile as he boarded the bus.

A trip to town could no longer be avoided when she needed groceries. While Josh was in school seemed the perfect time to go shopping. Shannon had quickly learned that six-year-old boys had a tendency to fill the grocery cart with sugary cereal and bags of chips while nobody was looking.

The trip had another purpose as well. She needed to start meeting people. Just because she'd decided she couldn't get close to anyone didn't mean she had to cut herself off from others completely. For Josh's sake, she had to make a place for them in Blessing. And that meant becoming a part of the community.

She'd just finished stowing her groceries in the trunk of her car when she heard her name called.

"Shannon. Shannon Whitney."

Shannon turned in time to see a sixtyish woman trotting toward her at a determined pace.

"Loretta Foster," the woman said, not waiting but taking Shannon's hand and pumping it vigorously. "It is you, isn't it? I recognized you right off from Gabe's description."

Shannon wasn't given time to puzzle over that one. "Oh, yes. Mrs. Foster. How do you do?"

"I'm doing just fine," the woman said. "I'm sorry I haven't been out to visit you. I've been minding my youngest daughter's twin boys while she was in the hospital having her third. Girl this time. Thank heavens. I always say God watches out for mothers. When He gives you two terrors the first time, He gives you an angel for the third. Those two like to run me ragged. This is the first time I've been in town in a week."

Breathless from that recital, Loretta paused and subjected Shannon to a shrewd stare. "Come on," she said, "let's get acquainted over a cup of coffee."

Before she knew what was happening, Shannon found herself being propelled along the sidewalk to a small diner.

Not waiting for a waitress to seat them, Loretta steered Shannon toward a comfortably shabby booth upholstered in green vinyl. Once seated, Loretta took her time studying Shannon, the open expression in her eyes inviting Shannon to do the same.

Loretta's plump face wore her age with pride, the wrinkles more a badge of honor than something to be concealed. Her eyes were alight with good-natured humor, giving an appearance of laughter even when her lips bore a stubborn set.

Unexpectedly, Loretta grinned. "Now that you're wondering just how old I am and I'm envying how young you are, we can get down to the important stuff. I'm the self-appointed town gossip, so I get the pleasure of finding out everything there is to know about you. Comes from not having my George around anymore," she added. Her sprightly smile held a trace of sadness. "But you don't want to hear about an old woman like me. Let's get to the good stuff, like how old you are and whether you're looking to get hitched."

Charmed and disarmed, Shannon settled back and prepared to be interrogated.

Loretta pumped Shannon about herself and Josh. By the time their coffee arrived, Shannon felt as if she'd been gently but thoroughly cross-examined. Much as she hated to lie to this friendly woman, Shannon kept her answers to a minimum and stuck to the story she'd settled on.

Loretta sat back. "Okay, we've got the pre-liminaries over with. Now tell me the truth. What do you think of Gabe Lambert?"

Shannon's silence drew a frown from the older woman.

"Is he giving you a hard time? If he is . . ."

Shannon shook her head. She sensed that beneath Loretta's fierce look lay a gen-uine liking for Gabe. The last thing Shannon wanted was to come between two friends. "He's been very . . . helpful."

"Helpful but not friendly. Right?"

"Right," Shannon admitted at last.

"We'll set him straight," Loretta said, every word thinned with exasperation. "Don't you fret over it. He can be a pain in the rear, but he has a good heart. He'll come around."

The last thing Shannon wanted was for him to "come around." Aside from that, she privately doubted that anyone could make Gabe do anything he didn't want to.

Seemingly satisfied with what she'd found out, Loretta proceeded to fill Shannon in on the town gossip. An hour later, Shannon reflected that she probably knew more about Blessing's residents than they knew about themselves.

The whole recitation was done with humor blended with such a generous dose of compassion that it was robbed of any sting of gossip. Loretta was in turns outrageous and endearing, and Shannon felt her liking for the older woman grow.

Loretta glanced at her watch and gave a yelp. "Listen to me yammering on, and me with a meeting to get to." She signaled for the check and pushed herself out of the booth. "Why don't you come with me? We're making plans for the town fair."

Shannon started to demur when she thought better of it. What better way to get involved in Blessing than to attend a town meeting?

Two hours later, she decided she'd lost her mind. What had possessed her to volunteer to head up the advertising committee for the fair? Granted, the town needed an infusion of cash. Blessing was dying. Even in the short time she'd been here, she could see that.

Well, she'd given her word she'd help so she'd better get busy working on some posters and flyers. The next meeting took place the following week. She'd promised to have some ideas ready to present then.

She heard the squeal of children's voices before the school bus came to a stop outside the house.

Josh bubbled over with first-day enthusiasm. "There's a playground. And we each have our own desks. And —"

"Whoa! How about the kids? Did you make a friend?" Shannon tried to keep her tone light, her words casual. She didn't want Josh to sense her anxiety over his first day at a new school.

"I made a lot of friends — Matthew, Tyler, Ricky. And Miss Winters. She's my teacher."

Shannon expelled a relieved breath. Nothing else mattered if Josh was happy. She could deal with anything. Unbidden, a picture of Sheriff Gabe Lambert formed in her mind. Or anyone.

# Chapter Three

Gabe had taken the hint to keep his distance from Shannon. He knew something had happened to scare her off, but he'd be darned if he knew what it was.

He'd tried to pinpoint when she'd turned the deep freeze on him.

If the lady didn't want him around, that was fine by him. He'd given her the space she obviously wanted. But he couldn't ignore the pull at his conscience that reminded him that a woman and child alone needed help to make a go of the Tyler place. Or the promise he'd made to Loretta to help his new neighbor.

Honesty forced him to admit that his decision to go by her place was more than a simple desire to be a good neighbor. He wanted to see her again.

Though he'd met her only twice, he'd learned enough about her to realize that the way to win her over was through her nephew. And he had just the thing to charm a six-year-old boy.

Shannon flexed her shoulders. Stripping the cabinets of their paint was more work than she'd anticipated. She'd promised to spend two hours on the project today before turning her attention to cleaning the house. Her mouth twisted at the thought of doing dishes. She'd be the first to admit that housekeeping was far down the list of her favorite things to do.

When the two hours were up, she stopped and looked at herself in distaste, reflecting that she might need sandpaper to remove some of the grime. Allowing herself a longer-than-usual shower, she reveled in the unaccustomed luxury. As she reached up to shampoo her hair, her shoulder muscles objected, and she winced.

When she'd finished the chores around the house, she decided she'd earned a treat. Impulsively, she unearthed her father's rifle from the trunk, running her fingers over its smoothly polished butt.

Her father had taught her how to handle and care for guns, and she had found a certain satisfaction in target shooting. Under his tutoring, she had become a competent markswoman, entering and winning several competitions.

Lost in her task of cleaning the rifle, she missed the first rap on the door. A second, more impatient one caught her attention, and she went to answer it.

Gabe stood there, more handsome than ever in jeans and a denim shirt.

"Can I come in?" he asked when she stared at him.

"I'm sorry." She opened the door wider and reminded herself to keep cool. She had nothing to be afraid of.

"I came to invite you to my place. I have something I think you might like to see."

"What's that?"

He grinned. "You have to come with me to find out."

She pulled a face. "You sure know how to get a girl's interest."

"So have I?" The words were light, but his tone held something different, something she wasn't sure she wanted to interpret.

She couldn't hide forever. And suddenly she realized she didn't want to. "Let me finish with this and I'll be ready."

He watched as she put the gun back together. "You're pretty handy with that."

"Thanks." She gave the rifle a final wipe with a soft cloth. "Okay."

He helped her into the pickup, his hand

57

warm at her waist. "Do you like dogs?" he asked as he steered the truck over the rough dirt road.

"Sure. Especially the big, sloppy kind with goofy grins."

A smile crept across his lips. "Good."

She didn't have time to wonder what he meant by that as he kept her busy answering questions about herself. She had to guard her tongue against saying more than she wanted. Lying was a lot of work, she decided, but she didn't want to risk anyone back home finding out where she and Josh were. She drew a relieved breath when he pulled into the long, winding driveway leading to his ranch.

When the house came into view, she gave a small gasp of pleasure. Wooden columns supported a two-story log home. Natural landscaping complemented the rustic look of the architecture.

"It's gorgeous," she said, taking in the cedar-shingled roof and wraparound porch.

"You like log cabins?"

"It's hardly a cabin."

"Some people think so."

She wanted to ask what he meant by that. Even more, she wanted to know what had suddenly put the shadows in his eyes. But she didn't have the right to ask personal questions, especially given her own refusal to answer the same kind, so she remained silent.

He helped her out of the truck and she had started to the house when he laid a hand on her arm, steering her to the barn. Puzzled and more curious than ever, she fell into step with him.

She squinted against the sudden change from morning light to the shadowy recesses of the barn. Stray beams of sunlight sifted through the rafters, catching dust motes in glittering gold.

"Back here," Gabe said, pointing to an empty stall.

At first she couldn't see anything. A series of high-pitched yips alerted her that the stall wasn't empty after all. In a corner lay a litter of puppies nestled around a huge black Lab. Greedily, they pushed one another out of the way as they fought for their place at their mother's side.

"Lunchtime," Gabe said, gently making room for the scrawniest of the pups between two of his greedier siblings.

Heedless of the straw and dirt lining the floor, Shannon knelt beside them. "They're adorable."

"I thought Josh might like one."

"He'd love it."

"If it's all right with you, then, I'll let him pick one out."

She watched as the smallest one was pushed out of the way, and she reached out to snuggle him to her. After a token protest, the puppy settled in her arms.

"Smart dog," Gabe said. "He knows a good thing when he sees it."

Her smile, as open as the Wyoming sky, erased whatever doubts he'd been entertaining.

Gabe hunkered down beside her, stroking the mother's massive head as she gently nudged her babies aside with a huge paw. "Smokey here's delivered more than a half dozen litters. I imagine she's getting kind of tired of being fought over."

Shannon returned the pup to his brothers and sisters. They tripped and tumbled over one another, their antics resembling those of circus clowns. She patted Smokey's neck. "Your babies are beautiful," she murmured.

She stood, brushing bits of straw from her jeans and shirt. "I'd better get back. When would you like us to come out for Josh to choose one?"

"Bring him out after school."

Impulsively, she pressed a kiss to his cheek. "Thank you."

The look in her eyes told him she was thanking him for more than the offer of a puppy. The lady was full of surprises. Maybe that was why he kept finding reasons to be with her.

Josh's reaction to having a puppy was predictably enthusiastic.

"Can I really have one?" he asked, practically dancing in excitement.

"You sure can," said Shannon, laughing at the boy's enthusiasm.

The ten-minute drive back to Gabe's ranch after school was filled with the boy's excited chatter. Josh couldn't wait to get to the barn and see the puppies.

"This one," he said when Gabe asked him which one he wanted, pointing to the friskiest pup of the litter. He buried his head in the glossy black coat.

The pup responded with a yip.

"What're you going to name him?" Gabe asked.

A thoughtful frown rested on Josh's face. "I dunno."

"He's going to be big."

"How can you tell?"

Gabe lifted a paw. "By this. Won't be long before he grows into the size of his feet."

"I'm gonna call him Samson."

Gabe traded a smile with Shannon. "Good choice," he approved.

They left Josh under the watchful eye of a ranch hand and headed to the house. Inside the kitchen, Gabe poured two glasses of lemonade.

She took a long drink. "Mmm. This is great." She glanced around the kitchen. Gleaming appliances coexisted comfortably with maple cabinetry and a plank floor.

"Would you like a tour?" Gabe asked.

"How did you know?"

"Your eyes. They give away all your secrets."

His words caused her to bite back a sharp gasp before she forced herself to relax. He didn't mean it literally.

"I'd love to see the rest of your home . . . if it's not too much trouble."

He steered her through an archway to the living room. A cathedral ceiling dominated the room. Woven rugs scattered over the hardwood floors and overstuffed leather furniture softened the austere lines of the room. A fieldstone fireplace took up one entire wall. A couple of pieces of sculpture — a stallion poised on the edge of a cliff and a hawk in flight — sat atop oak pedestals.

The overall effect was one of casual

comfort, inviting her to make herself at home.

"It's perfect," she said, slowly circling the room and noticing for the first time details like a pewter pitcher filled with eucalyptus and an oil painting of a nineteenth-century roundup.

"You like it?" His voice sounded oddly strained, as if her answer mattered.

"How could anyone not like it?" Her question didn't demand an answer, and she didn't wait for one. She was too busy running her fingers over the cedar mantel that topped the fireplace.

"Want to see the upstairs?" Taking her acceptance for granted, he steered her toward the open staircase. Rooms opened off a balcony that ran around the entire second floor. She counted four bedrooms, two baths, plus a large empty room.

"It was going to be a playroom," he said.

She waited, but he didn't offer any further explanation.

Her artist's eye immediately filled it with primary colors and blocks big enough for children to crawl through and over. "It's wonderful."

"You mean that, don't you?"

"Why wouldn't I?"

"No reason." He shrugged. "Some women wouldn't."

She was left to wonder what he meant by that. "I'd better go check on Josh."

When he took her hand, it seemed churlish to pull away. His hand closed around her own. She'd always been self-conscious about her hands. Years of working with ink and paint had left them permanently stained; she kept her nails short and unpolished.

As if he sensed her feelings, he lifted her hand to study it. "I've always thought you could tell a lot about a person by their hands. Yours tell me that you're not afraid to work."

The faint tremors that shivered up her arm had nothing to do with his touch. She was cold, she told herself, conveniently ignoring the fact that the temperature had hovered in the high nineties all day.

She was relieved when he suggested they head back to the barn. They found Josh snuggling the puppies to him. With Gabe's promise to bring Samson by as soon as he was weaned, Josh reluctantly agreed that they could go home.

After Josh was in bed that night, Shannon tried to analyze her response to Gabe. Hadn't she told herself that the smart thing to do was to avoid him?

She couldn't very well refuse to have anything to do with him, she defended herself. He was a neighbor, after all. And after his generous offer to give Josh the pup, she had more reason than ever to be grateful to him. She had nothing to fear from the town's good-looking sheriff.

Nothing at all.

When Loretta came by three days later to discuss ideas for advertising the fair, Shannon was still puzzling over her reaction to Gabe.

". . . and we'll need at least two dozen posters for the high school. . . . Shannon, are you with me?"

With an effort, Shannon dragged herself back to the present and to Loretta, who was watching her with concern.

There'd been a time when Shannon had dreamed of a future, a husband and children, a home of her own. She'd thought those dreams were safely shelved. And they had been . . . until recently.

"Are you all right, honey?" Loretta asked.

Shannon managed a smile. "I'm fine. Sometimes I just start daydreaming — you know how it is."

Loretta shook her head. "Can't say that I do. I guess I'm the down-to-earth type whose feet never get far off the ground." She aimed an admiring glance at the painting now occupying the easel in the corner. "I never had much of a creative bent. I sure never could do anything like that."

Uncomfortable with the older woman's praise, Shannon flushed. "Your creativity shows up in other ways. Look at the way you're working to bring the town back to life."

Loretta looked pleased. "Guess I am, at that." Her smile dimmed a bit. "Some people don't see it that way, though."

It didn't take much guesswork to know she was referring to Gabe.

"He hasn't been giving you any more trouble, has he?" Loretta asked, a fierce scowl at odds with her normally serene expression.

"No. In fact, he's gone out of his way to be helpful."

Loretta's look turned speculative. "He has, has he?"

"Don't go getting any ideas," Shannon warned her. "Gabe's just being neighborly." She didn't want anything more from him, she assured herself. *Couldn't* want anything more from him.

Involuntarily, her thoughts strayed to when her fiancé had demanded she make a choice between Josh and himself.

"I want a wife, not a ready-made family with someone else's kid to raise," Ron had said. "Why not let the old man have the boy? He could give the kid a heck of a lot more than you ever could."

She'd slipped the engagement ring from her finger and given it back to him with no regrets.

"Is that what you call it? Being neighborly?" Loretta asked, an arch look on her face.

Annoyed, more with her own thoughts than with Loretta's teasing, Shannon deliberately changed the subject.

"Take a look and tell me what you think."

They spent the next couple of hours going over ideas for the fair. Shannon produced a couple of sketches for posters and ads for the newspaper.

"These are great," Loretta said. She launched into an enthusiastic description of how they'd send copies of the posters to surrounding towns. "This ought to bring 'em in, if anything does. Now show me what you've been doing to the house."

Shyly, Shannon gestured to the kitchen. "I started in here. As you can see, I haven't gotten much done yet."

"I'd love to help."

"It's pretty exhausting work," Shannon began doubtfully, but the older woman's enthusiasm was contagious.

While Shannon collected the tools they'd need, Loretta looked through the easels piled against the wall. "Someday you're going to sell these and make a pot of money."

That produced a laugh from Shannon. Right now, she could barely afford to buy oils. They worked together companionably, scraping and sanding away the old paint. Loretta's witty observations of the Blessing townspeople caused Shannon to laugh more than she had in months.

When Shannon suggested they take a break, Loretta brushed aside her concerns.

"I'm as fit as I ever was. Now let's get back to work before I remember I'm an old woman."

"I didn't mean —"

Loretta's smile was as wide as the prairie. "I know you didn't, honey."

When a knock sounded at the door, Shannon welcomed the break. Though Loretta had staunchly maintained she wasn't tired, Shannon could see she was. The physical exertion had winded her to the point that she struggled to even her breathing.

Gabe stood there, a large box in his arms. "I thought you might be able to use these."

She looked inside the box to find clumps of bulbs. Nothing could have pleased her more. Uncaring of the dirt that clung to them, she gently pulled out the fat bulbs. She recognized daffodils, tulips, irises. If she'd been given a box full of jewels, she couldn't have been more excited.

She pressed a kiss to his cheek. "Thank you."

The world spun before coming to an abrupt stop. For a moment, she had forgotten about Loretta, forgotten that Gabe was the sheriff, forgotten everything but the feel of her lips against his slightly stubbled skin.

"You're welcome." As if he'd just now become aware of her presence, Gabe nodded toward Loretta. When he noticed her flushed face and labored breathing, he turned a scowl on Shannon.

"Don't go getting on your high horse, Gabe Lambert," Loretta said, slipping a protective arm around Shannon's shoulders. "I'm helping because I wanted to. I've never seen anyone work as hard as this girl has around this old place. Why, just look —"

"I'm sure Gabe isn't interested in all this," Shannon cut in quickly.

"Now that's where you're wrong," he said quietly. "I'm interested in everything that's ever happened to you."

Shannon hesitated, conscious of Loretta's gaze resting on them with bright speculation. "Well," she said after too long a pause. "I'm afraid nothing much has ever happened to me." She laughed self-consciously. "I'm really a boring person."

Gabe looked at her thoughtfully for a moment, but she did her best to ignore the questions clearly apparent in his eyes. "So what're you working on?" he asked.

Loretta launched into a blow-by-blow explanation of Shannon's plans for renovating the old house. Growing more embarrassed by the moment, Shannon tried to stop her friend's glowing description.

Loretta just patted her hand and continued. "After we get the cabinets done, she plans to rip out this window someday and put in French doors so the room opens onto the patio."

Gabe looked bemused. "What patio?"

Shannon could feel her cheeks growing warm. "That's just me dreaming."

"Everyone needs dreams," he said, so seriously that she looked at him in surprise.

"Do you have them? Dreams?"

"I did. A long time ago."

"I'd better be on my way," Loretta said, her sly smile earning a glare from Shannon. "I'll be by in a couple of days and we'll talk about" — she shot Shannon a teasing look — "things."

"What was that all about?" Gabe asked.

"Nothing," Shannon said shortly. She was going to have to talk to Loretta about letting her imagination get the better of her. There was nothing between herself and Gabe. Loretta's speculations could only embarrass them both.

"I'll be bringing Samson by pretty soon," he said. "Another week and he'll be weaned."

"Josh can hardly wait. He keeps asking when *his* dog is coming to live with us."

"You're welcome to bring him to the ranch any time to visit."

"Thanks. I may just do that."

Gabe tipped back his hat, a smile breaking across his face as he watched the

71

boy and dog together. He'd brought Samson over last week. Both boy and puppy had taken to each other with scarcely a moment's hesitation. Samson chased Josh around the yard. Or was it the other way around?

"Hey there, partner," Gabe called. "Looks like you and Samson are hitting it off."

"You bet." Josh trotted along beside him, the puppy cuddled against his chest. "We could never have a puppy before. Grandpa didn't like dogs. Then my mom got sick and . . ." His voice trailed off.

"Grandpa?"

"We lived with him. I don't remember him much. He and my mom used to fight a lot."

He started to ask Josh about it and then stopped himself. He was curious about Shannon and her nephew, but not so curious that he'd stoop to pumping a six-year-old for information. "You two keep it up. I'm going to see your aunt."

"Okay. See you later, Gabe."

He found her in the backyard, turning over a small flower bed that flanked the house. He spent a few minutes watching her, enjoying her smooth, economical movements.

She'd scooped her hair up, he saw. He supposed she thought the knot on top of her head was practical. Maybe it was, he mused, but the strands that fluttered and curled around her neck made the practical intensely feminine.

He decided he'd stared long enough and moved closer. "You look like you know how to handle a shovel."

She swiped at her cheek, smearing a streak of dirt across it. "I manage, but this dirt . . ." She stubbed at the hard clumps of dirt with her sneakered toe.

"The ground around here hasn't been worked in a long time." He took the shovel from her and began breaking up the bigger of the clumps.

"Josh mentioned something about living with his grandfather for a while."

The color blanched from her face, but she managed a brief nod. "After Grace's husband died, they moved in with her father-in-law. It didn't work out."

Anxious to turn his attention away from the matter, she gestured to the ground. "I know it's early for planting bulbs, but I couldn't wait. The idea of knowing something's growing — something that I planted . . ."

Light sparked his eyes, turning them

gold in the late summer sun. "I know what you mean."

The sincerity in his voice had her smiling. "I guess you would. This land would make anyone feel that way."

He looked surprised; then a cautious approval lit his eyes. "You like the emptiness?" He gestured to the seemingly endless prairie.

"I don't see it as empty. Awe inspiring, maybe. But not empty. It's much too alive — the colors, the sounds, everything — to ever be empty. I think I understand why you love this place. It's a place for dreaming." The meeting of land and sky, the colors that defied description, the sheer vastness, all pulled at her. What must they do for a man like Gabe, who'd spent his entire life here?

"You feel that?"

"Don't you?"

To emphasize her words, she picked up a handful of dirt and let it sift through her fingers. The dark soil smelled richly of humus and the tiny organisms that made their home there. She'd discarded her gloves earlier, preferring to feel the texture of the dirt between her fingers.

"Next spring," she said, picking up a trowel and attacking the smaller clumps, "this'll all be flowers. Reds and yellows and purples and pinks. I want color. Lots and lots of color. And a vegetable garden."

He lifted the shovel and resumed his task of turning over the ground. Companionably, they worked together, the land a bond between them.

A half hour later, muscles stiff with fatigue, she started to push herself up and groaned. Dropping the shovel, Gabe cupped her elbow and helped her to her feet.

"Thanks."

Unable to help himself, he drew her to him.

She smelled of newly turned earth and sunshine, as fresh and clean as a spring morning. With her face adorned by nothing more than a smudge of dirt and stray curls slipping from the untidy knot, she shouldn't have been so beautiful. She shouldn't have been, but she was. Transfixed, he couldn't look away.

As he stared, her cheeks flushed and her eyes widened slightly. Her reaction mirrored the churning in his gut. She was as deeply affected by him as he was by her. The knowledge, however, didn't do anything for his nerves.

Samson bounded through the freshly

turned earth with Josh not far behind. Josh skidded, nearly tumbling over the puppy, who had stopped to sniff at Shannon's feet.

Gabe steadied him with a hand on the shoulder. "Whoa, there, partner."

Boy and dog alike panted from the exercise.

"Thanks," Josh said between huffs. "Hey . . . Aunt Shannon . . . look what Samson can do." He picked up a stick and threw it as far as he could.

Samson chased after it and retrieved it, dropping it at Josh's feet. Tongue lolling, he pranced about.

Josh dropped to his knees and hugged the dog.

Instinctively, she looked at Gabe, wanting to share the moment with someone. His indulgent smile drew a matching one from her.

"Samson's my best friend," Josh said, his arms still around the dog's neck. "Except for Aunt Shannon."

Shannon swept him into her arms and rose to her feet. He wrapped his arms around her neck, grimy hands and all, and gave her a hug and a big, wet kiss on the cheek. Her smile put the sun to shame.

Gabe enjoyed watching the warm, relaxed way she had with Josh. She was a far cry from his own mother, who'd been more interested in protecting her skin from the sun than in playing with her small son.

Gabe didn't stay long after that, needing to get back to the office. Serving as Blessing's sheriff and mayor didn't require a lot of time, but the paperwork involved of any elected office, even in a small town, mounted quicker than the manure in old man Paget's barn. Smiling at the analogy, he reflected that Ralph Paget would probably take offense at having anything connected with his prize horses compared to bureaucracy-generated paperwork.

At the office, Gabe drummed his fingers on his desk, his thoughts far from the town council minutes he'd been reading. They strayed with increasing frequency to Shannon. She was making a go of the place, he mused with a touch of admiration. Of course, the house and land still needed a lot of work, but she seemed to relish the challenge.

He wanted to get to know her better. She intrigued him, which was more than he could say for any woman he'd met in years.

A frown furrowed his brow. He had the uneasy feeling that she was hiding something. Or running from something.

The latter idea took hold. He had viewed her reluctance to share her past as a natural reticence. But lately he'd got the feeling that it was something more than that. Why her fear — there was no other word for it — when she had learned he was sheriff?

Ms. Shannon Whitney had some explaining to do. He could wait for the answers, though. One thing police work had drilled into him was patience.

# Chapter Four

Rain greeted her the next morning. *Oh, no,* she groaned, thinking of how temperamental her car could be when wet. She'd planned to buy some oils and maybe a canvas or two. Maybe she could hitch a ride into town on the school bus with Josh. The driver had seemed friendly enough.

Rousing Josh proved to be a chore.

"Come on, honey," she coaxed. "If we hurry, we might have time to make waffles," she added, tempting him with his favorites.

That won his cooperation, and within record time they were dressed, breakfasted, and ready for the bus.

When Shannon hesitantly asked the driver for a lift, he nodded. "Be glad to, Ms. Whitney. We've plenty of room."

Mindful of the other children, Shannon refrained from giving Josh a good-bye kiss when they reached the school. "Have a good day," was all she said.

She headed toward the town's one craft

store, which, she had noticed earlier, carried a limited line of art supplies. Though her funds were limited and she wouldn't be able to buy much, she knew she needed the outlet that her art would bring. Just a few tubes of paint and some canvases would be enough to keep her occupied.

Intent on her errand, she failed to hear the voice that called her name. When at last she turned and saw Gabe striding toward her, she stopped.

"Where're you heading?" he asked.

"There," she said, pointing to Myra's Arts and Crafts.

"Mind if I tag along?"

She shook her head. Inside the store, she studied the prices for oils and canvas. Turning her back on him, she opened her wallet to see if she had enough money. Finally, she selected a couple of tubes of oil paint. Regretfully, she put back the larger of the canvases she'd looked at and settled for a smaller one. She took it to the checkout counter, then carefully laid out the correct amount of money.

Following her outside, he asked, "What are your plans now?"

"Waiting for the bus. I rode in with Josh on the school bus," she explained.

"That's a long wait. How about some

lunch with me and then I'll run you both home after school's out?"

With her hunger pangs growing, Shannon was tempted to agree. Caution won out, though. "No . . . thank you."

"It would be a kindness to a lonely man." Taking her hesitation for acceptance, he took her arm and led her to the diner.

After they were seated at a table, he summoned a waiter. "Frank, we won't need menus today. Two specials."

"Yes, sir, Mr. Lambert."

"The food isn't usually much here, but they do the best buffalo wings around," Gabe said. "I don't think you'll be disappointed."

When Frank returned shortly with a platter of buffalo wings, Shannon almost gasped. Each appeared to be as big as her hand.

"Just use your fingers," Gabe advised, observing her struggles with the knife and fork. "It's the only way."

Gingerly, Shannon picked up one and bit cautiously into it. "It's great," she said in some surprise.

They cleaned up the platter of wings, fries, and salad.

Remembering her manners, Shannon said, "Thank you for lunch."

"My pleasure. Are you any good with that rifle you were cleaning?" His abrupt question rattled her a bit.

"Yeah. I'm good."

A broad smile tilted the corners of his mouth. "No false modesty, huh?"

"I never saw the point in it."

"You ever enter any contests?"

She nodded, wondering what he was getting at.

"The fair always has a shooting contest. I think you'd stand a good chance of winning. In the women's division," he qualified. "There's a cash prize."

In spite of herself, Shannon was interested. "For how much?"

Smiling now that he had her attention, he said, "A hundred and fifty dollars for first place in the women's competition. Three hundred dollars in the main event."

"Are women allowed in that?"

"Technically, there's no rule against it, though no woman has ever entered it before." His eyes narrowed slightly. "Would you be thinking of entering that, too?"

"Is there a limit on how many contests one person can enter?"

"None that I know of." He regarded her

speculatively. "It should be interesting anyway."

Something in his tone made her uneasy. "What do you mean?"

"Just that I plan on entering the main competition. You may provide more competition than I've been accustomed to." He didn't sound worried.

"You're right — it'll be interesting. Now, I ought to be on my way. School's out in a few minutes."

"I offered you and Josh a ride home," he reminded her.

*Why not?* Josh would be thrilled at riding in the truck again.

"Thanks."

"Is Josh liking school here?" Gabe asked, gently taking her elbow as they left the restaurant.

"I think so. It's really too early to tell, but he seemed happy enough yesterday. I hope he can make some friends here and the other children will accept him."

"It must be hard taking care of him all by yourself."

"I manage."

The conversation was becoming far too personal. Shannon hunted around for another topic. "From what you said, you must win the contest every year."

"Usually. Of course, this year may be different." He shot her a teasing glance.

"I intend entering both events. And I'll do my best to win."

"I wouldn't have it any other way. In fact, I'll even bring the entry forms to you."

Shannon's thanks were cut short as they approached the school and heard the dismissal bell. Walking around to the first grade room, she looked for Josh in the stream of children spilling out onto the playground. At last, she saw him, standing by himself, facing the wall.

"Josh," she said, touching his shoulder. He refused to turn around. "Mr. Lambert is going to take us home today." Gently, she turned him to face her. "What is it, honey?" she cried in alarm as she saw the tears that formed tiny rivulets down his cheeks. "What happened?"

Gabe had kept his distance until now. He stepped forward and lifted Josh high onto his shoulder. With his other hand, he guided Shannon out of the school grounds. "This isn't the place," he said quietly.

He was right. Better to wait until they were home. Josh didn't protest at being carried by Gabe.

Settled in the front seat of the truck, with Josh in the middle, they rode in silence. Shannon put her arm around his shoulders and held him close to her.

"Some of the kids made fun of me," he burst out. "They said we're taking charity because we're living in the old Tyler house and Miss Loretta gave it to us."

The color drained from Shannon's face. She forced herself to answer in a calm, reassuring tone. "Josh, there's nothing wrong in not having much money. As long as we're honest, we have nothing to be ashamed of."

She ignored the yank at her conscience. She was a fine one to talk about honesty when she was living a lie. But she'd worry about that later; right now she needed to think of Josh.

"Do you understand?"

Slowly, he nodded.

Unsure of what to say next, she looked at Gabe.

He surprised her. "Josh, how about a trip over to see the new foals? We've got three right now, two colts and a filly. They're mighty pretty."

Josh's eyes widened in delight. "Could we, Aunt Shannon?"

"That sounds great." Her eyes thanked Gabe.

The foals enchanted Josh. Shannon, too, was charmed by their endearing awkwardness and growing awareness of their new world. How she would like to capture the gentle awakening and tentative testing of untried limbs in a sketch. Normally, she carried a small sketch book with her wherever she went, never knowing when or where she might find an interesting subject.

She noticed Gabe studying her intently. He then turned to one of the stable hands and spoke briefly to him, gesturing toward the house. The man, little more than a boy, really, turned and headed toward the homestead. Shortly, he returned and handed something to Gabe.

He beckoned to Shannon. Checking to see that Josh was all right — he was kneeling by the filly, seeming especially drawn to her — she obeyed his summons.

"Shannon Whitney, Jeff Hunter." He made the casual introductions. Laying his hand on Jeff's shoulder, he continued, "I noticed you were studying the foals, Shannon. You looked like you were trying to memorize the image. I've seen the same look on Jeff, usually right before he whips out a paper and pencil and starts to sketch." He handed her a tablet of paper and several pencils. "Not the proper equipment, of course, but I thought you might like to make a few drawings."

Surprised at his perceptiveness, Shannon thanked him shyly. "Jeff, why don't you try one, too?" she invited, handing him a pencil and sheet of paper.

He looked at Gabe, who nodded.

Shannon didn't start immediately, content to continue just admiring the lovely creatures for a while. Her first sketch didn't attempt an exact duplication of what she saw, but, rather, expressed the animals' fascinating mixture of grace and awkwardness, their desire for exploration checked by timidity. Her swift strokes caught the line of delicate legs, the dainty arch of the neck, the exquisite shape of the head.

Satisfied with the sketch, she started another, this time including Josh and the almost reverent way in which he touched the filly. Again, her emphasis was on feeling as she strove to portray the communion between the small boy and the beautiful animal.

Gabe kept apart, allowing Shannon the privacy he sensed she needed. Though unaware of it, she presented an adorable picture, absorbed as she was in her task, the tiny puckering of her brows indicating the degree of her concentration.

As if sensing his scrutiny, she looked up

and met his eyes, discovering an expression she couldn't fathom. Her gaze wavered, then dropped. Placing her drawings inside the sketch pad, she realized she'd forgotten the problems she and Josh had brought with them. Guiltily, she remembered Josh's hurt and bewilderment. How could she have lost herself in her own pursuits and abandoned him when he needed her most?

Her self-condemnation must have shown on her face, for Gabe chided her softly, "Don't beat yourself up. Josh's forgotten about it. At least, for now. It's done him good. And you, too. You needed to step away from it."

Again his discernment confused her.

"Did your drawings come out well?" he asked, indicating the sheaf of papers she clutched.

"They're just sketches, really; 'drawings' is much too grand a word for them."

"May I see them?" The usual note of command in his voice was absent now. He genuinely sought her permission.

She held them close, reluctant to expose them to his gaze, suddenly aware that his opinion was important to her. Too important. This was ridiculous. His sensitivity this afternoon had surprised her, that was all.

He watched the play of confusion and

doubt chase across her face. Her features were wonderfully expressive and revealed, with childlike candor, whatever she felt. The facade of independence and toughness that she fought so hard to maintain was just that. What had caused her to assume such a mask, he didn't know. At a guess, though, she had erected the barriers to hide her vulnerability. Or fear.

Aware that he was still waiting, Shannon gave the sketches to him hesitantly. "They're just impressions," she said, warning him not to expect too much.

Without haste, Gabe studied them. Though no expert, he realized the talent necessary to evoke feelings on paper as she had done. Even with her crude tools, she had caught the essence of her scenes, the engaging foal in wonder at his new surroundings, the total absorption of boy and horse in each other. Their simplicity caused the viewer to project part of himself when gazing at them. Good art, he'd always thought, invited an involvement between viewer and picture.

Unconsciously, Shannon held her breath and waited for his judgment.

"They're beautiful."

Warmed by his praise, she blushed in pleasure.

"Hey, Gabe, look at this," Josh called.

Gabe looked up to see Josh running a currycomb over the mare's mane. His lips pursed, he concentrated on his task.

"Don't worry, Ms. Whitney," Jeff said. "I'll keep an eye on him."

"Thank you." Her voice came out hoarse and raw, and she dipped her head. "Thank you, both."

Gabe fitted a finger beneath her chin, urging her to look at him.

Her lashes lifted slowly, and he saw the glisten of tears on them. He had a feeling very few people had ever seen Shannon cry. A protective streak he hadn't known he possessed surfaced, and he curved his hand over her shoulder, drawing her to him.

Gently, he ran his hand over her hair and heard her breath go out on a sigh as she leaned against him.

She looked up at him, surprise clear in her eyes — whether at his gesture of comfort or her acceptance of it, he couldn't be sure. His heart leapt when she didn't move away.

Josh tugged at her hand, demanding her attention. With a smile at Gabe, she stooped and listened to him.

Gabe heard Shannon murmur something to Josh, who was now smiling. The quiet cadence of her voice, her head bent close to the small boy's, touched something deep within Gabe. Try as he would, he couldn't recall any of this kind of loving attention from his mother.

He'd been well taken care of and had never lacked for the basics. Unless one considered love a basic.

It made him look more closely at Shannon. She gave love as easily as she breathed. For that reason, he should keep his distance. Love was the last thing he was looking for.

"Josh is lucky to have you," he said.

"I'm the lucky one."

He shifted his gaze to settle on the small boy, who was now nuzzling one of the colts. "I guess you are, at that."

"Thank you for inviting us here. We ought to be going."

After taking them home, Gabe seemed disinclined to leave. Shannon settled Josh in the kitchen, happily munching on the brownies she'd made yesterday. Leaving him to devour the treat, she joined Gabe in the living room.

Canvases piled two and three deep lined the walls. He gestured to them. "Yours?"

"Guilty."

"Can I take a look?" At her nod, he pulled one of the paintings away from the wall.

Bold colors, just on the edge of clashing, randomly crisscrossed the canvas. Not randomly, he corrected himself. The strokes, as bold as the colors, formed a design that shifted when he moved.

Intrigued, he put it back and picked up another one. This one, a landscape, was all blues and blacks. Not a typical landscape, it was of gnarled trees bent even more by a raging storm. He could all but feel the force of the wind, the rain on his face.

He flipped through the rest of the canvases — portraits, still lifes, all the traditional settings with none of the traditional trappings. Each contained what he was coming to recognize as her style — energy and passion mixed together in a riot of color. Her work wasn't restful; nor was it easy to turn away from. It demanded a response from the viewer.

"Why didn't you say something?"

"About what?"

He could only stare at her, shaking his head. She didn't know. The lady honestly didn't know what she had. She'd said she sketched some. An understatement if he'd ever heard one. But these . . . he knew people who would pay top dollar for such work.

"Why aren't you selling your work?"

"These are for myself. I don't paint professionally."

"Why the heck not?"

She shrugged.

He decided to back off.

"I appreciate your help this afternoon," she said.

"I'm glad I was there. If you take my advice, you won't make too much of it. Children are resilient, and Josh's no exception. He'll take his cue on how to respond from you." He watched her closely as she digested his words.

Recognizing the wisdom of his advice, she nodded. "I know you're right. But what happens the next time? Children can be cruel, especially when they parrot what their parents have said," she finished bitterly.

Realizing the intimacy of this conversation, she drew back, both physically and emotionally. "Please don't worry about us. I'll have to sort this out by myself."

"By myself," he mimicked her proud words. "Can't you accept help when it's offered?"

Frightened how close she had come to

confiding in him, to leaning on him, if just for a moment, Shannon backed away.

"What kind of life is this for a young woman? Scratching out an existence, trying to be both mother and father to a little boy? If not now, then soon, you'll break under the strain."

"Please go," she whispered. She wanted only to be alone, to lick her wounds in private.

Sensing how close she was to tears, Gabe left. To stay would deprive her of the release tears would bring. He checked an impulse to return and take her in his arms. Somehow, she had gotten under his skin. Whatever he felt for her — running the gamut from maddening exasperation to a protective tenderness — it wasn't indifference.

On the way home, Gabe felt the sudden chill of the empty truck with the prospect of a lonely evening ahead of him. Inviting Shannon and Josh to his place had been as much for his own sake as it had been to offer comfort to them.

Loneliness was an unfamiliar emotion.

He'd grown accustomed to being alone long ago. Normally he didn't mind. But loneliness was something different, something he hadn't allowed himself to feel for more years than he cared to remember.

He felt it now. It was more than the silence that even the radio failed to fill. It was more than knowing he was returning to an empty house. It was the realization that he wished things were different.

Shannon's house — he could no longer think of it as the old Tyler place — was more of a home than his house. It had nothing to do with the architecture or decor; it had everything to do with the love that saturated the rooms.

He'd built his house with the intention of sharing it with the woman he loved. His plans to fill it with children and laughter had evaporated with the end of his engagement.

Since then he hadn't given the idea of starting a family much thought. Until now.

Shannon pressed her fingers into the inner corners of her eyes, willing the tears not to come as she recalled Josh's distress. Her own pride had taken a beating when she'd accepted a home from the town, but she hadn't counted on Josh being subjected to the cruel teasing of children because of it.

How did she explain to a six-year-old boy that she couldn't afford a house because she'd had to leave her job to care for his dying mother?

At all costs, she must keep up her show of calm in front of Josh. Gabe had been right about one thing: Josh would model his reaction upon hers.

She was attracted to Gabe despite everything; she could no longer deny it. She would not, could not, though, succumb to the temptation of leaning on him, of drawing on his strength. To do so would be fatal. If her attraction to him had been only physical, she could have handled it. Her emotional reaction to him worried her far more. Talking with him was so easy, she forgot to be careful.

"Aunt Shannon," Josh called, interrupting her unhappy thoughts.

"Out here, honey. Come join me." Shannon had to smile at the picture he made — chocolate frosting outlined his mouth, and even his nose had a touch on it.

"I'm sorry I cried. I didn't mean to," he said.

"It's all right to cry. You don't need to be ashamed of tears. They can be good." She paused before continuing, "Do you remember when we talked about Mommy? I explained that she was very sick and couldn't be with us any longer. When she was sick, I quit work so that I could take care of her. That meant I couldn't earn any money."

"I can tell the kids that."

"Right," she said, relieved that he'd accepted something she had a hard time accepting herself. "Your mommy didn't want to leave us. She loved you very much. She still does."

"In heaven? With my daddy?"

"That's right. In heaven."

"She'd want us to be happy even when she can't be with us." Shannon's composure almost collapsed as she remembered her sister's last words.

Josh slipped his hand in hers.

"About the children at school — they don't mean to be unkind. Sometimes children, adults too, say things because they don't understand."

"But I want to be friends with them."

"I know that." She squeezed his hand. "They will, too. We just have to give them a chance. All right?"

"All right." His smile wobbled around the edges.

Again Shannon marveled at his acceptance and trust in her. She prayed she would never disappoint him. "What did you think of the foals?" she asked for a change of subject.

His rapt look answered her. "They were great. Do you think we could see them again?"

"It's up to Mr. Lambert. We could ask him," she suggested, though somewhat reluctantly.

"Why do you call him 'Mister'? He told me to call him Gabe."

"Sometimes adults are more formal with each other."

"But he called you Shannon," Josh pointed out with irrefutable logic.

"Yes, well, I don't know," she admitted at last. She sought to steer the conversation away from the disturbing Gabe Lambert. "I'd better get started on dinner. How would you like sloppy joes?"

"My favorite! Can I help?"

She pretended to think for a minute. "Well, I do need a taster to tell me if they're done." She looked him over with an experienced eye. "You look like you might be an official taster, but what's the test?"

Josh, too, knew the game. "Clean hands," he said, after imitating her pose of deep thought. With that, he scurried off to the sink to clean up.

It was a ritual that they went through for

every dinner. Shannon had devised a number of such games. They gave a feeling of security to Josh, their unchanging rules something that he could count on in a world where too many changes had already occurred in his short life.

Washing dishes later that evening, she determinedly tried to exorcise Gabe from her mind. When his handsome face appeared in the soapsuds, though, she gave up. Perhaps sleep would banish what willpower could not.

"I just came by to drop these off," Gabe said the next day, handing Shannon the entry forms for the shooting contest "— and to find out how Josh is feeling."

Gabe was not a man who made a habit of lying to himself. The flowers clutched in his other hand mocked the reasons he'd just given for his visit. He'd wanted to see Shannon. He'd been concerned about both her and Josh. Even more than concern, though, was need. The need to see Shannon — to be with her — was what had brought him here.

If Shannon was surprised at his visit, she didn't show it. Her smile was genuine. "He's fine. It's like you said — children are a lot stronger than we give them credit for.

Are those for me?" she asked, gesturing to the flowers he held at his side.

Disgusted with himself, he all but thrust the flowers in her face. "They reminded me of you."

Charmed, she bent her head, sniffing appreciatively. "Thank you."

"If you'll fill these forms out, I'll deliver them for you."

"Thanks."

Quickly, she wrote in the information and then noticed the line stating the fees. Twenty-five dollars for each event.

*Of course, there would be a fee,* she told herself angrily. The purpose of the fair was to raise money for the school. Why hadn't she realized that before? Regretfully, she pushed the forms away. Fifty dollars. She couldn't risk that much, not on a chance that she might win.

"You're worried about the fee."

The words jolted her, and she jerked around to find Gabe standing inside the door. There was no point in lying, and she nodded.

"Do you have the drawings you did yesterday?" he asked. "Get them for me, will you?"

She took them from the folder where she'd placed them and handed them to him.

He laid them on the table and studied them as he'd done yesterday. "Would you be willing to sell these?" he asked after several minutes.

Realizing his intention, Shannon picked them up and said with quiet dignity, "I don't take charity."

"And I'm not in the habit of offering it. As I said yesterday, these are beautiful. I'd like to buy them and hang them in my study."

She couldn't doubt the sincerity of his tone, but still she hesitated. "I don't know what they're worth —"

"In Laramie, drawings like these go for several hundred dollars apiece," he informed her. At her gasp, he said, "That's for known artists, of course. Do you think two hundred dollars for the pair would be fair?"

"M-more than fair," she stammered. "Are you sure? They're just quick sketches, like I said."

He drew out four fifty-dollar bills, handed three to her, then placed the other in the fold of the form. He glanced around. "You've been busy."

She grimaced. "The more I do, the more I discover how much needs to be done." She held up a hand. "Don't say it."

"That I told you so? Never."

"I've enjoyed it. It's like going on a treasure hunt and finding things you didn't know were there."

"That's a unique way of looking at it. Not many women would view it that way. All they'd see is the hard work involved."

"There's been plenty of that, too," Shannon admitted.

"How 'bout I give you a hand? I've got a couple of hours."

"You really want to spend your free time stripping floors?"

He didn't have any free time. Hadn't had any for more years than he cared to remember. But the opportunity to spend a few hours with Shannon was enough to have him ignore the chores that awaited him at the ranch and the paperwork that had piled up at the sheriff's office.

Removing the grime and grit of generations was a grueling job. When lunchtime came, she suggested they eat outside, away from the fumes of the chemical stripper they'd been using. They shared a picnic lunch under a tree in the front yard.

Bologna sandwiches washed down with soda didn't qualify as a romantic meal. Ants invited themselves to the impromptu picnic, and flies buzzed overhead with annoying frequency. None of it mattered as he watched Shannon.

She didn't clutter the conversation with meaningless chatter. Nor did he feel awkward when the silence stretched into minutes. Maybe the difference lay with the woman he was with.

# Chapter Five

The dry prairie breeze ruffled Gabe's hair, and Shannon found herself wanting to brush it off his forehead.

His first, gentle kiss took her by surprise. Her lips softened beneath his as a sweet longing coursed through her. When his mouth touched hers again, she was prepared.

Or thought she was.

Nothing could prepare her for the need that filled her, a need to give as well as to take. In the end, she did both. And understood for the first time what love meant.

Her use of the word — even silently — shook her to the core. Love? Since when had she been thinking in those terms? Love implied commitment. And that was something she wasn't ready to give, something she couldn't give. Not now. Not when her life was complicated with so many secrets.

Gently, she pulled away, needing the distance.

She'd been trying to decide, wondering

if she had the courage to tell him everything, wondering if she had the *right* to tell
him, trying to work out a way to begin,
when she was in his arms again.

After the surprise faded, it felt right.
Right and good and, most of all, safe to be
there, cradled against him in the brightness
of day.

She'd spent too long in the shadows.

She pressed closer against him, absorbing his strength, needing his warmth.

She felt as though nothing could harm
her, not when she was in the circle of his
arms. The thought shamed her, but she
welcomed it. For so long, she'd stood on
her own. Now, she was tempted to lean on
someone else.

He kissed her again. Her heart thudded,
the beat drowning out everything else as
she gave herself up to the moment.

He gave her time, if she wanted to back
away, space, if she needed it. She didn't
want time, didn't need space; all she
needed was him.

The realization was sobering.

Shannon knew a quiet joy at the pleasure
a kiss could evoke. She wanted to throw
herself into his arms and bury her face
against his neck, to breathe in the scent
that was uniquely his. Suddenly aware of

what she was doing, she pushed against his chest.

Gabe took the hint and dropped his hands. She noticed his breathing was not quite steady as he picked up an apple.

Her own breath came in ragged gasps. Desperately, she searched for an explanation for her behavior. She'd been under a lot of stress lately, and she was lonely.

But the rapid tattoo of her heart beating against her chest made a lie of the explanation. It was not loneliness she'd been feeling. Far from it.

"Tell me about your parents," she said, determined to keep him talking. When he was talking, he couldn't be doing other things. Things like kissing her, things like turning her inside out with needs she hadn't even known she had.

Until Gabe.

Gabe gave her a look that left little doubt that he saw through her ploy, but he obliged her. She soon forgot her own troubles as she listened to him. His description of his childhood sounded bleak — a mother who was more interested in herself than her child, a father too wrapped up in a failing ranch to pay attention to a small boy.

It was only when he described his grandparents that his face lit up. She listened as he reminisced about them. The love he described had her eyes filling with tears.

"They sound pretty wonderful," she said softly.

"They were. What they had makes anything else seem pretty second rate," he said, echoing her own feelings. "Would you want that someday? With the right man?"

She wanted to believe that his question was purely hypothetical, but something in his eyes told her it was more than that. *Stop it,* she ordered herself. She was reading something into his words that wasn't there.

She thought of her ex-fiancé, who'd refused to accept her and Josh as a package deal. What kind of man would want to raise another man's child?

She stole a look at Gabe. She saw the strength in his eyes, in the lines defining his face. Strength seasoned with compassion. And, for a moment, she let herself dream.

He didn't press the issue, for which she was grateful. His next words, though, made her wish he'd stayed with that topic.

"I know you're frightened of something, something you can't tell me. The trouble with secrets is that while you're trying to keep them in, you keep the people who care about you out."

"I don't —"

He put a finger to her lips. "Don't. Until you can tell me the truth, don't say anything."

She wanted to. Oh, how she wanted to. When he drew her into his arms, she went willingly.

She stayed there, needing comfort. But comfort soon changed to something more, something less easily defined, something that caused her to pull away.

"How about you? Isn't there someone special in your life?" she asked, wanting to turn the conversation away from herself. She couldn't believe that he was single by choice. A man like Gabe could have any woman he wanted.

He didn't answer but lowered his head and brushed his lips against hers. She felt the breath rush into her throat and stay there.

He left shortly after that. She wasn't sorry to see him go. Something had happened when he kissed her, something she wasn't ready to examine.

The following day, Loretta came over to finalize the ads for the town fair. When she admired the flowers that Shannon had arranged in a vase on the table, Shannon felt her cheeks growing hot.

"Give," Loretta said. "Who's the admirer?"

"Gabe brought them," Shannon admitted.

"Ooh."

Loretta was way off base in what she was thinking.

"It's not like that. He was just being neighborly." There was that word again. "He stayed to help me sand the floors."

"Gabe spent the day here? During the busiest season of the year? That's a lot more than neighborly, honey." A knowing smile settled over her lips. "You're being courted," she said as they sipped lemonade at Shannon's kitchen table.

"Courted?"

"The man brings you flowers, helps you dig up the garden, spends every spare moment with you. That's courting in my book." Loretta sat back with a satisfied smile.

Shannon tested the idea. It had been a long time since any man had paid attention to her in that way, not since her fiancé had dumped her.

She basked in the warmth of knowing a man found her attractive, before she caught herself. She had no right thinking — feeling — that way. Not when she was living a lie and had nothing to offer in return but more lies.

Loretta looked at her with eyes that missed nothing. "You've got it bad, girl."

Shannon bristled. "I —"

"Don't go denying it. I know the signs." The older woman patted her gray hair. "I know it doesn't look like it now, but I had my share of beaux." She sighed in reminiscence. "Men knew how to treat a girl back then. 'Course, Gabe's not too shabby in that area, either." She took Shannon's hand in her own. "He's a good man, a strong man. He needs a woman who'll stand by him."

More uncomfortable than ever, Shannon gently withdrew her hand. She wasn't that woman. Gabe was the finest man she'd ever met. He deserved someone who was free to give him her whole self. With the lie she was living, she wasn't free to do that. Might never be. All she could give him were bits and parts of herself. Intuitively, she knew that wouldn't be enough. Not for a man like Gabe.

With quick sensitivity, Loretta changed the subject. "Show me what you've been up to."

Shannon brought out the sketches for the posters and flyers for the fair. "What do you think?"

Loretta took her time studying them. "They're great. You've got a real flair. You sure you've never done this kind of thing before?"

Lying to her friend didn't set well with Shannon, but she thought it better to keep her former occupation a secret. People in hiding had been caught by letting things smaller slip.

She feigned a shrug. "I just like fiddling around with paints and stuff like that." That much, at least, was true.

Loretta gave her a long look but let it go.

Shannon had a feeling her friend saw a great deal more than she let on.

They spent a pleasurable afternoon going over plans for the fair and coming up with wild ideas of how Shannon would spend the prize money that Loretta was certain she'd win in the shooting contest.

Loretta kept up a steady stream of chatter, mentioning the PTA meeting the following evening. "I have to go because I'm on the school board." She gave her braying laugh. "Comes from being a nosey parker. You ought to come along."

Anxious to feel a part of the community,

Shannon agreed to attend. "I'll have to bring Josh."

"I'm sure he'd be fine, but he'd probably be very bored. Why don't I ask my oldest granddaughter? She's seventeen. I'm sure she'd be glad to tend him for a couple of hours."

"I don't know," Shannon demurred.

"She'd love to have Josh," Loretta said. "Let's see, you don't have a phone, do you?"

Shannon shook her head. "I'm afraid not. It seemed like an extravagance when I didn't know anyone to call."

"I'll come by and pick you up. Say about seven."

Loretta was a bulldozer in polyester, Shannon decided. Once set on course, the older woman didn't budge.

Clearing the table after dinner, Shannon let her thoughts wander back to Gabe. He hadn't had to bring by the forms, yet he'd gone out of his way to help her.

Maybe, just maybe, he was beginning to feel something different for her. A smile tugged at her lips as she considered the possibility. Not that she could afford to get involved with anyone right now, she reminded herself.

"Aunt Shannon." Josh's insistent voice

called her back to the present. He held up a drawing for her approval.

Two hours later, after she'd checked on Josh, who had fallen asleep halfway through his bedtime story, and finished cleaning up the kitchen, she sat at the kitchen table, her account book propped open in front of her.

No matter how she added up the figures, the numbers came out the same. She was rapidly running out of money. Outfitting Josh for school had cost more than she'd planned. Having the utilities hooked up had taken another chunk.

No doubt about it. The prize money would come in handy.

At her door the next evening, Shannon thanked Gabe for the ride home. Somehow, Loretta had finagled Gabe into taking Shannon home, saying she'd drop Josh off.

How she'd allowed herself to be maneuvered that way, Shannon didn't know. The older woman's intention was obvious. Apparently Gabe guessed it also, for he smiled wryly.

"Loretta's wearing her matchmaking hat again," he said.

His frank admission that he knew exactly what was going on relieved some of the tension, and Shannon found herself smiling. "Does she do that often?"

"Not so you'd notice. Not until . . ." He left the rest of the sentence hanging.

Afraid to ask what he'd been about to say, she gestured to the kitchen. "Would you like some coffee?"

"No, thanks. I've got an early morning and the caffeine would only keep me up." But he seemed in no hurry to leave and settled on the lumpy sofa.

After a brief hesitation, she sat beside him. When the kiss came, she wasn't surprised. Neither was she prepared. Not for the feelings it evoked within her. Not for the need with which she accepted it. Not for the intensity with which she returned it.

Why was it that this man should affect her so strongly, should cause her pulse to scramble and her heart to race?

It was the way he looked at her, she decided, as if he could see into her mind and know what she was thinking. She ran an unsteady hand through her hair. She didn't even know what she was thinking when he looked at her, so how could he?

"Someday we'll settle what's between us," he said. "And we won't need Loretta's — or anyone else's — help to do it." The intensity in his gaze made the words a promise.

Loretta arrived, then, with a sleepy Josh in tow.

"Let me get him," Gabe said as Shannon stooped to pick up Josh.

"I can manage."

"I know. But you don't have to. Not while I'm here." Again, she sensed his words held a deeper meaning. Gabe lifted Josh into his arms and carried him into the bedroom.

She raised her head to find Loretta watching her, a satisfied look in her eyes.

As she undressed for bed, Shannon reflected on the evening. It had been a disturbing one. Gabe had aroused feelings in her she hadn't even known existed. Sheer physical appeal, she could have handled. But it was more than that. Much more. But she couldn't let it go any further.

She couldn't risk what an involvement with him would inevitably bring. If she repeated that to herself enough times, she just might begin to believe it.

Three sleepless hours later, she acknowledged she'd been lying to herself. She'd do well to stay away from him. Not because he might discover the lie she was living, but because it would be all too easy to give him her heart.

The week passed quickly. In between doing jobs on the house, Shannon snatched spare hours to practice her shooting. By sheer will and working herself to exhaustion, she managed to keep her thoughts from Gabe.

As though aware of her need for space, he hadn't stopped by. She was by turns disappointed and relieved.

The morning of the fair dawned bright and clear, a magical kind of day when anything was possible. When Gabe arrived to escort her and Josh, she was about to refuse. But her resolve to keep her distance from him crumbled under the pleading in Josh's eyes.

"Thank you. Josh would like that."

"What about you?" he asked softly.

"I'd like it, too," she said and knew she'd spoken only the truth.

With Gabe at her side, they strolled through the fair, admiring the exhibits. A quilt display caught her eye, and she went to stare at the exquisite handiwork. One quilt, with a log cabin pattern, sported a first-place ribbon.

Absorbed in the quilts, she didn't notice when Gabe disappeared.

"Where'd Gabe get to?" she asked Josh.

He grinned. "It's a surprise." He tugged at her hand, dragging her to a fenced-off area.

Two men, stripped down to jeans, stepped into the makeshift arena. Her lips parted in surprise as she recognized Gabe. A squeal pierced the air as a young pig was released into the arena.

"It's a greased pig contest," Josh explained. "Gabe told me all about it."

Gabe and the other man chased the pig around the enclosure. The crowd roared as first Gabe and then the other man caught and then lost the squirming animal.

At last Gabe fell upon the pig, grasped it by the legs, and held it up.

The referee clapped Gabe on the shoulder. "This year's winner, Gabe Lambert."

The two opponents shook hands. After they'd washed off, they reappeared.

"Shannon Whitney," Gabe said, slipping an arm around her waist. "Meet my deputy, Ray McClellan."

Her ready smile died at the introduction. Meeting another lawman was the last thing she wanted — or needed. She'd come to terms with the fact that Gabe was the sheriff. Meeting his deputy forced her to remember what she preferred to forget.

The open admiration in the young man's eyes allayed some of her fears. "Glad to meet you, Ms. Whitney."

Aware that Gabe was watching her, she tried to smile and found her lips stiff. "You, too, Deputy."

"Ray," he said easily.

"Ray. And it's Shannon."

"Ladies and gentlemen," a voice squawked over the loudspeaker, "the shooting contest begins in thirty minutes."

"Come on," Gabe said, taking her by the elbow. "Let's get some lunch before it starts."

She ordered a hamburger for lunch but barely tasted it. Nerves and guilt combined to dry out her mouth and coat her hands with sweat. Dumping her hamburger in the trash, she headed back to where she'd stored her gun. She broke it apart, checked it, and put it back together.

"How many times have you done that today?" Gabe asked.

"A few."

"Let's walk," he said, draping an arm around her shoulders. "You need to work off those nerves."

It'd take a marathon to work off the case of nerves that had settled in her gut, but, after making sure Josh was all right with Loretta, she fell into step with Gabe.

He urged her along with a hand at the small of her back. He talked about ranching, about growing up in Wyoming, and about a dozen other things, until she felt herself relaxing.

He'd known what she needed and had quietly set about seeing to it. His sensitivity no longer surprised her. She was growing accustomed to the way he picked up on her feelings. What's more, she was starting to like it.

That wasn't in her game plan. Her shoulders tensed as she acknowledged how important Gabe was becoming to her.

"Hey, what's wrong?" he asked.

"Nothing."

"Don't give me 'nothing.' You were as soft as melted butter and now you're as tight as a bow."

Deliberately, she let the tension seep from her.

Apparently she succeeded, for he smiled. "That's better." He checked his watch. "Time to be getting back."

"Yeah." Did he hear the reluctance in her voice? She didn't want this time to end.

Loretta offered to watch Josh during the

contest. Shannon accepted gratefully and smiled nervously. Josh held up crossed fingers as a good-luck sign. Shannon blew him a kiss, then took her place in the sign-up line for the women's division. She shifted on her feet impatiently, the waiting honing a fine edge on her already strained nerves. A large hand gripped her shoulder.

"Steady, Shannon," Gabe said quietly. "Don't let this part rattle you. You'll do fine."

His words steadied her, and she whispered her thanks.

Ten women had entered the competition. Shannon was assigned the fourth position. She looked over the other contestants and wished she knew something of their ability. Each handled her rifle with ease and confidence, betraying none of the anxiety that had threatened to overwhelm her a few minutes earlier.

Shannon looked on with detachment as the first three women took their turns. They performed creditably, scoring 72, 70, and 69, respectively, out of a possible 75 points.

She wiped her palms against her jeans, an instinctive but unnecessary gesture, as they were already dry. An unnatural calm settled over her, leaving her feeling slightly removed from her surroundings.

The hubbub of excited chatter swarming about her was replaced by her father's voice. "Forget everything and everyone else, honey," he would say. "Concentrate on the target. Hold your gun steady and squeeze gently on the trigger. More shots have gone wild due to jerking the trigger than to poor aim." Deliberately, she avoided scanning the crowd for Gabe's face.

"Contestant number four," the loud-speaker squawked.

Shannon took her place, nodded when she was ready, and fired.

"Three rounds — each a perfect hit," the judging official announced, "for a score of 75 points."

A ripple of surprised approval swept through the crowd.

The target was removed; another, fifty yards farther away, was set in place. She fired, her score a perfect 75 again. As she withdrew, the crowd cheered. Friendly congratulations were pressed upon her as she made her way back to where Loretta stood with Josh.

Upon seeing her, Josh ran to her and hugged her legs. Shannon bent to kiss him.

"You were great, Aunt Shannon."

She managed a laugh. "Thanks. But I'm glad my part's over."

Loretta joined them, bubbling over with excitement. "No one else can touch you," she predicted. "You'll have to win."

Afraid to let herself count on it, Shannon shook her head. "Someone might tie with me."

The remaining six contestants took their turns, with the highest score a 74.

"The winner of the women's division is Ms. Shannon Whitney," a voice over the loudspeaker announced.

Josh let out a whoop and grabbed Shannon around the legs, nearly toppling her over.

Amid the cheers of the crowd, Loretta urged Shannon forward to accept her trophy and check. She whispered a hoarse "Thank you" and turned to find Gabe behind her.

"Congratulations. Let's celebrate," he suggested. "Treats are on me. What will you have, Shannon? Josh?"

Hungry now, she chose a hot dog with the works, a chocolate malt, and an order of onion rings. Josh asked for the same with the addition of a cone of cotton candy.

"I wish it were all over," Shannon said with a contented sigh as she finished the last of her malt.

Gabe nodded in understanding. "It's going to be rough all right."

They cleaned up their lunch scraps and headed back to the competition ring.

This time, Shannon was assigned the eighth position; she was the only woman among the twelve contestants. The targets were set farther back than in the women's competition and included one swinging bull's-eye.

Several men scored in the low 90s, out of a possible 100 points. She watched them in admiration and joined in the cheering. Finally, it was her turn. She practiced the same relaxation techniques as she had before. They served her well, and she scored 98, the highest score thus far.

Gabe was the final contestant. He approached the task before him as he did everything — with an air of easy confidence based upon skill. He scored a series of perfect bull's-eyes and brought in a score of 100.

Shannon cheered along with the rest, although she felt a brief stab of disappointment. Gabe met her eyes briefly. She smiled at him and gave him a thumbs-up sign.

"First place winner is Gabe Lambert," the same voice rasped over the loud-speaker.

Josh and Loretta crowded around Gabe and Shannon, thrilled by the double victory.

"You're a worthy opponent, Shannon Whitney," Gabe saluted her.

"As are you, kind sir," she said, returning the compliment.

A light flashed in her face and she blinked at the momentary blindness. When it passed, she saw a teenage boy with a camera.

"Hey, Gabe, how 'bout one of you and the lady together?" he asked.

Gabe looped an arm around her shoulders. "Smile."

She tried to wriggle away. "Please . . . I don't want my picture taken."

"You're a celebrity," the boy said. "Be a sport and let me get one of the both of you. Maybe I can sell it to the paper."

Realizing they'd attracted an audience, she didn't feel like making a scene. Despite the photographer's coaxing, she lowered her head. When he'd taken two more shots, she managed to make her getaway.

Gabe caught up with her. "What was that all about?"

"Nothing," she mumbled. "I just don't like having my picture taken."

She ignored the frown he directed at her and forced a smile. His eyes seemed to strip away the web of lies she'd spun around herself. Instinctively, she drew Josh closer to her, laying a protective hand on his shoulder. "I need to get Josh home. It's been a long day."

"You can catch up on your sleep tomorrow. Tonight we're going dancing."

She knew of the dance that capped off the fair activities, of course, but she hadn't planned on attending.

"Hey, we're friends, aren't we?"

"Of course, we are, but —"

"But nothing. Friends like to make each other happy. Right?"

"Right," she was forced to agree.

"So, will you make me happy by being my date at the dance tonight?"

"That's not fair," Shannon protested, laughing in spite of herself.

"Oh, I wouldn't say that. I like to get my own way. And I usually do."

"You're incorrigible, Gabe Lambert."

"So I've been told."

"There's Josh —"

"Loretta's offered to watch him. It's all arranged."

"How did you manage that?"

He twirled an imaginary mustache and leered at her. "I've got a way with older women."

"You've got a way with women of any age," she said, smiling at his nonsense. "And little boys as well. Josh mentions you about a hundred times a day."

She tried to put the incident with the picture-taking in perspective. An amateur picture in a small-town paper wasn't likely to make the big papers. Chances were the boy's photographs wouldn't even make the local paper.

Loretta, with Josh in tow, showed up. "Is it all set for tonight?" she asked Gabe.

"All set."

"Good." Her wide, mischievous smile invited a smile from Shannon in return.

At home, Shannon chuckled over Gabe and Loretta's scheming. Despite their high-handed methods, she couldn't be annoyed with them. She hummed to herself while dressing. It would be fun to go to a dance. She hadn't been to one since before Grace had died.

As the hour drew closer for Gabe to pick her up, her enthusiasm took a downswing. She could practically feel the tension humming along her nerves, the stork-sized butterflies flapping their wings in her stomach. She hadn't felt this way since her junior prom.

*Get a grip, girl,* she told herself. *It's a dance, for heaven's sake. Nothing to get so het up about.*

That said, she swallowed and prayed she could make herself believe it.

# Chapter Six

The dance at the local lodge was well under way when Shannon and Gabe arrived. The lodge hall buzzed with dozens of conversations, the festive air no doubt a result of the fair's success.

Gesturing toward the dancers, Gabe asked, "Shall we?" At her nod, he led her onto the dance floor.

Though slightly apprehensive that she would prove a poor partner, she found herself following his lead and moving with him as though they'd been dancing together for years. He led her with practiced ease, his hand warm on the curve of her waist. He drew her closer till she could feel the steady thud of his heart. Could he feel the erratic thumping of her own? The thought had her tensing slightly.

As though reading her thoughts, he murmured, "Relax. I won't eat you."

She laughed jerkily. "I know that."

"Then, let's enjoy ourselves. See how well we dance together."

She couldn't deny it. Their bodies fit together as if they'd been designed with that sole purpose in mind. In her heels, she nearly came to his chin, her head nestled comfortably on his shoulder. At the end of the dance, he escorted her to the refreshment table.

"Hi, Sheriff," Ray McClellan said. He turned his attention to Shannon. "Good to see you again, Ms. Whitney. Would you — would you dance with me? If it's all right with you, Sheriff?"

"It's up to the lady."

Though Ray was probably only a few years younger than herself, she felt ancient beside his fresh-faced youth. Aware that he was waiting, she said, "I'd be honored."

The blush started at his neck and worked its way up his face, making her want to hug him. With touching formality, he cupped a hand under her elbow and led her to join the other dancers.

"Have you known Gabe long?" The question came out before she realized she'd voiced her thoughts aloud.

"Most of my life," Ray said. "He went to school with my older brother. I could tell you stories . . ."

He spent the remainder of the dance regaling her with stories about Gabe.

The dance over, he led her to the refreshment table, where they were joined by Gabe.

Gabe cocked an eyebrow at Ray. "What lies have you been filling Shannon's head with?"

Ray exchanged a knowing smile with Shannon. "Just sharing some old stories."

"Then it's up to me to set the record straight." Gabe held out his hand. "C'mon, Shannon, before he starts spreading any more of his lies."

They circled the floor, his unwavering gaze rattling her a bit. He danced her out to the patio, where the air smelled of wild roses and honeysuckle. The summer night wrapped around them, the star-spangled sky the perfect canopy.

She felt a small crack around her heart as he held her. For tonight — tonight only — it was just the two of them. She laid her head against his shoulder as the night deepened around them and tried to remind herself of all the reasons she shouldn't — couldn't — love him. None of them seemed very important right now, with his hand fitted warmly against the small of her back, his breath softly caressing her cheek.

The music stopped, signaling the end of

the dance, but they continued to sway to music heard only in their hearts. When others spilled out onto the patio, Gabe reluctantly released her. They found a wrought-iron love seat secluded from view by a clump of bushes.

"Thank you for tonight," she whispered.

"Thank you." His lips curved, then softened against hers. The kiss was as soft as the summer night, as gentle as the breeze that caught her hair.

"Something's happening between us," he said. "You feel it, don't you?"

She couldn't think of lying. He had incredible eyes, the kind a woman could stare into for hours and never grow tired of. They were looking at her now, waiting, questioning, challenging. "I feel it." The hitch in her breath duplicated that in her heart.

"People who" — he hesitated, obviously choosing his words carefully — "care about each other share things."

Where was he heading? "Things?" she repeated cautiously.

"I know you're running from something, Shannon. Why won't you let me help you?"

Her stomach curled in tight coils as he came painfully close to the truth. It was already apparent he had questions, questions she had no answers for.

She pushed away from him. For a moment, she'd been in danger of forgetting the role she'd chosen to play.

Sighing heavily, he stood and offered her a hand up. "Someday, you're going to trust me enough to let me help you. In the meantime, we'll consider the subject closed. Okay?"

"Okay."

But it wasn't, and they both knew it.

Returning from a grueling ride the following evening, Gabe rubbed down Buck, frowning over the lather the gelding had worked up during their ride. Gabe had pushed them both hard in an effort to forget the mess he'd made with Shannon. She'd been wary and skittish when he'd brought her home from the dance. His probing had threatened the cautious friendship they'd shared and he found himself regretting it more than he thought possible. Now, she was likely to throw him out the door if he ever so much as tried to talk to her.

*Heck.* A man couldn't win no matter what he did.

He skipped dinner, preferring the solitude of the barn. He pulled an apple from his pocket and fed it to Buck. The big gelding whickered at the unexpected treat. "You know what you want, don't you, boy?" Unconsciously, he twined his fingers in Buck's mane and held on tight. The whinny of protest had him dropping his hand and murmuring soothing words.

He'd always enjoyed the way night deepened across the plain, the gradual darkening from dusk to blackness. Stars played hide-and-seek against the clouds. Night sounds — the hoot of an owl, the rumbling of cattle — stirred the stillness.

It was here that he found the peace he needed. Days were spent working, always working. A ranch the size of his didn't run itself. The calluses that ridged his palms were proof of that.

He didn't regret the hours, days, years it had taken to make the ranch into what it was today. Life was a trade, exchanging one commodity for another. He hadn't had money, so he'd used what he did have. Time.

For five long years, he'd put in eighteen-hour days, hiring out to other ranchers during the day and working his own ranch in the time remaining. Rising at three in the morning to take care of his stock so he could arrive by eight at whatever job he'd managed to find. Slowly, he'd rebuilt the ranch to what it had been in the early days.

Sleep had become a luxury and he'd snatched an hour here, an hour there, grateful that he had the strength to keep going, pouring every cent back into the land.

Wearily, he rubbed the back of his neck. Tension coiled the tendons there into knots. A woman's hands could undo the tightness, he thought.

Shannon's hands.

His thoughts had taken him full circle. He had to find out what she was running from. Until then, he feared they had no chance at a future together.

Gabe's investigation started at the office the following morning. He'd been hesitant to involve Ray, but the younger man was a whiz with the computer, and right now Gabe needed all the help he could get.

He'd been disappointed but not surprised to find there was no record of a Shannon Whitney in San Diego. Ray skimmed his fingers over the keys, bringing up another screen.

"No go, Sheriff."

Next, Ray turned to the criminal data bank. Gabe didn't know whether he was relieved or disappointed that no record of a Shannon Whitney showed up there either.

"So where do we go from here?"

"Have you tried asking her what she's running from?"

Apparently Gabe's grimace was answer enough, for Ray clamped his lips together. "I'm sorry. I mean, she's a real nice lady and all. . . ."

Gabe settled a hand on his deputy's shoulder. "Don't worry about it."

"We'll find out what's scaring your lady. I've got a friend in the department there who owes me a favor. Let me see what he can dig up."

"Thanks."

Shannon had lied. Gabe wasn't yet sure how far the lies went. Where she'd come from — maybe. Her name — probably.

When they'd gotten nowhere with the computer, Gabe headed out to Shannon's place. Maybe Ray was right. The direct approach had its advantages.

He found Shannon out back, shovel in hand, digging ditches to let rainwater drain away from the house. For a moment, he forgot what had brought him here and simply enjoyed watching her.

The sun had dusted her cheeks with freckles, making her look scarcely older than Josh. She stood and flexed her shoulders, the movement drawing his attention to the lithe lines of her figure. Shadows underscored her eyes, making her appear vulnerable. She worked too hard, he thought. When was she going to admit that the place was too much for her?

He knew the moment when she spotted him. Her posture stiffened and her chin angled up.

"Don't you ever get tired?" he asked.

He heard the censure in his voice. Apparently she did too, for her chin jutted out a fraction more.

"Sure. Only trouble is the rain doesn't know it. We're due for a big storm and I don't want water flooding the kitchen."

He took the shovel from her, and after a momentary tussle, she let him have it. Instead of sitting down and resting as he'd hoped, she began spreading mulch over the flower beds.

With a sigh he didn't bother to hide, he finished the ditch, all the while planning what he'd say to her.

He knew she had secrets. Secrets she wasn't willing to share. Secrets she wasn't able to share? The thought tumbled hard upon the first.

Instinctively, he knew the secrets had something to do with Josh.

If only she'd trust him. . . .

He pushed that thought aside. He hadn't time for wishful thinking. He sensed that whatever was frightening Shannon was coming to a head. If he was to help her, he needed to convince her to tell him the truth. And soon.

When he finished with the ditches, he led her to the porch step and gently pushed her down. Her eyes widened as he brushed his knuckles over her cheek. His carefully planned words fled as a sense of urgency filled him.

"I think you're in trouble, Shannon. I want to help you . . . if you'll let me."

She forced a laugh. "You've been reading too many mysteries."

"Have I?" He bent toward her, wanting to comfort, to take away the pain. Before he'd touched her, she backed away, the challenge in her eyes vanishing to be replaced by wariness. She wasn't ready to trust him yet.

It hurt.

The intensity of his gaze stopped her, robbing her of coherent thought. The expression she read in his eyes was deep concern.

He eased a tendril of hair off her neck. The feel of his fingers against her skin caused a catch in her throat, and awareness of him had the breath lodging there. The memory of dancing in his arms made her tingle. She could feel his warmth, his strength, his goodness.

The way he looked at her jumbled her thoughts. No one had ever looked at her in quite that way before. Suddenly, she wanted nothing more than to fall into his embrace, to feel those big arms holding her, protecting her from the nightmare of fear and distrust. She wanted to feel his strength and maybe, in it, bolster her own.

The direction her thoughts had taken caused her to stand, widening the space between them. She couldn't afford the luxury of leaning on him, even for a moment. Especially now, when Gabe's questions were increasing with every day. She knew Gabe cared for her. Maybe too much. Right now she couldn't afford that kind of caring. She was dangerously close to breaking her self-imposed isolation and confiding in him.

"What's got you so frightened?" he asked.

"Nothing," she said, trying to sound casual. But her voice had faltered to a mumble, and she lowered her head.

"I know you're running from something. I can see it in your eyes. All I ask is that you let me help you."

Unable to face the questions, she spun away. He closed the distance she'd so recently created and fitted a finger beneath her chin, gently forcing her head up so that her gaze met his.

In his eyes she read genuine concern, honesty, and a quiet insistence that she give the same in return.

He was asking too much, far too much.

With an impatient shake of his head, he pulled her into his arms. Reason told her to pull away. If he touched her, she knew she was lost. But need held her still.

When he lowered his head, she knew what was coming. Knew it and welcomed it. The kiss was gentle and so very, very sweet that it brought tears to her eyes. Longing swelled within her, a yearning so intense that it both thrilled and frightened her. When she thought she could bear no more, he ended the kiss but continued to hold her.

Rational thought returned slowly, and with it, a regret so sharp that she nearly crumpled beneath its weight. She remembered who she claimed to be.

Summoning her courage and determination, she forced herself to break away, turning her back to him to compose herself.

He turned her to face him as if she weren't resisting in the least. Part of her acknowledged how strong he was. And how gentle.

"Why won't you let me help you?"

The question simmered between them, a challenge that she couldn't meet.

She wanted to. She wanted to tell him everything and let him handle it. She had no doubt that he'd do anything he could to protect her and Josh.

But she didn't have the right. Telling Gabe meant involving him in the web of lies she'd spun around herself. Even worse, she might get him in trouble by confiding in him. Lee Winston had far-reaching contacts and wielded a power that he could easily use against a county official.

She tried to ignore the entreaty in Gabe's eyes, the silent plea that hung in the air between them.

"I appreciate your concern, but you're way off base." She hated the stiff formality of her words, the impersonal tone of her voice.

She couldn't ignore the pain that darkened his eyes, tightened his lips. But he was asking too much. Confiding in him —

in anyone — was a luxury she just didn't have.

Shannon drew a relieved breath as she watched Gabe withdraw from her. The man was dangerous. He'd almost convinced her to drop her guard and tell him everything.

The thought of what might have tumbled from her heart to her lips unnerved her. If she had the choice between saying too much and saying too little, she had to choose the latter.

Gabe was an honest man. A decent man. If he knew what she'd done, he might very well feel compelled to step forward and let Josh's grandfather know where he was. How did she explain her fear, a fear even she recognized as irrational but real nonetheless?

Though months had passed, she could still recall the terror in Grace's voice when she spoke of her father-in-law, the fear in her eyes.

Shannon shook her head. She couldn't risk it. If it was just herself she had to consider, she might have been willing to take the chance. But the stakes were much higher. Josh's life was at stake.

She couldn't — she wouldn't — gamble with that.

"I think you'd better go," she said, hoping her voice didn't sound as unsteady as she felt.

"Maybe I'd better," he said with a sigh.

She wondered why love had to hurt so much.

Once back home, Gabe returned to his musings. Given enough time, he felt sure he could convince Shannon to share whatever was frightening her.

What was scaring her so badly that her face went white when he started asking questions? Was she running from the law? Immediately, he rejected the idea. Shannon had too much integrity to break the law. But something was definitely frightening her.

He couldn't help her if she didn't tell him the truth. Not if he was to protect her and her nephew.

He recalled the way she looked at Josh, the love shining from her eyes. That she loved the boy was the one thing he knew for certain. She'd fight to protect him.

Gabe slammed his fist into his open palm. He'd fight to protect both of them.

# Chapter Seven

The rain came, great, heaving torrents of it, that flooded the arroyos carved into the prairie by thousands of years of wind and water.

Shannon kept a careful watch for flooding, but her home appeared safe. Gabe's help in digging the trenches had probably saved her from a flooded kitchen.

She had tucked Josh in bed hours before. The old house grated and rasped as the rain and wind battered it. The wooden shutters clattered against the walls and the roof creaked, but it held.

Her coffee grew cold and the ache between her shoulder blades was beginning to stab, but she remained where she was, unable to forget what had happened between Gabe and herself.

The last thing she'd wanted was to hurt him. And she had. She'd seen it in his eyes, heard it in the sigh in his voice when he'd acknowledged her refusal to open up to him.

It was almost eleven at night when she heard the pounding at the door. *Nobody comes calling at this hour,* she thought in alarm.

She let herself hope it was Gabe. Though it had been only hours since she'd seen him, it seemed much longer. She ran to answer the door, eager to clear up the misunderstandings between them and, if he were willing, to begin again.

Her pleasure turned to fear as she stared into Grace's father-in-law's eyes.

"Please, may I come in?" Lee Winston asked.

He'd aged in the last year, she noted. Shoulders stooped, he used a cane. Pain flickered in his eyes as he stepped inside.

Instinctively, she moved to help him. Surprisingly, he accepted her offer and allowed her to help him to the sofa. He lowered himself with difficulty, wincing as he did so.

This wasn't the same man who had so frightened her sister, Shannon realized. It wasn't just the obvious physical differences but something in his eyes. A plea that bordered on humility.

"You're wondering how I found you," he guessed.

She nodded.

"One of the San Diego papers picked up a picture of you at your town fair. From there, it was a simple matter to trace you."

That sounded more like the man she remembered. With limitless resources, he could obtain whatever information he wanted.

She squared her shoulders. "What do you want?"

His sigh surprised her. "I want to be part of my grandson's life." He held up a hand when she started to speak. "I've made mistakes in the past. First with my son, Lee, then with Grace. I don't want to lose Josh as well."

Shannon felt a glimmer of sympathy for the man who had everything in life but that which mattered most.

Love.

"I'm not getting any younger," he said. "I had a heart attack last year. It made me take a look at myself, and I didn't much like what I saw. I know you and Josh don't need me, but, I —" A hoarse cough interrupted whatever he'd been about to say, and he placed a hand on his chest before fumbling in his pocket for a bottle of pills.

She hurried to get him a glass of water.

"Thank you," he said, after swallowing a pill. "As I was saying, I need him. And you," he hurried to add. "You two are all the family I have left."

Tears pricked her eyes. She didn't have it in her to deny him a chance to be a part of his grandson's life. But she wasn't about to rush into anything.

"What did you have in mind?" she asked cautiously.

"If you could bring Josh to visit me once or twice a year — at my expense, of course — you'd make me a very happy man." He glanced around the small room. "I have everything a man could want, but . . ."

She stiffened at the mention of his wealth and power. Apparently sensing her reaction, he reached for her hand, but she backed away. This man had caused Grace so much pain. How could she be sure he'd changed?

He held up a hand. "Let me finish . . . please. I'd trade it all today if it could bring back Lee or Grace. I know I can't buy my way into your life, but" — the hacking cough interrupted him again — "I would like to share it. On whatever terms you choose."

"I think we might be able to manage that."

The look of gratitude in his eyes warmed her more than she would have thought possible. "Thank you." His wistful gaze strayed to the closed bedroom door. "I guess Josh is sleeping right now."

She nodded.

"I have a room at the motel. Maybe I could see him tomorrow?"

Tomorrow was Saturday. "If you want to come by around noon, maybe we could have lunch together."

"I'd like that." He pushed himself up, leaning heavily on his cane. "Thank you, Shannon. You've given me more than I had a right to ask."

"We're family," she said, echoing his earlier words.

*We're family.* She had cause to remember those words over the next few days as Josh and his grandfather got to know each other. The Lee Winston Sr. Grace had warned her about had disappeared. In his place was an old man who simply wanted to spend time with his grandson.

"Look, Grandpa. Watch how Samson can fetch." Josh threw a stick as far as he could. Samson bounded after it, retrieving it and dropping it at Josh's feet.

Lee Winston stooped to ruffle the dog's fur. The look he sent Shannon was filled with regret. "I wish I hadn't been such a hardheaded . . ." — a glance at Josh

halted whatever he'd been about to say —
". . . and let the boy have a dog when he
and Grace lived with me." He cleared his
throat and directed his gaze at Samson
again. "He's going to be a big one."

Josh tossed a ball this time. "That's what
Gabe said."

"Gabe?" Lee Winston gave Shannon an
inquiring glance.

"He's a neighbor," she said quickly.

"He's sweet on Aunt Shannon," Josh
added before racing off with Samson, who
had pounced on the ball.

"I take it he's somebody special."

"I don't know," she said honestly.

"Would you like him to be?"

She was saved from answering by the
arrival of the man in question.

Shannon made the introductions. The
questions she read in Gabe's eyes demanded an explanation.

"Mr. Winston —"

"Lee," he corrected. "Please," he added
when she hesitated.

"Lee, would you mind watching Josh
while I talk with Gabe?"

Tears glistened in the old man's eyes.
"You trust me with him?"

"We're family."

"Thank you." He nearly choked over the

two words before he headed off in the direction Josh and Samson had taken.

Gabe led her to the porch. "You want to tell me what this is all about?"

"I told you that Josh's mother died a couple of months ago."

He nodded.

"Before she died," — pressing her fingers against the inner corners of her eyes, Shannon tried to stem the tears that still came so easily when she remembered her sister — "she made me Josh's guardian. She asked me not to let Josh's grandfather get custody."

"I can see why she'd want someone younger to raise her son, but what did she have against the old man?"

"After Grace's husband died, she and Josh went to live with Lee. Since he held the purse strings, he thought he could dictate how they were going to live. He started telling her what to feed him, when to feed him, even had him signed up for a preschool when he was barely two years old. After a year, Grace couldn't take it anymore. She got out, but Lee was always after her, trying to get Josh back."

"What happened?"

"Grace moved back to her home and turned it into a day care center. She and

Josh were doing pretty good. Then" — her voice faltered, but she swallowed past the tears and went on — "a year ago, Grace started having fainting spells. She was weak and tired all the time. I made her go to the doctor. It was cancer. He said it was already advanced. I quit my job to take care of her. She decided against radiation and chemotherapy; and they could only prolong her life by a few months. And she'd have had to stay in the hospital, away from Josh.

"Grace made me promise to take care of Josh, not to let his grandfather gain custody. Even then, after almost four years, she was afraid of him. I gave her my word."

"That's why you've done everything you've done, isn't it? To safeguard Josh."

She nodded. "I took my mother's maiden name. My real name's Howard. Shannon Howard."

"Why were you so afraid of him?"

The question she had dreaded. "The last time I saw him, he was still trying to get control of Josh. All he cared about was making Josh his heir and turning him into some kind of miniature version of himself — someone whose only interest was money and power. When I lost my job, I knew I couldn't fight him in court."

"But you had legal custody."

"I was scared out of my mind. Don't you understand?"

Gabe took her hand, pressing it between his own. "Hey, I'm on your side, remember?"

"I'm sorry." She took a steadying breath. "Lee Winston buys and sells companies. He chews them up and spits them out. I didn't want that happening to Josh." Her eyes pleaded with him to understand.

"He showed up two nights ago. I've watched him with Josh since he's been here. He's changed, Gabe. He's really changed. All he wants is some time with his grandson. I couldn't say no."

Of course she couldn't. Just as she couldn't refuse her dying sister's request that Shannon take care of her child. Her heart was as big as the Wyoming sky — one of the reasons he loved her as he did.

He gave her his best imitation of a brotherly hug and reminded himself that what she needed right now was a friend. She'd gone through enough already without him telling her how he felt.

Back home, he stared out the window, digesting what Shannon had told him. The burden she'd carried for so long was far greater than he'd thought. If only she'd trusted him enough to share it earlier . . .

Well, she wasn't alone now. And if he had his way, she wouldn't be alone much longer.

With no more lies between them, Shannon hoped she and Gabe could reach a new understanding.

He'd taken to spending the evenings with her and Josh. During the quiet hours between dusk and dark, she felt herself growing more and more deeply in love with him. But while her feelings for him grew, he seemed to be distancing himself from her.

She believed that he had come to care for her, if only a little. Then she would remember that he treated Josh with the same casual affection and wonder if she'd imagined the whole thing.

After dinner one night, he talked football with Josh while she worked on a sketch she was doing of Gabe and Josh together. It was to be a surprise for him.

Shannon watched the two of them, her heart swelling with love at the picture they made, Gabe's blond head bent close to Josh's dark one as they looked at Josh's latest additions to his football card collection.

"I've gotta go, partner," Gabe said,

brushing a kiss on the top of Josh's head. "But I'll be back tomorrow."

"But, Gabe —"

"Don't you have school tomorrow?"

The barest of nods elicited a smile from Gabe.

"Then you need to get some sleep. Can't have a future star quarterback not making a pass because he didn't get enough sleep when he was six."

Josh digested that. "Yeah. I guess you're right."

Shannon waited, hoping that Gabe would spend some time alone with her, but he seemed oddly edgy. When she asked him about it, he shrugged the question off. Embarrassed, she murmured "good night" and watched as he left.

Gabe hoped that spending time with Shannon would open her eyes to the possibility of something more than friendship between them, that she'd come to see how much she needed him. Keeping his distance from her was proving harder than he'd ever imagined, but he'd made himself a promise. He wouldn't press her while she was still growing accustomed to the freedom of not worrying over Josh's grandfather.

Gabe had come dangerously close to

153

stepping over his self-imposed bounds. If it hadn't been for Josh's presence, he might have asked her things he had no right to ask of a vulnerable woman. He didn't want her like that.

She might have said yes. Would have said yes, he thought, and then regretted it, when the situation and her life were back to normal. Without the threat of a custody fight, she could return to San Diego and pick up her old life there.

*Face it, man.* It wasn't Shannon who needed him. He needed her — needed her with an intensity that frightened him. Vulnerability was something new to him, and he found himself unsure how to handle it.

He knew she was concerned about money. From what she'd told him about her sister's illness, he guessed she didn't have much, if any, savings left. That was one thing he could relieve her mind of.

Lee Winston had approached Gabe before he left, to let him know that he was settling a large amount of money upon Shannon and Josh.

"I didn't want to tell her," Josh's grandfather had said. "I made mistakes in the past, first with my son, then with Grace. But Josh is my own flesh and blood. I want to do something to help out. I *have* to."

The older man had taken Gabe's hand in a surprisingly strong grip. "Make her see that it's not charity. And there are no strings attached." His voice was rueful. "I've learned my lesson."

Shannon would never have to worry about money again.

When Gabe told her about it, she was oddly still. All but her eyes. They were shooting flames. Directly at him.

"Hey, you look like you've lost your best friend," he said, trying to rouse a smile from her.

"Let me get this straight. You and Lee got together and decided what was best for me and Josh?" Her voice was low, dangerously so.

He reached for her, only to have her back away. He watched as she carefully closed her eyes, plainly fighting to reclaim her self-control. It took several minutes. When she lifted her head to face him, the flames had stilled to glowing embers.

"What gave you the right to interfere? I don't want his money. I can take care of Josh on my own."

"If you're afraid that he'll use it to try to control you, you don't —"

"It's not that. Josh's grandfather has the right to give him whatever he wants to. But

155

I can't use it for me." Her hands twisted in agitation. He longed to take them in his and still them, but he kept his distance.

He could tell she didn't like it. And she still wasn't ready to accept it. Not any of it.

"It's not like that. You're taking care of Josh. It's only fair you should —"

"Don't you think I should be the one to decide that?"

"I'm sorry. I didn't mean to step on your toes." The words came across stiffly.

"All I ask is that you give me the chance to stand on my own. That you see me as an equal." Her voice, hoarse with feeling, scraped over his raw emotions.

"That's all I've ever seen you as."

"Is it?" she asked quietly.

"Of course it is," he said and then stopped. Is that how he truly saw her? He looked at her — really looked — and realized he'd lied. He saw the gentle curve of her cheek, the softness of her mouth, the fragile bone structure.

He looked again, this time more closely. Those things hadn't vanished, but he noticed different things as well: the quiet strength reflected in her eyes, the jut of her chin, the work-roughened hands. Shannon wasn't a hothouse flower. She'd proved that over and over. Maybe it was time he started believing what she'd been trying to tell him.

"Is it?" she asked again.

"No." The word couldn't have come from him. He wasn't a sexist male like some of the men in town. He never lumped women together; he saw them as individuals. But had he allowed the obvious physical differences between women and men to blind him to their strengths?

The challenge in Shannon's eyes convinced him he had.

"What do you want?" he asked.

"See me as me."

Had he mixed Melissa and Shannon in his mind? Shannon was small and delicately built like his ex-fiancée, but the similarities ended there. Melissa had reveled in the cosseting care of her father and had demanded, insisted, that Gabe provide the same. The role of helpless woman was so ingrained in her that he doubted she could have shed it if she'd wanted to. Which she clearly had not.

"I know you were trying to help," Shannon said, weariness replacing the anger in her voice. "Next time, ask me first. Okay?"

"Okay."

He left shortly after that.

Shannon stared after him, more troubled

than she wanted to admit. Somehow, they had to find a way to right what was wrong between them.

It went far beyond Gabe accepting her as a strong, capable woman. It went to the very core of how they regarded love. Love without respect wasn't enough. Until Gabe understood that . . . She shook her head, refusing to finish the thought.

When he showed up at her place the following morning, she ran to greet him, wanting to bridge the rift between them.

"I'm sorry," he said. "Will you forgive me for acting like an idiot?"

The simplicity of his words touched her more than any elaborate apology could have. "It's all right."

"No, it's not. I hurt you. I never wanted to do that."

"I know." Strangely, she did. Her anger faded as she realized how difficult this must be for him.

Clutching his hat awkwardly, he appeared more than a little uncomfortable.

"I suppose it's hard for someone like you to know what it's like," she said, wanting to put him at ease.

His mouth hardened. "What do you mean, 'someone like me'?"

Aware that she'd blundered, she rushed

on, "You know, someone who has every-thing —"

"You've got it all figured out, haven't you?" He jammed his hat on his head and turned on his heel.

Shannon grabbed his arm. "I'm sorry. I didn't mean it that way."

He peeled her fingers from around his arm. "How would you know what I have or haven't experienced?"

She shrank back at his tone. "I only meant —"

"I know what you meant. You think I was born with a silver spoon in my mouth." His lips twisted into a mirth-less smile at the guilty expression in her eyes.

"You weren't?"

"Hardly. Mine has always been a working ranch. What I have, I've worked for. And worked hard. Nothing was handed to me."

"I didn't mean —"

"I had to work my tail off to get the ranch out of hock when I came back from Denver. Eighteen-hour days for five years. Working for other ranchers and then coming home and doing the same thing all over again."

"I didn't understand."

"Of course you didn't."

He brushed the hair off her cheek. "Quit being such a stubborn little thing and let Lee — and me — help you. Pride is a lonely companion."

Ashamed, Shannon looked down at her scuffed boots. "I'm sorry."

"Hey, it's all right." He lifted her chin so that her gaze met his. The warmth she found there unsettled her more than ever.

Samson tumbled over his feet, skidding to a stop in front of Shannon. "You're just a big baby," she said, stooping to pick him up.

Gabe laughed. "You've got the big part right anyway."

She cuddled the puppy to her. Gabe was right. Already, Samson had doubled in weight. Pretty soon, she wouldn't be able to lift him, much less hold him to her as she was now.

Samson squirmed in her arms and she let him down, watching as he scampered away. If only her need for independence could be as easily satisfied.

His horsing around eased the tension between her and Gabe. More relieved than she could say, she relaxed enough to laugh at Samson's antics. They spent most of the day together and, gradually, began to reweave the strained threads of their friendship. The quarrel still hung between them, though, and she knew one day they'd have to settle their basic conflict.

She understood his anger over her dismissing what must have been a monumental task to get his ranch out of debt. He had a right to be proud of what he'd accomplished.

But he wasn't the only one with pride. She had her own share of it, too.

Shannon was whistling when Josh came home. She knew something was wrong the minute he stepped off the bus.

"What's wrong, honey?"

Josh tried to smile, but the sadness that came through twisted Shannon's heart into knots.

"Why'd God take away my mom and my dad?"

Hugging him to her, she fought to control her expression. How was she supposed to answer that? What could she say that wouldn't make Josh feel worse?

Before she was able to find the right words, Josh spoke again. "Gabe said he liked six-year-old boys."

It didn't take much effort to figure out the change of subject.

"Why don't you marry him?" Josh asked.

"Then you could have a little boy of your own."

The quiver in his voice tore at her heart a little more. "Hey," she said, kissing his brow, "I already have a big boy. Why would I need a little one?"

He snuggled closer. "I love you, Aunt Shannon."

"That makes us even," she whispered, " 'cause I love you, too."

"Gabe likes you."

"Yes," she agreed cautiously. "I think he does."

"Miss Loretta says he's stuck on you." A frown scrunched up his face. "How can he be stuck on you?"

"That just means that he likes me."

*Stuck on her?* She felt a smile tickle her lips at the old-fashioned term. Was he? Stuck on her, that is. At one time, she'd thought so. But lately he'd pulled back, distancing himself. She'd thought they'd cleared up the misunderstandings between them, but she was beginning to think she was wrong. Had she completely misjudged his feelings for her?

"You like him, don't you?" Josh persisted.

"Very much."

"Do you love him?"

162

She sighed. Josh wasn't going to give up. "I love him."

"People who love each other get married."

If only things were that simple. "Sometimes it's not always enough to love someone."

"Why?"

Why, indeed.

"Why are you so interested in Gabe and me getting married?"

"If you and Gabe got married, he'd be sort of like my dad."

"Would you like that?"

Josh hunched a shoulder, in a gesture so very much like what Grace had done when she'd tried to block out hurt, that it brought tears to Shannon's eyes. "It'd be okay, I guess."

She heard much more than the lukewarm words. She heard all the longing of a small boy for a dad and a family like other kids had.

She wanted to give that to him. More than anything, she wanted him to have everything he deserved.

*Face it,* she ordered herself. *You want it for yourself. You want a husband and children, a family. You want Gabe more than you've ever wanted anything or anyone.*

There. She'd admitted it. Now all she

had to do was convince Gabe that she needed his love, not his help. What she felt for him was the most important thing in her life. Then why was he erecting barriers between them?

# Chapter Eight

Feeling happier than she had in days, Shannon put away her packages. When Gabe had suggested they go shopping in Laramie, she'd accepted eagerly. The idea of spending the day with him was an unexpected gift.

Though he hadn't said anything more about their quarrel, she knew their differences weren't settled. By unspoken agreement, they'd shelved the subject — at least for now.

When she turned on the faucet to wash the dishes, water spurted out like a geyser. Convinced she'd lost her mind, Shannon turned the faucet off, then on. Again, the water gushed out.

"Hey, Aunt Shannon, you're all wet," Josh said.

"Yeah. Isn't it great?" She laughed and turned the water off.

"How come it works now?"

"I don't know," she said, a small frown pleating her brow. Only this morning, the water pressure had been lower than ever, barely producing a trickle when she turned on the shower.

For the rest of the afternoon, she wondered about it. Not one to complain about good fortune, she accepted it, but still she couldn't help wondering . . .

It wasn't until that evening that she found the work order tucked behind, rather than inside, the trash can. A work order with Gabe Lambert's signature on it.

Her anger grew as the truth sank in. Gabe had arranged it because he felt sorry for her. The shopping trip had been nothing but a ruse to get her out of the house.

He seemed determined to see her as a helpless female, someone who couldn't be trusted to take care of herself and a child.

She *was* grateful for his help, but that didn't mean she wanted him to continue to think of her as needing rescuing. He treated her with the same casual affection he gave Josh, as if she were six years old as well, she thought indignantly.

It was beginning to wear thin and she didn't intend putting up with it any longer. Mr. Gabe Lambert had a lot to learn about how to treat a woman. And she intended to make sure he learned it.

The following morning, after Josh left for school, she drove to his house. She'd worked herself into a fine temper by then. She found him in his den and slapped the work order down on his desk.

He folded his arms and tipped back his chair. "Okay. So you know."

"Why?"

"Because I couldn't stand seeing you in that ramshackle house with no water coming through the pipes. Did you even have enough to shower, to wash dishes, to do anything?"

"We had enough."

"When? Every day? Every other day?"

She angled her chin. "We were getting by."

He slammed a hand down on the desk, scattering papers everywhere. "You needed water."

"So you decided to do something about it."

"I decided to help you. What's wrong with that?"

"Everything," she shouted. More quietly, she said, "You arrange things behind my back, make decisions for me, all because you don't think I can cope on my own. How do you think that makes me feel?"

"That's not it —"

"Isn't it?" Her voice had quieted, but

anger and hurt still darkened her eyes. "I'm used to taking care of myself. It's frustrating to find things suddenly taken out of my control. Frustrating and . . . demeaning."

"I'm trying to help you." The words were clipped, and he winced at the harshness that edged them. Why did she insist upon throwing all his attempts to help her back in his face? Why couldn't she understand he only wanted to make life easier for her?

"Maybe I don't want your help."

"Don't be stu—" Appalled at what he'd been about to say, he stopped. Stared. "I didn't mean . . ."

"Didn't you?"

He didn't know what he meant anymore. All he knew was that he didn't want to see her try to make do without water. Or anything else, for that matter. Why couldn't she understand that, accept it?

"You were trying to take care of me. Just like you took care of me when Lee asked you to see to it that I took the money."

"So now you're going to tell me I shouldn't have interfered."

"That's right."

"I see." The words had a curiously flat sound to them.

*Do something about it,* he ordered him-self. *Show her how you feel.* He pulled himself together and reached for her. When she jerked away, he bit back the angry words that hovered on his tongue. Why couldn't she understand that he only wanted to take care of her? That was all he'd ever wanted.

"I'll always need you, Gabe. Just not the way you want me to." Her shoulders drooping slightly, she headed to her car.

Disappointment tattered his insides. She saw him as a friend. As soon as the thought had formed, he berated himself for being an idiot. She'd made it clear how she felt.

*Friend.* The word was too tepid for what he felt for her.

The residue of their earlier quarrel was still there inside him, gnawing away at his gut. Anger and frustration, fed by a large dose of hurt pride, had grown until he didn't trust himself to speak to her, especially when he remembered the things she'd said to him.

The lady was way off base. Reluctantly, he admitted that he could be a little over-bearing at times. But, darn it, couldn't she see he was only trying to help her, to take care of her?

What did she expect him to do? Sit on his hands and do nothing while she did without water? Thinking about it, he started getting angry all over again.

He loved her, but she didn't seem to understand how a man felt when he loved a woman, the overpowering need to protect and to cherish. He'd been taught that a man — a real man — took care of his woman.

Despite his misery, Gabe felt his lips curving upward. Shannon would have a fit if she heard herself referred to in those terms.

She paused before climbing into the car. For the space of a heartbeat, he let himself hope. She couldn't leave, he thought desperately. He needed her so much, more than he'd ever thought possible. But he couldn't tell her that. He didn't have the right to tell her. Not now. Not when she had a whole new life waiting for her.

He'd heard the rumor that Shannon had an offer to go back to her job in a San Diego ad agency.

*Fool.* He'd known she didn't belong here and he'd gone ahead and fallen for her anyway. The fact that he had no one to blame but himself didn't lessen the pain.

*Tell her. Tell her that you love her.* The words stuck in his throat. Need and conscience warred. He needed her here, with him, but she had opportunities he could never give her. In the end, conscience won.

Gabe closed his eyes. He could feel his heart trembling, yet all he could do was watch her drive away.

On the drive home, Shannon tried to understand what had happened. Independence wasn't some whim but a basic need — for a man or a woman. Gabe was a strong man, a man who would always try to protect those he cared for. But caring meant respecting. And until he could respect her and accept her need for independence, she feared there was nothing for them.

Once again, he had stepped in to solve her problems. Why couldn't he understand she didn't need someone to take care of her?

She just needed him.

Inside, she felt hollow. He'd given her his answer, in more ways than one. He'd proved to her just how unwilling he was to see her as a strong, independent woman, capable of making her own decisions. Why couldn't he understand that she needed him to see her as a partner, a helpmate, a wife?

She'd thought — hoped — that he had started to think of her as something more than someone needing to be rescued. She'd been mistaken.

Resolutely, she looked to the future. Now that there was no reason to hide her whereabouts, she'd contacted some of her friends in San Diego. She'd heard that her old job was vacant, and that the boss had been making noises about wanting her back.

She wouldn't be human if she weren't flattered by the news. Working in a big ad company had given her an opportunity to use her talent, even if it hadn't been the kind of painting she'd always dreamed of doing.

She stewed over the matter for the next few days. Maybe she'd send a letter to her former boss and see if he really did want her back. It wouldn't hurt to keep her options open.

A week later, she had a reply to her letter. The salary her old boss named was enough to have her gasping. Good sense dictated that she take it. She'd never be able to make that kind of money here.

She had reached an agreement with Josh's grandfather. The money he settled on Josh would be set up in a trust fund to be used for his education when the time came.

She'd lose the house, of course, and the friends she'd made while she'd been here.

Most of all, she'd lose Gabe. No, that wasn't right. You couldn't lose something you'd never really had.

Needing to think about something else, she pulled out her oils. When Loretta stopped by, Shannon put away the painting she'd been working on and wiped her hands on her jeans.

"Don't let me interrupt you," the older woman said.

"Believe me, you're not interrupting anything," Shannon said. "It's garbage."

It was true, she reflected, looking at the insipid landscape. She hadn't painted anything worthwhile since her argument with Gabe. She'd refused to admit to herself that the two were related, but it was hard to keep denying the obvious.

A visit from Loretta was always a welcome break. Today, though, Shannon sensed something behind the older woman's seemingly last-minute decision to stop by.

Loretta settled on the lumpy sofa and grimaced. "Honey, we've got to get you another sofa before I get lost in the lumps in this thing." Without missing a beat, she added, "Have you seen Gabe lately?"

"Not in the last couple of weeks," Shannon said cautiously. He'd kept his distance from her since their last disastrous encounter.

For all she knew he could have met someone else. Someone dependent and clinging who'd appreciate his overprotective attitude. She frowned at the catty thought. She ought to be happy for him if he'd found someone. Gabe was too decent, too caring a man, to remain alone. He deserved whatever happiness he could find — even if it meant sharing it with someone else.

*And if you believe that one,* she silently jeered, *maybe you'll buy some swampland in Florida and make a fortune.*

"You two having problems again?"

The frank question had Shannon wincing.

Loretta nodded, as if confirming something to herself. "If you don't want to talk about it, I understand. The last thing I want is for you to think of me as a meddling old woman."

"You're not —"

"Thank you, dear. But let's be honest. I *am* a meddling old woman. Fortunately, I've reached the age where it's acceptable." She smiled. "Or, at least, tolerated. If you want me to shut up, just say so. Otherwise, I'll say my piece."

Shannon felt an answering smile tug at her lips. "I don't mind."

"I've known Gabe since he was a boy. He and his pa didn't have an easy time of it. His mama didn't take to ranch living; she wasn't much of a wife and even less of a mother. When Gabe brought Melissa here, I hoped he'd found someone."

"Melissa?"

"His fiancée. She was beautiful. Looked a lot like you, she did. Small, with dark hair and blue eyes. Gabe went on a stock-buying trip back east and brought her back from Kentucky. She never took to ranch life, never really tried to fit in. Insisted that they live in town when they got married. She criticized the house Gabe built for her, claiming it was nothing but a log cabin. After a couple of weeks, she up and left him practically at the altar. Good riddance, I said."

Loretta looked at Shannon shrewdly. "You're wondering why I'm telling you all this. Right?"

Shannon lifted her hands. "I guess I don't see —"

"What it's got to do with you."

She nodded.

"Gabe seemed all right after she left, but it changed him. Oh, he dated some, but not seriously. He never really looked at another woman. Not until you." Loretta let her words sink in.

"And you think he's mixing me up with her."

"I think he needs you to love him." Loretta took Shannon's hand. "He has a lot of pride . . . too much, sometimes. He loves you, honey. He doesn't know it yet. But he does."

"How can you be so sure?"

"I've seen the way he looks at you, like you're the sun and the moon and the stars all rolled up in one. Don't give up on him."

Loretta's eyes were sympathetic, and that alone sent the emotion welling up in Shannon's throat. If she allowed herself, she'd wallow in the sympathy. She couldn't afford that luxury. She had a child who depended on her.

She wished she could believe Loretta was right, that Gabe loved her that way. She wished for a lot of things, things like a home and husband and enough children to make a baseball team. Things like loving and being loved in return. Things like . . .

Her smile was weak and she bit her lip, willing herself not to cry. She hated crying. Yet lately it seemed that was all she did. Love did that to a person. Love and a stubborn man who couldn't see past the end of his own nose.

Unwittingly, Loretta had helped her make her decision.

The sunset was gentle tonight, the sky pearled by the palest peach and lavender. She'd miss the land. It was a harsh task-master, but it held its own beauty. She could understand Gabe's commitment to it.

The land and the man were alike in more ways than one. Rough around the edges, exacting in their demands, solid and able to stand up to everything life threw at them. There was one important difference, though. Gabe's strength was tempered with compassion. The land gave no quarter. The man was strong enough to know strength could be gentle.

Tears crowded her eyes at the thought that she was leaving both.

When Loretta breezed into the sheriff's office early the next morning, Gabe scowled. The last thing he was in the mood for was a lecture, even one from an old friend.

"You're a fool, Gabe Lambert."

"Good to see you, too," he said, sighing as she poured some coffee and made her-self at home.

"What're you going to do about Shannon?"

"I don't see that that's any of your business."

Loretta made a rude noise, drawing a reluctant smile from him.

"That girl's planning to up and leave town. And it's your fault."

He didn't need this, Gabe thought. Hadn't he already called himself every name he could think of?

"Shannon's a strong woman," Loretta said. "She needs a strong man to love. And to be loved by."

"I do —"

"Someone strong enough to be there when she needs him and smart enough to recognize when she needs to stand on her own."

"What're you trying to say?"

"Your mama, God bless her soul, was weak. So was that fool girl you brought back here. Shannon's a different kettle of fish. It's time you realized it."

Loretta folded her arms sternly. "If you'd start thinking with your head instead of that misplaced pride of yours, you'd see that she loves you. Why do you think she's thinking of leaving?" She didn't give him a chance to answer but poked him in the chest with her finger. "You think about it. If you come up with the right answer, I figure you know what to do with it." She gave him one last look that left her last words in doubt and handed him a large folder. "Here. She asked me to give this to you."

Feeling like a small boy who'd been well and truly put in his place, Gabe saw her out, all the while wondering if she was right. Had he lost his chance with Shannon because of some distorted sense of male pride?

He opened the folder. A picture of himself and Josh stared back at him. The pen-and-ink drawing captured the rapt look on Josh's face, the tenderness on Gabe's. He remembered her sketching something while he and Josh had been looking at Josh's football cards.

It had been only a couple of weeks since he'd seen her, but he missed her as if years had passed. There was an ache in his heart that wouldn't go away, no matter how hard he tried to obliterate it with work.

He whistled silently into his fist as he acknowledged that even the sixteen-hour days he'd been putting in couldn't obliterate Shannon from his mind. Inevitably, he would recall things. Like how she looked with dirt smudged on her nose as she was planting bulbs. Her delight in

Samson's antics. The way she soothed away Josh's fears with a soft word, a gentle touch.

He missed her. And Josh. Boy, did Gabe miss that kid. Who would have thought that a child could steal such a big piece of his heart. Until he'd met Josh, Gabe had never given much thought to kids, had never really been around them much. Then, within a matter of weeks, his life had been suddenly filled by the presence of one small boy.

He didn't pretend to understand why he had fallen so hard for a six-year-old boy. Josh was in no way related to him. Yet he had awakened in Gabe some of the fiercest feelings he'd ever experienced. He felt the same protectiveness for Josh that he did for Shannon, the same need to cherish and . . .

The realization drew him up short.

Had *that* been what Shannon had been trying to tell him? That he was treating her in the same manner he did the child? All because of some distorted thinking and a large dose of masculine pride.

No wonder the lady had called him on it. It was a miracle she hadn't decked him. His lips curved slightly at the thought of Shannon punching his lights out. She could probably do it, too. Despite her small size, she had more than her share of guts.

Calling himself all sorts of a fool, he headed to her place. He'd find her, tell her that he'd been an idiot, and beg her to forgive him. Then, when he'd convinced her that he loved her and Josh and always would, he'd ask her to marry him.

A picture of the three of them together lodged in his mind. They'd be a family. Not a traditional one, perhaps, but a family just the same. It was love, not blood, that counted.

Later, there'd be other children. He'd like a houseful of them. His lips edged upward. A houseful and a heartful.

The image was so vivid that he could only stare in surprise when he arrived at Shannon's house and found it boarded up. As the significance of the abandoned house sank in, he let loose a string of curses that Loretta would have washed his mouth out with soap for.

# Chapter Nine

"Why're we running away?" Josh asked.

"We aren't —" She stopped short. Of course she was running away. First from Josh's grandfather. And now Gabe. Granted that the circumstances were different. But she'd been running for so long that she wasn't even aware of it.

With the help of a couple of teenage boys from town, she'd managed to load the car and board up the house last night. She'd dragged a grumbling Josh from bed and settled him in the front seat. Once she'd made up her mind, she hadn't given herself time to think about what she was doing.

Josh's question had changed that.

"What makes you think we're running away?"

"We're leaving Loretta and Gabe and all the friends I made at school. I *like* living in Blessing. Samson likes it, too."

Samson barked from the backseat.

"So do I," she said.

"I'm gonna miss Gabe."

"Me, too."

"So why're we leaving?"

Good question. The words galvanized her to action. Heedless of the traffic, she made a U-turn.

"We're going home," she told Josh.

"You mean San Diego?"

"I mean we're going back to Blessing. That's our home now."

Josh let out a whoop that had her grinning. Gabe Lambert had another thing coming if he thought he could treat her like some helpless idiot. She'd make him see her for what she was — strong and independent, a woman who wanted to spend the rest of her life with him.

He wouldn't be an easy man. He was too intense, too sure of himself, to make it easy. But she'd discovered something along the way. She didn't want easy.

She wanted him.

Shannon caught sight of the sheriff's car in the rearview mirror. Its driver seemed to be motioning her to pull over. Puzzled, she did as directed. Had the U-turn been illegal? She hadn't thought so, but . . .

She did as the driver directed, pulling the car to the side of the road and waiting.

When she saw the deputy approach, she rolled down her window.

"Sorry, Shannon, but I've got to ask you to come with me," Ray McClellan said.

Fumbling for her license and registration, she missed the hint of a smile in his eyes.

"I don't understand, Ray. Have I done something wrong?"

"If you'll just follow me."

Feeling she had no choice, she nodded.

"Aunt Shannon, what's happening?"

"We need to follow the deputy." She pointed to the uniformed man and started the car.

Excited at the prospect of being pulled over, Josh seemed to forget his sadness in leaving. "Are we being arrested? Were you speeding? Will we go to jail? Will they take our fingerprints?"

"I don't know," Shannon said, frustrated at the delay and concerned about what it might mean.

Josh's questions died away at her abrupt reply. He looked down at his hands. "I'm sorry," he said in a small voice.

Contritely, Shannon placed her hand on his. "No, honey. I'm the one who's sorry. I shouldn't have snapped at you like that. I guess I'm a little nervous."

"It's all right. I'll take care of you."

She smiled at that, touched by the seriousness of his reply. "I know you will."

Up ahead, she could see the sheriff's office. She pulled in alongside the deputy's car.

Ray held the door open, motioning for her and Josh to go inside. Josh clung to her hand, whether in reassurance or fear, she wasn't sure. Indicating chairs for them, the deputy offered her coffee, which she refused.

Shannon's anxiety mounted steadily; her grip on Josh's hand tightened until he tugged it away.

"You're hurting me."

Shannon looked down in dismay at the red marks on Josh's hand left by the pressure of her nails.

"I'm sorry," she apologized in a low voice. "I can't imagine what they want with us."

Finally, Ray approached them, smiling broadly. "If you'll just step back here."

Shannon didn't immediately stand up. She glanced at Josh. Interpreting her hesitation correctly, Ray reassured her. "There's no cause for alarm. And Josh" — he smiled at Josh — "can stay with me."

He ushered her into an office marked

PRIVATE. To her surprise, he didn't remain but backed quickly out, closing the door behind him.

No one sat at the room's solitary desk, and at first it appeared empty. A movement at the far corner caught her attention.

"No," she whispered. She hadn't seen him. Hadn't *felt* him. How could he be so close and she not feel it?

Looking exceedingly grim, Gabe walked toward her. With nowhere to run and unable to take her eye off him, Shannon remained still.

He stopped several feet short of her. His eyes were bloodshot, his skin was gray, and his clothes looked as if he'd slept in them. And she wanted nothing more than to hurl herself into his arms and feel his lips upon hers.

She did none of those things. All she could do was stare and drink in the sight of him. She couldn't seem to do anything but stare like a gawking idiot.

"Shannon."

Just the sound of his voice was the gentlest of caresses. She wanted so much to touch him, to trace the outline of his jaw, but she didn't dare. Even now, she couldn't be sure he wasn't a dream, something her imagination had conjured up because she'd missed him so desperately.

If he was real — and she still didn't trust herself to fully believe it — she didn't want him to disappear. So she concentrated on something safe to say, something that wouldn't make that cold, empty look return to his eyes. A shudder ran over her as she remembered the last time she'd seen him and the angry words they'd hurled at each other. She couldn't ask all the questions that she wanted to.

Instead, she asked, in what she hoped was a calm voice, "You had me brought here?" She couldn't wait for him to answer. "Why?"

"I put out your description and license number in a hundred-mile radius."

"It's illegal to track me down that way."

He hunched a shoulder. "A little." He closed the remaining steps between them, and she found herself in his arms, his lips pressed against her own.

"Why am I here?" she asked, when he lifted his head.

"Because I couldn't let you leave."

Her breath hitched in her throat and stuck there.

"You were leaving without saying goodbye."

"I thought you didn't care. I couldn't bear to be that close to you and know you didn't. . . ."

"Didn't what?"

"Didn't love me," she mumbled against his chest. Even as she said them, the words caught in her throat.

"And that matters to you?"

She could only nod.

"Look at me," he said. "I love you. Love you so much that it scares me. I tried to let you go, but I found I couldn't."

"Why? Why did you try to let me go?"

"I don't know if I can love you the way you need to be loved. I'll always want to take care of you, protect you. But I'll try not to smother you. I love you, Shannon. I have nearly from the first."

"Why couldn't you tell me?"

"I was afraid you'd leave, just like —"

"Like Melissa did," she finished for him. Tears rolled down her cheeks. She wasn't sure whom she was crying for. Gabe. Or herself. "You're afraid I'm the same as her."

"No. I *know* you're strong. You said it yourself. You don't need me. Not like I do you."

His admission humbled her. "You don't listen. I told you once that I'll always need you. That hasn't changed."

He gently rubbed the pads of his thumbs under her eyes before reaching down to take her hands in his. "I found out something important."

"What?"

"I can't live without you. I'd survive, but that's not living."

She said nothing, she couldn't, as her breath continued to lodge in her throat. But her eyes widened, and a new tear fell on their linked hands.

"Don't you know how much I love you?" she asked. "That's why I was turning around."

"I couldn't be sure. . . ." His thumb massaged the nape of her neck, destroying any power of thought she might possess. "You were coming back?"

She nodded. "I was going to make you see that you needed me."

"And how were you going to do that?"

"By doing this." She pressed a kiss to his neck. "And this." She brushed another one against his cheek. "And —" His lips caught hers.

"You're everything I've ever wanted. You and Josh. Could you be happy here? We don't have any of the things that a city offers. And we aren't likely to, either."

"Those things don't make a home. It's

the people you're with that count." She hesitated. "I still need to take Josh to San Diego to see his grandfather."

"Not without me, you don't."

"I was hoping you'd say that," she said, a smile hovering on her lips. The smile faded as she realized how close she'd come to losing him.

Shivers danced along her spine at the warmth in his eyes.

"What made you come after me?" she asked.

"This." He pulled her sketch from its folder. "I realized how much I loved Josh. And his aunt," he added with a teasing smile.

"Is that the only reason?"

He grimaced. "Loretta told me a few home truths. Things I would've figured out for myself if I hadn't been acting like such a macho fool. We'll make it work. I've been thinking of turning the back porch into a studio. It's got plenty of light and —"

She kissed him. "I love you for thinking of that. But I wouldn't care if we lived in a shack, as long as we're together."

"Are you asking me to marry you?"

"I was trying to."

He groaned and tightened his hold on her. "You put me through agonies."

"And what about me? Sometimes, I felt like you didn't even like me."

" 'Like' has always been too tame a word for what I feel for you."

Her hands reached up to twine around his neck. "It's all right now. Nothing matters but that we're together." Shannon snuggled against him and turned up her face for another kiss.

His lips brushed hers, a promise for today and all the tomorrows that followed.

Suddenly, she pulled away and looked up at him. "About Josh —"

"He'll be with us," Gabe said. "I've already started investigating how to go about adopting him. He'll be the start of our family. He'll make a good big brother for our other children."

"Our other children?"

"At least one of each. With dark curls and blue eyes like their mother."

"No," she contradicted. "They'll have blond hair and dark eyes like their father."

"Are you going to start arguing with me already?"

She shook her head. "I'll wait until after we're married." Her voice caught. "I love you so much it hurts."

"Not half as much as I love you."

He touched her face and cupped it between his fingers, fitting his palm to the curve of her jaw, as if to mold the shape of it in his mind. To remember her as she was at this moment. Eyes bright with anticipation, lips trembling, skin soft and luminous. "You're beautiful."

Soft color crept into her cheeks.

He'd embarrassed her. He was sorry for that. But he could no more keep the words back than will himself to stop breathing. She was everything he'd ever wanted.

He'd made mistakes. He probably would again. No one knew better than he that he was far from perfect. But he loved her. And Josh. And, if they'd let him, he'd spend the rest of his life proving just that.

"You're crazy," she said. "You know that, don't you?"

"Yeah. Crazy in love. Got a problem with that?"

"No problem. No problem at all."

A rap at the door interrupted what she had been about to say. Ray gave them an apologetic look. "Sorry to bother you, ma'am, Gabe, but this young fellow is feeling a mite lonely."

Josh, followed by Samson, bounded into the room, took in the situation, and threw his arms around their legs, nearly toppling them over.

They included him in the hug as Gabe whispered to her, "As I was saying —"

"Hey, Aunt Shannon, Gabe, I have to go. I have to go real bad." Josh's plaintive voice cut through their words of love.

They exchanged smiles. Gabe took Josh's hand. "Might as well get in practice."

Shannon watched them together, the small boy holding the large man's hand. Love had come, unexpectedly, wonderfully, in its own time.

# *About the Author*

**Jane McBride Choate** has been weaving stories in her head ever since she can remember, but she shelved her dreams of writing to marry and start a family. After her third child was born, she wrote a short story and submitted it to a children's magazine. To her astonishment, it was accepted. Two children later, she is still creating stories. She believes in the healing power of love, which is why she writes romances. Jane and her husband, Larry, live with their five children in Loveland, Colorado.

The employees of Thorndike Press hope you have enjoyed this Large Print book. All our Thorndike and Wheeler Large Print titles are designed for easy reading, and all our books are made to last. Other Thorndike Press Large Print books are available at your library, through selected bookstores, or directly from us.

For information about titles, please call:

(800) 223-1244

or visit our Web site at:

www.gale.com/thorndike
www.gale.com/wheeler

To share your comments, please write:

Publisher
Thorndike Press
295 Kennedy Memorial Drive
Waterville, ME   04901

# International Trade and Trade Policy

**International Trade and Trade Policy**

edited by
Elhanan Helpman
and
Assaf Razin

The MIT Press
Cambridge, Massachusetts
London, England

This book was set in Times Roman
by Asco Trade Typesetting Ltd., Hong Kong
and printed and bound
in the United States of America.

Library of Congress Cataloging-in-Publication Data

International trade and trade policy / edited by Elhanan Helpman and Assaf Razin.
    p.  cm.
  "Papers were presented in May 1989 at the sixth international conference of the Pinhas Sapir Center for Development at Tel Aviv University"—Pref.
  Includes bibliographical references and index.
  ISBN 0-262-08199-7 (hc)
  1. International trade—Congresses. 2. Commercial policy—Congresses. 3. Protectionism—Congresses. I. Helpman, Elhanan. II. Razin, Assaf.
HF1372.I58  1991
382'.3—dc20
                                                    90-13515
                                                      CIP

# Contents

## III STRUCTURAL ISSUES

# List of Contributors

Randic Boorstein
International Trade Commission
Washington, DC

Wilfred J. Ethier
Department of Economics
University of Pennsylvania

Robert C. Feenstra
Department of Economics
University of California, Davis

Harry Flam
Institute for International Economic Studies
University of Stockholm, Sweden

Gene M. Grossman
Department of Economics
Princeton University

Elhanan Helpman
Department of Economics
Tel-Aviv University, Israel

Arye L. Hillman
Department of Economics
Bar-Ilan University, Israel

Henrik Horn
Institute for International Economic Studies
University of Stockholm, Sweden

Ronald W. Jones
Department of Economics
University of Rochester

Kala Krishna
Department of Economics
Harvard University

Paul R. Krugman
Department of Economics
Massachusetts Institute of Technology

James A. Levinsohn
Department of Economics
University of Michigan

James R. Markusen
Deartment of Economics
University of Western Ontario, Canada

Peter Neary
Department of Political Economics
University College, Dublin, Ireland

Assaf Razin
Department of Ecoomics
Tel-Aviv University, Israel

Alasdair Smith
Department of Economics
University of Sussex, England

Robert W. Staiger
Department of Economics
Stanford University

Aaron Tornell
Department of Economics
Columbia University, USA

Anthony J. Venables
Department of Economics
University of Southampton, England

# Preface

The theory of international trade and trade policy has undergone major developments during the last decade. These developments have incorporated elements of industrial organization and political economy into the study of trade structure and the formation of trade policy. They have affected the interpretation of events as well as empirical evidence. This volume contains a collection of papers that describe research at the frontier of these developments.

The papers were presented in May 1989 at the sixth international conference of the Pinhas Sapir Center for Development at Tel Aviv University. Earlier conferences in this series were published in the following books: M. June Flanders and Assaf Razin (eds.), *Development in an Inflationary World* (Academic Press, 1981); Elhanan Helpman, Assaf Razin, and Efraim Sadka (eds.), *Social Policy Evaluation: An Economic Perspective* (Academic Press, 1983); Shimon Spiro and Ephraim Yuchtman-Ya'ar (eds.), *Evaluating the Welfare State: Social and Political Perspectives* (Academic Press, 1983); Assaf Razin and Efraim Sadka (eds.), *Economic Policy in Theory and Practice* (Macmillan, 1987); Elhanan Helpman, Assaf Razin, and Efraim Sadka (eds.), *Economic Effects of the Government Budget* (The MIT Press, 1988); and Yoram Weiss and Gideon Fishelson (eds.), *Advances in the Theory and Measurement of Unemployment* (Macmillan, 1989)

The book is divided into three parts, the first two dealing with trade policy and the third with structural issues. In the first part, devoted to the theory of trade policy, the papers are concerned with a broad spectrum of subjects. They deal with issues such as the formation of trading blocks, strategic trade policy, the political economy of protection, and growth-oriented trade policies. The second part consists of empirical studies dealing with voluntary export restrictions and European integration. In the third part we have collected papers on various structural issues: trade in services, intersectoral adjustments and the advantage of early entry.

In addition to the authors, conference participants included discussants and panel members—Joshua Aizenman, Zvi Eckstein, Arthur Fishman, Jacob Frenkel, Morris Goldstein, David Klein, Anne Krueger, Leonardo Leiderman, Yaakov Lifschitz, Dalia Marin, Liora Meridor, Lars Svensson, Dani Tzidon, and Joseph Zeira—who contributed importantly to the quality of the conference and the final drafts of the papers. We thank them all.

# International Trade and Trade Policy

## Introduction

Recent research in the area of international trade and trade policy has clarified many important issues related to the implications of industrial structure, competition, and the political economy of protection. Our understanding of the role of oligopolistic and monopolistic competition and their interaction with government policies has been enhanced, as has our understanding of expected government responses to market conditions and the credibility of policies. This literature has dealt with such diverse policies as tariffs, export subsidies, and voluntary export restraints (VERs) that are of the utmost practical importance.

A major conclusion from this literature is that the effectiveness of policies depends crucially on the nature of competition and market structure. Thus, for example, in some situations in which export subsidies prove to be welfare improving for the policy active country when the number of its exporters is small, an export tax may be needed in order to raise welfare when the number of exporters is large. Or, with a given number of domestic exporters an export subsidy may raise welfare when the exporters compete in quantities, while in the same economy an export subsidy may reduce welfare when the exporters compete in prices. In the latter case an export tax raises welfare.

The fragility of these policy implications leads to two complementary lines of exploration. First, more systematic theoretical studies have tried to identify additional channels of policy transmission in order to broaden the scope of policy analysis and have thus further clarified sources of the proliferation of possible outcomes. Second, empirical studies, mostly by means of simulations of theoretically based models, calibrated to empirical data, have attempted to assess the relative importance of specific features of these models and to produce estimates of welfare effects of various policies. These studies have been extremely useful in shedding light on major theoretical and practical problems. But, as might have been expected, in addition to the answers that have been provided they also have raised new questions and identified new problems. The importance of this work can hardly be overemphasized, as can the need for its further development.

The essays collected in this volume provide valubale new insights—theoretical as well as empirical—on these topics. A number of chapters represent early attempts to address new important theoretical questions, while others extend and clarify the existing literature. The empirical chapters provide new information on the quantitiative significance of restrictive trade policies.

Krugman (chapter 1) analyzes the welfare consequences of the number of trading blocks in the world economy, whereby each block imposes its optimal external tariff and maintains free trade within the block. In the symmetric Nash equilibrim of his policy game, the result is necessarily Pareto efficient when the world consists of a single trading block because this situation amounts to free trade. Consequently, starting with one block, initial increases in the number of blocks reduce welfare. On the other hand, if the world consists of many blocks, the monopoly power of each one becomes small, and so further inreases in the number of blocks raise welfare. The interesting result is that for plausible parameter values minimum welfare obtains when the number of blocks equals three. It seems therefore that a small number of blocks that is larger than one can be most harmful.

In competitive environments quotas have tariff equivalents in the absence of distortions. It has also been known for many years that in the presence of monopoly power, be it oligopolistic or otherwise, quotas do not have tariff equivalents. These result were derived in the absence of foreign direct investment. Levinsohn (chapter 2) shows that in the presence of direct foreign investment and an oligopolistic market structure, quotas often become equivalent to tariffs. This result is driven by the fact that to avoid trade taxes a foreign supplier shifts from arm's-length exports to supply the domestic market via its subsidiary. He uses the same route when the foreign supplier's exports are restricted by quotas.

Krishna (chapter 3) points out that the welfare level of a quota-imposing country may increase by granting a foreign monopolist who serves the domestic market some of the import licenses, even when they are given away free of charge. Here the point is that when the quotas are auctioned off domestically the foreign monopolist, who faces a vertical demand curve as a result of the quota, charges the consumer price, thereby reducing to zero rents of domestic importers. Consequently all quota rents accrue to the foreign monopolist. By granting the foreign monoplist some of the quota rights, his pricing decision takes also into account the return on his quota rights. As a result of this consideration he will typically price the good so as to generate positive quota rents, some of which will accrue to domestic holders of import licenses. This may be welfare improving relative to a situation in which all quota licenses are held by domestic residents. Naturally, if all licenses are given to the foreign monopolist, no gains accrue to the domestic importers.

Tornell (chapter 4) discusses the role of precommitment in trade policy. The mechanism of protection may lead to situations in which a plan for the future elimination of protection fails because enterprises take into account the inability of the government to precommit to its plan. The example employed in order to demonstrate this point is the government's desire to secure a minimal level of employment. Companies that are aware of this objective may underinvest in the initial phase in expectation of future protection, despite the plan to remove protection. And indeed, these expectations are self-fulfilling. When faced with a low capital stock, the government does not discontinue protection in order to avoid a decline in employment below the desired level.

The debate on the efficacy of export subsidies in oligopolistic markets with price competition is reexamined by Neary (chapter 5). As we mentioned before, it has been known for some time that export subsidies are desirable when firms compete in quantities and that export taxes are desired when firms compete in prices. These results are based on the notion that the government moves first, namely, that it chooses its policy before firms take action. The present chapter clarifies the differences between ex ante and ex post export tax and subsidy schemes. This amounts to a distinction between cases in which the government can precommit, and chooses its policy before companies determine pricing policies, and situations in which the government cannot or does not desire to precommit to a policy (to a tax or subsidy). In the latter case corporations' pricing strategies take into account the government's policy decision process. Neary shows that a higher level of welfare is attained in the ex ante game in which the best policy consists of an export tax rather than subsidy.

Flam and Staiger (chapter 6) discuss the role of infant industry protection in a less developed country with limited financial markets in which the domestic expected rate of return exceeds the cost of funds on international financial markets. Due to adverse selection and limited information of lenders, risky infant industries are underfunded and inhabited by excessively risky firms. In these circumstances protection may prove beneficial because it compensates to some extent for the underfunding of the industry at large and induces safer firms to enter. Naturally, in this case tariff protection is not the first-best policy, although it may prove useful in a limited dose. On the other hand, there exists an inherent time-inconsistency problem in this scheme because, once firms have entered and secured financing, the government has no longer any incentive to protect.

The link between lobbying activities to secure protection and the degree of an industry's concentration is examined by Hillman (chapter 7). Companies have limited managerial resources which they allocate between monitoring of business activities and lobbying activities. The effectiveness of individual contributions to lobbying for protection depends on the contribution of other firms in the industry. Hillman shows that in the Nash equilibria of such games there need not exist a positive association between the degree of concentration of an industry and its aggregate lobbying effort. This may contribute to the explanation of a certain body of evidence.

Grossman and Helpman (chapter 8) examine welfare implications of R&D subsidies and commercial policies in a growing economy. They show that tariffs and export subsidies have significant effects on long-run growth and welfare. Growth rates may increase or decrease in response to protection depending on whether the import competing or the exporting sector is promoted by the trade policy. They also show that even in cases where trade policy promotes growth, it may not raise welfare. A policy that promotes growth, which is undersupplied in their framework as a result of spillovers from current R&D efforts to future costs of R&D, may aggravate the misallocation of resources that results from monopolistic competition of innovating firms.

Trade policies affect not only the volume of trade but also its composition. In particular, quantitative restrictions lead to changes in the quality of imported goods, with the average quality being upgraded in response to the quantitative restriction. Boorstein and Feenstra (chapter 9) derive a measure of the welfare cost that results from such quality changes and apply it to the voluntary restraint agreement on U.S. steel imports in 1969–74. They report that this welfare cost amounted to 1% of the value of steel imports. This cost exists in addition to traditional welfare costs of protection that result from distorted relative price effects.

Smith and Venables (chapter 10) also measure the effects of VERs, this time for the European car market. In Europe the restraint on imports of Japanese cars is applied to market shares. They construct a model of oligopolistic competition, calibrate it to the European data, and simulate various policy experiments. They find, for example, that removal of the 3% share restriction of Japanese cars in France raises Japan's market share to over 13%, reduces the price of Japanese cars by about 34%, and reduces only slightly prices of other European cars. This would raise French consumers' welfare by about 6% of their expenditure on cars.

Trade in services is examined by Ethier and Horn (chapter 11). They treat services as differentiated specialized products that have to be combined with other inputs in order to manufacture final goods. In order to examine the role of services in foreign trade, they compare a number of regimes that differ in the degree of tradability of services. Since in their economies there exist several distortions that result from noncompetitive market structures, welfare rankings of alternative regimes require second-best considerations. They find, for example, that embodied service trade (whereby there is no direct trade in services but services are embodied in traded manufactures) yields higher welfare for the trading partners than complete autarky.

Markusen (chapter 12) examines the question of time lags in entry to a worldwide competitive industry. If one country develops such an industry first, will the lagging country be able to develop the same industry at a later point in time and thereby catch up with the leader? For a noncompetitive industry with entry costs and fixed operating costs, his answer is in the negative.

In the closing chapter (chapter 13) Jones and Neary examine the stability of the intersectoral allocation process for an open economy with factor price distortions. They develop a concept of "wage sensitivity" ranking between sectors and show how to use it in order to characterize stability in such economies. Their measure provides direct information about the direction of intersectoral capital movements.

The intent of this volume is to represent main strands of current research in international trade and trade policy. The chapters in this volume advance our knowledge in a number of important areas and open up new avenues for future explorations.

# I TRADE POLICY: THEORY

# 1 Is Bilateralism Bad?

**Paul R. Krugman**

In the 1980s the process of trade liberalization through multilateral negotiations within the GATT framework seems to have run ground. Major areas where conventional trade restrictions remain legion, such as agriculture and services, appear resistant to major progress. Meanwhile the "new protectionism" of voluntary restraint agreements, antidumping actions, and so on, has eroded the effectiveness of the GATT in dealing with trade in manufactures. The result has been increasing disillusionment with the multilateral process, and an increasing focus on alternative trade strategies.

Perhaps the most important of these strategies has been the turn to bilateral or regional arrangements for trade. The most important agreements on trade in the past decade have been the "completion of the internal market" that the European Community has agreed to achieve by 1992 and the free trade agreement between the United States and Canada. Regionalism is also apparent in the enlargement of the European Community to include several semi-industrialized countries on Europe's rim. Japan, while not explicitly engaging in regional trading pacts, has recently sharply increased its manufactures imports from East Asian NICs; it is widely argued that the de facto protectionism that results from Japan's cartelized distribution system is being selectively dismantled for nearby countries in which Japanese direct foreign investment is increasingly significant. With growing discussion of further enlargement of the Economic Community and of the possibilities for special trading arrangements between the United States and Mexico, many economists and business managers have begun to raise the possibility that the multilateral GATT trading system is giving way to a world of three main trading blocs.

One might expect that experts in trade negotiation would be at least fairly positive about the bilateral and regional trade liberalization that has taken place in recent years. Worldwide liberalization might be better still, but isn't half a loaf better than none? In fact, however, there are widespread misgivings. While it is difficult to get a very explicit statement of the concern, in general what trade policy experts seem to be worried about is the possibility that countries that join trading blocs will be more protectionist toward countries outside the blocs than they were before, so world trade as a whole will be hurt more than helped by moves that at first sight seem to be liberalizing in intent. The clearest example of this concern is the widespread discussion of the possibility that 1992 will lead to the creation of "Fortress Europe," an increasingly closed market to the rest of the world.

A full analysis of the costs and benefits of bilateral trading arrangements would require a healthy dose of political science and a careful analysis of the process of bargaining in trade negotiations. It would also require some realism in modeling the actual participants in the game. As a first step, however, it may be useful to have a minimal model in which the concerns about formation of trading blocs can be expressed in order to give us some more foundation for our intuition about the subject. That is the purpose of this chapter. I offer a simple approach to modeling trade liberalization and trade conflict in which the tension between the benefits of special trading arrangements and their negative effect on the world trading system can be clearly seen. In answer to the question posed by the title of this chapter, whether bilateralism is bad or good depends; but as we will see, in the context of a simple model we can get a pretty good idea of what it depends on.

This chapter is in four sections. The first reviews some of the existing theory on preferential trading arrangements and sets out the basic logic of this analysis in an informal way. The second section sets out a simple economic model that can be used to offer a more precise treatment of the issue, in which we can show how the outcome of trade policy at a world level varies with the number of trading blocs into which the world is organized. The third section examines the welfare implications of changes in the number of trading blocs. Finally, the chapter concludes with a brief discussion of an extended model in which there are "natural" trading blocs defined by transportation costs, and asks how the presence of such natural blocs alters the results.

## 1.1   Preferential Trading Arrangements: General Considerations

A naive view would be that since free trade is better than protection, any movement toward freer trade must be a good thing; that preferential trading arrangements are at any rate a step in the right direction. It is a familiar and indeed famous result, however, that this is not always true— half a loaf may be worse than none. In the celebrated analysis of Viner (1950), it was shown that a customs union may cause losses because it leads to "trade diversion" instead of "trade creation"—that is, instead of specializing more and increasing efficiency, countries that form a trading bloc may substitute each others' more expensive goods for goods from outside the bloc, leading to a loss of efficiency. Thus at one level we could argue that bilateral or regional trading arrangements could be destructive if they lead to trade diversion instead of trade creation.

As a general source of concern, however, the risk of trade diversion seems a weak point. It shows that under certain circumstances a customs union could be a mistake—but this is true of many economic policies, and policy concern based on the possibility of widespread stupidity by governments may be realistic though not very interesting. Also, while a customs union with a *given* external tariff may be harmful to the members, a customs union that adjusts its tariff optimally is always beneficial; while optimal adjustment may be unlikely in practice, again this seems to reduce the concern over bilateralism to a fear that governments will make mistakes.

The point that a customs union is always potentially beneficial to its members has been made formally by Kemp and Wan (1976). It may be useful to state the point informally. Suppose that two countries that happen to have the same tariff rate form a customs union. If they did not alter their external tariff rate, the increased trade within the union would represent a mixture of trade creation and trade diversion. Since the trade diversion would be harmful while the trade creation would be beneficial, the overall welfare effect would be ambiguous. (There may also be a terms of trade effect, to which we return below). The Kamp-Wan point, however, is that by adjusting the external tariff, the members of a customs union can always ensure a gain. Specifically, by reducing the tariff to the point at which external trade remains at its preunion level, the countries can ensure that there is no trade diversion. Also, since at this reduced tariff rate the offer to the rest of the world would be unchanged, the terms of trade of the customs union would also remain the same. So the welfare effect of a customs union that lowers its external tariff enough to prevent trade diversion is unambiguously positive. Now, in general, the customs union may choose to have a different tariff level than this; but if it does so, it is because this other tariff level yields still higher welfare. Thus a customs union is always potentially beneficial.

So far as good. But the last point—that a customs union may choose a tariff rate that is different from the one that leaves external trade at its preunion level—raises a potential negative possibility. The reason is that almost surely the optimal tariff rate for the customs union will be higher than this constant-trade level because the customs union will want to take advantage of its size to improve its terms of trade. Indeed, we may expect as a general presumption that a customs union, being a larger unit with more market power than any of its constituent members, will have an optimal external tariff that is higher than the preunion tariff rates of the member nations. Thus while our proof of potential gains relies on the hypothetical case of a customs union that does not lead to any trade diversion, in fact a customs union ordinarily will choose policies that *do* lead to trade diversion.

But this means that the formation of a customs union, while necessarily beneficial to the members, will certainly be harmful to the rest of the world and may reduce the welfare of the world as a whole (if such a measure can be defined).

Now let us return to the concern over bilateral and regional trading arrangements. One way to rationalize the concern of the trade negotiation professionals is the following: They fear that there may be a Prisoner's Dilemma at work in the formation of trading blocs. Imagine a world consisting of four countries, A, B, C, and D. Let A and B form a customs union; then other things equal they will be better off. However, they will have an incentive to improve their terms of trade by maintaining an external tariff that induces trade diversion—indeed, probably an external tariff that is higher than either of them would have on their own—and which therefore leaves C and D worse off. Similarly, C and D will be better off, other things equal, if they form a customs union, but their optimal external tariff will similarly induce trade diversion in the effor to achieve improved terms of trade. What could happen is that the resulting tariff war will induce enough trade diversion to leave everyone worse off than if they had not formed the customs unions.

This story is, of course, a caricature of the actual process of tariff-setting. I have described a world in which trade policy of nations is set to maximize national welfare and in which trading blocs behave noncooperatively. This makes internal politics look better and external relations worse than they are in fact. In reality nations set trade policy in a fashion that reflects internal conflicts of interest more than promotion of national interest vis-à-vis foreigners, and international trade policy reflects a fair degree of bargaining. However, this story does capture the basic idea that formation of trading blocs, while advantageous in itself, may have an adverse effect on the multilateral system and in the end be harmful. Thus, although we will eventually need a more realistic story, this seems like a useful starting point.

The story also points us toward an interesting question: How does world welfare vary with the number of trading blocs into which the world is organized? Absent any market imperfections, the *optimal* number of trading blocs is, of course, one: free trade. One might at first suppose that this implies that the fewer trading blocs, the better. However, in the general second-best logic that prevails here, that is far from clear. If a world consisting of many small trading blocs, each of which is very open to external trade, consolidates into a somewhat smaller number of blocs, each of which is still very open to external trade, most of the expansion of intrabloc trade may come from trade diversion rather than trade creation. Thus when the number of blocs is reduced from a very large number to a still fairly large number, it would not be surprising to find that world welfare falls. Conversely, when there are only a few trading blocs, doing only limited trade with each other, most of the expansion of intrabloc trade when they consolidate into a still smaller number of blocs will represent trade expansion, and welfare will probably rise. Thus the number of trading blocs at which world welfare is minimized—henceforth referred to as the *pessimal* number—will probably be some moderate number of blocs. A world that is either more or less fragmented will have higher welfare.

This is about as far as informal argumentation can take us. To firm up the intuition and to provide further insight, we now turn to a formal model.

## 1.2 Trading Blocs and Tariff-Setting: A Formal Model

In order to make the analysis of the problem of bilateralism tractable, I consider a very special model. In this model all nations and trading blocs appear symmetrically so that we can meaningfully describe the world in terms of the representative nation or trading bloc. Also it turns out to be helpful to assume particular functional forms. Thus this model is illustrative rather than conclusive. However, it does, as we will see, yield some striking insights.

Consider, then, a world whose basic elements are geographic units which I will refer to as "provinces." There are a large number $N$ of such provinces in the world. A country, in general, consists of a number of provinces. For the analysis here, however, I will basically ignore the country level of analysis, focusing instead on "trading blocs" that contain a number of countries (perhaps only one), and thus a larger number of provinces. Specifically, there are $B < N$ trading blocs in the world. These trading blocs will be assumed to be symmetric so that each contains $N/B$ provinces; the integer constraint is ignored. A main purpose of the analysis will be to find how world welfare depends on $B$.

Each province is specialized in the production of a single good that is an imperfect substitute for the products of other provinces. All provinces will be assumed to be the same economic size, so without loss of generality I will choose units so that each produces one unit of its good. All provinces have the same tastes, into which the products of all provinces enter symmetrically, with the specific functional form

$$U = \left[ \sum_{i=1}^{N} c_i^{\theta} \right]^{1/\theta}, \qquad 0 < \theta < 1, \tag{1}$$

where $c_i$ is the province's consumption of the good of province $i$. This is of course a CES utility function, where the elasticity of substitution between any two products is

$$\sigma = \frac{1}{1 - \theta}. \tag{2}$$

The resemblance between this setup and standard monopolistic competition models of trade is obvious and not coincidental; indeed this formulation was suggested by an analysis of optimal tariffs in a monopolistically competitive world by Gros (1987). If you like, you may regard a "province" as an area with fixed resources that specializes in a limited number of differentiated products because of increasing returns. However, this interpretation is not necessary, and the model may also be viewed as arising from a perfectly competitive environment.

A trading bloc is a group of provinces with internal free trade and a common external ad valorem tariff. The external tariff rate is chosen so as to maximize welfare, taking the policies of other trading blocs are given (because of the symmetry among provinces there are no internal income distribution effects). This is a standard problem in international economics: The optimal tariff for a bloc is

$$t^* = \frac{1}{\varepsilon - 1},$$ (3)

where $\varepsilon$ is the elasticity of demand for the bloc's exports.

To determine $\varepsilon$, consider the imports of the rest of the world from a representative trading bloc. The "rest of the world" consists of the $N(1 - B^{-1})$ provinces that are not part of the bloc; given the symmetry of the model, the price of the goods produced by all these provinces will be the same. Let $y^W$ equal the volume of output of the rest of the world, equal to

$$y^W = N(1 - B^{-1}).$$ (4)

Also let $d^W$ be the volume of rest-of-world consumption of rest-of-world products, and $m^W$ be rest-of-world imports from our trading bloc. Then we must have

$$d^W + pm^W = y^W,$$ (5)

where $p$ is the price of our bloc's output relative to rest-of-world output on world (not internal) markets.

Now consider the effects of a change in $p$, holding the ad valorem tariff rates constant. Placing a "hat" over a variable to represent a proportional change, we have

$$(1 - s)\hat{d}^W + s(\hat{p} + \hat{m}^W) = \hat{y}^W = 0$$ (6)

where $s = pm^W/y^W$ is the share of imports from our bloc in income at world prices. Also with ad valorem tariffs internal prices will change in the same proportion as external; therefore given the constant elasticity of substitution, we have

$$(\hat{d}^W - \hat{m}^W) = \sigma\hat{p}.$$ (7)

Combining (6) and (7), and rearranging, we have

$$\hat{m}^W = -[s + (1 - s)\sigma]\hat{p},$$ (8)

which implies that our bloc faces an elasticity of demand for exports

$$\varepsilon = s + (1 - s)\sigma$$ (9)

and therefore that the optimal tariff rate is

$$t^* = \frac{1}{(1-s)(\sigma - 1)}. \tag{10}$$

There are two interesting things to notice about this expression. First is that the optimal tariff is increasing in $s$; that is, the larger the share of a trading bloc's exports in rest-of-world expenditure, the higher the tariff it will charge. On the other hand, no matter how small the share, the optimal tariff does not go to zero; as $s$ goes to zero, $t^*$ goes down only to $1/(\sigma - 1)$. This is because there are no "small countries" in the sense of price-takers in this model: Even an individual province produces a differentiated good and therefore has a positive optimal tariff. As Gros (1987) has pointed out, this is normally the case in monopolistically competitive models, where the optimal tariff for a small country equals the markup of price over marginal cost.

The share variable $s$ is of course endogenous, depending for a given number of trading blocs on the tariff rate. Thus we turn next to the determination of $s$.

Let $y$ be the volume of output of a representative trading bloc; we know that

$$y = \frac{N}{B}. \tag{11}$$

Let $m$ be the volume of this trading bloc's imports and $d$ the volume of consumption of its own goods. In a symmetric equilibrium, in which all blocs have the same tariff rate, the goods of all regions will sell at equal prices on world markets. Thus the budget constraint for a representative bloc is

$$m + d = y. \tag{12}$$

Next consider the relative demand for goods produced inside and outside of the bloc. There are $N/B$ goods produced by provinces inside a representative trading bloc, implying $N(B-1)/B$ goods produced outside. If consumers faced the world prices of these goods, which are equal, then given the symmetrical way in which the goods enter into demand we would have $m/d = B - 1$. Since consumers must pay a tariff rate of $t$ on extrabloc goods, however, and since the elasticity of substitution is $\sigma$, we have

$$\frac{m}{d} = (1+t)^{-\sigma}(B-1). \tag{13}$$

From (11)–(13) we find that

$$m = \frac{y}{(1 + t)^\sigma/(B - 1) + 1} = \frac{N/B}{(1 + t)^\sigma/(B - 1) + 1}. \tag{14}$$

This determines the imports of a representative bloc. Because trade must be balanced, however, imports equal exports (i.e., $m = m^{\mathrm{W}}$). Thus the share of bloc exports in nonbloc income is

$$s = \frac{m}{y^{\mathrm{W}}}$$

$$= \frac{m}{N(1 - B^{-1})}. \tag{15}$$

Substituting and rearranging, we have

$$s = [(1 + t)^\sigma + B - 1]^{-1} \tag{16}$$

so that the share of bloc exports in nonbloc income is decreasing in both the tariff rate and the number of blocs.

Figure 1.1 shows how equations (10) and (16) simultaneously determine the tariff rate and the export share for a given number of blocs $B$. The downward-sloping curve $SS$ represents (16); it shows that the higher the

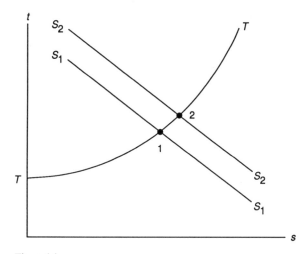

Figure 1.1

tariff rate of a representative bloc, the lower is the share of each bloc in rest-of-world income. The curve $TT$ represents (10); it shows that the tariff rate levied by blocs is higher, the larger their export share. Equilibrium is at point $E$, where each bloc is levying the unilaterally optimal tariff.

Now consider the effect of a change in the number of blocs. Suppose, for example, that there are a series of negotiations between pairs of blocs that reduces the number of blocs from some initial number $B_0$ to $B_0/2$. It is immediately apparent what the result will be. For any given tariff rate, the effect of the reduction in $B$ is to shift $SS$ up; at a given $t$ each bloc will have a higher $S$. Thus in figure 1.1 $S_1 S_1$ shifts up to $S_2 S_2$. As a result the tariff rate rises as equilibrium shifts from 1 to 2.

It is clear that this process will reduce the volume of trade between any two countries that are in different blocs. Even at an unchanged tariff, the removal of trade barriers between members of the expanded bloc would divert some trade that would otherwise have taken place between blocs. This trade diversion will be reinforced by the rise in the tariff rate.

Thus this model suggests that there is something to the concern of trade specialists that bilateral trade pacts may impair multilateral trade. The obvious next question, however, is whether this is actually bad for welfare.

## 1.3   The Number of Trading Blocs and World Welfare

The effect of the tariffs levied by trading blocs is to distort the consumer choice between intrabloc and external goods. The utility function (1) may be written as

$$U = [N(1 - B^{-1})(c^{\mathrm{W}})^\theta + NB^{-1}(c^{\mathrm{D}})^\theta]^{1/\theta}, \tag{17}$$

where $c^{\mathrm{W}}$ and $c^{\mathrm{D}}$ represent a province's consumption of a representative good produced outside and inside the bloc, respectively. After a little manipulation we can show that

$$c^{\mathrm{W}} = \frac{B/N}{(1 + t)^\sigma + B - 1} \tag{18}$$

and that

$$c^{\mathrm{D}} = \frac{[B(1 + t)^\sigma/N]}{(1 + t)^\sigma + B - 1}. \tag{19}$$

For evaluating how welfare changes when the number of trading blocs changes, the number of regions $N$ is unimportant; so it is harmless to simplify by normalizing $N$ to equal 1. Under this assumption welfare equals

$$U = \left[\frac{B}{(1 + t)^{\sigma} + B - 1}\right][(1 - B^{-1}) + B^{-1}(1 + t)^{\sigma\theta}]^{1/\theta}. \tag{20}$$

If trade were free, we would always have $U = 1$. Since the tariff rate is also a function of $B$, (20) together with (10) and (16) allows us to determine how welfare varies with the number of trading blocs.

Rather than attempting to prove general results here, since the model is so special in any case, it makes more sense to adopt a numerical approach. This is especially true because the model has only one parameter: $\sigma$, the elasticity of substitution in world trade. Thus we can plot welfare as a function of $B$ for a number of plausible values of $\sigma$. In what follows I use three values of $\sigma$: 2, a rather low estimate; 4, a somewhat high estimate; and 10, which is much higher than any empirical estimates.

As an initial step, figure 1.2 plots equilibrium tariff rates as a function of

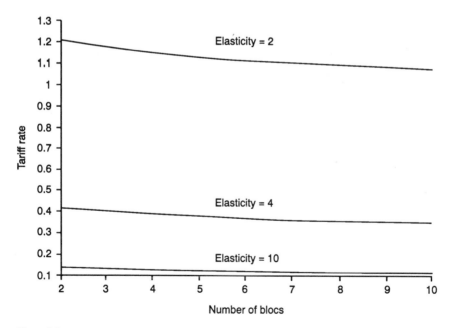

Figure 1.2

*B*. We note that the tariff declines as B is increased, but not to zero as already pointed out. Two other points are worth noting. First, the actual relationship between *B* na *t* is rather flat. This is because when there are fewer blocs, trade diversion tends to reduce interbloc trade, and thus leads to less of a rise in *s* than one might expect. Second, except in the case of a very high $\sigma$, the tariff rates are much higher than the actual rates of protection on trade among advanced nations. This is a useful caution on taking this model too seriously; actual relations among trading blocs are clearly far more cooperative than envisaged here.

We now turn to the level of welfare as a function of the number of trading blocs, shown in figure 1.3. In each case world welfare is maximized with free trade (i.e., with *B* = 1). The costs from lack of free trade are larger, the lower the elasticity of substitution. As suggested informally in section 1.1, the relationship between welfare and the number of blocs is U-shaped, with the pessimum at a moderate number of blocs. The surprise is that the pessimal number is the same for all plausible elasticities of substitution. Three trading blocs is the number that minimizes world welfare.

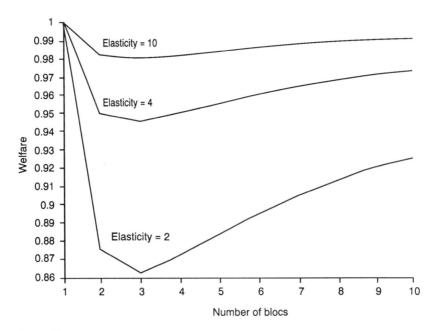

**Figure 1.3**

This is an interesting result, since many observers suggest that the world is in fact evolving precisely into a three-bloc economy. Before we put too much weight on the result, however, we should examine why we get it and whether it is really plausible.

The basic explanation of the result is the following: In the model as stated so far, there are no natural trading blocs. That is, except for the effect of tariffs, each province tends to consume the products of all provinces equally. Even with tariffs, as long as there are more than a few trading blocs most of each province's consumption comes from provinces outside its own bloc. The result is that as long as there are more than a few blocs, the trade diversion that results from consolidation outweighs the trade creation. Notice that if there were no tariffs, consumption from outside the bloc would exceed intrabloc consumption as soon as the number of blocs exceeds two. The presence of tariffs alters this, but it is not surprising that the number of blocs at which trade diversion begins to outweigh trade creation is small—though it is still fairly remarkable that the number always turns out to be three.

It is apparent from this intuitive story, however, that the result that a three-bloc world represents a pessimum is crucially dependent on the assumption that there are no natural trading blocs. The final argument of this chapter will be that this result does not hold up if transportation costs give rise to the existence of natural regions.

## 1.4  Natural Trading Blocs

To get a fix on the issue of natural trading blocs, let us now imagine a world in which there is a structure of transportation costs. Specifically, we now assume that the $N$ provinces in the world are located on three "continents": $X$, $Y$, and $Z$. Each continent contains $N/3$ provinces.

The structure of production and preferences will be assumed exactly the same as before. Also we continue to assume that there are zero transportation costs within each continent. However, we now suppose that there are transportation costs between continents. These take Samuelson's "iceberg" form: Of a unit of a good shipped from one continent to another, only a fraction $1 - \gamma$ arrives. Thus the continents in effect form natural trading regions, with the extent of natural regionalism determined by the transport cost $\gamma$.

Suppose next that each continent is initially divided into two equal-sized trading blocs. What will happen to world welfare if each bloc reaches an agreement with its neighbor, consolidating each continent into a single trading bloc?

We can immediately see that the result depends on intercontinental transportation costs. Consider first the case where $\gamma = 0$ so that there are no transportation costs. In this case we are back to the symmetric case studied before, where three trading blocs represents the pessimal trading structure for all plausible parameter values. So in this case the bilateral deals end up reducing world welfare. On the other hand, consider the case where $\gamma$ is close to one, so that transport costs are nearly prohibitive. In this case intercontinental trade is unimportant. Thus in effect each continent is a world unto itself, which moves from two blocs to one—which we know is welfare improving.

The result then is that the assessment of regional trading arrangements depends on whether there is enough inherent regionalism in the structure of transportation costs. If trading arrangements follow the lines of natural trading regions, they will have a much better chance of improving welfare than trade arragements between "unnatural" partners.

## 1.5    Conclusions

Is bilateralism (or more accurately, regionalism) in trading arrangements bad? This chapter has shown that in the context of a highly stylized model, it might be. Although a world that consolidates into trading blocs could simultaneously reduce tariffs so as to avoid trade diversion, the optimal noncooperative behavior of the blocs is actually to increase external tariffs. Thus a reduction in interbloc trade is the normal outcome of the formation of regional trading blocs.

In the simplest version of the model presented here it is also highly likely that the net effect of regionalization will be to reduce world welfare. This is a fragile result. The result might be softened considerably by either a realistic appreciation of the role of transport costs (as shown here) or a recognition that real-world trade policies are set through negotiation, not through wholly noncooperative actions. Nevertheless, the analysis given here suggests at least some grounds for the widespread concern over the apparent trend toward regionalization of international trading arrangements.

## References

Gros, D. 1987. A note on the optimal tariff, retaliation, and the welfare loss from tariff wars in a model with intra-industry trade. *Journal on International Economics* 23: 357–367.

Kemp, M., and Wan, H. 1976. Elementary proposition concerning the formation of custom unions. *International Economic Review* 6: 95–97.

Viner, J. 1950. *The Customs Union Issue*. New York: Carnegie Endowment for International Peace.

# 2 Strategic Trade Policy and Direct Foreign Investment: When Are Tariffs and Quotas Equivalent?

James A. Levinsohn

The equivalence of tariffs and quotas in a perfectly competitive world is well understood. It is by now equally well known that the presence of a monopoly may destroy the tariff–quota equivalence. These are informative limiting cases, however; much international trade is conducted in markets that lie somewhere between the extremes of pure competition and monopoly. This trade is often characterized by large, frequently multinational, players who recognize their influence on markets and hence act strategically. Recent developments in trade theory have explored how trade policy works in this setting. This work is nicely surveyed in Grossman and Richardson (1985).

Most of the recent work on trade policy with imperfect competition has looked at various tariff-subsidy schemes. By concentrating on prices rather than quantities as policy instruments, researchers have made an important choice. Under perfect competition there would be an equivalent quota associated with any tariff, but this is not necessarily the case under imperfect competition. Bhagwati (1965) first noted this point. He showed that a tariff might dominate a quota, or vice versa, depending on the basis for comparison (same imports or same total consumption) and on where the monopoly was located: The existence of a competitive fringe is an essential element of Bhagwati's model.[1] In contrast, the asymmetric foreign supply response to a tariff and a quota is at the heart of the nonequivalence result. Under a tariff the foreign producer can still increase output, whereas under a binding quota it cannot.

Krishna (1983) was among the first to investigate quotas in an oligopoly setting. Her analysis provides yet another example of nonequivalence between tariffs and quotas. Using a game-theoretic framework in which firms play strategically against other firms but take government actions as given, Krishna shows that a quota might serve as a facilitating device while a tariff would not. She demonstrates that in a Bertrand duopoly setting, each firm would like to raise its price if it were sure that its rival would do likewise. Under a quota it is irrational for a firm to lower its price in order to gain market share since quotas would bind. Quotas then allow firms to

Expanded version of a paper published in the *Journal of International Economics*, vol. 27, pp. 129–146. Reprinted by permission of Elsevier.

credibly precommit to higher prices. Like Bhagwati's results, Krishna's exploit the lack of a foreign supply response imposed by a quota but not by a tariff.[2]

In Krishna's introduction, she writes:

Most of the literature has dealt with the two polar cases of monopoly and perfect competition, neglecting the strategic interaction crucial to the analysis of oligopoly. Such interaction between firms is a dominant feature of many markets, especially in some international markets in which large multinationals operate.

Her work, though, like much of the analysis of tax based policies, ignores the possible multinational aspects of the game firms play. In this chapter I consider the tariff quota equivalence question in a setting that explicitly accounts for the possibility of direct foreign investment (DFI).

The absence of a foreign supply response under a quota, so critical to the analysis of the differential impact of tariffs and quotas under imperfect competition, is called into question by the potential occurrence of DFI. The credible precommitment permitted by a government-imposed quota is crucial to Krishna's analysis. Yet when the possibility of DFI exists, the key assumption of no foreign supply response to a quota may no longer hold. Even if a foreign producer is not able to increase local exportable output due to a binding quota, the firm can produce the additional output in the home country. In this case a quota is no longer a facilitating device, and many of the strategic interactions that differentiate a quota from a tariff disppear.

The chapter is organized as follows. Section 2.1 presents a diagrammatic analysis of tariff–quota comparisons in the presence of DFI. This section provides a useful taxonomy for the general model of section 2.2. Section 2.1 also provides some intuition about the results of section 2.2. In that section a general oligopoly model with DFI is developed. The generality extends to the number of firms and their mode of conduct. In this setting the tariff–quota nonequivalence of Bhagwati and Krishna is reconsidered. In particular, the optimal profit-shifting tariff is compared to the optimal profit-shifting quota. Section 2.3 entertains the notion that trade policy might be motivated by considerations of domestic employment. Allowing this to be the case, equivalence results are reexamined. Section 2.4 relaxes assumptions about firm's cost functions and reconsiders the results of section 2.2. A brief summary is given in section 2.5.

## 2.1   A Diagrammatic Analysis of Tariff–Quota Comparisons

Consider a market in which a foreign monopolist is the sole supplier of a
good in the home-country market.[3] Figure 2.1 represents the market for
the foreign good in the usual space of own price and quantity. The foreign
monopolist faces the demand schedule $D$ and the corresponding marginal
revenue schedule $MR$.

Figure 2.1 shows the well-known result that when the optimal tariff is
positive, the home country can improve its welfare by extracting monopoly
rents from the foreign country in excess of the lost consumer surplus.[4] This
result requires only that $MR$ be more steeply sloped than the linear $D$. It
is noteworthy that some positive tariffs are welfare improving. Since it is
rational to impose such a tariff, (non)equivalence results are meaningful in
a way they might not be if the imposition of a tariff was itself economically
irrational. For example, the equivalence of tariffs and quotas in the perfectly
competitive paradigm begs the question of why the tariff or quota is present
in the first place.

Initially, the foreign firm produces only in the foreign country (this will
be referred to as foreign production) at constant marginal cost $MC^{for}$. The
assumption of constant marginal cost is not incidental. Although it simplifies the analysis, it is also the logical choice. If marginal cost were increasing,
one might ask why additional plants, foreign or domestic, do not already

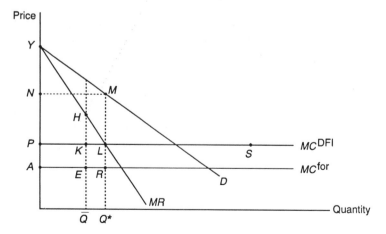

**Figure 2.1**

exist. This analysis, like its predecessors, glosses over the implications of large fixed costs. An exception to this is Horstman and Markusen (1988). They consider a market in which home and foreign firms produce at equal constant marginal costs, but there is a fixed cost to DFI. Their results highlight the importance of how fixed costs are (or are not) modeled. If marginal costs were decreasing, a new set of issues for strategic trade policy arises.[5]

Now let us introduce the possibility of DFI by the foreign firm in the home country. DFI production is assumed to be a perfect substitute for non-DFI production. For example, the consumer is assumed to be in-different between a Honda Accord built in Ohio and the same model manufactured in Japan. The marginal cost of production under DFI, $MC^{DFI}$, also is assumed to be constant. $MC^{DFI}$ must be at least as high as $MC^{for}$. If this were not the case, cost minimization would preclude any domestic production. The optimal rent-extracting tariff may be either at least as large as or smaller than the difference in marginal costs.[6] I will compare tariffs and quotas for each case.

With inverse demand represented by $p = a - bx$ and the constant marginal cost by $c$, the optimal rent-seeking tariff absent the possibility of DFI is given by $a - c/3$. This tariff and the difference between $MC^{DFI}$ and $MC^{for}$ are exogenous to the policymaker. Whether or not the optimal tariff is greater than the difference in marginal costs is a function only of tastes and technologies.[7]

Some terminological clarification is useful. A tariff of $EH$ that was optimal before the possibility of DFI is termed the no-DFI optimal tariff. The tariff that is optimal after DFI is introduced is termed the cum-DFI optimal tariff.

CASE 1    *The optimal tariff, neglecting the possibility of DFI is at least as large as the difference in marginal costs.*

Such a case is given in the figure by a tariff equal to $EH$. In the absence of DFI, the quota yielding the same level of imports is given by $\bar{Q}$. Now introduce the possibility of DFI at $MC^{DFI}$. DFI constrains the optimal tariff to a level of $AP$.[8] Any larger tariff induces DFI, and no revenue is raised.

There is no cum-DFI tariff that ensures imports of $\bar{Q}$, whereas a quota does just that. While this is an obvious nonequivalence, it is not a very meaningful one, since a quota of $\bar{Q}$ in the presence of DFI is not optimal. At a quota of $\bar{Q}$ the foreign producer faces a kinked $MC$ schedule given by

*AEKLS*. Quota licence revenue is given by *APKE*. When imports equal $\bar{Q}$, the amount *KL* is produced via DFI in the home country. Total consumption of the good is $Q^*$. Home welfare is given by consumer surplus and licence revenue. This is area *MNY* plus *PKEA*. A quota of $Q^*$, which corresponds to the cum-DFI optimal tariff, yields the same consumer surplus but gives strictly greater licence revenue by amount *KLRE*. The cum-DFI optimal tariff is equivalent to the cum-DFI optimal quota.

Simple jumping of a quota such as $\bar{Q}$ leads to DFI concurrent with home production, even though marginal costs are constant. Without quantity restrictions, such behavior is incompatible with standard cost minimization. Seen from a different angle, the very presence of DFI as quota jumping is evidence that the quota is set at a suboptimal level.

With imperfect compeition DFI may be welfare worsening, for it may undermine optimal rent-extracting trade policies.[9] Although it is not obvious from the geometry of figure 2.1, a revealed-preference argument shows that DFI is welfare worsening since the cum-DFI policies were feasible but not chosen when selecting the no-DFI optimal policies.

CASE 2   *The optimal tariff is less than the difference in marginal costs.*

In this case previously considered, tariff–quota comparisons[10] hold except that the marginal cost of DFI imposes an upper bound beyond which a quota will provoke a supply response in the form of DFI. If the cost function of DFI is similar to the cost function of domestic production, the difference in marginal costs will be small, and it becomes less likely that case 2 will obtain.

## 2.2   A More General Analysis of Tariff–Quota Comparisons

The previous section demonstrated that in a fairly specific setting, if the no-DFI optimal tariff exceeded the difference in local and DFI marginal costs, then the introduction of DFI made the optimal rent-extracting tariff and the optimal rent-extracting quota equivalent policies. In section 2.1 there was a foreign monopolist facing a linear demand schedule. In this section I generalize the diagrammatic results by considering a differentiated-product oligopoly in which firms face general demand schedules and market conduct is not restricted. This latter generalization is of some significance, as Eaton and Grossman (1986) have shown that choice of market conduct is often key to characterizing optimal policies.

I consider tariff–quota equivalence in the presence of DFI when firms compete only in the home market. The restrictive assumption that is in part carried over from section 2.1 is that marginal costs must be constant in the neighborhood where production actually occurs. The reasons are the same as before. With upward-sloping marginal costs, one must consider why another plant does not already exist. (The ramifications of upward sloping marginal costs are discussed in section 2.3.) With downward-sloping marginal costs, an entirely new set of issues arises, and these may obscure the original intent of the analysis.

The more general setting described above is of more than just theoretical interest as it describes the U.S./Japanese automobile market fairly accurately. U.S. and Japanese cars are certainly differentiated products. They are produced with constant marginal costs by a small number of very large firms in each country. These firms compete with each other almost solely in the U.S. market. Furthermore the market has been subject to tariffs and, more recently, quotas.[11] Completing the picture, DFI in the United States by Japanese firms is a rapidly growing phenomenon.

**The Setup**

It is useful to establish some notation at the outset. Let

$n_1$ = number of domestic firms,
$n_2$ = number of foreign firms.

I consider a symmetric market structure in which firms within a country are identical. DFI production represents an increase in output but it is not an increase in the number of firms. Output is given by

$q_1$ = output of a firm in industry 1,
$q_2$ = output of a firm in industry 2,
$q_2 = q_{2f} + q_{2d}$,

where $q_{2f}$ is production by foreign firms in the foreign country and $q_{2d}$ is DFI production.
Let

$Q_1 = n_1 q_1$,
$Q_{2d} = n_2 q_{2d}$,
$Q_{2f} = n_2 q_{2f}$ and $Q_{2d} + Q_{2f} = Q_2$.

Cost functions are

$$C^1 = c(q_1),$$
$$C^2 = c(q_{2f}, q_{2d}).$$

ASSUMPTION 1    Marginal costs, denoted $c_1$, $c_{2d}$, and $c_{2f}$, are constant and $c_{2d} > c_{2f}$.

Let $v_{ij}$ be firm $j$'s conjecture of firms $i$'s quantity response to a change in its own quantity $(i, j = 1, 2)$. The conjectural variations (CV) parameter is used in this context as a flexible parameter that can represent myriad market conducts. It is no more than a convenient parameterization.

The home country's utility function is given by $U = U(Q_1, Q_2)$ Inverse demands are

$$\frac{\partial U}{\partial Q_1} = P^1(Q_1, Q_2) \quad \text{and} \quad \frac{\partial U}{\partial Q_2} = P^2(Q_1, Q_2).$$

Supercripts on $P^1$ and $P^2$ will denote partial derivatives.

Before DFI is introduced, the home country is able to freely set a specific tariff $t$ on imports and a specific subsidy $s$ on home production. Finally I make the following two assumptions:

ASSUMPTION 2    The no-DFI optimal tariff is profitably jumped. (This corresponds to case 1 of the diagrammatic analysis.)

ASSUMPTION 3    Home welfare is continuous and strictly concave in policy tools. This assumption holds in the linear cases (as in section 2.1) and is a natural extension thereof. The assumption is restrictive in that it disallows cases in which, as one goes from no tariff to the optimal tariff, welfare falls and then rises.

*Proof of Tariff–Quota Equivalence*    I prove that the optimal tariff and quota are equivalent in two steps. In step 1 I characterize the optimal tariff and subsidy combination. It is important to consider subsidy schemes. A subsidy will generally be needed, in addition to a tariff, to attain a first-best optimum. This is true with or without DFI because one needs two instruments to control optimally for two targets. One of these targets is the price–marginal cost gap in the production of home firms; the other is the strategic distortion that gives rise to profit shifting. Without DFI, the production subsidy addresses the first target, and trade policy addresses the second. Because the no-DFI optimal tariff is, by assumption 2, profitably jumped, the no-DFI optimal tariff raises no revenue in the presence of DFI. In this sense DFI constraints tariff-setting to a level no greater than the difference in foreign marginal costs. Since the possibility to DFI blunts the efficacy of the tariff with respect to the profit-shifting objective, there will be an additional motive for employing the subsidy. The approach here follows Dixit (1984, 1986).

In step 2, I characterize the optimal quota and subsidy combination. DFI does not constrain quota-setting as it constrains tariff-setting. Hence the home country has an unconstrained policy tool for each quantity involved. I prove that the ability to set a binding quota has no value in terms of home-country welfare. Furthermore the solution to the optimal tariff/subsidy scheme will always be the solution to the optimal quota/subsidy scheme. This equivalence will be shown to be independent of the number of firms on either side of the market and independent of the mode of market conduct.

I then extend the equivalence by proving that the optimal tariff and quota are also equivalent when no subsidy is available.

**Step 1: The Optimal Tariff Subsidy Scheme**

Firms choose outputs strategically but take government policies as given. The government maximizes national welfare conditional on firm's profit maximization.

I first consider firms' profit-maximizing behavior. By assumption 2, the cum-DFI optimal tariff must be no greater than $c_{2d} - c_{2f}$. (Were it greater, no revenue would be raised). Because marginal costs are constant by assumption 1, cost minimization precludes DFI concurrent with domestic production. Thus $q_2 = q_{2f}$.

Firm's profit functions are given by

$$\pi_1 = P^1(Q_1, Q_2)q_1 - C^1(q_1) + sq_1, \tag{1}$$

$$\pi_2 = (P^2(Q_1, Q_2) - t)q_2 - C^2(q_2). \tag{2}$$

An interior solution to an individual firm's profit maximization implies that

$$\mu^1 = \frac{\partial \pi_1}{\partial q_1} = 0$$

$$= P^1(Q_1, Q_2) + s - c_1 + q_1(P_1^1(Q_1, Q_2)g_0 + P_2^1(Q_1, Q_2)g_1), \tag{3}$$

$$\mu^2 = \frac{\partial \pi_2}{\partial q_2} = 0$$

$$= P^2(Q_1, Q_2) - t - c_{2f} + q_2(P_1^2(Q_1, Q_2)h_1 + P_2^2(Q_1, Q_2)h_0), \qquad (4)$$

where

$$g_0 = [1 + (n_1 - 1)v_{11}],$$
$$g_1 = n_2 v_{21},$$
$$h_0 = [1 + (n_2 - 1)v_{22}],$$
$$h_1 = n_1 v_{12}.$$

These $g$ and $h$ terms reflect the mode of market conduct and the number of firms. They are treated as constants, although making them functions of quantities does not affect any of the equivalence results.

Some comparative statics analysis on firm's profit maximization will be useful for the later welfare analysis. It will be helpful to introduce some new notation. Arguments of partial derivatives of the inverse demand functions will be omitted for brevity. Let

$$\Omega_1(Q_1, Q_2) = \frac{P_{11}^2 h_1 + P_{12}^2 h_0}{n_2},$$

$$\Omega_2(Q_1, Q_2) = \frac{P_{12}^2 h_1 + P_{22}^2 h_0}{n_2},$$

$$\Omega_3(Q_1, Q_2) = \frac{P_{12}^1 g_0 + P_{22}^1 g_1}{n_1},$$

$$\Omega_4(Q_1, Q_2) = \frac{P_{11}^1 g_0 + P_{12}^1 g_1}{n_1},$$

This set of terms is related to the degree of concavity or convexity of the inverse demand functions. With linear inverse demands, these terms all become zero. A second set of terms deals with conjectures aggregated to an industry level. These terms are

$$R_1(Q_1, Q_2) = \frac{P_1^1 g_0 + P_2^1 g_1}{n_1},$$

$$R_2(Q_1, Q_2) = \frac{P_1^2 h_1 + P_2^2 h_0}{n_2}.$$

Using this notation, firms' first-order conditions simplify to

$$P^1 + Q_1 R_1 - c_1 = -s, \tag{3'}$$

$$P^2 + Q_2 R_2 - c_{2f} = t. \tag{4'}$$

Equations (3') and (4') implicitly define a one to one mapping between policy tools $s$ and $t$ and quantities $Q_1$ and $Q_2$. As policy tools change, firms respond by adjusting quantities. This relationship is given by totally differentiating (3') and (4') to give the following system:

$$\begin{pmatrix} P_1^1 + R_1 + Q_1 \Omega_4 & P_2^1 + Q_1 \Omega_3 \\ P_1^2 + Q_2 \Omega_1 & P_2^2 + R_2 + Q_2 \Omega_2 \end{pmatrix} \begin{pmatrix} dQ_1 \\ dQ_2 \end{pmatrix} = \begin{pmatrix} -ds \\ dt \end{pmatrix}. \tag{5}$$

Conditional on assumptions 1 through 3 and firm's profit maximization, the home country sets $s$ and $t$ to maximize home welfare. Home welfare is given by consumer surplus, domestic profits, and net trade taxes. Hence

$$W = U(Q_1, Q_2) - P^1 Q_1 - P^2 Q_2 + n_1 \pi_1 + t Q_2 - s Q_1$$

$$= U(Q_1, Q_2) - P^2(Q_1, Q_2) Q_2 - c_1 Q_1 + t Q_2. \tag{6}$$

This implicitly defines welfare as a function of $s$ and $t$. That is,

$$W = f(Q_1(s, t), Q_2(s, t), t). \tag{7}$$

I proceed by characterizing the optimal policy pair $(s^*, t^*)$. The home production subsidy is not constrained by the potential of DFI. Hence $s$ is set such that

$$\frac{\partial W}{\partial s} = 0 \quad \text{for any tariff } t. \tag{8}$$

The tariff, though, is constrained in that any tariff greater than the difference in marginal costs induces DFI and hence raises no revenue. If follows from assumption 3 that $\partial W / \partial t > 0$ for a tariff set below the the difference in marginal costs. The optimal cum-DFI tariff then is the largest tariff that does not induce DFI. Hence $t^* = c_{2d} - c_{2f}$.

Equation (8) implicitly defines the optimal subsidy coupled with the cum-DFI optimal tariff. Using $t = c_{2d} - c_{2f}$ and substituting (3') into (8) yields

$$\frac{\partial W}{\partial s} = 0 = [-s - Q_1 R_1 - P_1^2 Q_2] \frac{\partial Q_1}{\partial s} + [c_{2d} - c_{2f} - P_2^2 Q_2] \frac{\partial Q_2}{\partial s}.$$

Using system (5) to solve for $\partial Q_1/\partial s$ and $\partial Q_2/\partial s$ and solving for $s$ gives

$$s^* = -Q_1 R_1 - Q_2 P_1^2 - \frac{[c_{2d} - c_{2f} - Q_2 P_2^2][P_1^2 + Q_2 \Omega_1]}{P_2^2 + R_2 + Q_2 \Omega_2}. \tag{9}$$

The optimal subsidy is a function of market conduct, number of firms, tastes, and technology. It is not in general possible to sign the expression. For the special case of Cournot competition and linear inverse demands,

$$\frac{\delta s}{\delta(c_{2d} - c_{2f})} = \frac{P_1^2}{P_2^2 + R_2} < 0.$$

This accords with intuition. As the difference in marginal costs contracts, the cum-DFI optimal tariff becomes more constrained. Since the profit-shifting ability of the tariff is more constrained, the home production subsidy acts to capture some of the foreign oligopoly rents that the tariff no longer can.

### Step 2:  The Optimal Quota/Subsidy Scheme and Its Equivalence to The Optimal Tariff/Subsidy Scheme of Step 1

The home government may set two policy tools—a quota on $Q_{2f}$ and a subsidy on home production.[12] As in the tariff/subsidy scheme I assume that $c_{2d} - c_{2f}$ is less than the no-DFI optimal tariff. The dual of this assumption is that DFI, if it existed, would occur at the no-DFI optimal quota. Unlike the case of the tariff, the difference in foreign marginal costs does not constrain the choice of the quota. This corresponds to the diagrammatic case in which no tariff could ensure imports of $\bar{Q}$, whereas a quota did just that. The cost differential $c_{2d} - c_{2f}$ now sets the maximum price a foreign firm would be willing to pay for a quota licence. So that comparison with the tariff/subsidy scenario is valid, I assume that quotas are auctioned to foreign producers.

As in step 1, I first consider firms' profit maximization and then characterize optimal policy conditional on firms' optimizing behavior. Since foreign firms pay $c_{2d} - c_{2f}$ for the quota license on non-DFI production, a foreign firm's profit function is now given by[13]

$$\pi_2 = [P^2(Q_1, Q_2) - (c_{2d} - c_{2f})]q_{2f} + P^2(Q_1, Q_2)q_{2d} - C^2(q_{2f}, q_{2d}). \tag{10}$$

A home firm's profit function is unchanged from (1) as is its first-order condition—equation (3) or (3′).

The foreign firms maximize profits only with respect to $q_{2d}$. They take $q_{2f}$ as given since the quota binds and is exogenously set. Foreign profit maximization then implies that

$$\frac{\partial \pi_2}{\partial q_{2d}} = 0 = P^2 - c_{2d} + q_2[P_1^2 h_0 + P_2^2 h_0], \quad \text{and} \quad q_2 = q_{2f} + q_{2d}, \quad (11)$$

$$= P^2 - c_{2d} + (Q_{2d} + Q_{2f})R_2. \quad (11')$$

Equations (3') and (11') implicitly define a mapping between policy tools $s$ and $Q_{2f}$ and free quantities $Q_1$ and $Q_{2d}$. As the government changes policies, quantities adjust. For foreign firms this relationship is represented by totally differentiating (11'). This gives

$$[P_1^2 + (Q_{2d} + Q_{2f})\Omega_1]dQ_1$$

$$+ [P_2^2 + (Q_{2d} + Q_{2f})\Omega_2 + R_2][dQ_{2d} + dQ_{2f}] = 0. \quad (12)$$

As quantities change, $P^2$ changes. Since $dP^2(Q_1, Q_2) = p_1^2 dQ_1 + P_2^2 dQ_2$, (12) can be written

$$dP^2 = (-Q_2\Omega_1)dQ_1 - (Q_2\Omega_2 + R_2)dQ_2. \quad (13)$$

Finally, (12) can be manipulated to show how free quantities change as the quota is adjusted. This gives

$$dQ_{2f} = -\frac{P_1^2 + Q_2\Omega_1}{P_2^2 + Q_2\Omega_2 + R_2}dQ_1 - dQ_{2d}. \quad (14)$$

Equations (13) and (14) will be useful for the home welfare maximization, to which I now turn.

Home welfare is given by consumer surplus, domestic profits, and license revenues.

$$W = U(Q_1, Q_2) - P^1 Q_1 - P^2 Q_2 + n_1 \pi_1 + (c_{2d} - c_{2f})Q_{2f} - sQ_1. \quad (15)$$

Unlike the tariff case, revenue is possible in the presence of DFI; hence $Q_{2d}$ need not equal zero. An incremental change in welfare is given by

$$dW = (P^1 - c_1)dQ_1 - (Q_{2d} + Q_{2f})dP^2 + (c_{2d} - c_{2f})dQ_{2f}. \quad (16)$$

Equation (16) implies a possible first best situation since there is an unconstrained policy tool for each of the free quantities $Q_1$ and $Q_{2d}$.

Substituting (3'), (13), and (14) into the welfare maximand (16) and simplifying gives

$$dW = \left( -Q_1 R_1 + s + (Q_2)^2 \Omega_1 - [(Q_2)^2 \Omega_2 + Q_2 R_2 + c_{2d} - c_{2f}] \right.$$

$$\left. \times \left[ \frac{P_1^2 + Q_2 \Omega_1}{P_2^2 + Q_2 \Omega_2 + R_2} \right] \right) dQ_1 + (c_{2f} - c_{2d}) dQ_{2d}. \tag{17}$$

The second term in (17) in very informative. Since $c_{2d} > c_{2f}$, DFI enters negatively in home welfare. The ability to set a strictly binding quota that provokes DFI then is of no benefit to domestic welfare. Indeed, given the assumptions of this model, the existence of DFI in a constant marginal cost imperfectly competitive industry is evidence of suboptimal trade policy. At a welfare optimum, $Q_{2d}$ equals 0. The quota on $Q_{2f}$ is set such that revenue $Q_{2f}(c_{2d} - c_{2f})$ is collected but no DFI is provoked.[14] This is exactly what the cum-DFI optimal tariff accomplishes.

The first term in (17) implicitly defines the optimal subsidy that is coupled with the optimal quota. Setting the term multiplied by $dQ_1$ equal to zero, and solving for $s$ gives the optimal subsidy. Straightforward calculations show that this optimal subsidy is identical to the optimal subsidy in the tariff/subsidy scheme of step 1. Again, the optimal subsidy depends on the number of domestic and foreign firms and their mode of market conduct.

The tariff/subsidy scheme is completely equivalent to the quota/subsidy scheme. This result is independent of the number of firms, their market conduct, and the inverse demand system they face.

For some modes of market conduct, the optimal production subsidy associated with the optimal cum-DFI tariff or quota will be positive. Subsidizing domestic oligopolists, though, may often be politically infeasible. I next show that restricting the home production subsidy to zero does not affect the equivalence of the optimal tariff and optimal quota demonstrated above. That is, the ability to set a binding quota that provokes DFI provides no benefit to home welfare, even when a home production subsidy in unavailable.

From assumption 3 it still follows that $\partial W/\partial t > 0$ for any DFI-constrained tariff. The cum-DFI optimal tariff then is still $c_{2d} - c_{2f}$. I next show that the optimal quota is equivalent to this optimal tariff.

Foreign firms' profit functions and their respective first-order conditions are unchanged by restricting a home production subsidy to zero. Hence (11'), (12), and (13) still obtain.

A home firm's profit function is now

$$\pi_1 = P^1(Q_1, Q_2)q_1 - C(q_1). \tag{18}$$

Its first-order condition at an interior solution is given by

$$P^1 - c_1 + Q_1 R_1 = 0. \tag{19}$$

Home welfare is still given by (15), and an incremental change in it by (16). Substituting (19), (13), and (14) into (16) now yields:

$$dW = \left[ -Q_1 R_1 + (Q_2)^2 \Omega_1 - [(Q_2)^2 \Omega_2 + Q_2 R_2 + c_{2d} - c_{2f}] \right.$$
$$\left. \times \left[ \frac{P_1^2 + Q_2 \Omega_1}{P_2^2 + Q_2 \Omega_2 + R_2} \right] \right] dQ_1 + (c_{2f} - c_{2d})dQ_{2d}. \tag{20}$$

Since $c_{2f} < c_{2d}$, DFI enters negatively into home welfare even when the subsidy is constrained to zero. The ability to set a binding quota that provokes DFI confers no welfare benefit to the home country.

As was the case in when a subsidy was allowed, the quota on $Q_{2f}$ is set such that $Q_{2f}(c_{2d} - c_{2f})$ is collected as license revenue, but no DFI is provoked. This is equivalent to the DFI-constrained optimal tariff scenario.

∎

## 2.3  Domestic Employment Considerations and Tariff–Quota Equivalence.

Section 2.2 showed that the existence of DFI in a constant marginal cost imperfectly competitive industry is evidence of suboptimal trade policy. DFI, though, is often praised for the increased employment associated with it. I ask in this section how the equivalence results of section 2.2 are affected by domestic employment concerns.

I assume the employment associated with production in the home country $(Q_1 + Q_{2d})$ enters national welfare but does not directly enter firms' profit functions.[15] The approach used in this section is intentionally agnostic as to why this might be the case.[16]

Let $\phi = \phi(Q_1 + Q_{2d})$ be a flexible function that measures how society values a dollar of wages relative to a dollar of trade tax revenue or consumer surplus. $\phi$ is normalized such that $\phi = 1$ implies that society is indifferent between a dollar paid in wages and a dollar of consumer surplus. $\phi = 0$

implies that wages do not enter national welfare. This was the implicit assumption throughout section 2.2. This might be a logical choice if there is no involuntary unemployment in the home economy. $\phi$ may be constant ($\phi' = 0$). In this case the first dollar of wages is just as important as the $n$th. Similarly $\phi$ may be concave or convex in employment. One might well imagine that the home country derives decreasing marginal benefits to increasing employment.

Employment enters national welfare in the following way:[17]

Benefits to home country employment $= \phi(Q_1 + Q_{2d})\alpha w[Q_1 + Q_{2d}]$,

where

$\alpha =$ the assumed constant input coefficient an labor,

$w =$ the assumed constant wage.                                        (21)

Firms' first-order conditions and comparative statics on them are unchanged since employment considerations do not enter profit functions. A tariff/subsidy scheme then still imposes a bang-bang solution to the firms' cost minimization problem. While a quota/subsidy scheme does not force this behavior, the optimal quota/subsidy scheme of section 2.2 does. I next investigate whether introducing employment concerns into the home welfare function alters this equivalence.

With a quota/subsidy scheme, home welfare is now

$$W = U(Q_1, Q_2) - P^1 Q_1 - P^2 Q_2 + n_1 \pi_1 + (c_{2d} - c_{2f})Q_{2f}$$
$$- sQ_1 + \phi(Q_1 + Q_{2d})\alpha w[Q_1 + Q_{2d}]. \tag{22}$$

An incremental change in welfare is given by

$$dW = [P^1 - c_1 + \phi\alpha w + Q_1\alpha w\phi']dQ_1 - Q_2 dP^2 + (c_{2d} - c_{2f})dQ_{2f}$$
$$+ [\phi\alpha w + Q_{2d}\alpha w\phi']dQ_{2d}. \tag{23}$$

Using the same substitutions as in step 2 of section 2.2 yields

$$dW = \left[ 1 - Q_1 R_1 - s + (Q_2)^2 \Omega_1 + \phi\alpha w + Q_1\phi'\alpha w - [(Q_2)^2\Omega_2 \right.$$
$$\left. + Q_2 R_2 + c_{2d} - c_{2f}] \left[ \frac{P_1^2 + Q_2\Omega_1}{P_2^2 + Q_2\Omega_2 + R_2} \right] \right] dQ_1$$
$$+ (c_{2f} - c_{2d} + \phi\alpha w + Q_{2d}\phi'\alpha w)dQ_{2f}. \tag{24}$$

Tariff–quota equivalence now depends on whether the welfare benefits to employment are constant over the relevant range of output.

## Case 1: $\phi' = 0$.

In this case tariff/subsidy and quota/subsidy schemes are equivalent. Due to constant marginal costs, firms either completely jump a tariff or engage in no DFI. Tariff revenue per unit of $Q_{2f}$ is $c_{2d} - c_{2f}$. The welfare benefits to DFI are $\phi \alpha w$ per unit $Q_{2d}$. If $\phi \alpha w > c_{2d} - c_{2f}$, the home country prefers to collect to tariff revenue and instead induce DFI and its attendant employment benefits. If $\phi \alpha w < c_{2d} - c_{2f}$, the home country prefers no DFI and instead collects tariff revenue $(c_{2d} - c_{2f})Q_{2d}$. The bang-bang solution hinges on $c_{2d} - c_{2f}[>$ or $<]\phi \alpha w$.

The optimal quota hinges on exactly the same inequality. This is evident by examining the second term in (24). At $\phi' = 0$, if $\phi \alpha w > c_{2d} - c_{2f}$, $Q_{2d}$ enters welfare positively—and the more DFI the better. The optimal quota will set $Q_{2f}$ at zero and induce only dfi while raising no licence revenue. If $\phi \alpha w < c_{2d} - c_{2f}$, DFI enters welfare negatively, and it will be optimal to collect license revenue but provke no dfi.

## Case 2: $\phi' = 0$

In this case a nontrivial binding quota may be optimal, and tariff–quota equivalence fails to hold. At a welfare optimum

$$\phi \alpha w - c_{2d} + c_{2f} + Q_{2d}\phi' \alpha w = 0. \tag{25}$$

From (11), we know that

$$Q_{2d} = \frac{c_{2d} - P_2}{R_2} - Q_{2f}.$$

Substituting this into (24) and solving for $Q_{2f}$ yields the optimal quota:[18]

$$Q_{2d}^* = \frac{\phi}{\phi'} + \frac{c_{2d} - P^2(Q_1, Q_2)}{R_2} - \frac{c_{2d} - c_{2f}}{\phi' \alpha w}. \tag{26}$$

For some specifications of $\phi$, the optimal quota will involve DFI concurrent with foreign production. This is intuitive when $\phi$ is very concave in employment. The welfare benefits of the first few hours of employment are very large but diminish quickly as domestically produced output expands. No DFI in this case may be suboptimal since the forgone welfare benefits for the first bit of extra employment will be very large relative to the licence revenue collected. All DFI, on the other hand, may also be suboptimal, for the increase in domestic employment will be so large that the marginal benefits of such employment are negligible. A quota allows the home country to ensure DFI at a level somewhere between the all or nothing levels imposed by the tariff/subsidy scheme. In this case the home welfare associated with an optimal quota will never be less than that associated with the optimal tariff.

## 2.4 Increasing Marginal Costs and Tariff–Quota Nonequivalence: An Example

Throughout this chapter marginal costs have been assumed to be constant. In this section I show that this assumption is essential to the general equivalence results. This is done by the use of of a numerical counter-example. I consider a simple Cournot duopoly.

Let firms' cost functions and marginal costs be given by

$$TC_1 = 10 + \tfrac{1}{2}(Q_1)^2, \qquad\qquad c_1 = Q_1,$$

$$TC_{2f} = 10 + \tfrac{1}{2}(Q_{2f})^2, \qquad\qquad c_{2f} = Q_{2f}, \qquad\qquad (27)$$

$$TC_{2d} = 10 + 3Q_{2d} + \tfrac{1}{2}(Q_{2d})^2, \qquad c_{2d} = 3 + Q_{2d}.$$

As in section 2.2 the marginal cost schedule of DFI lies strictly above the marginal cost schedule of foreign local production. Inverse demands are given by

$$P^1 = 10 - 0.1Q_1 - 0.05Q_2,$$

$$P^2 = 10 - 0.05Q_1 - 0.1Q_2. \qquad\qquad (28)$$

It is no longer useful to use the taxonomy of the constant marginal cost case when calculating optimal policies. Even in the tariff is greater than $(c_{2d} - c_{2f})$, DFI and foreign local production might coexist. Another difference relative to the constant marginal cost case is that the value of a quota license will depend on the quantities being produced. In particular, a licence will be worth the difference in marginal costs at the equilibrium quantities. With these points in mind, it is straightforward to calculate optimal policy schemes using the same methodology explained in section 2.3. Using the

**Table 2.1**
Optimal tariff/subsidy and optimal quota/subsidy schemes with increasing marginal costs

| | Free trade | Tariff/subsidy | Quota/subsidy |
|---|---|---|---|
| Optimal subsidy | — | 1.127 | 1.061 |
| Optimal tariff | — | 3.687 | (value of license) 4.229 |
| Optimal quota | — | — | 2.115 |
| DFI ($Q_{2d}$) | 4.291 | 4.806 | 3.344 |
| Total imports ($Q_2$) | 11.582 | 8.745 | 5.549 |
| Domestic production ($Q_1$) | 7.851 | 8.909 | 8.990 |
| $P^1$ | 8.636 | 8.671 | 8.828 |
| $P^2$ | 8.450 | 8.680 | 9.005 |
| $\pi_1$ | 26.980 | 37.619 | 38.494 |
| $\pi_2$ | 29.200 | 6.952 | 2.351 |
| Consumer surplus | 14.335 | 11.687 | 7.984 |
| Home welfare | 41.316 | 64.524 | 55.422 |

cost functions and inverse demands from (27) and (28), resulting equilibria are given in table 2.1.

Table 2.1 illustrates several points. First, the optimal tariff/subsidy scheme is not equivalent to the optimal quota/subsidy scheme. This is due to the very differet ways a tariff and a quota affect the foreign firm's profit function. In free trade the profit-maximizing foreign firm will produce where $c_{2d}(Q_{2d}) = c_{2f}(Q_{2f})$ at an interior solution. This implies that $Q_{2f} > Q_{2d}$ since $c_{2d}(\cdot) > c_{2f}(\cdot)$. A tariff shifts $c_{2f}$ upward, but the foreign firm continues to produce where $c_{2d} = c_{2f} + t$. As output expands past the point at which DFI becomes profitable, the foreign firm minimizes cost by dividing production between DFI and foreign local production. When a binding quota is in place, the foreign firm cannot divide output between its two plants. Instead, the firm must on the margin produce only via DFI. This results in marginal costs that rise more quickly per unit of output. Whereas with a tariff the foreign firm could in effect spread the increased marginal costs between two plants, now only one plant may produce output beyond the amount of the quota. This is why in table 2.1 the foreign good price is higher and foreign output and profits are lower with the quota than with the tariff. The lower $Q_2$ associated with a quota yields a larger $P^1$. While this increases domestic profits, this does not offset the loss in consumer surplus and trade tax revenue relative to the tariff scheme. Net home welfare is lower with the optimal quota/subsidy than with the optimal tariff/subsidy.

Second, table 2.1 dramatically illustrates the concept of profit-shifting trade policy. Foreign profits fall from 29.2 with free trade to 6.95 with a tariff and 2.35 with a quota. Home welfare in turn rises from 41.31 to 64.52 with a tariff and to 55.42 with a quota.

The results of table 2.1 are a specific example of tariff–quota non-equivalence. They are not a general comparison of tariffs and quotas with increasing marginal costs. The results of table 2.1 are sensitive to the mode of market conduct and the functional forms used.

## 2.5  Summary

Recent work on tariff–quota nonequivalence under imperfect competition has ignored the possibility that the firms concerned might be multinational. Introducing the possibility of DFI, which is often associated with multinational firms, greatly simplifies the tariff–quota comparison. Many of the strategic interactions that are difficult to model in a general way disappear when DFI is introduced into the model.

Section 2.1 analyzed the equivalence issue in a linear foreign monopoly model. Using a diagrammatic analysis, optimal tariffs and quotas were shown to be equivalent when the cum-DFI optimal tariff exceeded the difference between the marginal cost of DFI production and the marginal cost of foreign production.

Section 2.2 extended the equivalence to a general demand system, general market structure, and general mode of market conduct. The restrictive assumption maintained was that of constant marginal costs.

Section 2.3 introduced domestic employment considerations into the general model of section 2.2. It was shown that tariff–quota equivalence depends on exactly how employment enters the home country's welfare function.

Section 2.4 relaxed the assumption of constant marginal costs. A numerical counterexample proved that the equivalence of section 2.2 breaks down under increasing marginal costs.

There are at least two broad areas for extending the analysis presented in this chapter. Recent empirical work on strategic trade policy by Dixit (1988) and Baldwin and Krugman (1988) has been restricted to the investigation of price-based policies. The results of this chapter should facilitate investigation of quantity-based policies when the restrictive assumptions of section 2.2 apply. The results of this chapter are applicable to an empirical analysis of the current U.S. quota on Japanese automobiles. This is the subject of current research. Finally, this model does not consider dynamic effects of DFI. In an uncertain world DFI might preempt future protectionist trade policy.

## Notes

I have benefited from the insightful comments and suggestions of Alan Deardorff, Avinash Dixit, Robert Feenstra, Gene Grossman, Ronald Jones, Jim Markusen, Dani Rodrik, and two anonymous referees. An abbreviated version of this chapter appears in the August, 1989 issue of the *Journal of International Economics* under the title, "Strategic Trade Policy When Firms Can Invest Abroad."

1. If a monopolist does not face a fringe of competitive suppliers, tariffs and quotas will be equivalent. That is, if the monopolist is a world, as opposed to domestic, monopolist, Bhagwati's result does not hold.

2. Sweeney (1985) recently studied tariffs and quotas in a conjectural variations oligopolistic setting. He noted that quotas in effect change a firm's conjectures in a way that tariffs do not. This is because the rational firm's conjectures will be conditioned on the type of policies its competitors face. Although there are problems in trying to model a sequential and hence dynamic process using conjectural variations, the underlying idea of the CV approach is the same as Bhagwati's and Krishna's. That is, there is no foreign supply response to a binding quota, though such a response exists for a tariff.

3. As stated in note 1, the optimal tariff and optimal quota are equivalent in this case when DFI is not possible, since there is no competitive fringe and the monopolist is a global, as opposed to domestic, monopolist. Nevertheless, this framework provides a very useful taxonomy for the more general oligopoly model of section 2.2.

4. This and related results have been demonstrated in a series of papers by Brander and Spencer. The flavor of these results is in Brander and Spencer (1984).

5. Krugman (1984) has shown that with increasing returns to scale, an advantage given to a firm in one market via trade or industrial policy may spill over into advantages in another market. Introducing direct foreign investment into this scenario is an interesting problem, but it obscures the more basic issues this chapter addresses.

6. It should be stressed that this chapter focuses on comparing *optimally set* policies. In this sense the equivalence results are fairly narrow. On the other hand, assuming optimizing behavior is a fairly standard premise.

7. As section 2.2 will prove, the linearity of this example is not necessary to the argument presented here. Even in a general model, the optimal policies will be functions of only tastes and technology.

8. Actually, the optimal tariff is constrained to a level of $AP$ minus epsilon. Throughout the analysis, the open set aspect of the optimal tariff will be ignored.

9. Similar conclusions have been reached in perfectly competitive models by Grossman (1984) and Rodrik (1987).

10. These comparisons will depend on market structure. The relevant comparisons are Bhagwati (1965) if the rest of the world forms a competitive fringe, Krishna (1983) if the rest of the world has few firms, and the result in note 1 if the there are no foreign producers.

11. The model, though, assumes that quota rents acrue to the home country. This is not the case with voluntary export restrictions on Japanese auto exports to the United States.

12. The modeling of the quota implicitly assumes that a quota on overall imports translates into a fixed ceiling on the exports of each foreign firm. This is a reasonable assumption if either the foreign government allots exports among the foreign firms based on prequota production levels (and the quota was not well anticipated) or the quota acts as a focal point around which the foreign firms can coordinate their actions.

13. It is well known that an equilibrium in pure strategies may not exist for Bertrand behavior in the presence of a quota. Krishna then shows an equilibrium will exist in mixed strategies. Nonexistence of equilibria in pure strategies is not a problem when DFI occurs. To understand why, it helps to understand why a pure strategies equilibrium in the presence of a quota might fail to exist in the first place. A binding quota acts like a binding capacity constraint. Firms playing Nash in prices may cycle endlessly around the capacity constraint or quota. Introducing DFI is analogous to removing the capacity constraint that is causing the cycling behavior. An equilibrium in pure strategies will exist when the quota is jumped via DFI.

14. Proof that this assignment does indeed achieve the optimum relies on assumption 3. We know DFI enters welfare negatively, yet license revenue, like the constrained tariff revenue, enters welfare positively. Hence the optimum is at the knife-edge described in the text. It is not possible to set $\partial W/\partial s$ and $\partial W/\partial t = 0$ to explicitly solve for the optimal quota because price is a general function of quantities.

15. Employment associated with the production of $Q_{2d}$ enters national welfare in the same way as the employment associated with the production of $Q_1$. It is unclear why this might not be the case. Nonetheless, the (non)equivalence results of this section are unchanged by letting only employment associated with DFI production enter welfare consideration via (21).

16. This approach is in the spirit of Atkinson's work on modeling attitudes concerning inequality in optimal tax problems.

17. The modeling approach does not address the possible endogeneity of the employment externality. That is, I do not account for the idea that the existence of protection may lead to a divergence between the actual and the shadow wage. Resulting unemployment in this case is endogenously determined with policy. Neglecting this endogeneity may result in misguided policymaking. See Rodrik (1986) on this issue.

18. One should note that for some modes of market conduct the optimal quota may not be well defined. This is because the optimal quota may be negative. While it is clear that a negative tax is a subsidy, a negative quota is somewhat trickier.

## References

Bladwin, Richard, and Paul Krugman. 1988. Market access and international competition: A simulation study of 16K random access memories. In *Empirical Methods for International Trade*, ed. R. Feenstra. Cambridge: MIT Press.

Bhagwati, Jagdish. 1965. On the equivalence of tariffs and quotas. In *Trade, Growth, and the Balance of Payments*, ed. R. Baldwin. Chicago: Rand McNally.

Brander, J., and B. Spencer. 1984. Tariff protection and imperfect competition. In *Monopolistic Competition in International Trade*, ed. H. Keirzkowski. Oxford: Oxford University Press.

Dixit, A. 1984. International trade policy for oligopolistic industries. *Economic Journal* 94: 305–312.

Dixit, A. 1986. Comparative statics for oligopoly. *International Economic Review* 27: 107–122.

Dixit, A. 1986. Optimal trade and industrial policies for the U.S. automobile industry. In *Empirical Methods for International Trade*, ed. R. Feenstra, Cambridge: MIT Press.

Eaton, J., and G. Grossman. 1986. Optimal trade and industrial policy under oligopoly. *Quarterly Journal of Economics* 101: 383–406.

Grossman, G. 1984. The gains from international factor movements. *Journal of International Economics* 17: 73–83.

Grossman, G., and J. D. Richardson. 1985. Strategic trade policy: A survey of issues and early analysis. Special Papers in International Economics, No. 15. International Finance Section, Department of Economics, Princeton University.

Harris, R. 1985. Why voluntary export restraints are "voluntary." *Canadian Journal of Economics* 18: 799–809.

Horstman, I., and J. Markusen. 1988. Endogenous market structures in international trade. Mimeo. University of Western Ontario.

Krishna, K. 1983. Trade restrictions as facilitating practices. Discussion Papers in Economics No. 55. Princeton University, Woodrow Wilson School.

Rodrik, D. 1987. The economics of export performance requirements. *Quarterly Journal of Economics* 102: 633–650.

Sweeny, G. 1985. Import quotas and oligopolistic interactions. Working Paper No. 84-W17. Vanderbilt University Department of Economics.

# 3 Making Altruism Pay in Auction Quotas

**Kala Krishna**

One of the most common criticisms of voluntary export restrictions (VERs) and the way that quotas are currently allocated is that they allow foreigners to reap the rents associated with the quantitative constraints. It has been suggested that auctioning import quotas would remedy this—that this would deliver the higher profits to the U.S. economy rather than abroad.[1] The big winner, as Alan Blinder has argued in *Business Week*, is the U.S. Treasury: "Auctioning import rights is one of those marvelous policy innovations that creates winners, but no losers, or, more precisely, no American losers."[2] An article in *Time* magazine quotes C. Fred Bergsten as saying that "quota auctions might bring in revenues as high as $7 billion a year."[3]

A Congressional Budget Office (CBO) memorandum estimates quota rents possible in 1987 to be about $5 billion.[4] It compares this to the Bergsten et al. (1987) estimate for the Institute for International Economics (IIE) of $9 billion. Part of the difference, $2.2 billion, arises because the CBO does not include a VER on automobiles while the IIE does. The remainder of the difference arises from differences in procedure. Both estimates assume perfect competition everywhere. Takacs (1987) points out that proposals to auction quotas have become increasingly frequent.[5] She states: "Commissioners Ablondi and Leonard of the U.S. International Trade Commission (ITC) recommended auctioning sugar quota licenses in 1977. The ITC recommended auctioning footwear quotas in 1985. Studies by Hufbauer and Rosen (1986) and Lawrence and Litan (1986) suggested auctioning quotas and earmarking the funds for trade adjustment assistance."[6] There is even a recent book (Bergsten et al. 1987) devoted entirely to auction quotas.

Despite the importance of the issues involved, the intuition behind such statements and the procedure used in the estimates is based on models of perfect competition.[7] In such models the level of the quota determines the domestic price, and the difference between the domestic price and the world price determines the price of a license. If the country is small, then the world price is given. If the country is large, then the world price changes with a quota. How the world price changes is determined by supply and demand conditions in the world market.

However, when markets are imperfectly competitive, this analysis is misleading. The reason is that in such environments, prices are chosen by producers, so there is no supply curve. Producers' responses to the constraint must therefore be taken into account when determining the price of an auctioned license. For example, if profit-maximizing producers adjust their prices upward to exactly clear the quota-constrained market, there is no benefit to be derived from owning a license to import, so its auction price must be zero!

In previous work (Krishna 1988, 1988a, 1989, 1989a) I develop a series of models of monopoly and oligopoly that show how the way in which licenses are sold, demand conditions, and market structure influence the resulting price of a license. The results indicate that the price of a license in imperfectly competitive industries may be much lower than that indicated by applying models of perfect competition. Revenue estimates such as those of the IIE and CBO may thus be far too large. I further show that *no* revenues are raised from auctioning quotas in the absence of uncertainty unless they are quite restrictive.

In this chapter I show that giving away a portion of the import licenses to the foreign firm is one way of raising revenue from the auctioning of quota licenses. This, in turn, affects the comparison between the optimal policy and free trade, and between auctioning existing quotas and a VER. Both comparisons are dealt with below.

The point that "altruism" may be in the nation's best interest is made in the simplest possible model—that of foreign monopoly. The model used is basically that of Krishna (1989). The main point is that the home country, in giving some of the licenses away, affects the foreign producer's pricing decision. The producer must now consider not only gross profits but also the value of licenses received from the government. Forfeiting some of the quota licenses would make it more costly for the firm to extract the quota rents from the domestic market by raising prices, so it restrains from any attempts to do so. This in turn raises the price of licenses that remain in the hands of the government. I show that such policies can lead to a *Pareto improvement* over free trade. The reason for this is that if the equilibrium price of a license is positive, the quota allows the foreign monopolist to effectively segment the domestic and foreign markets. The price to consumers at home differs from that to consumers abroad by the amount of the license price. This price discrimination raises world welfare, while the license allocation causes a positive license price that allows segmentation and permits redistribution of gains in a Pareto-improving manner.

In this way the chapter is part of a small but growing literature that examines the optimal behavior of a small open economy facing a foreign monopoly supplier. The adjective "small" refers to the fact that the home country cannot directly affect the monopolist's objectives and cost conditions, or the demand it faces in other foreign markets that it serves.

The early literature implicitly assumed that markets were internationally segmented, so, with constant costs, the home country's policies could be considered independently of demand conditions abroad.[8] I pursue here an approach pioneered by Jones and Takemori (1987) in which markets are "naturally" integrated: There are no transport costs or other impediments to goods arbitrage, but trade policy can potentially induce market segmentation. In the case of a tariff, such as considered by Jones and Takemori (1987), this raises the potential of a welfare gain whenever the monopolist can be induced to discriminate in favor of the home country. In my study it raises the potential of a positive price for quota licenses, which allows for some market segmentation. The results of the two studies are therefore related.

In this chapter I assume that the market for licenses is competitive and thus side step many interesting issues raised by the auction design literature. I do this because this literature is not well suited to my purpose. The main problem is that it deals with an exogenously specified distribution of values of object(s) being auctioned.[9] However, these valuations are better specified as endogenous here as they are derived from the operation of a secondary market—that for the imported good. In this setup valuations cannot be defined independently of the allocation of the object. Thus one would need to deal with endogenous valuations and multiple objects in the design of auctions. Since my interest here is on the behavior of producers, I choose to avoid the implications of strategic behavior in the market for licenses by assuming competition.[10]

In section 3.1 the model is set up. I show that if markets are segmented, license revenues remain zero even when the monopolist obtains some of the licenses. Section 3.2 analyzes the case when markets are not segmented. I first examine the base case where the monopolist gets all the licenses. I show that if home demand is more elastic than that abroad, a license will have a zero price unless the quota is quite restrictive.[11] If the reverse is true, a license has a positive price, and markets are effectively segmented by the quota. In the first case the price charged by the firm rises with a quota, and in the second case it falls. This is related to Jones and Takemori's result in that in the former case the price charged by the firm is unchanged for a small tariff, but can fall for a large enough tariff, and in the latter case it falls for all tariffs.

Section 3.3 briefly discusses the effect of varying the allocation of licenses as well as the level of the quota, and sets the ground for the discussion of two policy questions. The first is whether existing quotas should be auctioned. The second is when the optimal quota scheme is worth implementing. If the home demand is more elastic than the rest of the world's demand, then no allocation of licenses can raise welfare. If the reverse is true, then auctioning quota licenses can lead to a Pareto improvement over free trade. Section 3.4 contains some simulation results for this case. The optimal levels of the quota and the share of licenses to the monopolist are calculated so as to maximize a weighted sum of license revenues and consumer surplus. Their sensitivity to parameter values is also calculated.

Section 3.5 summarizes the results, draws out their implications, and suggests directions for future work.

## 3.1   The Model

Let $Q(P)$ and $q(p)$ denote the demand functions facing the foreign firm in the home market and in the rest of the world, respectively. Let $C(q + Q)$ denote its cost function, and assume that constant marginal costs equal to $C$. Similar results obtain when marginal costs are not assumed to be constant.

Assume that the firm's profit function in the domestic country, $R(P)$, is concave in $P$ and is maximized at $P^M$. Similarly let $r(p)$ be the profits from sales in other market(s), and let $r(p)$ be maximized at $p^m$. It is easy to see that $P^M = [E/(E - 1)]C$ and $p^m = [e/(e - 1)]C$, where $E$ and $e$ are the respective demand elasticities. In the absence of arbitrage the monopolist would choose to charge a higher price in the market with less elastic demand. With costless arbitrage the monopolist will choose one price that will be between the two prices that would be set in the absence of arbitrage possibilities. The optimal price maximizes $\pi(P) = R(P) + r(P)$ and is given by

$$P^* = \frac{\bar{E}}{\bar{E} - 1}C,$$

where $\bar{E} = \theta E + (1 - \theta)e$ and $\theta = Q/(q + Q)$. This is the free trade price $P^*$. The monopolist chooses the price as if faced with one market where the elasticity of demand is a share weighted combination of the elasticities of the two markets. Of course the existence of a monopoly is a distortion, so the free trade equilibrium is not first best. The question then is how a quota affects the price charged by the monopolist when the quota licenses are auctioned off. I first consider the base case where the monopolist receives all the licenses.

At this point it is important to be clear about exactly what constitutes a license, how licenses are sold, and what the timing of moves is. With market segmentation, a license is defined as a piece of paper that entitles its possessor to buy one unit of the product in question at the price charged by the seller in the license-holder's market. If arbitrage is possible, then the possessor buys at the lower of the prices charged by the seller in the home and the world market. However, it is a dominated strategy for the monopolist to attempt to charge different prices in his different markets, since sales will only be made at the lower of the two prices. For this reason the monopolist can be restricted to choosing only one price.

The licenses are sold in a competitive market to either competitive domestic retailers with zero marginal costs of retailing or directly to consumers. I assume that the timing of moves is as follows. First, the government sets the quota and allocates the licenses. Then the monopolist sets a price and chooses how many licenses to use. Finally, the market for licenses clears. This timing is consistent with the idea that the market for licenses clears *more* frequently than the monopolist sets his choice variables, and that the government sets the quota even less frequently than the monopolist sets prices.

The model is then solved backwards as usual. First consider the market for licenses. If the price charged by the monopolist is $P$ and the price of a license is $L$, then the demand for licenses must be the same as the demand for the good at price $P + L$, $Q(P + L)$. The total number of licenses is $V$, the level of the quota. The monopolist gets a proportion $\lambda$ of these and chooses a fraction $u$ of these to use.[12] Hence he chooses $u \leq \lambda V$. The remainder of the licenses, $(1 - \lambda)V$, are always put on the market by the government. The equilibrium price of a license is given by $L(P, u; \lambda, V)$.[13] $L(\cdot)$ is defined by the market for licenses clearing: $Q(P + L) = V(1 - \lambda) + u$. Notice that if $Q(P) < (1 - \lambda)V + u$, then $L(\cdot) < 0$ as defined thus far. However, since a quota is not binding if such a high price is charged, $L(\cdot)$ is defined to be zero in this case. Let $P(u; \lambda, V)$, the "virtual price" that corresponds to the quota level $(1 - \lambda)V + u$, be defined by $Q(P) = (1 - \lambda)V + u$

so that $L(P, u; \lambda, V) > 0$ and the quota is binding if $P \leq P(u; \lambda, V)$. By the definition of $L(\cdot)$, it is apparent that if $P < P(\cdot)$, then demand at home equals $V(1 - \lambda) + u$, although this is less than $Q(P)$. $P(u; \lambda, V)$ is the virtual price of the quota level $(1 - \lambda)V + u$. It is the price at which the amount offered for sale, $V(1 - \lambda) + u$, is demanded.[14]

The monopolist chooses $P$ and $u$, which is constrained to be weakly below $\lambda V$, to maximize total profits, which include license revenues for the given levels of $\lambda$ and $V$. Note that the price charged by the monopolist, $P$, is weakly below the price that consumers face, the virtual price $P(\cdot)$ which equals $P + L(\cdot)$.

## 3.2 Giving Away All the Licenses

Before we analyze how the monopolist sets $P$ and $u$ in the base case where the monopolist receives all the licenses ($\lambda = 1$) and markets are not segmented, consider what their optimal values would be were the markets already segmented. Since markets are already segmented, there is no gain in using a positive license price to segment them. It is therefore optimal for the monopolist simply to choose $P$ and $u$ so as to appropriate all the license rents available. For any value of $\lambda$, and for any $V$ below the free trade level $Q(P^*)$, the monopolist chooses to use all of licenses ($u = \lambda V$), and sets price at $P(V)$ where $Q(P(V)) = V$. Because all licenses are sold ($u = \lambda V$) and the price is set so that the market exactly clears, $L(\cdot) = 0$.

Now turn to the base case where markets are not segmented and $\lambda = 1$ It is useful to consider the cases of $e > E$ and $e \leq E$ separately.

### Case A: $e > E$

Here the home market demand is less elastic than that abroad. In this case figure 3.1a depicts the profits in the two markets and total profits under free trade. $P^M$, the profit-maximizing price for the home market alone, lies above $P^*$, the free trade price, which in turn lies above $P^m$, the profit-maximizing price for the rest of the world alone.

Consider the profits of the firm if it chooses to use $u$ licenses and charge price $P$ when the quota is set at the free trade level, $V^* = Q(P^*)$:

$$\pi(P, u; 1, V) = r(P) + (P - C)Q(P + L(P, u) + L(P, u)u \qquad \text{if } P \leq P(u),$$

$$= r(P) + R(P) \qquad \text{if } P \geq P(u),$$

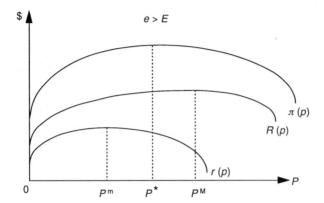

**Figure 3.1a**

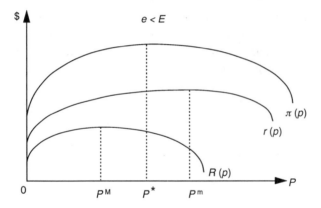

**Figure 3.1b**

where $L(P, u) \equiv L(P, u; 1, V)$ is defined by $Q(P + L(\cdot)) = u$ as long as it is positive, and by zero otherwise. Note that if $P$ exceeds the virtual price, then $L(\cdot) = 0$. $P(u) \equiv P(u; 1, V)$ is defined by $Q(P(\cdot)) = u$.
Hence

$$
\begin{aligned}
\pi(\cdot) &= r(P) + [P(u) - C]u \qquad \text{if } P \leq P(u), \\
&= r(P) + R(P) \qquad\qquad\ \text{if } P \geq P(u).
\end{aligned}
\tag{1}
$$

As $[P(u) - C]u$ can be represented by $R(P)$, the optimal $u$ and $P$ are apparent by inspection. Since $[P(u) - C]u$ is the only component of profit that depends on $u$, $u$ should be set at the level that maximizes profit subject to $u \leq V$. As is apparent from figure 3.1a, this corresponds to $u = Q(P^M)$ if $V = V^*$. Given this, the optimal choice of $P$ maximizes $r(P)$ (i.e., is $P^m$). This yields a license price of $L = P^M - P^m$. Notice that the profits under this policy are exactly those of a price-discriminating monopolist. These policies are optimal for all $V \geq V^*$; that is, the monopolist ignores being "allowed" to sell more than he would have chosen to in the absence of the quota.

If $V < V^*$, but more than $Q(P^M)$, the profit-maximizing policies are unchanged as is the maximized level of profits. If $V < Q(P^M)$, then it is optimal to set $u = V$, and $P = P^m$ so that $L(\cdot) = P(V) - P^m > P^M - P^m$. However, the maximized level of profits falls with $V$.

**Case B: $e \leq E$**

If, on the other hand, $e \leq E$, then $P^M < P^* < P^m$, as depicted in figure 3.1b. The monopolist would like to discriminate in favor of the home country but cannot under either free trade or a quota. In this case it is again optimal to choose $u$ to maximize $[P(u) - C]u$. As this occurs when $Q(P^M) = u$, this level of $u$ exceeds $V$ when $V = V^*$. Hence the optimal level of $u$ equals $V^*$. However, this reduces profits of the firm below its free trade level for $P \leq P^*$ and makes $P^*$ the optimal price. Hence $L(\cdot) = 0$ if $V = V^*$. It is easy to verify that that optimal $P$ and $u$ are as follows:

| $V$ | $P$ | $u$ | $L$ |
|---|---|---|---|
| $V \leq Q(P^m)$ | $P^m$ | $V$ | $P(V) - P^m$ |
| $Q(P^m) < V < V^*$ | $P(V)$ | $V$ | $0$ |
| $V^* \leq V$ | $P^*$ | $V^*$ | $0$ |

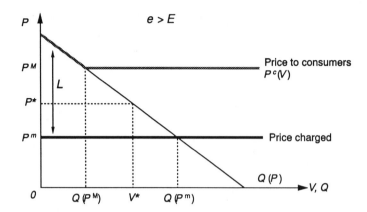

**Figure 3.2a**

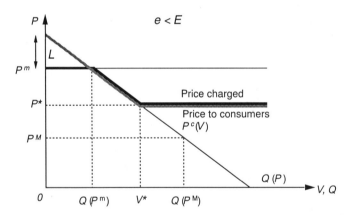

**Figure 3.2b**

Figures 3.2a and 3.2b depict the path of optimal price charged by the firm for every $V$ and the price paid by consumer.

The main results so far are summarized in Proposition 1.

PROPOSITION 1    If $e > E$ and $\lambda = 1$, the license price is positive for all $V$. If $e \leq E$ and $\lambda = 1$, the license price is zero unless $V < Q(P^m) < V^*$.

The consideration of these base cases, and the use of continuity arguments, shows that the government derives revenues from the auction of licenses for $\lambda$ close to 1 if $e > E$, but not if $e \leq E$, unless $V$ is small.

## 3.3    Varying the Quota and the Proportion Given to the Monopolist

When $e > E$ and all licenses are allocated to the monopolist, the monopolist acts like a price-discriminating monopolist and obtains the profits of such a monopolist by allowing the license price to be positive. However, in this case the government earns no revenues. The question then is whether the license price remains positive when the government retains some licenses. If this is so, the government can obtain nonnegative revenues by retaining some licenses. In Krishna (1990) I characterize the profit-maximizing solution for this more general problem. I prove the follow proposition:

PROPOSITION 2    If $E > e$, then even if the level of the quota and the share to the foreign firm are set optimally, welfare cannot rise from the free trade level.[15]

However, if the monopolist's price falls below the free trade price and much of the license revenue accrues to the government, welfare may rise above its free trade level. Notice in addition that if the price charged by the monopolist falls, consumers in the rest of the world gain. If the license price is positive, the monopolist can effectively price discriminate. Hence, if $\lambda$ is high and $L(\cdot) > 0$, the monopolist's profits could also rise. Therefore it is possible that only domestic consumers lose. If aggregate welfare rises, they can be compensated for this loss.[16]

The possibility that all parties could gain from such policies can be understood by noting that perfect price discrimination by a monopolist leads to maximization of world welfare. Since quotas, when the license price is positive, allow price discrimination, world welfare could rise. This gain could possibly be distributed between the home country and the rest of the world so that in some cases all parties gain by the appropriate allocation of licenses.

There are two policy questions that need to be clearly differentiated. First, for a given level of a quota, is auctioning all of the quota better than not auctioning it? The second concerns the optimal levels of $\lambda$ and $V$.

In considering the first question, it is important to be clear about what constitutes the status quo, as the answer to whether auctioning off quotas is a good idea depends crucially on this.

I offer two alternative interpretations of the status quo. Which one, if either, seems more appropriate depends on exactly how existing quotas are implemented.[17] It is often claimed that the present system gives the quota license rents to foreigners. Should this be taken to mean that the status quo would coincide with $\lambda = 1$?[18] If we interpret the status quo as $\lambda = 1$, and auctioning all quotas as $\lambda = 0$, auctioning all quota licenses is quite attractive when $V$ is close to $V^*$. Whether $\lambda = 0$ or $\lambda = 1$, license revenues to the government are zero. Hence we need only look at the price to consumers when $\lambda = 0$ as opposed to when $\lambda = 1$ to determine welfare effects. If $e > E$, domestic consumer prices are lower when $\lambda = 0$ than when $\lambda = 1$ as $P(V) < P^M$. If $e < E$ and $V$ is close to $V^*$, the price charged is the same when $\lambda = 1$ and $\lambda = 0$, and equals $P(V)$. Hence, when the status quo is $\lambda = 1$, and $V$ is close to $V^*$, auctioning existing quotas raises welfare if $e > E$, and does not affect welfare if $e < E$.

The interpretation that the status quo corresponds to $\lambda = 1$ could be argued to be inappropriate on the grounds that licenses are *not* awarded to the foreign firm. A more reasonable description might be that the firm is just constrained not to sell more than the quota. If it charges a low price and demand at this price exceeds the quota, whoever is lucky enough to get the good can resell it at the market-clearing price and reap the implicit license rents. This corresponds to allocating licenses to foreign or domestic retailers or domestic consumers who resell the good, thereby effectively selling these licenses in the competitive market, and reap any license revenues that exist.

With this interpretation the status quo corresponds to the case where $\lambda = 0$, but the government does not get any license revenues: If these exist, they go to whoever gets the goods. In this case auctioning off licenses for existing quotas with $\lambda = 0$ does not affect the firm's behavior. It can transfer rents to the government if the license price is positive. However, the license price with $\lambda = 0$ is unlikely to be positive unless the quota is very restrictive. Moreover, even if the license price is positive, the transfer of rents to the government is a net increase in welfare only if it comes at the expense of foreigners, rather than from domestic agents. For this reason auctioning *all existing* quotas (i.e, $\lambda = 0$), will never raise welfare if all the goods were allocated to domestic agents under the status quo, and will raise welfare from the status quo if some of the goods were allocated to foreign agents in the status quo and $L(\cdot) > 0$. This, however, requires the quota to be restrictive.

However, if auctioning the quota involves setting $\lambda$ optimally, auctioning an existing quota becomes much more attrative: Welfare when $\lambda$ is set optimally weakly exceeds that when $\lambda = 0$ or 1. Hence it is always weakly better to auction the quota. Moreover, if the quota is not too restrictive and $e > E$, it is possible for welfare to even exceed that under *free trade* when $\lambda$ is set optimally. In fact it is possible for such a policy to be Pareto improving! If $e < E$, the ability to set $\lambda$ optimally for a given quota is less valuable because the firm cannot segment the markets and the quota cannot be welfare improving. Notice that it is not necessary for license revenue to be positive for auctioning quotas to be better than the status quo.

The second policy question, to which the simulations are addressed, is what the optimal levels of $\lambda$ and $V$ are, and how they vary with domestic and foreign market size, demand elasticity, and the weight placed on revenue. Let $N$ and $n$ denote the number of home and foreign consumers. The home and foreign nations have a constant elasticity demand function given by $NP^{-E}$ and $nP^{-e}$, respectively. Let $\beta$ denote the weight on revenue raised in welfare. $\beta$ can be thought of as an estimate of the cost of raising revenue from alternative sources. I then examine how the optimal $\lambda$ and $V$ change with $\beta$. This addresses the desirability of auctioning quotas for revenue-raising reasons without eliminating consumer welfare from the objective function. $\beta \to \infty$ corresponds to the revenue-maximizing case, whereas $\beta = 1$ corresponds to maximizing the usual welfare function. Here I focus on the level of welfare when $\lambda$ and $V$ are set optimally compared with that under free trade. Welfare $W$ is the usual sum of consumer surplus and revenue and is given by

$$W(\lambda, V) = U(Q(\lambda, V)) - (P(\lambda, V) + L(\lambda, V))Q(\lambda, V) + \beta(1 - \lambda)VL(\lambda, V),$$

where $U(\cdot)$ is the utility function,

$$Q(\lambda, V) \equiv u(\lambda, V) + (1 - \lambda)V$$

and

$$L(\lambda, V) = L(P(u(\lambda, V)), u(\lambda, V); \lambda, V).$$

$P(\lambda, V)$ and $u(\lambda, V)$ are of course the profit-maximizing values of $u$ and $P$ chosen by the firm.

In the simulations I first explore the conditions under which welfare rises from free trade. Then, given a weight $\beta$ on revenues, I find how the welfare-maximizing policy varies with $\beta$. This addresses the question of how large $\beta$ has to be to make auction quotas better than free trade. The simulations were run for the interesting case, namely, when $e > E$. Recall that when $e \leq E$ and $\beta = 1$, free trade is optimal by proposition 2.

## 3.4   Simulation Results

First consider the effect of raising $n$, shown in figure 3.3. Depicted there are the optimal quota level as a fraction of free trade imports, the proportion of licenses used, and the maximized level of welfare as a proportion of free trade welfare. Note first that the quota is set close to the free trade level and that most licenses allocated are used. This keeps the price consumers face close to that under free trade so that consumer surplus loss due to the quota is limited. The excess of welfare above free trade welfare comes from license revenue. Second, note that welfare relative to free trade first rises and then falls, as the foreign size $n$ increases. The extent of welfare gains is limited to about 5%. License revenues, not shown here, also rise and then fall as $n$ increases. This occurs because when $n$ is very small it is hard to obtain any license revenues. In this case the home market is very important to the foreign firm, and it sets prices so as to capture license revenues as in the market segmentation case. However, when $n$ becomes very large, $P^*$ gets close to $P^m$ so that the possible license revenues become small, though it is easier to capture them. For this reason license revenues and welfare first rise and then fall with $n$. Hence, when $\beta = 1$, such policies are most desirable for large, but not too large, countries.

However, it is often argued that there are greater costs of raising revenues from other sources because of induced efficiency losses, so $\beta$ typically

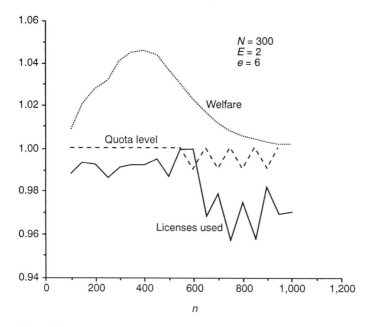

**Figure 3.3**

exceeds unity. It is commonly thought to lie between 1 and 2 in developed countries,[19] though it may be higher for developing countries. Figure 3.4 depicts the effect of changing $n$ as $\beta$ varies. Two points are worth noting. First, for a given $n$, welfare gains are fairly limited until a critical $\beta$, after which they rise more swiftly with $\beta$. The critical value of $\beta$ lies between 1 and 2 for $n$ between 1,000 and 10,000, and $N = 300$. Second, welfare gains tend to rise more quickly with $\beta$ when $n$ is large compared to when $n$ is small.

The reason for this seems to be that reducing $V$, given $\lambda$, raises the license price by more when $n$ is large. This works toward having a more restrictive quota when $n$ is large and greater license revenues at the cost of a greater consumer loss. As $\beta$ rises, these revenues are weighted more heavily in welfare, which tends to make welfare gains rise faster for high $n$. Thus these simulations suggest that optimally setting auction quotas could significantly raise welfare if the economy is distorted so that $\beta$ exceeds unity.

Figure 3.5 summarizes the simulation results when $e$ changes and $\beta = 1$. As before, the optimal quota is close to free trade and most licenses are used. Also the extent of welfare gains are limited to about a 6% increase.

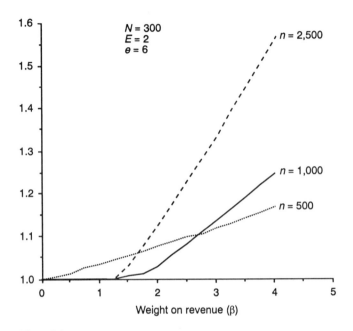

**Figure 3.4**

Welfare relative to free trade first rises and then falls with $e$. On the one hand, this occurs because possible gains due to price discrimination rise with $e$. On the other hand, foreign sales under this parametrization tend to fall with $e$. This makes the home market more important for the foreign firm, limiting the extent to which the government can appropriate the license revenues. While the former works in favor of raising welfare above free trade in the simulation, the latter works against it! For small $e$ the first effect seems to predominate, whereas for large $e$, the second does. However, $e$ needs to be quite large, more than three times $E$, for the second to dominate, and we restrict attention to the first case below.

Figure 3.6 shows the simulation results for varying $e$ when $\beta$ changes. Notice that the critical $\beta$ (at which $W/W^F$ starts diverging from unity) lies between 1 and 3 and rises as $e$ falls, and that $W/W^F$, after the critical $\beta$, is steeper for lower $e$'s. Thus optimally designed quota auctions seem to be relatively desirable for an undistorted economy ($\beta = 1$) when $e$ is neither too large nor too small. They are desirable when $e$ is low only for a very

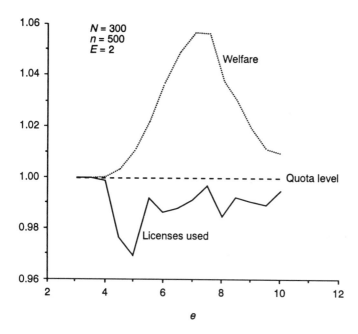

**Figure 3.5**

distorted economy. If *e* is not very low, they can raise welfare for even a
slightly distorted economy.

## 3.5   Conclusion

Auctioning quota licenses when product markets are imperfectly competitive involves taking into account the strategic response of producers to the
policy. This makes the details of the implementation of such policies crucial
in determining their effects. In this chapter I have shown that the distribution of license revenues between the government and a foreign monopolist
can play a role in raising revenues and can even lead to a Pareto improvement over free trade.

This is clearly only a beginning in explaining how the details of implementation of auctioning quota licenses affect the outcome of such policies.
More work on this aspect is needed to help understand how such policies
should be implemented. Clearly the results will depend on the market

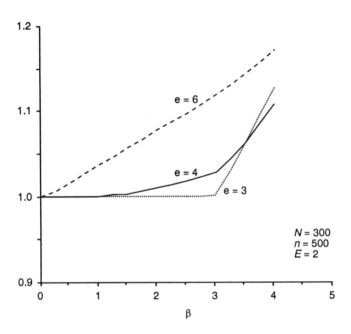

**Figure 3.6**

structure in the product market and in the auction market, the form of the quotas—global versus nonglobal—as well as on the demand structure and possibility of market segmentation. For example, when product markets are oligopolistic, allocation of licenses to producers affects their pricing incentives. The interaction of firms' behavior then determines equilibrium. Hence the allocation of licenses would affect the equilibrium and could raise revenues with or without market segmentation. Work on examining this is also underway.

The allocation of licenses could also be designed to affect market structure in the license market. A question that needs to be addressed is whether making the market for licenses imperfectly competitive so as to create "countervailing power" to the market power in the product market is a good idea. In addition more work on the design of optimal quota auctions is needed although this is likely to be quite difficult. The implications of these issues must be understood for a fully informed analysis as to the actual benefits of auctioning quotas to be made.

## Notes

Financial support from the World Bank and the Center for International Affairs at Harvard is gratefully acknowledged as is support from the National Science Foundation under Grant No. SES8822204. I am indebted to Phillip Swagel for excellent research assistance, and to Peter Neary for very valuable comments on an earlier draft.

1. *Business Week*, March 16, 1987, p. 64.

2. Ibid., March 9, 1987, p. 27.

3. *Time*, March 16, 1987, p. 59.

4. Memorandum of February 27, 1987, from Stephen Parker (CBO) on revenue estimates for auctioning existing import quotas (publicly circulated).

5. The interested reader should consult Bergsten et al. (1987) and Takacs (1987) for a historical and institutional perspective of work in this area.

6. See Takacs (1987), n. 7.

7. Macmillan (1988) surveys the auction literature to highlight its implication for quota auctions. However, as I argue later, this literature is not suited to the analysis of this problem when product markets are imperfectly competitive. Also see Feenstra (1988) on the possibility of foreign responses to quota auctions.

8. See, for example, Katrak (1977), de Meza (1979), Svedberg (1979), and Brander and Spencer (1984).

9. Milgrom (1985) nicely summarizes the work on optimal auctions. Wilson (1979) deals with multiple auctions, but considers a "share" auction, and deals with exogenous valuations. Maskin and Riley (1990) deal with multiple object auctions but consider exogenous valuations. The only work I am aware of in the auction literature that can deal with endogenous valuations is that of Bernheim and Whinston (1985); however, they do not deal with sequential auctions. In their model objects need not be identical so that their model is more general than the one needed to study endogenous valuations. They also focus on the complete information case.

10. See Krishna (1989a) for some preliminary work on these issues.

11. How restrictive it must be for a license to have a positive price depends on the demand elasticities at home and abroad and on relative market size.

12. The firm is allowed to choose not to use all its licenses. If it were forced to use them all then the virtual price would be independent of $\lambda$ and equal $P(V)$. Notice that in this case the pricing behavior of the firm and the price charged to consumers would not correspond to that given below.

13. To denote that $P$ and $u$ are choice variables for the monopolist, they appear before the semicolon in $L(\cdot)$ and $P(\cdot)$. That $\lambda$ and $V$ appear after the semicolon indicates that these are choice variables for the government and are taken as given by the firm.

14. See Neary and Roberts (1979) for the use of the "virtual" price.

15. This result obtains even if $u$ is not a choice variable and must equal $\lambda V$. The reason is the same: that the price charged in this case must exceed the free trade price.

16. It is easy to show that if $u$ cannot be chosen, and must equal $\lambda V$, then it is always possible to do better than free trade if $E < e$. This can be achieved by setting $V = V^*$ and $\lambda$ such that the price charged is a bit below the free trade price. This keeps consumer surplus unchanged from that under free trade but raises some license revenues. If $u$ is chosen, welfare need not necessarily rise.

17. In reality, the implementation of VERs differs across products. VERs for footwear have explicit licenses associated with them. The VERs on autos do not.

18. $\lambda = 1$ can be the status quo even if no formal licneses exist if *under the quota* firms can price exports to the restricting country higher than exports to the rest of its markets. This of course presumes that the quota is implemented so that the firm has the sole ability to export (i.e., that transhipments from other markets are not possible).

19. This is evident from estimates of excess burden in public finance. Hausman (1985), in the *Handbook of Public Economics*, suggest that the ratio of deadweight loss to tax revenue for a 10%–30% income tax is about 15%–20%. A figure of 20% gives $\beta = 1/(1 - 0.20) = 1.25$.

## References

Bergsten, C. F., Kimberly, A. E., Schott, J. J., and Takacs, W. E. 1987. Auction quotas and United States trade policy. *Policy Analyses in International Economics*, vol. 19. Washington, DC: Institute for International Economics. September.

Bernheim, B. Douglas, and Whinston, Michael D. 1986. Menu auctions, resource allocation, and economic influence. *Quarterly Journal of Economics* 107 (February): 1–32.

Brander, J., and Spencer, B. 1984. Trade Warfare: Tariffs and cartels. *Journal of International Economics* 16: 227–242.

de Meza, D. 1979. Commercial policy towards multinational monopolies: Reservations on Katrak. *Oxford Economic Papers* 31: 334–337.

Feenstra, R. 1988. Auctioning U.S. import quotas, foreign response and alternative policies. NBER Working Paper No. 2839.

Hausman, J. 1985. In *Handbook of Public Economics*, vol. 1, A. Auerbach and M. Feldstein (eds.) Amsterdam: North Holland, ch. 4.

Hufbauer, G., and Rosen, H. 1986. Trade policy for troubled industries. *Policy Analyses in International Economics*, vol. 15. Washington, DC: Institute for International Economics.

Jones, Ronald W., and Takemori, Shumpei. 1987. Foreign monopoly and optimal tariffs for the small open economy. *European Economic Reivew*, forthcoming.

Katrak, H. 1977. Multinational monopolies and commercial policy. *Oxford Economic Papers* 29: 283–91.

Krishna, K. 1988. Auction quotas with uncertainty. Mimeo. Harvard University.

Krishna, K. 1988a. The case of the vanishing revenues: Auction quotas with oligopoly. NBER Working Paper No. 2723.

Krishna, K. 1989. The case of the vanishing revenues: Auction quotas with monopoly. NBER Working Paper No. 2840. Forthcoming in *American Economic Review*, 1990.

Krishna, K. 1989(a). "Auction Quotas with Endogenous Valuations." Mimeo, Harvard University, July.

Krishna, K. 1990. Making altruism pay in auction quotas. HIER Working Paper No. 1468.

Lawrence, R. Z., and Litan, R. E. 1986. *Saving Free Trade*. Washington, DC: The Brookings Institution.

Macmillan, John. 1988. Auctioning import quotas. Mimeo. Graduate School of International Relations and Pacific Studies, University of California, San Diego.

Maskin, Eric, and Riley, John. 1990. Optimal multi-unit auctions. In *The Economics of Missing Markets; Games and Information*, F. Hahn (ed.). Oxford: Oxford University Press.

Milgrom, P. 1985. The economics of competitive bidding: A selective survey. In *Social Goals and Social Organizations*, L. Hurwicz, D. Schmeidler, and H. Sonnenschein (eds.). Cambridge: Cambridge University Press, ch. 9

Neary, J. P., and Roberts, K. W. S. 1980. The theory of household behavior under rationing. *European Economic Review* 13: 25–42.

Svedberg, P. 1979. Optimal tariff policy on imports from multinationals. *Economic Record* 55: 64–67.

Takacs, W. E. 1987. Auctioning import quota licenses: An economic analysis. Institute for International Economic Studies, University of Stockholm. Seminar Paper No. 390. September.

Wilson, R. 1979. Auctions of shares. *Quarterly Journal of Economics* 93: 675–689.

# 4 On the Ineffectiveness of Made-to-Measure Protectionist Programs

Aaron Tornell

Recently, there has been an emergence of arguments justifying the implementation of industrial policies. According to these arguments, trade protection or investment subsidies provide domestic firms with the time and resources to undertake cost-reducing investments that will give them a strategic advantage over foreign firms. However, in many cases the performance of protectionist programs has been grim. Industries have not adapted, and protection has had to be renewed again and again.

Granting protection to a firm is justified on the ground that in the absence of protection, the marginal cost of investing the socially or politically optimal level is greater than the marginal benefit. Protection must be granted to induce this investment level.

A common assumption made in these arguments is that government authorities can credibly precommit to end protection in the future. This is a very strong assumption. In fact government actions are not exogenous. Government authorities maximize a welfare function or they react to political forces, as stressed in the public choice literature.[1] Therefore, if these authorities grant protection in the present, it is unlikely that they will not grant it in the future, in the event that the targeted firm would not have adapted.

The inability of government to precommit to the unconditional elimination of protection generates a trade-off for the firm. If during the program the firm does not invest sufficiently, it will receive a renewal of future protection. In addition it would save the opportunity cost of capital, but it would loose the benefits derived from cost reductions. Since, by construction, at the socially optimal level of investment, the latter two are equal, it follows that the firm will choose not to invest sufficiently. Therefore a protectionist program that was intended to be temporary becomes time inconsistent. This happens because the original plan of eliminating protection will no longer be optimal when the future finally arrives, so government will have to renew protection.

In this chapter I analyze whether time inconsistency is eliminated when the program consists of subsidies that are granted only if investment takes place (investment-contingent subsidies).

Obviously, if authorities could credibly precommit to grant only investment-contingent subsidies in the future, then these subsidies would bring about time consistency because the above-mentioned trade-off would disappear: Although a reduction of current investment would induce a renewal of protection, such protection would only be obtained by investing in the future. However, since this deviation implies a delay of investment, as well as a delay in obtaining the additional investment-contingent subsidy, the firm would not find it profitable to reduce investment.

Note, nevertheless, that a protectionist program cannot just promise to grant investment-contingent subsidies in the future because it takes time for investment to reduce costs and because firms in "need" of protection are not able to obtain resources from the capital market. The program must also consider that in case of failure there would be a need for a "bailout" to allow the firm to operate in the short term. This bailout should consist of a general and front-end-load subsidy, which should be granted before investment takes place—namely, the bailout (BO) cannot be an investment-contingent subsidy (ICS).

Since a protectionist program cannot be of the form ICS–investment–ICS but has to be ICS–investment–BO, and since firms have the possibility of inducing future bailouts, it follows that time inconsistency is not eliminated by investment-contingent subsidies that just equalize marginal costs to marginal benefits at the socially or politically optimal level of investment.[2] The reason for this is that the net gain from deviating is equal to the rents generated by the renewal of protection; the rents are not investment contingent.

The above point is important because it is customary in the literature to design protectionist programs that assume away the possibility that firms can induce future bailouts. As a result these programs fail to induce the targeted firm to invest sufficiently in cost reductions.

Staiger and Tabellini (1987) and Matsuyama (1987) have also analyzed time inconsistency problems. Staiger and Tabellini show that when protectionist policies are time inconsistent, it might be optimal for government authorities to choose tariffs over production subsidies. Matsuyama addresses the issue of whether there exists a game-theoretic credible government threat in the future that can support the pair {protect, invest} in a subgame-perfect equilibrium. His result is similar to that of this chapter. He shows that an equilibrium in pure strategies does not exist if each player is restricted to choose the same move facing the same circumstances.

In section 4.1 I present the model and prove the basic time inconsistency result. In section 4.2 I address the issue of whether there is an investment-contingent subsidy high enough to eliminate time inconsistency. I show that this can be achieved by setting the oversubsidization rate equal to the present value of all future bailouts the firm might induce. However, at such a high subsidy rate, it would not be optimal to grant protection to begin with. In section 4.3 I draw some conclusions.

## 4.1   The Model

Instead of modeling the political process that leads to protection, I will concentrate on a particular firm and assume that due to some political pressures the firm has to maintain at all times a certain level of employment: the negotiated employment level $\bar{N}$. Once $\bar{N}$ has been set, government authorities will implement a protectionist program that will ensure that the level of employment is never lower than $\bar{N}$.

By considering employment as their political objective rather than protection government authorities' hazard the possibility that in the long run protection will be eliminated if the firm adapts even if the political process that had led to protection does not change.[3] The negoitated employment level is in line with Baldwin's (1985, 31) view that "the pattern of inter-industry protection is influenced not only by differences among industries in their ability to succeed in the political marketplace but in their ability to compete in economic markets since the latter factor affects the perceived need for protection."

The notion of a negotiated employment level encompasses a variety of cases. Before introducing the model, lets look at three commonly discussed cases:

1. The case of injured or infant industries that need time and resources to make cost-reducing investments that will allow them in the future to compete more effectively in the world market.[4] Targeting a higher $\bar{N}$ is equivalent to demanding higher competitiveness, which in turn is equivalent to having a higher marginal product of labor.

2. The case of strategic trade and industrial policy, according to which, at the present employment level, protection enables firms to capture a larger share of the world market in rent-earning industries. The desired share can be interpreted as $\bar{N}$.

3. The case of sunset industries in which protection is intended to allow the targeted industry to contract more gradually, and thereby to reduce the costs related with the reallocation of the specific resources it employs. In this case $\bar{N}$ represents displaced labor effectively reemployed in other

sectors. Protection is intended to allow workers to be retrained (i.e., to induce investment in human capital).

To focus on the essentials, I consider in the model a profit-maximizing firm that is a domestic monopolist but faces a perfectly competitive international market. To model the fact that this firm has low competitiveness, I assume that its marginal product of labor is so low that, in the absence of an import tariff, its employment level would be lower than $\bar{N}$.

In this section I consider only two periods. At the beginning of time $t_0$ the political process occurs and $\bar{N}$ is set for the targeted firm. Once this has occurred, the government implements a protectionist program that is supposed to end at time $t_1$. The program consists of two parts: an investment-contingent subsidy granted at $t_0$ and an announcement that protection will elapse in $t_1$. The firm chooses the level of cost-reducing investment and receives the investment-contingent subsidy according to this investment level. If the firm invested sufficiently at time $t_0$, the increase in the marginal product of labor will be such that at $t_1$ it will employ $\bar{N}$ without protection. In this case the protectionist program will be successful, and protection will not have to be renewed.

Government authorities cannot precommit to eliminate protection because if the firm does not invest in reducing costs, its marginal cost curve will not shift downward. Thus at time $t_1$, when the program is scheduled to come to an end, authorities will have to impose an import tariff in order to raise the domestic price and induce $\bar{N}$. This renewal of protection is not investment contingent, it is a bailout.

Now we will describe the technology: The firm produces a homogeneous good, using a neoclassical production function for transforming labor and capital.[5] There are no installment costs of capital, investment increases the capital stock with a one-period lag, there is no depreciation domestic demand is not binding, and no resale market for capital exists. Under these assumptions all investment will be bunched at time $t_0$. Therefore we can express the firm's profits as

$$\Pi = r[\Phi(K_1,\mu)] - (r - s)I_0, \tag{1}$$

with

$$\Phi(K_1,\mu) = \max_{N_1} \{p[1 + \mu]F(N_1,K_1) - wN_1\},$$

$$K_1 = K_0 + I_0.$$

In the first period the firm chooses its investment level $I_0$, it incurs an opportunity cost of $I_0$, and it receives a subsidy of $sI_0$ (the investment-contingent subsidy). In the second period, taking as given the capital stock and the domestic price $p(1 + \mu)$, the firm chooses an employment level $N_1$ that will maximize profits in the shortrun. The term $\mu$ represents the gains from a renewal of protection, which will be analyzed next.[6]

### Renewal-of-Protection Function

The renewal-of-protection function arises from the asymmetric bargaining power of both parties at time $t_1$. Government authorities are weak because they have to ensure a level of employment not lower than $\bar{N}$. In contrast, the firm is strong because at time $t_1$, it has accumulated $K_1$ since investment has increased the capital stock with a one-period lag. Thus the firm can credibly threaten to employ fewer than $\bar{N}$ if it does not receive protection.

The argument is as follows: At time $t_1$ the firm will optimally choose employment to equalize the marginal product of labor to the real wage, as shown in figure 4.1:

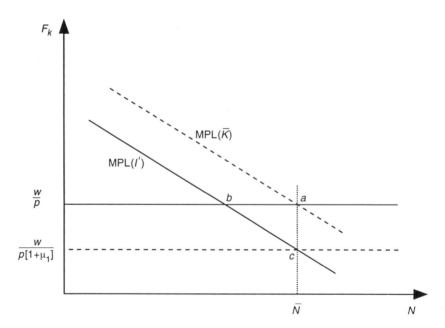

**Figure 4.1**

$$F_n(N_1; K_1) = \frac{w}{p(1 + \mu_1)}.$$  (2)

If $\mu_1$ is equal to zero, the firm would employ $\bar{N}$ at time $t_1$ only if it has invested at time $t_0$ an amount equal to[7]

$$\bar{K}(\bar{N}) = F_n^{-1}\left(\frac{w}{p}; \bar{N}\right).$$  (3)

If the firm chooses at time $t_0$ an investment level $I'$ lower than $\bar{K}$, then its labor productivity curve at time $t_1$ will lie to the left of the curve $\text{MPL}(\bar{K})$ in figure 4.1. Since this curve is fixed in the short run, authorities will be forced to alter their original plan and set $\mu_1 > 0$ to make employment equal to $\bar{N}$ (i.e., move the equilibrium from point $b$ to point $c$).

This implies that when choosing its investment level at time $t_0$, the firm behaves as a Stackelberg leader who faces the following renewal-of-protection function:

$$\mu(I_0) = \begin{cases} \dfrac{w}{pF_n(\bar{N}, I_0)} - 1 & \text{for } I_0 < \bar{K}, \\[2mm] 0 & \text{for } I_0 \geq \bar{K}. \end{cases}$$

Since $F_{nk} > 0$, this function is decreasing with investment, which means that less investment ultimately results in more protection.

### Determination of the Investment-Contingent Subsidy

We assume that at the end of the protectionist program, the authorities' objective is that the targeted firm will will employ $\bar{N}$ in the absence of protection. That is, the program is of the form $\{s, \mu = 0\}$.[8]

In this subsection we set the investment-contingent subsidy $s$ equal to its "made-to-measure" level, as Corden has named it.[9] This is the case generally used in the literature. In terms of our model this is the subsidy that government authorities impose in order to render $\bar{K}$ the most profitable choice for the firm. In other words, it is the subsidy that would be granted if the possibility of future bailouts was disregarded. In section 4.2 we set the investment-contingent subsidy at a higher rate.

At the margin the made-to-measure investment-contingent subsidy equates the opportunity cost of capital with the benefits derived from lower future costs. Formally, it is defined by the following maximization problem of the government authorities:

$$\max_{s} U^g = U(N_1), \qquad \text{where } U'(\bar{N}) = 0, \quad U''(N) < 0, \tag{5a}$$

subject to

$$\bar{K} = F_n^{-1}\left(\frac{w}{p}; \bar{N}\right) \quad \text{and} \quad r - s = rpF_k(\bar{N}, \bar{K}), \tag{5b}$$

which, given our assumption that domestic demand is not binding, implies that

$$s^{mtm} = r[1 - pF_k(\bar{N}, \bar{K})]. \tag{6}$$

The first equation in (5b) defines the level of investment that makes $\bar{N}$ the optimal employment level for the firm at time $t_1$. The second equation represents the optimality condition of a firm that believes that protection will be eliminated unconditionally at time $t_1$.

It is clear from the model that if the firm cannot bail out and thus believes that protection will be eliminated at time $t_1$, then an investment-contingent subsidy at a rate of $s^{mtm}$ will induce the firm to invest $\bar{K}$ at time $t_0$ and employ $\bar{N}$ at time $t_1$. In other words, the protectionist program will be time consistent, and protection will end at time $t_1$.

### Time Inconsistency of Made-to-Measure Protectionist Programs

The existence of a renewal-of-protection function introduces a trade-off for the firm. On the one hand, by lowering its investment at time $t_0$, the firm gains because it induces a higher protection rate at time $t_1$. On the other hand, it loses due to a lower labor productivity. It also loses part of the investment-contingent subsidy.

Proposition 1 states that if protection is made to measure, then the gains from having protection renewed are greater than the losses. Therefore the firm will always set $I_0 < \bar{K}$, making the protectionist program time inconsistent.

PROPOSITION 1    Protectionist programs based on the made-to-measure principle are time inconsistent.

*Proof*    See the appendix at the end of this chapter.

To get the intuition behind proposition 1, consider the firm as acting under two mutually exclusive regimes: a nonprecommitment regime (*NP-*

regime) in which the firm faces the renewal-of-protection function (4), and a precommitment regime (P-regime) in which authorities can credibly precommit to eliminate protection. The P-regime is an ideal construct under which bailouts do not exist (i.e., $\mu(I) = \mu'(I) = 0$) for all levels of investment.

From the standpoint of the firm, investment is more expensive under the $NP$-regime. This is because under the $NP$-regime an increase in investment reduces future protection, whereas under the P-regime it does not. In different terms, under the P-regime the cost of investment is $r$, whereas under the $NP$-regime it is $r - rp\mu'F > r$. The term $rp\mu'F$ is the value of protection forgone by investing an additional unit of capital.

Consider a firm that made its decision under the P-regime and set $I_0 = \bar{K}$. Now suppose that suddenly the firm finds itself in the $NP$-regime. Will it reduce its investment? The gains of reducing investment from an initial position $\bar{K}$ are

1. an increase in the domestic price faced during $t_1$: $[-rp\mu' \cdot F(\bar{N}, \bar{K})]dI_0$, and
2. a reduction in costs: $(r + rw \cdot dN_1/dI_0)dI_0$.

The losses are

3. a reduction in the investment-contingent subsidy received at time $t_0$: $sdI_0$, and
4. a reduction in protection (bailout) received at time $t_1$ due to lower production: $rp[1 + \mu(I_0)]dF$.

Given that initially the firm's production is at an optimum level (i.e., $I_0 = \bar{K}$), the gains in condition 2 equal the losses in conditions 3 and 4. Therefore the firm will benefit from reducing investment starting at $\bar{K}$. Its net gains will be those given in condition 1. To see why conditions 2, 3, and 4 cancel out, we will make use of the envelope theorem. First, substract conditions 3 and 4 from condition 2, noting that $\mu(\bar{K}) = 0$, and that $dF = F_n dN + F_k dI$:

$$r(w - pF_n)dN_1 + (-s + r - rpF_k)dI_0. \tag{7}$$

Now consider the optimality conditions of the firm:

$$pF_n(\bar{N}, \bar{K}) = w \quad \text{and} \quad s + rpF_k(\bar{N}, \bar{K}) = r.$$

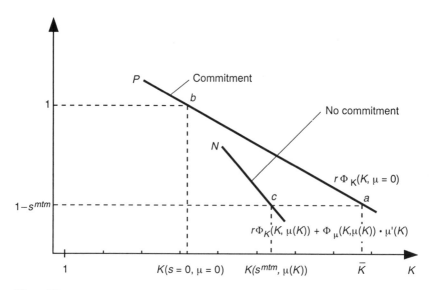

**Figure 4.2**

In the first equation note that the first two terms in (7) have vanished, and in the second that the next three terms have vanished. Starting from $\bar{K}$, the renewal of protection effect will dominate, and the firm will optimally choose a lower level of investment. Therefore made-to-measure protectionist programs are time inconsistent. This is illustrated graphically in figure 4.2.[10] The $PP$ and $NN$ curves represent marginal revenues under the $P$-regime and $N$-regime, respectively. Under the $P$-regime the firm would invest less than $\bar{K}$ (point $b$) if no investment subsidy is granted. In order to induce $\bar{K}$, a subsidy of size $s^{mtm}$ is necessary (point $a$). However, since due to the renewal-of-protection effect ($p\mu' F$) marginal benefits are lower under the $N$-regime than under the $P$-regime, a subsidy of the size $s^{mtm}$ induces an investment lower than $\bar{K}$ (point $c$).

## 4.2  Oversubsidization Programs

So far I have shown that a protectionist program will fail to induce $I_0 = \bar{K}$ if the investment-contingent subsidy is designed in such a way that the firm has no possibility of inducing bailouts (i.e., if $s = s^{mtm}$). In this section we analyze whether by oversubsidizing investment (by setting $s \gg s^{mtm}$) the firm could be induced to set $I_0 = \bar{K}$, and thus eliminate the time inconsistency. This scheme would be effective if authorities could precommit not to oversubsidize in the future. By offering an investment-contingent subsidy higher than the made-to-measure investment-contingent subsidy, by an amount only greater than the value of a bailout, the firm would be deterred from investing less than $\bar{K}$. By doing so, the firm would lose an investment-contingent subsidy that is higher than the value of the bailout it would receive.

We need to recognize, however, that it is difficult for government authorities to precommit not to oversubsidize in the future. If it is optimal to grant a high investment-contingent subsidy in the present, it will also be optimal to oversubsidize in the future. To model this correctly, we need to lengthen the horizon. By taking two periods, we are implicitly assuming that authorities can precommit not to grant investment-contingent subsidies in the future. In what follows we will let the horizon be infinite, and we will set the level of oversubsidization constant over time (i.e., $s_t = s$ for all $t$).

Under the new assumptions it is clear that a low level of oversubsidization will not eliminate time inconsistency. This is because the lost oversubsidization $s$ can be recuped by investing at anytime in the future. Thus, if $s$ is not high enough, the firm could profitably make the following deviation: (1) at time $t_0$ set $I_0 < \bar{K}$, forgoing a subsidy of $s[\bar{K} - I_0]$, and (2) at time $t_1$ receive a bailout subsidy of $\mu pF$ and invest $\bar{K} - I_0$, recuperating $s[\bar{K} - I_0]$.

Now we will analyze what level of oversubsidization renders unprofitable the above-mentioned deviation. To do this formally, we will write the profits of the firm as

$$-I_0(1 - s) + r\{[1 + \mu(I_0)] \cdot F(\bar{N}, I_0) - (\bar{K} - I_0) \cdot (1 - s) - w\bar{N}\} \tag{8}$$

$$+ \sum_{j=2}^{\infty} r^j[F(\bar{N}, \bar{K}) - w\bar{N}], \qquad \text{where} \quad K_j = K_{j-1} + I_{j-1}, \quad K_0 = 0.$$

It follows that the value of $s$ that makes a one-period deviation unprofitable is determined by the derivative of (8) with respect to $I$, evaluated at $I_0 = \bar{K}$:

$$0 = -(1 - s) + r\{[1 + \mu(I_0)] \cdot F_k + \mu'^- F + (1 - s)\}. \tag{9}$$

Since the unprofitability of a one-period deviation implies the unprofitability of longer deviations, the value of $s$ that makes $I_0 = \bar{K}$ optimal is defined by (9). Noting that when $I_0 = \bar{K}$ the bailout subsidy $\mu$ is equal to zero, it follows that

$$s^{tc} = 1 - \frac{r}{1-r}[F_k(\bar{N}, \bar{K}) + \mu'^- F(\bar{N}, \bar{K})]. \tag{10}$$

Just for comparison note that in this case the made-to-measure investment-contingent subsidy (that which assumes away the possibility of bailouts) is given by

$$s^{mtm} = 1 - \frac{r}{1-r}F_k(\bar{N}, \bar{K}). \tag{11}$$

From (10) and (11) it is clear that the oversubsidization rate needed for the elimination of time inconsistency is $(r/1-r)\cdot \mu'^- F(\bar{N}, \bar{K})$, which is equal to the discounted present value of all future bailouts from $t_1$ until infinity. The greater the firm's discount factor, the greater is the oversubsidization rate. In the limit, if $r = 1$, then it is impossible to design a time-consistent protectionist program (i.e., $s = \infty$).

## 4.3 Conclusions

When government authorities cannot credibly precommit to eliminate protection, the targeted firm has the ability to induce a renewal of protection by not investing sufficiently in cost reductions. The firm will choose to do so and render the program time inconsistent if the rents it would obtain from a renewal of protection are greater than the profits it would get by competing in the world market.

The introduction of investment-contingent subsidies does not necessarily eliminate time inconsistency. When a renewal of protection is necessary, investment-contingent subsidies would include a bailout, which would have to be granted before investment takes place. This would allow the firm to operate in the short term.

If, as is customary, the design of the investment-contingent subsidy assumes away the possibility of future bailouts, the firm will find it profitable not to invest sufficiently, and thus will induce a renewal of protection. This problem can be worked out by oversubsidizing investment. However, for oversubsidization to be effective, it has to be higher than the present value of all future bailouts, and this could be very costly.

This chapter does not imply that all protectionist programs are ineffective, nor does it contradict successful protectionist experiences such as that of the Japanese. If the oversubsidization rate is sufficiently high, the program will be time consistent from the outset. Japan, for example, has solved the problem by promising subsidized loans or government procurement contracts only to those firms within the targeted industries that will lower costs and develop new products thus encouraging vigorous competition among domestic firms (Carliner 1986). It should be noted that Japan has also experienced trouble with protectionism in its aluminum, chemical, and steel industries. To allow these industries to contract more gradually, a so-called temporary law to stabilize industries in recession was enacted in 1978. However, despite subsidies and permission to form cartels, firms with declining markets were none to anxious to reduce their capacities. When this law expired in 1983, it was necessary to renew it for another five years under a new name: the law to promote industrial structure. (Yamamura 1986).

## Appendix:   Proof of Proposition 1

I will prove proposition 1 by showing that the firm maximizes profits at an investment level lower than $\bar{K}$. The proof consists of two steps. First, I show that the left-hand side derivative of profits, under the $NP$-regime, with respect to investment is negative at $I_0 = \bar{K}$. Then I will show that for $I_0 > \bar{K}$ profits are lower than for $I_0 = \bar{K}$ (see figure 4.2).

From (1) it follows that

$$\frac{\partial \Pi_0^{np}}{\partial I_0} = (s_0^{mtm} - r) + rp\{[1 + \mu(I_0)]F_k(\bar{N}, I_0) + \mu'(I_0) \cdot F(\bar{N}, I_0)\}. \tag{A1}$$

The equation's sign is ambiguous since the second and fourth terms are negative, while the others are positive. To determine its sign, note that the first three terms are equal to $\partial \Pi_0^p / \partial I_0$, which by construction of $s^{mtm}$ equals zero at $I_0 = \bar{K}$. Also note that $\mu(I)$ evaluated at $\bar{K}$ is zero. Therefore the limit of (A1) as $I_0$ tends to $\bar{K}$ from the left is

$$\frac{\partial \Pi_0^{np}}{\partial I_0} = rp\mu' \cdot F(\bar{N}, \bar{K}). \tag{A2}$$

This expression is negative provided that $F_{nk} > 0$ because

$$\mu'(I_0) = -\frac{wF_{nk}(\bar{N}, I_0)}{p[F_n(\bar{N}, I_0)]^2} < 0 \qquad \text{if } I_0 < \bar{K}. \tag{A3}$$

To finish the proof, we just need to show that $\Pi^{np}(I > \bar{K}) < \Pi^{np}(I = \bar{K})$. Note first that for $I > \bar{K}$ profits under the $P$-regime and the $NP$-regime coincide $[\Pi^{np}(I > \bar{K}) = \Pi^p(I > \bar{K})]$ because $\mu_1(I \geq \bar{K}) = 0$. Second, note that under the $P$-regime, profits are maximized at $I = \bar{K}$. Thus, $\Pi^p(I = \bar{K}) > \Pi^p(I > \bar{K})$.[11]

## Notes

I thank Jagdish Bhagwati, Max Corden, Rudi Dornbusch, Elhanan Helpman, Paul Krugman, and Lars Svensson for helpful suggestions.

1. The notion that protection reflects not national welfare maximization but rather pressures by special interest groups has been formalized by Bhagwati and Srinivasan (1980), Brock and Magee (1980), Findlay and Wellisz (1982), Krueger (1974), and Rodrik (1986). For recent surveys see Bhagwati (1988), Baldwin (1985), and Hillman (1989).

2. This statement is valid for subsidies that are continuous functions of investment.

3. By contrast, in interest-group models the government acts only as an intermediary between economic groups.

4. This argument relies on the existence of externalities or on a capaital market imperfection that does not allow firms to finance their projects.

5. The production function has the standard properties $F_n > 0$, $F_k > 0$, $F_{nn} < 0$, $F_{kk} < 0$, and $F_{nk} > 0$.

6. Note that (1) does not contain a term corresponding to $\mu_0$. From a $t_0$ perspective $\mu_0$ is a bailout that is not contingent on $I_0$. Therefore the choice of $I_0$ is independent of $\mu_0$.

7. We will set $K_0 = 0$ to simplify notation.

8. In a more complete model $\mu$ need not be zero. The optimal choice of $\mu$ and $s$ would depend on the costs associated with them.

9. According to the made-to-measure principle, "the tariff structure would be tailored so that no industry or product is protected more than is 'necessary,'" Corden (1974, 220).

10. This figure was suggested by Lars Svensson.

11. The concavity of $\Pi^p$ does not imply the concavity of $\Pi^{np}$. However, the concavity of $\Pi^{np}$ is not necessary for the validity of proposition 1. Note that $\Pi^{np}_{kk} = \Pi^p_{kk} + \mu F_{kk} + 2\mu' F_k + \mu'' F$. Since the first two terms are negative, a sufficient condition for $\Pi^{np}_{kk}$ to be negative is that $\mu'' < 0$, which is equivalent to $F_{nkk} \cdot (F_n)^2 > 2F_{nk}$.

## References

Baldwin, R. 1985. *The Political Economy of US Import Policy*. Cambridge: MIT Press. 1988.

Bhagwati, J. 1988. *Protectionism*. Cambridge: MIT Press.

Bhagwati, J., and Srinivasan, T. 1980. Revenue seeking: A generalization of the theory of tariffs. *Journal of Political Economy* 88: 1069–1087.

Brock, W., and Magee, S. P. 1980. Tariff formation in a democracy. In J. Black and B. Hindley (eds.), *Current Issues in Commercial Policy and Diplomacy*. New York: St. Martin's Press.

Carliner, G. 1986. Industrial Policy for Emerging Industries. In P. R. Krugman (ed.) *Strategic Trade Policy and the New International Economics*. Cambridge: MIT Press, pp. 147–168.

Corden, M. 1974. *Trade Policy and Economic Welfare*. Oxford: Clarendon Press.

Findlay, R., and Wellisz, W. 1982. Endogenous tariffs, the political economy of trade restrictions, and welfare. In J. Bhagwati (ed.), *Import Competition and Response*. Chicago: Chicago University Press.

Hillman, A., *The Political Economy of Protection* (Chur, Switzerland: Harwood Academic Publishers, 1989).

Krueger, A. 1974. The political economy of the rent seeking society. *American Economic Review* 64: 291–303.

Krugman, P. R. 1986. New thinking about trade policy. In P. R. Krugman (ed.), *Strategic Trade Policy and the New International Economics*. Cambridge: MIT Press, pp. 1–22.

Matsuyama, K. 1987. Perfect equilibria in a trade liberalization game. Mimeo. Northwestern University.

Rodrik, D. 1986. Tariffs, subsidies and welfare with endogenous policy. *Journal of International Economics* 21: 285–300.

Staiger, R. and Tabellini, G. 1987. Discretionary trade policy and excessive protection. *American economic review* 77: 823–836.

Yamamura, K. 1986. Caveat emptor: The Industrial policy of Japan. In P. R. Krugman (ed.), *Strategic Trade Policy and the New International Economics*. Cambridge: MIT Press, pp. 169–209.

# 5 Export Subsidies and Price Competition

Peter Neary

The traditional case against export subsidies is twofold: In a small open economy no type of trade intervention can be first best, and in a large economy, which can affect its terms of trade, there is a presumption that its exports should be taxed rather than subsidized in order to raise their world prices. However, these arguments have been extensively reexamined in recent years. Feenstra (1986) and Itoh and Kiyono (1987) have shown that even under competitive circumstances subsidies to some exports may be desirable if as a result the terms of trade of other exports are improved. More surprisingly, Brander and Spencer (1985) have shown that if the market structure is a Cournot duopoly, an export subsidy is always optimal because it raises the profits of the home firm at the expense of the foreign.[1]

Such a startling and clear-cut departure from orthodoxy as the Brander-Spencer result has naturally attracted a great deal of attention. However, recent work has shown that it is not very robust. In particular, Eaton and Grossman (1986) have shown that if firms are assumed to be Bertrand price competitors rather than Cournot quantity competitors, then the optimality of an export tax is restored.[2] More recently still, this result has been challenged by the work of Carmichael (1987) and Gruenspecht (1988). Carmichael argues that the traditional method of modelling export subsidies diverges from practice in the real world in two important respects: First, subsidies are typically related to the *price* secured on an export contract rather than to the *volume* of export sales, and, second, the level of the subsidy is typically determined not *before* but only *after* an export contract has been secured and a price agreed between the exporting firm and the foreign buyer. Taking this empirical paradigm as given, Gruenspecht proceeds to show that subsidies may be optimal when firms are price competitors for plausible parameter values.

The objective of this chapter is to examine these novel arguments and to show that they do not in fact rescue the optimality of export subsidies in markets where firms compete on price. In section 5.1 I introduce the framework to be adopted and compare the effects of output and price subsidies. Section 5.2 explores the Carmichael-Gruenspecht model, and section 5.3 shows that subsidies are never a dominant policy.

## 5.1 Price versus Output Subsidies

The framework I consider is a Bertrand duopoly model in which a home and a foreign firm produce differentiated products, whose output levels are denoted $x$ and $y$, respectively. To clarify the issue, I concentrate throughout on the case where there is no home consumption and the foreign government does not subsidise its own country's firm. The home government can impose either an output subsidy, which effectively reduces the home firm's unit costs by an amount $s$, or a price subsidy, which reduces the price charged by the home firm by an amount $\sigma$. Letting $p$ and $q$ denote the home and foreign prices (not including the subsidy), the demand functions may therefore be written as

$$x = x(p - \sigma, q) \quad \text{and} \quad y = y(p - \sigma, q), \tag{1}$$

The home and foreign firm's profits are

$$\pi = [(p + s)x - C(x) \quad \text{and} \quad \pi^* = qy - C^*(y)], \tag{2}$$

where $C(x)$ and $C^*(y)$ are the home and foreign cost functions, respectively.

As I note at the beginning of this chapter, two alternative assumptions can be made about the timing of subsidy decisions. First, there is the conventional assumption (adopted by Brander and Spencer 1985, among many others) that the government chooses the value of the subsidy before any decision is taken by firms. I will refer to the resulting game as the ex ante game. Second, there is the assumption whose realism is argued by Carmichael (1987) whereby the government chooses the level of the subsidy after the firms have played among themselves. Forward-looking firms anticipate this of course, so they choose prices in the first stage of the game in the knowledge of how the government will react in the second stage. I will refer to this game as the ex post game.

With two alternative assumptions concerning the order of moves in the game and two alternative assumptions concerning the type of instrument used by the government, there are in principle four different combinations to be considered. In the remainder of this section, I consider some general issues that arise in each case.

### Case 1: Output Subsidy in the Ex Ante Game

This is the standard combination of assumptions made by most authors, whether they consider output competition (as in Brander and Spencer 1985;

Dixit 1984) or price competition (as in Eaton and Grossman 1986). We know from this work that when only two firms compete on price, the optimal subsidy is negative (i.e., the optimal policy is an export tax).

### Case 2:  Price Subsidy in the Ex Ante Game

This combination of assumptions does not appear to have been examined by any writers, although it might appear more natural when firms are Bertrand price competitors. However, it is easily seen that it is in fact fully equivalent to the combination considered in case 1. To see this, write $P$ for the *net* price of the home good, $p - \sigma$, in the demand functions (1). It may now be seen that the two types of subsidy operate in exactly the same way. In particular, both have identical effects on the two firms' profits:

$$\pi = P + s + \sigma x(P,q) - C\{x(P,q)\}, \tag{3}$$

$$\pi^* = qy(P,q) - C^*[y(P,q)]. \tag{4}$$

Evaluating and differentiating the first-order conditions shows that changes in the two types of subsidy have identical effects on the equilibrium:

$$\begin{bmatrix} \pi_{pp} & \pi_{pq} \\ \pi^*_{qp} & \pi^*_{qq} \end{bmatrix} \begin{bmatrix} dP \\ dq \end{bmatrix} = \begin{bmatrix} -x_p \\ 0 \end{bmatrix} (ds + d\sigma). \tag{5}$$

Hence, provided that both firms take the levels of the subsidy rates as given in choosing their prices (or, what amounts to the same thing, provided that the home firm negotiates with foreign buyers on the basis of the net price $P$ only), the two types of subsidy are fully equivalent. Of course this is not surprising. If the two subsidies operated in different ways, the home government would have two independent policy instruments at its disposal and, with only two target variables to control ($x$ and $y$), would be able to implement any desired pattern of output.

### Case 3:  Output Subsidy in the Ex Post Game

Consider next the paradigm about the timing of moves proposed by Carmichael, whereby firms set their prices in the anticipation that the government will respond by granting an ex post optimal subsidy to the home firm. Logically this paradigm could be examined for the case where the subsidy is an output subsidy, but in fact it does not make sense in this case. The reason is that since demands depend only on the prices $p$ and $q$, output levels are determined before the government makes its choice of subsidy, so intervention would be redundant. Consider the welfare function which, with no domestic consumption, is simply the level of home profits less the cost of subsidy payments:

$$W = \pi(p, q, s) - sx. \tag{6}$$

Substituting from the profit function (2), the level of subsidy payments cancels:

$$W = px(p, q) - C[x(p, q)]. \tag{7}$$

This shows that social welfare is independent of the output subsidy level. Therefore, if prices are set by firms in the first round of the game, there is no optimal policy. Hence, although the issues of whether subsidies are related to the home firm's output or price and whether the game is ex ante or ex post are distinct in principle, they are related in that the ex post game makes sense only with price subsidies.

**Case 4: Price Subsidy in the Ex Post Game**

Turning finally to the case considered by Carmichael, a difficulty arises even there if the welfare function is defined in the usual way (i.e., as in (6) except that $\sigma$ replaces $s$):

$$W = \pi(p, q, s) - \sigma x. \tag{8}$$

The problem here is that there is no upper bound on the price that the home firm may charge: The government is indifferent between extra profits and extra subsidy disbursements, but the firm is not. To avoid the implausible implication that subsidies should be increased without bound, I follow Gruenspecht in introducing a parameter $\delta$, which is assumed to be greater than unity, to measure the opportunity cost of public funds:[3]

$$W = \pi(p, q, \sigma) - \delta\sigma x. \tag{9}$$

This ensures that the ex post optimal subsidy is bounded and has the plausible implication that an extra pound of subsidy payments reduces welfare by more than an extra pound of profits increases it. (Note that the addition of the $\delta$ parameter does not resolve the difficulty with an output subsidy in the ex post game. The welfare function now becomes

$$W = [p + (1 + \delta)s]x(p, q) - C[x(p, q)]. \tag{7'}$$

instead of (7)). This welfare function is no longer independent of $s$, unlike

**Table 5.1**
Implications of alternative assumptions about the type of subsidy and the nature of the subsidy game

|                     |         | Type of subsidy        |                        |
|---------------------|---------|------------------------|------------------------|
|                     |         | Output ($s$)           | Price ($\sigma$)       |
|                     |         |                        | Same as                |
|                     | Ex ante | Eaton-Grossman         | Eaton-Grossman         |
| Nature of the game  |         |                        |                        |
|                     | Ex post | Intervention redundant | Carmichael-Gruenspecht |

(7). However, its derivative with respect to $s$ is constant (since $p$ and $q$ are predetermined) and negative (for $\delta$ greater than one). This implies that the optimal value of $s$ is minus infinity—once again, a conclusion that makes no sense.

The conclusions of this section may now be summarized in table 5.1. Essentially the choice of instrument in the ex ante game does not of itself raise any substantive issues, and an output subsidy is redundant when the government moves after rather than before firms in determining the subsidy level. Since I wish to compare the two types of game on an equal footing, these conclusions allow me to concentrate in the remainder of the chapter on price subsidies.

Before proceeding to the analysis, a difficulty that must be faced is that exact results cannot be obtained for the general specification of demand and costs given by (1) and (2). In the second stage of the game the government maximizes (9) for given prices $p$ and $q$. This implies a subsidy function, which can be written as $\tilde{\sigma}(p, q)$. Foreseeing this, both firms in the first stage of the game maximize their profits, taking only the other's price as given. Thus the home firm's problem is

$$\max_{p} \pi[p, q, \tilde{\sigma}(p, q)], \tag{10}$$

whereas the foreign firm's problem is

$$\max_{q} \pi^*[p, q, \tilde{\sigma}(p, q)]. \tag{11}$$

From these equations, it is clear that to solve for the actual value of the price subsidy that will obtain in equilibrium, it is necessary to have information concerning the third derivatives of the demand and cost functions. It is essential to assume a much simpler specification of demand and costs. Therefore I will adopt a specification similar to that assumed by Gruenspecht; specifically I assume that demands are determined not by (1) but as follows:

$$x = \alpha - \beta(p - \sigma - q) \quad \text{and} \quad y = \alpha + \beta(p - \sigma - q). \tag{12}$$

This implies that the demand conditions facing firms are symmetric and that the total market is fixed at $2\alpha$, the role of the relative price $p - \sigma - q$ being merely to determines the firms' market shares. In addition I assume that both firms have zero fixed costs and identical marginal costs that are fixed independently of the level of output at a level $c$. For later use these assumptions imply that the values of prices, outputs, and profits in the free-trade equilbrium are

$$\bar{p} = \bar{q} = \mu + c, \tag{13}$$

$$\bar{x} = \bar{y} = \alpha, \tag{14}$$

$$\overline{W} = \bar{\pi} = \bar{\pi}^* = \alpha\mu. \tag{15}$$

(In the absense of intervention, home welfare $\overline{W}$ equals just home profits $\bar{\pi}$.) Here I have introduced the parameter $\mu$, defined as $\alpha/\beta$, the relative price $(p - \sigma - q)$ at which the foreign firm captures all of the market.

## 5.2   Post-contract Choice of Subsidies

In this section I reexamine the model of Gruenspecht and try to provide additional intuitive explanations for his results. To explore the solution of this game, it is necessary as usual to solve first for the second stage, assuming that the firms have already chosen their prices in the first stage. The government therefore chooses $\sigma$ to maximise the welfare function (9), taking $p$ and $q$ as given. For the particular specification of demand and costs assumed, the welfare function becomes

$$W = (p - c - \delta\sigma)[\alpha - \beta(p - \sigma - q)]. \tag{16}$$

Maximizing this by choice of $\sigma$ yields the following function of $p$ and $q$:

$$\tilde{\sigma}(p, q) = -\frac{\mu}{2} + \frac{1}{2}(p - q) + \frac{1}{2\delta}(p - c). \tag{17}$$

(Recall that $\mu$ equals $\alpha/\beta$.) Equation (17) shows that a higher subsidy is warranted, the greater the existing gross price differential $p - q$ (since this reduces exports and so welfare) and the greater the home firm's price-cost margin $p - c$ (since this makes it more profitable to encourage an expansion of output). Thus a rise in $p$ tends to raise $\sigma$ on two counts, but because of the lower social valuation placed on profits than on government revenue, the government only partly compensates for a price rise with an increase in the subsidy. A rise in the home firm's price is therefore partly (though never fully) passed on to consumers:

$$\frac{\partial}{\partial p}[p - \tilde{\sigma}(p,q) - q] = \frac{\delta - 1}{2\delta}, \tag{18}$$

which is increasing in $\delta$ and lies between zero and 0.5.[4]

Whereas the government takes both prices as fixed in the second stage of the game, the firms set prices in the first stage in the anticipation that a subsidy will be provided according to formula (17). Thus, with its profits given by (2) (setting $s$ equal to zero), the home firm's first-order condition may be written as

$$\frac{d\pi}{dp} = \frac{\partial \pi}{\partial p} + \frac{\partial \pi}{\partial \sigma}\frac{\partial \tilde{\sigma}}{\partial p} = 0. \tag{19}$$

Since a higher price induces a higher subsidy, which raises profits, the firm will always, for a given price charged by the foreign firm, set a higher price than it would if it did not anticipate a change in the subsidy. Writing (19) explicitly gives the home firm's reaction function:

$$2(\delta - 1)p - \delta q = \delta\mu - (2 - \delta)c. \tag{20}$$

Surprisingly, similar incentives face the foreign firm, which implies that both firms gain from the mere existence of the subsidy program. This follows from the corresponding equation for the foreign firm:

$$\frac{d\pi^*}{dq} = \frac{\partial \pi^*}{\partial q} + \frac{\partial \pi^*}{\partial \sigma}\frac{\partial \tilde{\sigma}}{\partial q} = 0. \tag{21}$$

Since a rise in $q$ will cause the home government to lower the subsidy, the foreign firm's profits will rise. Hence it will also (for given $p$) charge a higher price than in the absence of the subsidy program. Writing (21) explicitly gives the foreign firm's reaction function:

$$-(\delta - 1)p + 2\delta q = 3\delta\mu + (1 + \delta)c. \tag{22}$$

Equations (20) and (22) can now be solved for the equilibrium prices that arise from price competition between firms in the first stage of the game:

$$\tilde{p} = c + \frac{5\delta}{3(\delta - 1)}\mu \quad \text{and} \quad \tilde{q} = c + \frac{7}{3}\mu. \tag{23}$$

Given what has been said, it is not surprising that both prices exceed their common value in the nonintervention case $\bar{p}$ and $\bar{q}$ (see (13)). Substituting these prices into (17), we obtain the following explicit expression for the optimal subsidy in this game:

$$\tilde{\sigma} = \frac{5(3 - \delta)}{6(\delta - 1)}\mu. \tag{24}$$

This gives one of Gruenspecht's principal results: The optimal subsidy is positive for values of $\delta$ less than 3. Though the values of $p$ and $\tilde{\sigma}$ vary with $\delta$, the net price paid by consumers does not; at the optimum the relative price is independent of $\delta$ and is positive. (It equals $\mu/6$.) This implies that whatever the shadow price of government funds, the effect of the subsidy program is to bring about the same pattern of sales, one that moreover gives a larger market share to the foreign firm: Home output is $5\alpha/6$, whereas foreign is $7\alpha/6$. Thus both firms gain from the subsidy program, the foreign firm because its larger market share raises its profits and the domestic because it benefits directly from the subsidy.

Finally, does the home government gain from the subsidy program? Substituting into (16), the expression for welfare at the optimum is

$$\tilde{W} = \alpha\mu\frac{25}{36}\delta. \tag{25}$$

Welfare is increasing in $\delta$: As the shadow price of government funds rises, the government gains more by having access to an increasingly efficient source of tax revenue. Nevertheless, for values of $\delta$ in the range 1.44 ($= 36/25$, the value at which $\tilde{W}$ equals $\overline{W}$) and 3, the optimal policy is a positive subsidy, and it yields a higher level of welfare than does the absence of a subsidy program. Since this range is consistent with many empirical estimates of $\delta$, a plausible case for the optimality of an export subsidy when firms are price competitors would appear to have been established.[5]

## 5.3   The Relative Optimality of Ex Post and Ex Ante Subsidies

So far I have followed Gruenspecht in assuming that subsidies are offered on an ex post basis, with both firms anticipating the effects of the prices they set on the government's choice of subsidy level. But it is not enough to compare the outcome of this game with the level of welfare in the absence of any intervention. We must also examine whether it leads to a higher level of welfare than in the ex ante game where the government first sets the level of subsidy and the firms take this as a parameter in their decisions. Since this sequence of decisions is the standard one considered in most writings on export subsidies, we already know a good deal about its implications. In particular, we know from Eaton and Grossman (1986) that at least when $\delta$ equals unity, the optimal policy in this game is an export tax rather than a subsidy. However, it is necessary to reexamine its properties under the parameterisation adopted in this chapter in order to determine which of the two games yields a higher level of welfare.

Consider first the decision problem of the home firm. With demand given by (12), it chooses its price to maximize profits, taking the foreign firm's price and the level of the subsidy as given. This yields the following first-order condition, which is also the home firm's reaction function:

$$2p - q = \mu + c + \sigma - s. \tag{26}$$

A similar series of derivations for the foreign firm yields

$$-p + 2q = \mu + c - \sigma. \tag{27}$$

Solving for $p$ and $q$ from (26) and (27),

$$p = \mu + c + \frac{\sigma}{3} \quad \text{and} \quad q = \mu + c - \frac{\sigma}{3}. \tag{28}$$

Hence a subsidy raises the price received by the home firm and lowers that charged by the foreign firm,[6] while on balance it lowers the relative price of home output:

$$p - \sigma - q = -\frac{\sigma}{3}. \tag{29}$$

Now, consider the first stage of the game in which the government chooses $\sigma$ to maximize (16), in the knowledge that firms will react as shown by (28). Calculating the solution for $\sigma$ yields

$$\sigma^0 = -\frac{3(3\delta - 2)}{2(3\delta - 1)}\mu. \tag{30}$$

This is negative and decreasing in $\delta$, which extends the result of Eaton and Grossman (who implicitly assumed a value of unity for $\delta$): In the ex ante game the optimal policy is always an export tax, irrespective of the value of $\delta$. From (29) it follows that the net relative price of home output is raised by the export tax. Hence in this game, too, the effect of the optimal subsidy is to cause the home firm to lose market share. Indeed this effect is considerably more pronounced than in the ex post game: Home output is 16.6% lower than without intervention in the ex post game but (depending on the value of $\delta$) between 25% and 50% lower in the ex ante game. The values of home output at the optima of the two games (to be compared with the free trade value, from (14), of $\alpha$) are

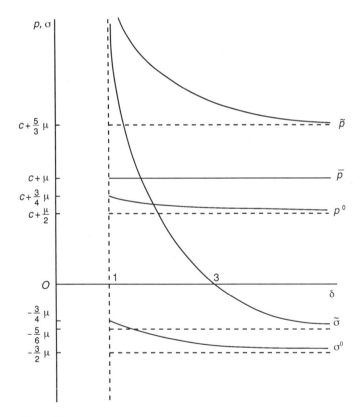

**Figure 5.1**
Values of home price and of the optimal subsidy as a function of $\delta$ in the ex ante and ex post games

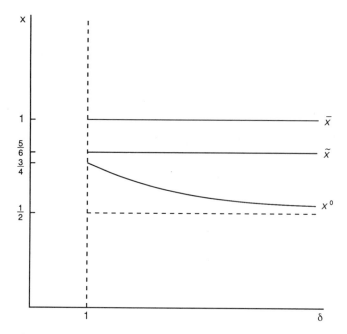

**Figure 5.2**
Values of home output as a function of $\delta$ in the ex ante and ex post games. Numbers on the vertical axis are in multiples of $\alpha$

$$\tilde{x} = \frac{5}{6}\alpha \quad \text{and} \quad x^0 = \frac{3\delta}{2(3\delta - 1)}\alpha. \tag{31}$$

The values of $p$ and $\sigma$ in the two games are compared in figure 5.1, while figure 5.2 compares the values of home output.

Finally, what do these results imply for the level of home welfare? Substituting into (16) leads, after some manipulations, to the following:

$$W^0 = \alpha\mu\frac{9\delta^2}{4(3\delta - 1)}. \tag{32}$$

Welfare is increasing in $\delta$, reflecting once again the advantage to the government of having a source of tax revenue which is more highly valued than corporate profits. More significantly, it is always greater than the level of welfare in the ex post game, given by (25). Thus it is not true to say that the government can gain by playing the ex post game: This is true only if the alternative is to avoid intervention altogether, not if it can play the ex ante game instead.

Why then would an ex post game be adopted? An obvious incentive favoring it can be seen by considering the levels of profits by both firms in both games. In the ex post game these are

$$\tilde{\pi} = \alpha\mu \frac{25}{18(\delta - 1)} \quad \text{and} \quad \tilde{\pi}^* = \alpha\mu \frac{49}{18}, \tag{33}$$

whereas in the ex ante game they are

$$\pi^0 = \alpha\mu \left[ \frac{3\delta}{2(3\delta - 1)} \right]^2 \quad \text{and} \quad \pi^{*0} = \alpha\mu \left[ \frac{9\delta - 4}{2(3\delta - 1)} \right]^2. \tag{34}$$

Recalling from (15) that profits of both firms in the symmetric no-intervention case are $\alpha\mu$, a number of important results follow from these

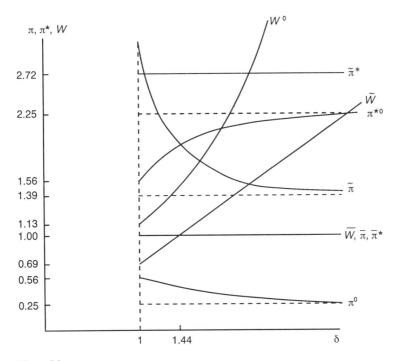

**Figure 5.3**
Values of home welfare and of home and foreign profits as a function of $\delta$ in the ex ante and ex post games. Numbers on the vertical axis are multiples of $\alpha\mu$

equations. The principal one is that both firms have higher profits in the ex post game than in either the ex ante game or the no-intervention case. Therefore in the truly ex ante situation of "choosing between games," the incentives facing firms are exactly opposite to those facing the home government. Both firms would prefer the ex post game to be adopted. This suggests that my earlier result that the home government attains a lower level of welfare when this game is played is not inconsistent with the empirical evidence adduced by Carmichael. However, the interpretation of this evidence is not that governments have been well advised in their choice of the "rules of the game" but rather that the national interest has been subordinated to the interests of the firms. Bearing in mind that the "government" in real-world situations is typically a specialist export credit agency (e.g., the ExIm Bank in the U.S.), this interpretation is fully consistent with the theories of Stigler and Posner that government agencies, rather than seeking to maximize some measure of general welfare, are typically "captured" by the very private sector actors whose actions they are intended to oversee.

All these results are illustrated in figure 5.3, where the vertical axis is measured in multiples of the benchmark level of welfare and profits ($\overline{W} = \overline{\pi} = \overline{\pi}^* = \alpha\mu$). Note that the foreign firm gains from both types of export subsidy, whereas the home firm actually has lower profits in the ex ante game than in the no-intervention case.

## 5.4   Conclusion

The main result of this chapter is that positive export subsidies cannot be justified on welfare maximization grounds if home and foreign firms compete on price. This conclusion was also reached by Eaton and Grossman (1986), but only in the context of the standard theoretical paradigm of how export subsidies are administered in practice—namely, a two-stage game where the government fixes the subsidy level in the first stage, knowing that that will affect firms' decisions in the second stage. However, the realism of this paradigm has been challenged by Carmichael (1987), who argues that the policy of the U.S. ExIm bank may be better characterized as a game where firms move first, choosing their prices in the knowledge that a predictable level of subsidy will be provided by the government in the second stage. This reversal of the standard assumption about timing in the choice of export subsidies has been shown by Gruenspecht (1988) to imply that under plausible circumstances a positive export subsidy may lead to a level of welfare higher than in the absence of intervention.

Although I am not disputing these results, I have shown that welfare is always higher in the ex ante subsidy game where the government moves first than in the ex post subsidy game. The government's first-mover advantage is clear-cut therefore: To the extent that it can influence the choice of subsidy regime (or the "rules of the game"), it should opt for an ex ante rather than an ex post type of program. Precommitment to a subsidy level rather than to a subsidy rule is always welfare enhancing. Of course, as I have noted, this is not necessarily in conflict with the empirical evidence presented by Carmichael. However, it suggests a very different interpretation of that evidence: Lobbying by firms rather than welfare maximization is the likely explanation for the adoption of ex post subsidy programs.

Naturally, since the results of sections 5.2 and 5.3 have only been obtained in a special model, their robustness needs to be investigated. (By contrast, the results of section 5.1, concerning the distinction between price and output subsidies in either game, hold under general specifications.) One final reflection seems justified by the conclusions of this chapter: The term "rent shifting" is clearly inappropriate as a description of the possibility of raising welfare by subsidizing a home firm that competes in an oligopolistic market with a foreign firm. It is of course true that the potential for raising the home firm's profits provides a source of welfare gain not present in competitive models. But "shifting" profits (or rents) from foreign to home firms is a consequence of optimal intervention only in the Cournot quantity competition case considered by Brander and Spencer (1985). In the cases considered in this chapter, optimal intervention shifts rents from foreign consumers toward both firms in the ex post subsidy game, whereas in the ex ante subsidy game the optimal policy (an export tax) raises the foreign firm's profits and lowers the home firm's. Thus no clear guidelines can be drawn about the desirability of using government policy to shift rents toward home firms at the expense of their foreign competitors.

## Notes

I am grateful to George Bulkley, Arje Hillman, Michael Hoel, Harmen Lehment, Assaf Razin, and participants in seminars at Exeter University, the Kiel Institut für Weltwirtschaft, the Norwegian School of Management, University College Dublin, the European Research Workshop in International Trade at Bergen, an International Economics Study Group Conference at Gregynog, Wales, and the Tel Aviv conference for helpful comments.

1. In Neary (1988) I have argued that the Brander-Spencer result can be understood as reflecting the same kind of considerations as those that underlie the Feenstra and Itoh-Kiyono results. In all of these cases an export subsidy has a direct effect of worsening the terms of trade of the subsidized commodity and an indirect effect that may improve the terms of trade in the markets for related goods. In the Cournot duopoly case the direct effect is exactly offset by the additional profits earned by the home firm, while the indirect effect must be welfare improving since (under plausible restrictions) the output of the foreign firm falls, which tends to improve the home country's terms of trade.

2. The Brander-Spencer result has also been shown to be sensitive to relaxations of the assumptions of only two firms (Dixit 1984), barriers to entry (Markusen and Venables 1988), and exogenously determined costs (Dixit and Grossman 1986).

3. Carmichael dealt with this problem by postulating an arbitrary upper bound on the contract price, but this begs the question of how the government agency chooses the limit. Carmichael's analysis also fails to justify an export subsidy.

4. By contrast, the home government always raises the subsidy to offset exactly half of a price cut by the foreign firm.

5. Browning (1987) provides estimates for the United States of the marginal welfare cost of taxes on labor earnings, equivalent to $\delta - 1$ (assuming that changes in export subsidies are matched by changes in labor taxes). His estimates (see his table 2, p. 21) imply a value for $\delta$ between 1.10 and 4.03, with his preferred estimates lying between 1.32 and 1.47.

6. By contrast, an output subsidy in this game reduces both firms' prices, the home price faster than the foreign. Of course these differences in the operation of the two types of subsidy are in fact illusory since they have identical effects on the net price of home output $p - \sigma$, and thus on the relative price of the two goods. This reflects the result found for the general specification of demand and costs in section 5.1, that output and price subsidies are equivalent in the ex ante game.

## References

Brander, J. A., and B. J. Spencer. 1985. Export subsidies and international market share rivalry. *Journal of International Economics* 18: 83–100.

Browning E. K. 1987. On the marginal welfare cost of taxation. *American Economic Review* 77: 11–23.

Carmichael, C. M. 1987. The control of export credit subsidies and its welfare consequences. *Journal of International Economics* 23: 1–19.

Dixit, A. 1984. International trade policy for oligopolistic industries. *Economic Journal* (suppl.) 94: 1–16.

Dixit, A., and G. M. Grossman. 1986. Targeted export promotion with several oligopolistic industries. *Journal of International Economics* 21: 233–249.

Eaton, J., and G. M. Grossman. 1986. Optimal trade and industrial policy under oligopoly. *Quarterly Journal of Economics* 101: 383–406.

Feenstra, R. C. 1986. Trade policy with several goods and "market linkages." *Journal of International Economics* 20: 249–267.

Gruenspecht, H. K. 1988. Export subsidies for differentiated products. *Journal of International Economics* 24: 331–344.

Itoh, M., and K. Kiyono. 1987. Welfare-enhancing export subsidies. *Journal of Political Economy* 95: 115–137.

Markusen, J. R., and A. J. Venables. 1988. Trade policy with increasing returns and imperfect competition: Contradictory results from competing assumptions. *Journal of International Economics* 24: 299–316.

Neary, J. P. 1988. Export subsidies and national welfare. *Empirica—Austrian Economic Papers* 15: 243–261.

# 6 Adverse Selection in Credit Markets and Infant Industry Protection

**Harry Flam and Robert W. Staiger**

A common justification for infant industry intervention in LDCs is that the workings of private capital markets are imperfect and can be improved upon. If such an argument is to provide a convincing rationale for intervention, two criteria must be met: First, the infant industry must be underfunded in the absence of intervention, and, second, intervention must increase the availability of funds in a way that is welfare improving.

In discussing this case for infant industry intervention, Baldwin (1969) argues that while the first criterion is likely to be met in the fledgling industries of LDCs, the second criterion is not. Baldwin has in mind a situation in which potential investors are initially overly pessimistic about the riskiness of new undertakings in the nontraditional sectors of the LDC and set overly high loan rates as a result. The high loan rates, in turn may choke off some or all of the potential infant industry activity: Protection can enable firms to overcome this handicap and pay the high loan rates initially demanded by investors. As Baldwin notes:

If this high return over a period of time is all that is needed for investors to acquire sufficient knowledge about the industry for the lending rate to be bid down to a rate reflecting actual risk levels in the industry, then a temporary tariff may be socially desirable. However, while some information about earning prospects is likely to be conveyed to investors by their payments experience, it is doubtful if the full information that is socially profitable in terms of investment in knowledge acquisiton will ever be conveyed to them simply by this sort of costless experience. The mere fact of tariff protection will make it difficult for investors to infer from their payments experience that they are overestimating investment risks in the industry. If this is so and the spillover problem also exists when outlays to obtain information are made, a temporary tariff cannot be relied upon to move production in the infant industry to a socailly optimal level. (p. 303)

We argue in this chapter that temporary protection in the presence of asymmetric information about risk can be desirable, not because investors learn about the risk characteristics of projects through experience gained by firms operating behind a tariff wall but because the tariff will alter the risk characteristics of the average entrant into the infant industry and, in so doing, internalize an important externality that keeps the degree of entry in an infant industry undesirably low. The logic is seen most simply by considering the case where all potential entrants into the infant industry share a common expected return but differ with respect to their probability of default. If banks are unable to distinguish individual firm default probabilities, the loan rate offered to potential entrants will include a premium that reflects the average default risk of the loan pool and that prevents profitable entry by the safest firms. Protection encourages the entry of these safer firms, lowering the average riskiness of projects in the infant industry. Accordingly, in the presence of protection, competitive investors will reduce their loan rates to infant industry firms. The favorable impact of the marginal firm's entry decision on the loan rate faced by all firms in the industry is a externality that can be internalized by a tariff. As we demonstrate below, a small amount of protection in the infant industry will be Pareto improving, and in general the optimal tariff for the infant industry is strictly positive.

Moreover we argue that informational symmetries may reverse the standard welfare ranking of tariffs and production subsidies as policy instruments for addressing production distortions. Specifically, if it is common knowledge that the government has access to information about the risk characteristics of individual firms that is not shared by potential foreign lenders, then it may be in the social interest for the government to commit not to use this private information when designing its infant industry policy. Because the benefits of a tariff are inherently nonselective with regard to the firms of an industry, while production subsidies can and often are administered on a "targeted" firm-specific basis, committing not to collect and exploit such private information may be less costly for the government under the former than under the latter program. Hence tariffs may dominate production subsidies as policy instruments for aiding the infant industry in this context.

We characterize the infant industry of an LDC as an industry in which norms have not yet been established, either in production or in financial relationships. Thus we have in mind the situation of a technological breakthrough that might allow domestic production of an import-competing good for the first time. Firms are new to the technology, and relationships between firms and banks are in their infancy, making the cost of bankruptcy to the firm less than if a long-term relationship between bank and firm already existed. Finally, firms are limited in their ability to collateralize loans. This is the setting within which adverse risk selection of the type studied in Stiglitz and Weiss (1981) is most likely to arise, and it is essentially the Stiglitz and Weiss framework within which our analysis is carried out. However, while Stiglitz and Weiss focus on credit-rationing equilibria, we focus on equilibria in which credit rationing does not arise. Hence our results depend only on the general properties of adverse selection in credit markets, and not no special conditions that lead to credit rationing.[1]

The chapter proceeds as follows: Section 6.1 lays out the basic model. Section 6.2 explores the properties of the equilibrium absent government intervention, and establishes that infant industry firms will be underfunded in the presence of adverse risk selection. Section 6.3 then examines the effect of tariff intervention and derives the optimal tariff for the infant industry. Section 6.4 considers several extensions, including the presence of projects with different expected returns and the role of production subsidies in the infant industry. Section 6.5 concludes the chapter.

## 6.1   The Model

The model we use to explore these issues is partial equilibrium and similar in spirit to the adverse selection model of Stiglitz and Weiss (1981). There are three players in the development of the infant industry under consideration: domestic firms who choose whether or not to take out a loan and enter the infant industry, foreign banks who choose the interest rate at which to make loans available to infant industry firms, and the domestic government who may choose to intervene. We consider each in turn.

### Firms

We assume that a continuum of potential infant industry entrants (firms) are indexed by $\theta \in [0, 1]$, with $G(\theta)(g(\theta))$ providing the distribution (density) of firms by $\theta$. Each firm is risk neutral and has at its disposal a stochastic technique for producing the infant industry good. One can think of the population of potential infant industry entrants as the set of entrepreneurs who have hit upon an idea of how to produce the infant industry good. All techniques require a fixed capital input $K$, an assumption we discuss in more detail below. This initial investment must be made prior to production, and it yields a plant with a capacity of one unit. While the prices of variable factors of production, such as labor, are fixed by conditions in the rest of the economy, variable factor inputs for unit production in firm $\theta$ are random, reflecting the riskiness of the particular production technique. Thus unit variable costs for firm $\theta$ are a random variable $c \in [0, 1]$ with mean $\bar{c}$, distribution function $F(c, \theta)$, and density function $f(c, \theta)$, where greater $\theta$ corresponds to greater risk in the sense of mean preserving spreads. Formally, $\theta' > \theta''$ implies that

$$\int_0^1 cf(c, \theta')\,dc = \int_0^1 cf(c, \theta'')\,dc \equiv \bar{c}, \tag{1}$$

and for $x \in [0, 1]$, that

$$\int_0^x F(c, \theta')\,dc \geq \int_0^x F(c, \theta'')\,dc. \tag{2}$$

Finally, all production will sell domestically at the price $P = (1 + \tau)$, where $\tau$ is the ad valorem tariff to be chosen by the domestic government, and the fixed world price has been normalized to one. Note that since variable unit costs $c$ will never exceed the domestic product price for $r \geq 0$, production for each firm that enters will always be set to capacity (one unit).[2] Thus each firm has only a single decision: whether or not to enter.

To enter the infant industry (build a plant), a firm must borrow the amount $K$ facing collateral requirements $m$ and loan rate $r$. We take $K$ as technologically fixed for each firm (entrepreneur) in the industry and, without loss of generality, assume that it is the same for all firms. The assumption of Leontief technologies is unnecessarily extreme but is sufficient to rule out the possibility noted in Midle and Riley (1988) of banks sorting firms by riskiness on the basis of loan size. We assume further that because of costly monitoring, banks do not offer loan rates that are contingent on the final outcome of the project.[3] The collateral requirment $m$ can be thought of as the maximum collateralization that firms in the infant industry can achieve. For simplicity, we assume that it is the same for all firms. Bester (1985) has shown that banks may be able to screen projects by risk by offering contracts that specify the loan rate and level of collateralization, provided that firms face no collateral constraint. Here we assume that firms are collateral constrained in the weak sense that $m < (1 + \delta)K$, with $\delta$ the bank cost of funds, and that it is costless for a firm to provide the collateral amount $m$. This ensures that no screening on the basis of collateral is feasible.[4]

While admittedly ad hoc, this list of assumptions is sufficient to ensure that the effects of asymmetric information between firms and bank cannot be eliminated by appropriate private contracts. This of course is a necessary starting point for a consideration of whether such informational asymmetries can give rise to a role for government intervention. However, it is clear that the restrictions we have placed on the ability of private markets to contend with informational asymmetries limit the applicability of our analysis to situations where the workings of private credit markets are themselves relatively undeveloped. Thus we reiterate here our belief that these conditions are most likely to be met in the relatively restrictive environment of LDCs.

A firm will default on its loan if the project return (net of variable factor payments) plus collateral is insufficient to pay off the loan, or if

$$(1 + \tau) - c + m \leq (1 + r)K. \tag{3}$$

Thus, if a firm has variable cost realization $c$, the firm's net profits will be

$$\pi(r, \tau, c) = \max[(1 + \tau) - c - (1 + r)K; -m], \tag{4}$$

whereas the bank's (gross) return on the loan will be

$$\rho(r, \tau, c) = \min[(1 + \tau) - c + m; (1 + r)K]. \tag{5}$$

The expected profit for firm $\theta$ is then given by

$$E\pi(r, \tau, \theta) = \int_0^1 \max[(1 + \tau) - c - (1 + r)K; -m] \, dF(c, \theta). \tag{6}$$

The expected (gross) return to the bank from this loan is

$$E\rho(r, \tau, \theta) = \int_0^1 \min[(1 + \tau) - c + m; (1 + r)K] \, dF(c, \theta). \tag{7}$$

**Banks**

Banks are located in the rest of the world and are assumed to be risk neutral.[5] Each firm's production technique is known by the banks to share the common expected variable unit cost $\bar{c}$, but banks do not observe individual firm $\theta$s. Thus the riskiness of a firm's production plan is unobserved by banks, who only observe the distribution $G(\theta)$ of firms by riskiness.

Banks compete for loan customers in the domestic infant industry facing a fixed cost of funds. The bank cost of funds is given by $\delta$ and is determined by credit conditions in the (large) world credit market. As discussed above, collateral levels are set at their maximum level of $m$. This implies that banks compete for infant industry borrowers by offering the lowest loan rate compatible with an expected return on loans to infant industry firms that is equal to the bank cost of funds.

## Government

We will consider explicity the effects on the infant industry of a tariff on imports and a production subsidy to infant industry firms. We measure the welfare effect of the tariff (production subsidy) by considering its impact on the sum of domestic producer and consumer surplus in the infant industry, plus tariff revenue (minus the cost of subsidy payments).

## 6.2  Equilibrium in the Absence of Intervention

In this section we characterize equilibrium in the absence of government intervention. With $\tau$ set to zero by assumption, the expected profit of an infant industry firm of type $\theta$ facing collateral requirements $m$ and loan rate $r$ is given by (6) as

$$E\pi(r, \tau = 0, \theta) = \int_0^1 \max[1 - c - (1 + r)K; -m] \, dF(c, \theta). \tag{8}$$

Since firm profits (given in (4)) are convex in $c$, expected firm profits increase with risk $\theta$. Thus for a given $r$, there may exist a level of riskiness $\tilde{\theta}(r, \tau = 0)$, below which expected profits become negative and firms choose not to enter.[6] For $r$ in the range that yields an interior solution $\tilde{\theta}(r) \in (0, 1)$, the critical value of $\theta$ is determined by the condition

$$E\pi(r, \tau = 0, \tilde{\theta}) = 0. \tag{9}$$

The adverse risk selection effect of higher interest rates can be seen by asking how $\tilde{\theta}$ changes with $r$. Total differentiation of (9) yields

$$\frac{d\tilde{\theta}}{dr} = -\frac{\partial E\pi/\partial r}{\partial E\pi/\partial \theta} \quad \text{for } \tilde{\theta}(r) \in (0, 1), \tag{10}$$

which is positive since expected firm profits are decreasing in $r$ but, as noted above, increasing in $\theta$.[7] Thus higher loan rates increase the riskiness of the applicant pool of entering infant industry firms.[8]

Finally, the expected (gross) return of a bank from a loan of size $K$ that lends at the loan rate $r$ is

$$E\rho(r, \tau = 0) = \frac{\int_{\tilde{\theta}(r, \tau=0)}^{1} E\rho(r, \tau = 0, \theta) \, dG(\theta)}{1 - G(\tilde{\theta}(r, \tau = 0))} \tag{11}$$

Since bank returns on a loan to firm $\theta$ (given in (5)) are concave in $c$, we have $dE\rho(r, \tau, \theta)/d\theta < 0$. With $d\tilde{\theta}/dr > 0$ by (10), $E\rho(r, \tau)$ as defined in (11) must be increasing in $r$ for $r$ close to zero but may be nonmonotonic in $r$ elsewhere, namely, when $\tilde{\theta}(r) \in (0, 1)$. We assume that conditions are such that there exist choices of $r$ that make $E\rho(r, \tau = 0) \geq (1 + \delta)K$. If this were not true, then banks would not lend to the infant industry at any interest rate, a situation referred to as "redlining" in Stiglitz and Weiss (1981). We focus here on the case in which neither redlining nor credit rationing are a problem.[9]

Given a fixed cost of funds $\delta$, perfect competition in the banking sector ensures that the equilibrium loan rate to infant industry firms will be bid down to the lowest $\hat{r}$, satisfying

$$\frac{E\rho(\hat{r}, \tau = 0)}{K} \equiv \frac{\int_{\theta(\hat{r}, \tau=0)}^{1} E\rho(\hat{r}, \tau = 0, \theta) \, dG(\theta)}{[1 - G(\hat{\theta}(\hat{r}, \tau = 0))]K} = 1 + \delta. \tag{12}$$

Equilibrium condition (12) determines the equilibrium loan rate faced by infant industry firms, $\hat{r}$, and through $\hat{\theta}(\hat{r}, \tau = 0)$, the risk characteristics of the entering infant industry firms.

We conclude this section with a result that implies that the infant industry will be underfunded in the absence of intervention and will characterize the capital market imperfection that may give rise to the possibility of welfare-improving policies of infant industry intervention.

PROPOSITION 1    If $\hat{\theta}(\hat{r}(\tau = 0), \tau = 0) < 1$, then $(1 - \bar{c})/K > 1 + \delta$.

*Proof*  With $E\rho(r, \tau, \theta)$ decreasing in $\theta$ and $E\pi(\hat{r}(\tau), \tau, \hat{\theta}) = 0$, equilibrium condition (12) implies that

$$\frac{E\rho(\hat{r}(\tau), \tau, \hat{\theta})}{K} + \frac{E\pi(\hat{r}(\tau), \tau, \hat{\theta})}{K} > 1 + \delta, \tag{13}$$

which, using (6) and (7), reduces under free trade to

$$\frac{1 - \bar{c}}{K} > 1 + \delta. \blacksquare \tag{14}$$

Proposition 1 states that a necessary condition for any lending to occur in the infant industry, $\hat{\theta} < 1$, is that the expected social return of infant industry projects be strictly positive, $1 - \bar{c} - (1 + \delta)K > 0$. Thus we can state the following:

COROLLARY    If $\hat{\theta}(\hat{r}(\tau = 0), \tau = 0) \in (0, 1)$, then there exist infant industry firms with socially desirable projects that, in the absence of intervention, fail to get funded.

Typically, $\hat{\theta}(\hat{r}(\tau = 0), \tau = 0)$ will be strictly greater than zero. This is because the possibility of default leads banks to raise the loan rate $r$ above the cost of funds $\delta$ in order to secure an expected return that covers the cost of funds. Since banks don't observe individual firm default probabilities, the increase in the loan rate must reflect the *average* default probability of the loan pool. Consequently firms with low default probabilities (low $\theta$s) may find their projects unprofitable at the prevailing loan rate, even though their expected project returns exceed the social cost of funds $\delta$. This is the sense in which adverse risk selection may lead to under funding of the infant industry.

Proposition 1 has an externality interpretation in the spirit of Greenwald and Stiglitz (1986). In particular, the low $\theta$ (safer) firms that choose not to borrow at the loan rate $\hat{r}(\tau)$ do not internalize the favorable effect that their entry would have on the average default risk for the loan pool and hence on the competitive loan rate offered by banks to all infant industry firms. In this sense there is too little entry into the infant industry. Hence policies that encourage entry into the infant industry may, by reducing the bank loan rate, increase the level of domestic welfare from the no-intervention equilibrium. We turn now to an analysis of the effects of intervention.

## 6.3    The Effects of Protection

In this section we examine the effects of government intervention in the infant industry in the form of a tariff on imports into the infant industry. We begin by showing that a small tariff will be welfare improving, and then we derive an expression for the optimal tariff. Welfare in the domestic infant industry is measured as the sum of domestic producer surplus, domestic consumer surplus, and tariff revenues, and can be written as a function of the tariff $\tau$ as

$$W(\hat{r}(\tau), \tau) = E\pi(\hat{r}(\tau), \tau) + \left[ \int_{1+\tau}^{\infty} D(p)\, dp \right] + [\tau(D(1 + \tau) - Q(1 + \tau))], \quad (15)$$

where $E\pi(\hat{r}(\tau), \tau) \equiv \int_{\theta(\hat{r}(\tau), \tau)}^{1} E\pi(\hat{r}(\tau), \tau, \theta)\, dG(\theta)$ is domestic producer surplus, $D(\cdot)$ is domestic demand for the infant industry good, and $Q(\cdot)$ is domestic supply, and where the large number of infant industry firms eliminates aggregate (industrywide) uncertainty.

PROPOSITION 2   If $\hat{\theta}(\hat{r}(\tau = 0), \tau = 0) \in (0, 1)$, then $\left. \dfrac{dW}{d\tau} \right|_{\tau=0} > 0$.

*Proof*  Using equilibrium condition (12), domestic producer surplus can be written as

$$E\pi(\hat{r}(\tau), \tau) = [(1 + \tau) - \bar{c} - (1 + \delta)K]Q(1 + \tau). \quad (16)$$

Substituting (16) into (15) and differentiating at $\tau = 0$ yields

$$\left. \frac{dW}{d\tau} \right|_{\tau=0} = -[(1 - \bar{c}) - (1 + \delta)K]g(\hat{\theta}) \left. \frac{d\hat{\theta}}{d\tau} \right|_{\tau=0}. \quad (17)$$

From proposition 1 we know that $(1 - \bar{c})$ must be strictly greater than $(1 + \delta)K$ if $\hat{\theta} < 1$, that is, if any lending takes place absent intervention. Thus the sign of $\left. \dfrac{dW}{d\tau} \right|_{\tau=0}$ is opposite that of $\left. \dfrac{d\hat{\theta}}{d\tau} \right|_{\tau=0}$, which is readily shown to be negative (i.e., a small tariff induces domestic entry).   ∎

Finally, it is straightforward to derive the optimal tariff for the infant industry

$$\hat{\tau} = \left[ \frac{(1 - \bar{c}) - (1 + \delta)K}{D'(1 + \hat{\tau})} \right] g(\hat{\theta}) \frac{d\hat{\theta}(\hat{r}(\hat{\tau}), \hat{\tau})}{d\tau}, \quad (18)$$

which is strictly positive. Expression (18) makes clear the point that the welfare-enhancing role of the infant industry tariff stems from its entry-promoting effects, $d\hat{\theta}(\hat{r}(\hat{\tau}), \hat{\tau})/d\tau < 0$, in an industry where expected social returns to further entry are positive, $[(1 - \bar{c}) - (1 + \delta)K] > 0$. This benefit must be weighted at the margin against the costs of distortions in consumption, $D'(1 + \hat{\tau}) < 0$.

We close this section with several comments. First, since it is not immediately apparent from the optimal tariff formula in (18), it deserves re-emphasis that the *entire* domestic welfare gain from infant industry intervention comes in the form of a reduction in the loan rate faced by all infant industry firms.[10] As such, time consistency issues are likely to arise in the implementation of this infant industry program. In particular, the government has an incentive to announce high tariffs to secure low-interest loans for its firms but to renege on the promised protection once plants are built and production begins. Such incentives would tend to undermine the credibility of the announced program, and could lead to underutilization of infant industry protection in this context.[11] Second, in the context of infant industry protection, the question of how the industry "grows up" naturally arises. Although a formal analysis of this question would require a dynamic model, it seems natural to think of the accumulation of profits and the subsequent relaxation of the collateral constraint as the central mechanism by which the capital market imperfection that provides the rationale for the infant industry policy would over time disappear.[12] Finally, as with optimal taxation generally, to set the tariff optimally, the government must have information about the key parameters. Among other things the implementation of the optimal tariff in (18) requires knowledge of the industry product demand function and the distribution of firms in the industry by risk type. In applying a welfare-improving small tariff, on the other hand, the government need only observe that the loan rate fall to know that its infant industry intervention has increased welfare.

## 6.4  Extensions

In this section we consider several extensions to the analysis of the previous section. We begin by relaxing the assumption that all projects in the infant industry share the same expected return. We show that a welfare-improving role for infant industry intervention generally remains, though the sign of that intervention can be reversed if the selection effect of the loan rate by expected return becomes sufficiently dominant to overwhelm the selection effect by risk that was the focus of the previous sections. We then comment on the role of production subsidies in the development of the infant industry.

### Multiple Expected Returns

It is straightforward to show that the role for infant industry protection laid out above is largely preserved in the presence of variation in the expected return of projects in the infant industry. If banks can distinguish between projects of different mean return, then the analysis of the previous sections will apply directly to each observationally distinguishable group. In particular, proposition 1 will hold so that any group receiving loans under free trade will have a strictly higher expected return than the social cost of funds. Therefore, if there exists a loan group $i$ with $\hat{\theta}_i(\hat{r}_i(r = 0)$, $r = 0) \in (0, 1)$, then there exists infant industry firms with socially desirable projects that, in the absence of intervention, fail to get funded. Hence a small tariff will be welfare improving.[13]

If banks can only distinguish dichotomously between projects whose expected social returns exceed the cost of funds, on the one hand, and projects whose expected social returns fall short of the cost of funds, on the other, then again the analysis of the previous section will apply to each observationally distinguishable group. In particular, suppose that banks can identify those projects for which, if firm type could be observed, a loan contract could be written that would be acceptable to both parties.[14] This will be the group of projects with socially worthwhile expected returns. Absent intervention, loans will be made, if at all, only to this group of projects, at a loan rate reflecting the average risk and return characteristics of the pool. If there exist relatively safe projects whose expected social returns, while greater than cost, are not sufficient to cover the risk premium associated with the competitive loan rate, then these socially worthwhile projects will fail to get funded, and a small tariff will be welfare improving.

It is only when banks are unable to distinguish between projects whose expected social returns exceed the cost of funds and those that do not that the possibility arises of "too much" entry absent intervention. In particular, in this case it is possible that in equilibrium the distribution of marginal borrowers by expected returns is such that banks (and thus society since profits of the marginal firms are zero by definition) make negative expected returns on loans to this marginal group and yet earn a competitive expected return overall due to an inframarginal distribution of loan types skewed heavily toward high expected return firms. When this is the case, there is too much entry in the infant industry, and an entry-deterring infant industry import subsidy would be called for. Thus an important element in the design of appropriate policy in this context is an understanding of the nature of the private information that firms possess, and of its relative importance for assessing project riskiness and expected returns.[15] Even here, however, there is at least in principal a simple very to engineer a welfare-improving program of infant industry intervention: Simply adopt a "small" amount of intervention in whatever direction results in a fall in the bank loan rate to infant industry firms. A small tariff (subsidy) will lead to a fall in the equilibrium bank loan rate if and only if, on average, the social return of marginal entrants induced into (out of) the infant industry by the intervention is strictly positive (negative).

**Production Subsidies**

The capital market imperfection that we have analyzed above results in a production distortion in the infant industry because a socially deficient level of entry occurs under free trade. A tariff, which is a combination production subsidy/consumption tax, can partially address this production distortion but is potentially inferior as a policy tool to a direct production (or capital) subsidy for two reasons:[16] First, the tariff finances its production subsidy with a distortionary tax on domestic consumers of the infant industry good, whereas a direct production subsidy may be financed by a less distortionary means if such taxes are available, and, second, the tariff taxes domestic consumers at a rate that raises more revenue than is needed to finance its subsidy to infant industry producers (the excess being the tariff revenue), and thus utilizes the distortionary consumption tax excessively as compared to the revenue needs of the production subsidy.

The notion that a tariff is a second-best policy for addressing a production distortion for the two reasons outlined above comes directly from the theory of targeting in the presence of distortions. However, in the present context there is a third relevant distinction between tariffs and subsidies, which is that the latter can be offered selectively to a subset of firms in the infant industry, whereas the former cannot.[17] In this subsection we consider the use of production subsidies in the infant industry, focusing on this third distinction. Specifically, we ask under what conditions the government, rather than following a uniform production subsidy policy in the infant industry, would choose to collect firm-specific information about domestic infant industry firms and to target specific firms with production subsidies.[18] We then show that when the government would prefer instead to pursue a uniform nonselective subsidy policy, it may have difficulty establishing a credible commitment to do so, and a tariff may represent a relatively low-cost way of achieving such commitment.

If the government has collected firm-specific information and is selectively subsidizing firms on the basis of its knowledge of firm type, the effects of its intervention on bank-lending activity are altered dramatically from the previous analysis. In particular, each firm's collateral constraint is effectively lifted as the government's firm-specific subsidy level becomes the firm's collateral. This in turn implies that banks can now offer screening contracts that sort firms according to type. Such contracts specify pairs of subsidy levels and loan rates that exploit the systematic dependence of government preferences over subsidy/loan rate combinations on the risk characteristics of each firm. We begin by characterizing these screening contracts and show that they will in fact be the only contracts offered by banks when the government is selectively subsidizing firms.

To show this, we suppose that each domestic firm's private knowledge about its own $\theta$ can be revealed to the domestic government at a cost $v$, but that foreign banks continue to know only the risk characteristics of the applicant pool as a whole. Suppose further that if the government chooses to subsidize production in the infant industry, banks can observe whether a particular loan applicant received a subsidy and, if so, the level of the subsidy. Finally, we simplify the ensuing analysis by restricting our attention to a special case of the model of the previous sections in which there are only two types of firms, indexed by $\theta = \{1, 2\}$. Both types of projects share the same expected return, but type-1 projects are perfectly safe while type-2 projects are risky. Moreover, for simplicity, we set the collateral supplied by the firm, $m$, equal to zero.

If the government learns firm types, it can design a type-specific subsidy program, $s(\theta)$. We assume that the government does not have available to it lump-sum tax instruments, so financing the subsidy payments (and learning costs) is achieved through some form of distortionary taxation in the LDC economy. For simplicity, we let the distortionary costs of government finance be constant so that the cost of generating a dollar of government revenue is given by $(1 + q)$ with $q > 0$.

Once the government has paid the amount $v$ to learn domestic firm types, its expected return from subsidizing a firm of type $\theta$ at the rate $s(\theta)$, given a loan rate $r$, is given by the expected firm profits net of the cost of subsidy payments, or

$$E\pi(r, s(\theta), \theta) - (1 + q)s(\theta) = \int_0^1 \max[1 - (c - s(\theta))$$

$$- (1 + r)K; 0]dF(c, \theta) - (1 + q)s(\theta)$$

$$= \int_0^1 \max[(1 - c) - (1 + r)K - qs(\theta);$$

$$-(1 + q)s(\theta)]dF(c, \theta). \tag{19}$$

The important point to note from (19) is that the government's expected return from subsidizing firm $\theta$ at the rate $s(\theta)$ given $r$ is exactly the expected profit of firm $\theta$ facing a loan rate $r$ and collateral requirements $s(\theta)$ and a cost $q$ per dollar of collateral generated. Thus the banks' problem is identical to that studied in Bester (1985) in which banks offer a menu of loan rate and collateral combinations to firms that face a common per unit cost of raising collateral. As such, a bank that offers screening contracts defining different combinations of the loan rate and collateralization can sort firms by risk (through the implicit collateralization $s(\theta)$ determined by the government subsidies). Moreover banks will only offer such contracts since any other loan contracts would be unprofitable.

To establish this, we first characterize screening contracts involving the minimum (nonnegative) subsidy requirements and then show that these are the only contracts that banks will offer when the government is known to be selectively subsidizing its firms. Since subsidies perform the role of collateral as confirmed by (19), the government will find loan contracts with high subsidy requirements relatively unattractive for its risky firms. Thus competitive screening contracts for safe firms will stipulate a riskless loan rate $\delta$ and a subsidy requirement $\hat{s}$ that is sufficiently high to prevent the government from getting an expected return with its risky firms from a "safe" loan contract with $(r = \delta, s = \hat{s})$ that exceeds $[(1 - \bar{c}) - (1 + \delta)K]$, the expected return for risky projects under an alternative "risky" loan contract with a zero subsidy requirement and competitive loan rate for risky firms. Using (19), $\hat{s}$ is thus defined implicitly by

$$E\pi(\delta, \hat{s}, \theta = 2) - (1 + q)\hat{s} = [(1 - \bar{c}) - (1 + \delta)K].$$

Explicit calculation yields

$$\hat{s} = \frac{\int_{\underline{c}(\hat{s})}^1 [(1 + \delta)K - (1 - c)]dF(c, \theta = 2)}{q + [1 - F(\bar{c}(\hat{s}), \theta = 2)]}, \tag{20}$$

where $\underline{c}(\hat{s})$ is the realization of $c$ at which a risky (type-2) firm goes bankrupt, when facing a loan rate $\delta$, and is given explicitly by

$\underline{c}(\hat{s}) = 1 + \hat{s} - (1 + \delta)K.$

A stipulation by banks that firms must secure a subsidy $\hat{s}$ in order to qualify for the riskless loan rate $\delta$ ensures that the government will have no incentive to masquerade its risky firms as riskless by offering them a subsidy $\hat{s}$. To see that only such screening contracts will be offered by banks when the government can selectively subsidize, note that for $q > 0$ any pooling contract must have $(s < \hat{s}, r > \delta)$.[19] But with government returns from subsidizing risky and safe firms equalized at $(\hat{s}, \delta)$ by the definition of $\hat{s}$, any pooling contract with $s < \hat{s}$ and $r > \delta$ and yielding a competitive return to the bank must have the government receiving on risky projects more than it would receive from a screening contract and on safe projects less than it would receive from a screening contract. Thus, if banks can offer screening contracts, poling contracts will not survive because they will attract only risky firms and thus be unprofitable to the banks.

Finally, ignoring for the moment the government's cost of collecting information $(1 + q)v$, the government return associated with each type of firm under the equilibrium screening contracts will be given by (19) as

$$E\pi(r(\theta), s(\theta), \theta) - (1 + q)s(\theta) = \begin{cases} [(1 - \bar{c}) - (1 + \delta)K] - q\hat{s} & \text{for } \theta = 1, \\ [(1 - \bar{c}) - (1 + \delta)K] & \text{for } \theta = 2. \end{cases}$$

Provided that this return is positive for both firm types, the government will choose, given information about firm types, to support full entry of all domestic infant industry firms. The total subsidy requirement to support full entry of infant industry firms when the government offers firm-specific subsidies based on its knowledge of firm type will then be given by

$$\hat{S} = \gamma N \hat{s}, \tag{21}$$

where $N$ is the total number of domestic firms in the infant industry and $\gamma$ is the fraction of type-1 (safe) projects. Since $\hat{s}$ is independent of $\gamma$, (21) implies that when the government can target specific infant industry firms on the basis of its knowledge of firm types, the subsidy requirements $\hat{S}$ necessary to induce complete funding of the infant industry will be rising linearly out of the origin as a function of the proportion of safe projects $\gamma$.

Now consider the subsidy requirements to support complete funding of the domestic infant industry when instead the government chooses not to collect firm-specific information but rather to offer a common subsidy to all domestic firms in the industry. With the possibility of screening contracts now precluded, banks will offer pooling contracts to domestic firms. We have established above that a pooling contract must have $(s < \hat{s}, r > \delta)$. Moreover competitive banks will offer that pooling contract which contains the smallest subsidy requirement. This contract will offer the greater surplus to the government since it minimizes the deadweight loss associated with the subsidy finance distortion $q$, subject to providing banks with a competitive expect return on the loan. Finally, we have also established that safe firms receive a lower expected return than risky projects for any pooling contract with $(s < \hat{s}, r > \delta)$. Thus the competitive pooling contract $(\tilde{s}, \tilde{r})$ will be a subsidy/loan rate combination with the lowest subsidy such that safe firms make nonnegative profits on the loan and banks make competitive expected returns when all firms (and firm types) are borrowing. Explicit calculation yields the following expression for $\tilde{s}$:

$$\tilde{s} = [(1 - \gamma) \cdot \int_0^{c(\tilde{s})} (\bar{c} - c) dF(\underline{c}(\tilde{s}), \theta = 2)] - [(1 - \bar{c}) - (1 + \delta)K]. \tag{22}$$

The first term in brackets on the right-hand side of (22) is strictly positive, and the second term in brackets is just the expected social return of the project which, by assumption, is strictly positive as well. Since this subsidy must be offered nonselectively to all firms, the total subsidy requirements needed to achieve complete funding of the domestic infant industry when the government offers a uniform subsidy to all infant industry firms is given by

$$\tilde{S} = N\tilde{s}. \tag{23}$$

Using (22), expression (23) implies that when the government is offering uniform subsidies, the subsidy revenues required to support full funding of the domestic infant industry are falling linearly in the proportion of safe firms in the industry and go to zero at some $\tilde{\gamma} < 1$.

Having derived expressions for the total subsidy payments required to achieve complete funding of the domestic infant industry both when the government is offering uniform subsidies $\tilde{S}$ and when it is targeting selected firms $\hat{S}$, we now plot in figure 6.1 the values of $\tilde{S}$ and $\hat{S}$ as linear functions of $\gamma$, the proportion of safe firms in the domestic industry. As depicted in the figure, there exists a critical $\hat{\gamma} \in (0, \tilde{\gamma})$ such that the subsidy payments required to fully fund the domestic industry will be lower for a government that follows a uniform subsidy policy if and only if $\hat{\gamma} \in (\hat{\gamma}, 1)$, that is, if and

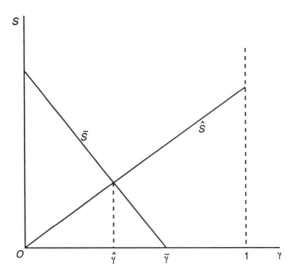

**Figure 6.1**

only if the proportion of safe firms is sufficiently high. Intuitively this result reflects the fundamentally different role played by the government subsidy under the two assumptions about government behavior. When the government selectively subsidizes based on its firm-specific knowledge, it ends up subsidizing safe projects to facilitate screening, and this will imply low subsidy costs in funding the infant industry when the number of safe projects is relatively small. Alternatively, when the government announces a uniform subsidy offered to all firms, then the subsidy is required to reduce the risk to banks of an average loan to the point where the competitive loan rate allows safe firms to enter. If there are many safe firms and few risky firms, then only a small subsidy per firm (if any at all) will be needed to reduce the risk premium to the required level.

   Provided the government's cost of information collection is not too large, it is clear from figure 6.1 that there will exist a critical $\bar{\gamma} \in (0, \hat{\gamma})$ below which the savings in subsidy finance costs associated with targeting, $q(\hat{S} - \tilde{S})$, outweight the cost of information gathering required for the targeting policy, $(1 + q)v$, and the government will choose to pursue a policy of targeting over a uniform subsidy in the infant industry. For $\gamma \in (\bar{\gamma}, 1)$ a uniform subsidy program is preferable. Thus a policy of targeting selected infant industry firms rather than offering uniform subsidies to all firms in the industry will be most beneficial when the proportion of risky firms in the industry is high.

Finally, although the government will wish to commit to a uniform subsidy policy whenever $\gamma > \bar{\gamma}$, it may not find such commitments costless. In particular, as we have noted above in the context of a tariff, the entire benefit of the uniform subsidy program comes in the form of a lower bank loan rate for domestic firms than they would receive absent government intervention. For a *fixed* loan rate there is no externality, domestic firms make the correct entry decisions, and there is no need for government intervention. Thus, if foreign banks can not monitor the government's promise to offer subsidies to all firms, the government will have an incentive to secretly acquire information about firm types and, regardless of its announced intentions, to follow through with subsidy offers selectively to only those firms that would be profitable absent a subsidy at the prevailing loan rate.[20] Such a selective subsidy policy would raise expected domestic profits net of subsidy payments above that associated with a uniform subsidy at the expense of foreign banks. Of course, aware of this incentive, foreign banks would discount government statements to the contrary and offer loan contracts that yield a competitive return under the assumption that the government does collect firm-specific information and is selectively subsidizing. Thus, absent some mechanism by which to commit to a uniform nonselective subsidy program, the government may become trapped in the suboptimal position of offering targeted subsidies to selected infant industry firms even if $\gamma \in (\bar{\gamma}, 1)$.[21]

In practice, for $\gamma \geq \tilde{\gamma}$ full funding will be achieved in the absence of any subsidy at all so that a commitment to uniform treatment (no subsidy) seems straightforward. However, for $\gamma \in (\bar{\gamma}, \tilde{\gamma})$ full funding requires *some* subsidy program, and a commitment to subsidize uniformly across all firms of the industry may be difficult to enforce. A tariff is one way to commit to the uniform treatment of domestic firms, with the cost of the commitment to a uniform subsidy via a tariff coming in the form of consumption distortions induced by the associated consumption tax. Whether a tariff is the least costly way of achieving this commitment depends on the cost of the alternative. However, as $\gamma$ rises toward $\tilde{\gamma}$, the tariff required to support full funding approaches zero, and the distortionary costs associated with the tariff—and thus the cost of commitment via the tariff—approach zero as well.

## 6.5 Summary and Conclusion

We have shown that in an industry where firms have expected returns higher than the cost of funds on the world capital market, and where investors have no information about the riskiness of individual firms and are unable to employ contracts that would screen firms according to riskiness, the industry will typically be underfunded in the sense that some socially worthwhile firms do not enter. A small tariff on competing imports would allow relatively safe firms to enter, lowering the cost of borrowing for all firms, and would consequently increase welfare. The optimal tariff balances this gain against the cost of the usual distortion in consumption. Moreover, although generally a uniform production subsidy to infant industry firms will be a better policy than a tariff, we have shown that if the proportion of risky firms in the infant industry is sufficiently high, a government targeting policy may be better yet. However, if the proportion of risky firms is low, and if the government has difficulty committing not to collect and use firm-specific information in its infant industry subsidy program by other means, a tariff may be an attractive alternative to achieve this commitment and may dominate a production subsidy on that basis (see also chapter 4 by Tornell for a discussion of the role of commitment in industrial policy).

We argue that the setting that is required for these results is typical for an infant industry in an LDC. The infancy of the industry means that little information exists about firms, and the low level of income and general scarcity of capital in LDCs implies that relatively little risk capital is available. Our model should therefore not be taken as a general argument for intervention in infant industries anywhere since the collateral constraints central to our arguments are presumably less important in developed countries.

In addition to the sensitivity of these results to the nature and relevance of private information possessed by firms, our case for infant industry protection is open to a general point of criticism of arguments for intervention, namely, that it does not incorporate all the aspects of intervention and therefore does not make a correct comparison of two alternatives. In particular, it does not incorporate general equilibrium or political economy aspects and associated costs (see chapter 7 by Hillman on the latter point). It is possible that when such costs are taken into account the scope for welfare-improving intervention becomes much smaller or even nonexistent.

Still, even if this is the case, our model points to an important externality that may exist in infant industries in LDCs and to a welfare gain that should be included in complete account of the gains and losses from intervention.

## Notes

This paper has benefited from the very helpful comments of Gene Grossman, Daniel Tsiddon, two anonymous referees, and seminar participants at the Institute for International Economic Studies in Stockholm and the Pinhas Sapir Center for Economic Development in Tel-Aviv. Staiger gratefully acknowledges financial support from the Institute for International Economic Studies and the Center for Research in International Studies and Flam from the Bank of Sweden Tercentenary Foundation.

1. DeMeza and Webb (1987) have pointed out that the conclusions of Stiglitz and Weiss (1981) are sensitive to the particular way in which private information enters the model, a theme that also arises in this chapter. Our results, however, differ form those of DeMeza and Webb in that we focus on characterizing the appropriate use of specific policy instruments (i.e., tariffs and targeted subsidies) that are of particular interest in the context of infant industry intervention.

2. Allowing realizations of variable costs to exceed price, in which case firms would choose not to produce, will not alter the analysis in any important way. Also, defining $\tau$ as a tariff implies that the infant industry is import competing. Alternatively, $\tau$ could represent an advalorem export subsidy to an export-oriented infant industry without any change in the analysis and the results.

3. Townsend (1979) demonstrates that costly state verification can make complete risk sharing suboptimal. A debt contract is a way to economize on state verification costs since there is only one state (bankruptcy) that must be monitored. Since the addition of monitoring costs in the event of bankruptcy to our formal model has no effect on the nature of our results, provided only that expected monitoring costs are nondecreasing in the riskiness of the loan, we leave monitoring costs out in what follows.

4. It is straightforward to show that with $m < (1 + \delta)K$ and costless to provide, the incentive compatibility and competitive bank return conditions required for each loan under screening are made inconsistent by the convexity of firm profits in the returns of the project.

5. The location of banks becomes important only when we consider the government's incentives in offering production subsidies in section 6.4.

6. See Stiglitz and Weiss (1981), thm. 1.

7. See Stiglitz and Weiss (1981), thm. 2.

8. We focus here on the risk selection effect of changes in the loan rate rather than selection by expected project return. In reality both effects are likely to be present, and in section 6.4 we take up this issue. See also DeMeza and Webb (1987).

9. Credit rationing in the sense of Stiglitz and Weiss (1981) could never occur in this model, given our assumption that credit is available in infinite supply at the rate $\delta$. See Tomlinson (1987) for a treatment of the role of infant industry protection in a model where the presence of moral hazard leads to credit rationing absent intervention.

10. The gain associated with the fall in the loan rate is embodied, however, in the additional entry it induces. In particular, the gain is not a terms-of-trade effect, as can be seen by noting that whether banks are foreign or domestic is immaterial to the welfare effect of the tariff.

11. For a related point in a more general context, see Staiger and Tabellini (1989).

12. Of course, as the political economy literature on protection has pointed out, this in no way implies that protection *will* be temporary, but only that it "ought" to be.

13. An implication of proposition 1 is that a small tariff could never induce bank funding of a new socially inefficient group of firms as long as banks can distinguish between project groups of different mean return.

14. This will be possible if the firm-specific information unknown to the bank is not relevant for assessing the expected return of the project but only its riskiness, or more generally if the observable firm characteristics allow a sufficiently complete characterization of expected project returns.

15. This point is also made in DeMeza and Webb (1987).

16. In the simple model we have analyzed here, production and capital subsidies are equivalent, though see also note 20.

17. The selectivity distinction between tariffs and production subsidies has been made previously by Rodrik (1986) in a different context.

18. We continue to assume that such information gathering is prohibitively costly for foreign banks.

19. This is because any pooling contract with $r < \delta$, or with $r = \delta$ and $s \leq \hat{s}$, would be unprofitable to banks, whereas any pooling contract with $r \geq \delta$ and $s > \hat{s}$ or with $r > \delta$ and $s \geq \hat{s}$ would be rejected by the government in favor of a screening contract $(\hat{s}, \delta)$. This leaves pooling contracts with $s < \hat{s}$ and $r > \delta$ as the only remaining possibility.

20. There is also the additional question raised in the previous section of whether the government, once loans have been granted and plants built, would actually follow through on its subsidy promise. This time consistency issue could be avoided with a capital rather than a production subsidy.

21. Note that a simple law that made it illegal to offer targeted subsidies to selected firms could be quite a costly way to achieve the commitment since it would preclude targeting even when targeting is the preferred policy, that is, when $\gamma \in (0, \bar{\gamma})$.

## References

Baldwin, Robert E. 1969. The case against infant-industry tariff protection. *Journal of Political Economy* 77: 295–305.

Bester, Helmut. 1985. Screening vs. rationing in credit markets with imperfect information. *American Economic Review* 75 (September): 850–855.

DeMeza, David, and David C. Webb. 1987. Too much investment: A problem of asymmetric information. *Quarterly Journal of Economics* 102 (May): 281–292.

Greenwald, Bruce G., and Joseph E. Stiglitz. 1986. Externalities in economies with imperfect information and incomplete markets. *Quarterly Journal of Economics* 101 (May): 229–264.

Milde, Hellmuth, and John G. Riley. 1988. Signaling in credit markets. *Quarterly Journal of Economics* 103 (February): 101–129.

Rodrik, Dani. 1986. Tariffs, subsidies and welfare with endogenous policy. *Journal of International Economics* 21 (November): 285–299.

Staiger, Robert W., and Guido Tabellini. 1989. Rules and discretion in trade policy. *European Economic Review* 33 (August): 1265–1277.

Stiglitz, Joseph E., and Andrew Weiss. 1981. Credit rationing in markets with imperfect information. *American Economic Review* 71 (June): 393–410.

Tomlinson, Steven R. 1987. Developing countries in the international capital market: An information based infant industry argument. Unpublished manuscript. Stanford University. November.

Townsend, Robert. 1979. Optimal contracts and competitive markets with costly state verification. *Journal of Economic Theory* 21 (October): 265–293.

# 7 Protection, Politics, and Market Structure

**Arye L. Hillman**

The profits of an enterprise can increase as the consequence of monitoring of production activities by residual claimants (owners of firms) or as the consequence of changes in economic policies that affect the value of claims to factor ownership. In this chapter, I present a model in which residual claimants within an Alchian-Demsetz firm (Alchian and Demsetz 1972; Demsetz 1988) choose between engaging in monitoring activities that increase the returns from their capital ownership and undertaking political activities that yield gains via protectionist policies. The model describes the endogenous determination of an industry's level of protection via the decision to allocate scarce managerial and entrepreneurial skills between political and economic activity, and yields predictions that can be used to shed light on a question central to the literature concerned with endogenous protection: Do the diverse protectionist outcomes that are observed across industries reflect collective action by self-interested coalitions seeking to exert political influence on the determination of trade policy? Or does an explanation based on social insurance or altruism underlie protectionist policies that redistribute income domestically?[1]

The political-influence model of endogenous protection is based on the concept of "cohesive coalitions" (see Mancur Olson 1965). A predicton that has been associated with the model is that market structure will affect an industry's level of protection, since cohesion will be reflected in the concentration of industry. In accord with this interpretation, more concentrated industries should, ceteris paribus, be more successful in securing favorable protectionist responses. Yet the empirical evidence has not consistently indicated this to be so. Empirical evidence confirms the role of political-support motives in explaining trade policy decisions by elected representatives. However, from the perspective of the attributes of beneficiaries of protection, greater concentration of industry has not been revealed to be consistently associated with greater protection.[2]

This chapter interprets the evidence on the relation between market structure and protection in the setting of an Alchian-Demsetz approach to the theory of the firm, with the added distinction between the private gain from monitoring of the firm's internal production activities and the collective or public-good nature of the benefit from lobbying to secure protection. The role of market structure in influencing protectionist outcomes is investigated when cohesion is reflected both in the number of firms in an industry and in industry concentration ratios based on market shares of a designated number of leading firms. The results reveal that the predictions of a political-influence model of endogenous protection are compatible with the empirical relationships that have been reported between market structure and industry levels of protection. In particular, higher concentration ratios are shown not necessarily to imply that more resources will be allocated to increasing the political influence of an industry seeking protection.

The chapter proceeds as follows: Section 7.1 sets out the model. Sections 7.2 and 7.3 demonstrate the characteristics of noncooperative and cooperative equilibria in contributions to political activity. Section 7.4 establishes the relation between protection and market structure when the number of firms is an indicator of industry cohesion. In section 7.5 the same relation is investigated when the indicator of industry cohesion is an industry concentration ratio. Section 7.6 applies the model to an interpretation of the results of previous empirical studies.

The model that follows assumes that protectionist policies are determined in an institutional setting of representative democracy.[3] That is, voters delegate authority with regard to the determination of trade (and other) policies to elected representatives. Since the behavior of elected representatives can be only imperfectly monitored by voters, a principal-agent problem arises with respect to policy determination. Pareto-inferior protectionist policies can as a consequence be chosen by elected representatives. A theory of endogenous protection under the alternative assumption of direct democracy would view protectionist outcomes as the direct expression of voters' preferences and would use a decision rule such as the median-voter theorem to establish the equilibrium trade policy.[4] A direct-democracy model of endogenous protection can of course explain the differential levels of protection achieved by different industries if voters have been presented with the opportunity to express their preferences regarding the levels of protection they would want for each industry. However, in the economies from which the empirical studies draw their data, international trade policies are not determined through direct democracy. A framework consistent with these studies thus requires a setting of representative democracy.

## 7.1   The Model

### The Beneficiaries of Protection

I begin by formulating a model that is distingusihed from previous analyses of politically endogenous determination of trade policy in that it focuses on the discretionary activity of residual claimants to the profits of import-competing firms. The theory of the firm adopted here[5] emphasizes the monitoring and coordinating role of residual claimants. This perception of the firm stresses that the incentive to organize production within the firm derives from the claim to the rewards from successful coordination of the firm's production and marketing activities. The incentive to engage in monitoring and coordinating activities arises because of the obstacle to team production (i.e., production within firms) arising from shirking by hired inputs. The claim to the profits deriving from the enterprise's business activities constitutes the reward from monitoring and provides the incentive for the organization of production within the firm. Agents in this view do not seek to separate ownership and control but rather seek to use control to monitor the firm's operations and thereby to secure the gains from ownership.[6] Residual claimancy will, in what follows, be associated with direct monitoring by owners of firms' production and marketing activities.

Extending beyond the Alchian-Demsetz framework to encompass political activity, residual claimants can also seek to increase the value of their enterprise by influencing protection or trade liberalization decisions.[7] A choice thus arises between monitoring and managing the enterprise's productive activities and coordinating political activies that benefit the firm by restricting access of foreign goods to the domestic market. Political activities are undertaken at the expense of a reduction in attention to activities that sustain the internal efficiency of the firm. The opportunity cost of political activity is therefore the inferior internal economic performance of the enterprise.[8]

The returns to political activity will differ across countries, and also within countries, at different points of time, depending on the degree of politicization of policy making. Where politicization is low, there may be little that can be achieved by political activity, and the rewards secured by residual claimants then principally derive from their roles as monitors of the firm's internal production activities. Where politicization is high, there may conversely be substantive returns from political activity. The establishment and ongoing maintenance of appropriate political ties then overshadows the rewards from monitoring the enterprise's business activites.

An industry's market structure has a bearing upon the decision to engage in political activity. Internal monitoring yields a private return exclusively appropriable by the firm's residual claimants. However, political activity where successful yields a public-good-type benefit in the form of increased protection for all firms in the domestic import-competing industry. The number of fims, and the distribution of market shares among firms, influence the decision to privately contribute toward the collective industry benefit of evoking protectionist policies.

**The Decision Problem**

To portray the decision problem confronting firm owners, I consider a domestic import-competing industry that faces a given world price for its output. Domestic firms in the industry purchase factor services in competitive domestic factor markets. A firm is characterized by an endowment $h_i$ of entrepreneurial or monitoring ability of its residual claimants. The value of $h_i$ is indicative of potential managerial and entrepreneurial ability of firm $i$. The endowment $h_i$ can differ among firms, reflecting the superior abilities of owners of some enterprises relative to others.

Abilities as reflected in $h_i$ will affect market shares. A higher concentration ratio of market shares for an industry does not here imply greater concentration of market power but the superior efficiencies of some firms emanating from owners' abilities to secure larger market shares.[9]

The political mechanism affords residual claimants the opportunity to influence trade policy. The level of protection achieved by an industry is determined by the total effort made by industry interests in seeking or maintaining political influence.

Denote the political activity of the owners of firm $i$ by $a_i$, and let $m_i$ denote internal monitoring activity within the firm. The firm's entrepreneurial and managerial abilities are allocated between political and economic activity, such that

$$h_i = a_i + m_i. \tag{1}$$

Let the instrument of protection be a tariff.[10] Denote by $P$ the domestic tariff-inclusive price of the industry's output. The level of protection increases with aggregate political activity A undertaken by $n$ firms in the import-competing industry, such that

$$P = P(A) = P\left(\sum_{i=1}^{n} a_i\right) \tag{2}$$

$$= P^* A^\beta, \qquad P \geq P^*, \qquad 0 < \beta < 1, \tag{2'}$$

where $P'(A) > 0$, $P''(A) < 0$.[11] $P^*$ is the international market price of the industry's output, and $\beta$ is a parameter characterizing the susceptibility of policy decisions to political influence. The greater is $\beta$, the greater is the politicization of economic decision making.

Endogenous protection as expressed by (2) encompasses various activities. For example, rather than attending to the operations of their business enterprise, owners of firms may find it useful to spend time in the national capital to maintain political connections. Or elected officials may be brought on study missions to the localities where the enterprise's plants are located. It may be necessary to prepare documentation supporting claims of unfair trading practices by foreign producers or injury incurred because of imports. Or in countries where nepotism is present, $a_i$ encompasses the activities directed at seeking and maintaining an appropriate marriage partner who can provide via family ties the requisite political connections to influence policy decisions that affect the firm's profitability.[12]

Although protection has a public-good character, firms do not benefit equally from protection (as individuals in general do not benefit equally from consumption of a public good). A firm's benefit from protection of course increases, the greater are its sales.

The production technology of firm $i$ is

$$q_i = \alpha(m_i)F(V_i), \tag{3}$$

where $F(V_i)$ has neoclassical properties and $\alpha(m_i)$ indicates the efficiency with which factors of production $V_i$ are employed by the firm. This internal efficiency depends upon monitoring, via

$$\alpha(m_i) = m_i^\rho, \qquad 0 < \rho < 1. \tag{4}$$

Thus $\alpha'(m_i) > 0$, $\alpha''(m_i) < 0$. The parameter $\rho$ reflects the returns to monitoring activity.

For given factor-input prices $w$ a firm's profits are

$$\pi_i = P(A)\alpha(m_i)F(V_i) - wV_i = \pi_i[P(A)\alpha(m_i), w]. \tag{5}$$

## 7.2   Noncooperative Equilibria

Let us assume that no trade organization coordinates the industry's political activities, nor is there covert collusion, so owners of firms undertake political activities independently. The domestic industry confronts import competition at the world price plus whatever tariff is levied on imports. We confine ourselves to tariffs that allow imports, and hence there is no potential for gain from domestic collustive activity with respect to price or quantity. The owners of each firm independently choose an allocation of $h_i$ between political and economic activity and a level of inputs $V_i$ to maximize profits as given by (5).

In choosing $a_i$ independently, a firm $i$ takes as given the contribution to political activity, denoted as $A_i$, of all other firms in the industry. Substituting $A = (a_i + A_i)$, the profit function (5) can be expressed as $\pi_i[P(a_i + A_i)\alpha(h_i - a_i), w]$, and profit-maximizing choice of $a_i$ consequently entails

$$\frac{\partial \pi_i}{\partial a_i} = \pi_i'[\alpha(m_i)P'(A) - \alpha'(m_i)P(A)] \leqq 0, \qquad a_i \frac{\partial \pi}{\partial a_i} = 0. \tag{6}$$

There is of course no presumption that an equilibrium will be characterized by all firms contributing to the quest for protection. On the contrary, one expects that "free riding" may occur. If a firm does not contribute to political activity, it follows from (6) that

$$h_i \leq \mu A, \tag{7}$$

where $\mu \equiv \rho/\beta$. $\mu$ expresses the effectiveness of internal monitoring relative to political activity as means of increasing firms' profits and is assumed common to all firms. By its public-good nature the industry's equilibrium level of political activity is also common to all firms. Less capable firms, with managerial and entrepreneurial abilities less than $\mu A$, are indicated by (7) to free ride.

For firms making positive contributions to political activity, (6) implies that

$$a_i = h_i - \mu A \tag{8}$$

and

$$m_i = \mu A. \tag{8'}$$

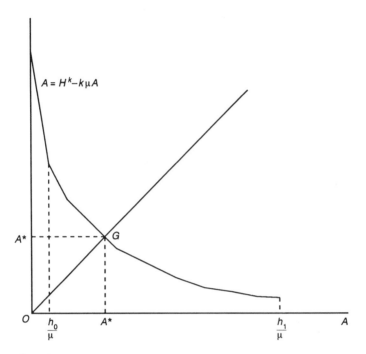

**Figure 7.1**

It follows therefore from (8′) that, with $a_i > 0$, firms are choosing the same internal monitoring allocations. Differing abilities $h_i$ among owners of firms are thus reflected in different political allocations. The more capable firms devote greater effort to influencing the political process, but no more effort than the less capable to monitoring the internal operations of the enterprise.

Figure 7.1 provides a characterization of the Nash equilibrium. In an industry with $n$ firms, let $k \leq n$ make positive contributions to the political activity underlying the industry's quest for protection. Thus in equilibrium $A^* = \sum_k a^*$. Summing over contributing firms in (8) yields

$$\sum_k h_i - A^* = k\mu A^*,                                                      \tag{9}$$

and therefore, with $H^k \equiv \sum_k h_i$,

$$A^* = H^k - k\mu A^* = \sum_i \max[h_i - \mu A^*, 0].                              \tag{10}$$

Equilibrium is portrayed in figure 7.1 at the fixed point $G$ for firms with a distribution of abilities ranging from a lower bound of $h_0$ to an upper bound of $h_1$. Reflecting (7), a firm that fails to contribute to the industry's political activity exhibits a level of ability sufficiently low such that $h_i/\mu \leq A^*$, while reflecting (8) a firm making a positive contribution to political activity has a level of ability sufficiently high, such that $h_i/\mu > A^*$.

### The Two-Firm Case

As an expository example, consider the case where the domestic industry consists of but two firms. Substituting $m_i = (h_i - a_i)$ and $A = (A_i + a_i)$ into (8') yields the solution in the two-firm case:

$$a_1 = \frac{h_1 - \mu a_2}{1 + \mu}, \qquad a_2 = \frac{h_2 - \mu a_1}{1 + \mu}. \tag{11}$$

The reaction functions are thus linear, with negative slopes that are the inverse of one another.

Let the firms in particular be identical, with common abilities $h$. Then the reaction functions of figure 7.2 yield a unique stable symmetric equilibrium at the common level of political activity $a^*$.

Suppose, on the other hand, that the firms were to differ in their abilities, with $h_1 > h_2$. Then

$$\frac{h_1}{\mu} > \frac{h_2}{1 + \mu}, \tag{12}$$

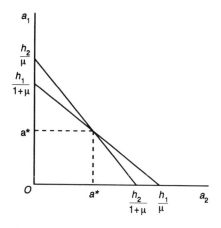

**Figure 7.2**

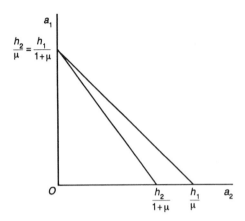

**Figure 7.3**

$$\frac{h_1}{1 + \mu} \gtrless \frac{h_2}{\mu},$$ (13)

and the nature of the equilibrium hinges on (13). If $h_1/(1 + \mu) < h_2/\mu$, an asymmetric interior equilibrium obtains where both firms contribute to political activity. But, if as in figure 7.3 $h_1(1 + \mu) \geq h_2/\mu$, then only the firm with the more able residual claimants undertakes political activity.

The sufficient condition for both firms to choose to engage in political activity can be expressed as

$$\frac{h_1}{h_2} < 1 + \frac{\beta}{\rho} = 1 + \frac{1}{\mu}.$$ (14)

Greater politicization of the tariff determination process, relative to the return to monitoring the enterprise's production activities, thus makes for outcomes where, ceteris paribus, the less efficient firm with the smaller endowment of monotoring and managerial skills also engages in political activity.

**Political Connections and Comparative Advantage**

Comparative advantage in political and monitoring activity is introduced via variation in $\mu$ among firms. With $\beta$ common to all firms, let $\rho$ be firm specific, thereby allowing different firm-specific values of $\mu$. Firms characterized by a lower $\mu$ then have residual claimants who are relatively more

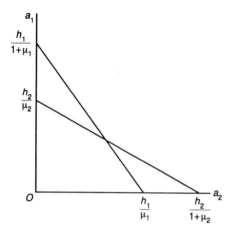

**Figure 7.4**

effective in influencing political choice of economic policy than in application of monitoring skills to ensuring efficient internal operation of the business enterprise.

It is evident that in (11) a lower value of $\mu$ counterbalances a high $h$. Thus, for example, if two firms have the same endowment of entrepreneurial and managerial ability, the firm with the lower $\mu_i$ undertakes more political activity. It is straightfoward to confirm that if one firm exhibits a sufficiently strong comparative advantage in political acitivity then that firm will undertake all the political activity. Nevertheless, a less able firm will undertake political activity if (as expressed in a sufficiently low relative value of $\mu_i$) it is better connected politically than the entrepreneurially and managerially more competent firm.

If the less-competent firm has, as a consequence of better political connections, a comparative advantage in political activity, then a stable equilibrium may not exist. In figure 7.4, $h_1 > h_2$ and $\mu_1 > \mu_2$, which is consistent with $h_1/\mu_1 < h_2/(1 + \mu_2)$ and $h_1/(1 + \mu_1) > h_1/\mu_2$.

## 7.3   Cooperative Equilibria

Suppose now that there is cooperation in political activity. For example, a trade organization may coordinate political activity. Or, political activity could still be decentralized. Guttman (1985, 1987) has, for example, proposed independent matching behavior as consistent with jointly optimal contributions to a public good. Or, cooperation may arise as an equilibrium from independent behavior in the repeated game entailed in pursuit of the common protectionist objective.

With cooperative political activity, the objective is to maximize joint profits, which are given by

$$\pi = \sum_j \pi_j = P(A) \sum_j \alpha(m_j) F(V_j) - \sum_j w V_j. \tag{15}$$

Maximizing (15) subject to

$$A = \sum_j h_j - \sum_j m_j \tag{16}$$

and assuming no firm is specialized to political or internal monitoring activities yields the condition for joint-profit maximization:

$$\sum_j P'(A)\alpha(m_j) = P(A)\alpha'(m_1) = P(A)\alpha'(m_2) = \ldots = P(A)\alpha'(m_n). \tag{17}$$

This is a familiar public-good efficiency condition: Joint profits are maximized when the collective benefit from political activity equals the marginal cost, which is the loss in efficiency at the firm level due to reduced monitoring of productive activities.

We now turn to consider how levels of protection are related to market structure characterized by (1) the number of firms and (2) a measure of concentration based on the distribution of market shares among a given number of firms.

## 7.4   The Number of Firms as an Indicator of "Industry Cohesion"

For the purposes of considering the relation between protection and the number of firms, we can impose symmetry so that firms are identical. In a symmetric equilibrium the choice of the level of political activity by the firm's residual claimants follows from (8) as

$$a_i = a = \frac{h}{1 + n\mu}. \tag{18}$$

Total political activity by industry interests is then

$$A = na = \frac{H}{1 + n\mu}, \tag{19}$$

where $H = nh$ is industrywide monitoring capability.

Political activity, by the individual firm and in aggregate by the industry, accordingly decreases with the ratio $\mu \equiv (\rho/\beta)$. A greater $\beta$ indicates greater marginal return from political activity; a higher value of $\rho$ indications a greater reward from monitoring of the firm's internal activities. Equations (18) and (19) thus confirm that the level of political activity undertaken by firms individually and by the industry at large responds positively to the marginal reward from such activity and negatively to the marginal opportunity cost.

The relationship between political activity and the number of firms follows from establishing how changes in $n$ affect $a_i$ and $A$ in (18) and (19). The outcome depends upon whether $h$ or $H$ is constant. The two possibilities introduce considerations relating to factor specificity.

### Specific Factors

Let us interpret $H$ as the fixed quantity of an industry-specific input. The returns to residual claimants then constitute sector-specific rents. Since firms are characterized by a value $h$, differing numbers of firms entail different firm assignments of the given industry-specific monitoring capability.

Equations (18) and (19) reveal that, with $H$ given, a reduction in $n$ increases both $a_i$ and $A$. That is, the firm and the industry levels of political activity both increase when the number of firms declines. Fewer firms therefore imply greater protection. This is consistent with the conventional wisdom: greater cohesion or smaller numbers in the group noncooperatively contributing toward collective benefit in the influence over policy yields a superior protectionist response.

### Mobile Factors

However, we can interpret $H$ as an intersectorally mobile factor that is subject to change via the entry and exit of firms from the industry. There are thus no barriers to entry; nor are there barriers to exit, in that residual claimants can exit to apply their managerial and entrepreneurial capabities in other industries. In equilibrium the return to $h$ is thus equalized across sectors.

Proceeding with the symmetric case where owners of firms have a common endowment $h$ of entrepreneurial and managerial skills, (19) can be reexpressed as

$$A = \frac{H}{1 + n\mu} = \frac{h}{1/n + \mu}. \tag{19'}$$

From (18) political activity at the firm level increases as $n$ declines. However, (19') indicates that for the industry as a whole, the level of political activity decreases. Fewer firms in this case therefore imply less protection.

**The Cooperative Case**

The above assumes noncooperative choice of levels of political activity. Joint-profit-maximizing levels of political activity follow from (17) as

$$a = \frac{h}{1 + \mu}, \tag{20}$$

$$A = \frac{H}{1 + \mu} = \frac{nh}{1 + \mu}. \tag{21}$$

Let $H$ be industry specific. Since $h = H/n$, (20) reveals the level of political activity at the firm level to be decreasing in $n$. However, (21) indicates that the aggregate industry level of political activity is independent of $n$. Thus, if political activity is undertaken cooperatively and managerial and entrepreneurial abilities are industry specific, the industry's joint-profit-maximizing political activity is independent of the number of firms.

Alternatively, view $H$ as intersectorally mobile. Then political activity undertaken by firms is independent of the number of firms, but aggregate political activity by the industry decreases as the number of firms declines. Fewer firms therefore now imply lower levels of protection.

**Diversity of Outcomes**

Diverse outcomes are therefore revealed for the relationship between industry cohesion as reflected in the number of firms and industry levels of protection. The effect on protection of fewer firms is summarized as

|                                    | Nash | Cooperation |
|------------------------------------|------|-------------|
| Industry-monitoring capability     | +    | No change   |
| Firm monitoring capability fixed   | −    | −           |

In particular, the inference of greater protection from greater cohesion, manifested in a positive relation between protection and the number of firms, only arises if managerial and entrepreneurial capability is industry specific and levels of political activity are chosen independently.

## 7.5   Industry Concentration and the Level of Protection

Cohesion can also be interpreted in terms of industry concentration ratios based on market shares. The prediction is that industries that exhibit greater cohesion, as reflected in more concentrated market shares, will succeed in securing higher levels of protection. We now consider whether this prediction is confirmed by the model.

### Determination of Market Shares

Given the total monitoring capability of the industry and a distribution of abilities among firms, the residual claimants of each firm decide on an allocation of their managerial and entrepreneurial abilites between the internal monitoring of firm activities and political activities. A firm's marginal cost of output depends on this allocation via

$$MC_i = \frac{w}{\alpha(m_i^*)F'(V_i^*)} \qquad i = 1, \ldots, n, \tag{22}$$

where $m_i^*$ and $V_i^*$ are equibrium values of internal monitoring and factor inputs. The choice of $m_i^*$ implies a choice $a_i^*$, which specifies the domestic tariff-inclusive price as

$$P(A^*) = P\left(\sum_{j=1}^{n} a_j^*\right). \tag{23}$$

Together (22) and (23) determine the market share of firm $i$ as $q_i/Q$ in figure 7.5.

### All Firms Politically Active

Suppose now that all $a_i$'s are positive (all firms are undertaking political activity), and consider a firm's profit function, which we can express as

$$\pi_i = P(a_i + A_i)\alpha(m_i)F(V_i) - wV_i. \tag{24}$$

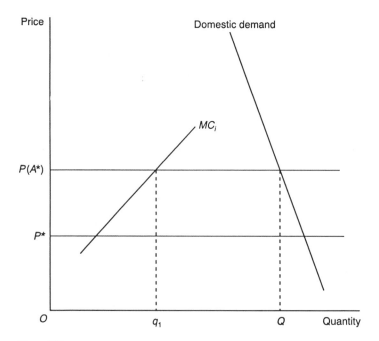

**Figure 7.5**

Substituting $a_i = (h_i - m_i)$ yields the expression for profits

$$\pi_i = P(h_i + A_i + m_i)\alpha(m_i)F(V_i) - wV_i \tag{24'}$$

$$= P(J_i - m_i)\alpha(m_i)F(V_i) - wV_i,$$

where

$$J_i \equiv h_i + A_i \tag{25}$$

is the total input of monitoring capabilities used to the firm's advantage, consisting of the firm's own endowment $h_i$ and the political activity $A_i$ undertaken by other firms to the advantage of firm $i$ via the public-good nature of such activity.

Profits in (24') depend only upon the sum $J_i$ and not upon the composition of $J_i$ between $h_i$ and $A_i$. The owners of a firm are understandably indifferent between a marginal decrease in their own managerial and entrepreneurial capability $h_i$ and marginal increase in the political activity $A_i$

undertaken by other firms, provided that $a_i > 0$. The reason is that because of the pure public-good nature of political activity, there is perfect substitution between the firm's own political activity and the political activity undertaken by other firms in the industry.

Consider now the Nash equilibrium that obtains when firms maximize (24') subject to (25). Let the equilibrium yield $a_i^* > 0$ for all firms, and with $H$ given make the change $\Delta h_i = -\Delta h_j$. The interpretation of such a change is that the residual claimants or owners of firm $i$ become more capable at the expense of firm $j$. Now let.

$$\Delta A_j = -\Delta h_i = \Delta h_j = -\Delta a_i. \tag{26}$$

These responses are consistent with the same equilibrium as obtained initially. The profit functions of firms $i$ and $j$ remain

$$\pi_i = P(J_i - m_i)\alpha(m_i)F(V_i) - wV_i, \tag{27}$$

$$\pi_i = P(J_j + m_j)\alpha(m_j)F(V_j) - wV_j. \tag{28}$$

Nor therefore is there any change in the equilibrium choices of political activity.

For example, with two firms we effect a change $dh_1 = -dh_2$, with $(h_1 + h_2) = H$. Let the response of firm 2 be $da_2^* = dA_1 = -dh_2$. Therefore $dJ_1 = dh_1 + dA_1 = 0$. But only $J$ and $w$ appear exogenously in firms' profit functions. Therefore the best response of firm 1 subsequent to the redistribution of $H$ remains $a_1^*$, which implies that $da_1^* = dh_1$. Firm 2 responds conversely and symmetrically. Hence the sum $a_1^* + a_2^*$ is invariant to the redistribution of entrepreneurial and managerial abilities between the firms.

Equilibrium choices of political activity thus depend upon $H$ but are neutral with respect to the distribution of capabilities among firms, if $a_i > 0$ for all firms.[13] The equilibrium values $m_1^*$ are then also independent of the distribution of abilities among firms, as are consequently firms' equilibrium marginal costs of output given by (21). Firms' equilibrium marginal costs, however, determine market shares, and thereby values of concentration ratios.

It follows then that in the case where each firm is individually choosing a positive level of political activity, the political activity undertaken by an industry, and thereby the industry's level of protection, depends upon the extent to which the formulation of the industry's trade policy is subject to influence via the political process and the effectiveness of internal monitoring but is unrelated to market shares and hence concentration ratios. Under the maintained assumption of common technologies, market shares are moreover equal, and no variation can be exhibited in industry concentration.

### Asymmetric Market Shares

The result that the equilibrium level of political activity is invariant with respect to concentration ratios in protected industries has limited usefulness in application to explaining differences in protection among industries, since it is based on sufficiently small differences in the distribution of abilities among firms to ensure strictly positive contributions by all firms in an industry to political activity. In more likely or plausible circumstances, industries are expected to be characterized by an asymmetric distribution of entrepreneurial and managerial abilities among firms, with some firms' residual claimants being capable and others' less so. As we have seen, the more capable firms choose positive $a_i^*$'s; the less capable choose equilibrium values of $a_i^* = 0$.

With firms now no longer necessarily identical and with $k \leq n$ firms choosing $a_i^* > 0$, the industry level of political activity follows from (9) as

$$A^* = \frac{\sum_k h_i}{1 + \mu k} = \frac{H^k}{1 + \mu k}. \tag{29}$$

The value $H^k$ of abilities of firms contributing to political activity thus determines $A^*$, in conjunction with $\mu \equiv \rho/\beta$ and $k$. The industry's equilibrium level of political activity is thus independent of the distribution of $H^k$ among the $k$ politically active firms, reflecting the outcome observed from $k = n$ (all firms contributing). However, denote by $H^f$ the total capabilites of the other or fringe firms choosing $a_i^* = 0$, and consider a redistribution $-dH^k = dH^f$. Via (29), $A^*$ then falls if no firm that previously did not contribute to political activity is led to make a positive contribution and if the $k$ originally politically active firms continue to contribute.

Political activity thus declines in an industry where concentration is declining if the lower concentration derives from smaller fringe firms improving their market shares at the expense of larger established firms. Conversely, increased concentration due to enhanced abilities of leading firms who increase market shares at the expense of smaller producers suggests outcomes of increased protection.

### The Relation between Concentration and Protection

Increasing concentration therefore here makes for greater protection, in the sense that entrepreneurial and managerial abilities are more concentrated in the group of dominant rather than fringe firms. On the other hand, decreasing concentration expressed in the limit in an equal distribution of abilities ensures that all firms contribute to the collective activity of seeking to influence the determination of trade policy. But then, in this special limiting case, market shares and levels of protection are mutually independent.

Further, indicated empirical relations will also reflect the manner of computation of industry concentration ratios. Observe that the number of firms $k$ in (29) need not (and in general will not) equal the number of leading firms that constitutes the basis for evaluation of industry concentration ratios. For example, concentration ratios are often based on the leading four firms. But from (29) it is the combined characteristics of the leading $k$ firms that determine the industry's level of political activity, and thereby the level of protection achieved.

## 7.6   Competing Hypotheses and Empirical Evidence

The model portrayed in this chapter has viewed trade policy as determined by the resources allocated by the beneficiaries of protection to influencing policy outcomes. An alternative hypothesis is that income distribution consequences of trade policy decisions reflect social-insurance motives. In this latter view policymakers intervene to protect low-income, unskilled, underprivileged individuals who are concentrated in a particular import-competing sector and who, in the absence of protection, would suffer declines in income because of shifts in comparative advantage. In formulating protectionist responses, governments are proposed to be implicitly acting in accord with insurance contracts that individuals would have sought, had risk sharing been facilitated by private insurance markets.[14]

Although motives differ, the behavior of policymakers predicted by the political-influence and social-insurance models of endogenous trade policy is in significant respects observationally equivalent. Both models in particular are consistent with protectionist responses for declining industries.[15]

Reservations have been expressed about both models. The criticisms of the social-insurance model are theoretically founded. As demonstrated by

Avinash Dixit, governments are not to be expected to be more successful in resolving problems due to insurance-related market failures that can arise in the context of international trade (moral hazard, adverse selection, and imperfectly observed behavior) than private insurance markets.[16] The reservations concerning the political-influence model of endogenous protection have, on the other hand, not been based on considerations concerned with theoretical consistency but on purported inconsistency with the empirical evidence. Market-structure characteristics have been the primary feature differentiating the political-influence and social-insurance models of endogenous protection, and how well the models perform in explaining differences in levels of protection across industries has accordingly been judged in terms of whether higher levels of protection are, ceteris paribus, associated with fewer firms and greater concentration.[17] The empirical studies for the most part confirm the negative relationship between the number of firms and levels of protection predicted by the model. However, the relation between industry concentration and protection is consistently neither positive nor negative.[18] If cohesion is necessarily associated with higher concentration ratios, the latter results compromise the political-influence model and suggest support for an alternative explanation of endogenous protection.

The model formulated in this chapter encompasses the reported empirical results when political-influence motives underlie protectionist policies. The relationship between the number of firms in an industry and the industry's level of protection has been shown to depend upon whether managerial and entrepreneurial abilities are industry-specific and upon whether political activity is undertaken independently or cooperatively. If managerial and entrepreneurial ability is industry specific, a decline in the number of firms is associated with increased protection when political activity is undertaken independently and is independent of the number of firms when political activity is undertaken cooperatively. If managerial and entrepreneurial ability is firm-specific but not industry-specific, fewer firms implies less protection without regard for whether political activity is undertaken independently or cooperatively. As a result the negative relationship between the number of firms and protection that is generally revealed in the empirical studies suggests independent behavior by residual claimants with industry-specific abilities.

When industry concentration is the indicator of cohesion of the protectionist coalition, the hypothesis in empirical studies has been that holding the number of firms constant, the greater is concentration as measured by the share of the few largest firms in an industry, the greater will be the industry's level of protection. The model set out in this chapter has, however, revealed a number of subtle complexities in the relation between concentration ratios and differences in levels of protection across industries. If all firms in an import-competing industry are active in seeking to influence policy, the total effort directed at political acitivity is independent of the industry concentration ratio. If firms' abilities are asymmetrically distributed, concentration of market shares (reflecting firms' abilities) does affect efforts directed at securing protection. Moreover, no particular significance can be attached to measures of industry concentration based on the market shares of a designated number of leading firms in an industry. For example, a concentration ratio based on the four largest firms could be an appropriate explanatory variable if only the four largest firms were making positive contributions to activities directed at increasing the political influence of the industry. However, as the model reveals, this would occur in very special circumstances since the number of leading firms included in the computation of the industry concentration ratio is endogenously determined.

## 7.7 Conclusion

It would appear that formalizations of the concept of "cohesion" in past empirical studies of the determinants of industry levels of protection have not been sufficiently refined to capture the distinction between the political-influence and social-insurance models of endogenous protection. Embedding political activity directed at influencing trade policy in a residual claimant theory of the firm that distinguishes the private gain from internal monitoring from the collective gain from evoking protectionist responses, and applying the model to investigating the relation between market structure and protection, has been demonstrated to yield results on the endogenous determination of protection that are consistent with the diverse outcomes reported in empirical studies. In particular, the ambiguous or haphazard relation revealed between industry concentration ratios and levels of protection has been shown to be consistent with the political-influence model of endogenous protection. Indeed, given that protection benefits the industry at large so that contributions to achieving a protectionist response entail private provision of a public good, the monitoring model predicts that concentration ratios based on an arbitrary number of leading firms will, for large numbers, exhibit the random relationship with industry levels of protection that is revealed by the data.

**Notes**

This chapter has benefited from the comments of Avinash Dixit, Gene Grossman, and Hal Varian. I also thank seminar participants at the Hebrew University of Jerusalem, UCLA, the University of California at San Diego, Princeton University, the University of Michigan, and participants in the Sapir Conference on International Trade at Tel-Aviv University.

1. On these alternative protectionist motives, see my 1989a paper.

2. On the empirical evidence, see the surveys by Robert Baldwin (1984), Hillman (1989, ch. 11).

3. On policy choice and the institutional political structure, see Bernholz (1966, 1974), Baldwin (1988), and Hillman (1989b). Previous models of endogenous trade policy under representative democracy include Cassing and Hillman (1986), Young and Magee (1986), and Hillman and Ursprung (1988).

4. Such a model of the endogenous determination of a protective tariff under direct democracy has been formulated by Mayer (1984).

5. Alchian and Demsetz (1985) and Demsetz (1988).

6. For substantiating evidence on concentration of ownership in U.S. industry, and the implied incentives for monitoring and the relationship to profits, see Demsetz and Lehn (1985).

7. Grossman and Levinsohn (1989) confirm a positive relation between protection and the market value of assets of a number of U.S. corporations.

8. I shall abstract from the use of hired inputs for political activity. Lobbyists can of course be hired. However, as hired inputs, lobbyists are subject to monitoring by residual claimants in the manner of hired inputs in general. Political activity would thus encompass the diversion of scarce entrepreneurial and managerial inputs to the monitoring, direction, and coordination of lobbyists' activities, at the same opportunity cost of internal monitoring of the enterprise.

9. On the perception of industry concentration coefficients as reflecting superior managerial and entrepreneurial abilities, see Demsetz (1970).

10. We hereby avoid considerations having to do with political choice of the means of protection. On the factors entering into political choice of how protection is provided, see my survey (1989b, ch. 9). In assuming here a tariff as the instrument of protection, I abstract from the influence that can be exerted by foreign interests on a country's trade policy. On foreign interests and trade policy in a setting of representative democracy, see Hillman and Ursprung (1988).

11. The specification (2') implies for consistency with protectionist outcomes choice of units such that $A > 1$. The assumption in (2) is that all individual contributions to the collective benefit associated with political influence are reflected in the aggregate contribution. For alternative formulations, see Jack Hirshleifer (1983).

12. These are all examples of activities that have been the focus of the rent-seeking literature and entail resource use in quests to affect income distribution rather than adding to the value of output. On rent seeking and trade policy, see, in particular, Baldwin (1984). A principal concern of the rent-seeking literature has been the relation between the value of contested prizes and resources expended in rent-seeking quests. On this relation, see, for example, Tullock (1980) and Hillman and Riley (1989).

13. An analogue to this type of neutrality result, it should be stressed, is well-established in the theory of voluntary private provision by consumers of public goods. The parallel result (Bergstrom, Blume, and Varian 1986; Cornes and Sandler 1986) is that the total quantity of a pure public good provided in a Nash equilibrium is independent of the distribution of income among consumers making strictly positive contributions to provision of the public good. The demonstration of this outcome for the consumer rests upon the invariance of the budget constraint with respect to marginal income transfers. The firm transacts in both product and factor markets and has of course no analogous budget constraint. However, the analogous neutrality result arises because monitoring capabilities of the firm's residual claimants are constrained.

14. For models of trade policy as social insurance, see Eaton and Grossman (1985), Cassing, Hillman, and Long (1986), and Hillman (1989b).

15. See Hillman (1982).

16. See Dixit (1987, 1989a, 1989b).

17. For example, Baldwin (1985, 146) describes the essence of the political self-interested model as follows:

*The key point* in the common interest group model is that an industry's success in achieving protection by exerting political pressure on elected officials depends on its ability to organize into an effective political pressure group. The ability to overcome the free-rider problem and organize effectively depends in turn on the relative size of firms within the industry and their degree of concentration.

18. See Baldwin (1988, 579, table 1).

## References

Alchian, Armen, and Harold Demsetz. 1972. Production, information costs, and economic organization. *American Economic Review* 82: 777–795.

Baldwin, Robert E. 1984. Trade policies in developed countries. In Ronald W. Jones and Peter B. Kenen (eds.), *Handbook of International Economics*. Amsterdam: North Holland, pp. 572–619.

Baldwin, Robert E. 1984. Rent seeking and trade policy. *Weltwirtschaftliches Archiv* 120: 662–677.

Baldwin, Robert E. 1985. *The Political Economy of U.S. Import Policy*. Cambridge: MIT Press.

Baldwin, Robert E. 1988. *Trade Policy in a Changing World Economy*. Oxford: Harvester Wheatsheaf.

Bergstrom, Theodore, Laurence Blume, and Hal Varian. 1986. On the private provision of public goods. *Journal of Public Economics* 29: 25–49.

Bernholz, Peter. 1974. On the reasons for the influence of interest groups on political decision making. *Zeitschrift fur Wirtschafts und Sozialwissenschaft* 94: 45–63.

Bernholz, Peter 1966. Economic policies in a democracy. *Kyklos* 19: 48–80.

Cassing, James H., and Arye L. Hillman. 1986. Shifting comparative advantage and senescent industry collapse. *American Economic Review* 76: 516–523.

Cassing, James H., Arye L. Hillman, and Ngo Van Long. 1986. Risk aversion, terms of trade variability, and social-consensus trade policy. *Oxford Economic Papers* 38: 234–242.

Cornes, Richard, and Todd Sandler 1986. *The Theory of Externalities, Public Goods and Club Goods*. Cambridge: Cambridge University Press.

Demsetz, Harold. 1970. Industry structure, market rivalry and public policy. *Journal of Law and Economics* 16: 1–10.

Demsetz, Harold. 1988. The theory of the firm revisited. *Journal of Law, Economics and Organization* 4: 141–162.

Demsetz, Harold, and Ken Lehn. 1985. The ownership structure of corporations: Causes and consequences. *Journal of Political Economy* 93: 1155–1177.

Dixit, Avinash. 1987. Trade and insurance with moral hazard. *Journal of International Economics* 23: 201–220.

Dixit, Avinash. 1989a. Trade and insurance with imperfectly observed outcomes. *Quarterly Journal of Economic* 104: 195–203.

Dixit, Avinash. 1989b. Trade and insurance with adverse selection. *Review of Economic Studies* 56: 235–248.

Eaton, Jonathan, and Gene M. Grossman. 1985. Tariffs as insurance: Optimal commercial policy when domestic markets are incomplete. *Canadian Journal of Economics* 18: 258–272.

Grossman, Gene M., and James A. Levinsohn. 1989. Import competition and the stock market return to capital. *American Economic Review* 79: 1065–1087.

Guttman, Joel M. 1985. Collective action and the supply of campaign contributions. *European Journal of Political Economy* 1: 221–241.

Guttman, Joel M. 1987. A non-Cournot model of voluntary collective action. *Economica* 54: 1–19.

Hillman, Arye L. 1982. Declining industries and political support protectionist motives. *American Economic Review* 72: 1180–1187.

Hillman, Arye L. 1989a. Policy motives and international trade restrictions. In Hans-Jurgen Vosgerau (ed.), *New Institutional Arrangements for the World Economy*. New York: Springer-Verlag, pp. 284–302.

Hillman, Arye L. 1989b. *The Political Economy of Protection*. New York: Harwood Academic Publishers.

Hillman, Arye L., and Heinrich Ursprung. 1988. Domestic politics, foreign interests, and international trade policy. *American Economic Review* 78: 729–745.

Hillman, Arye L., and John Riley. 1989. Politically contestable rents and transfers. *Economics and Politics* 1: 17–39.

Hirshleifer, Jack. 1983. From weakest link to best shot: The voluntary provision of public goods. *Public Choice* 41: 371–386.

Mayer, Wolfgang. 1984. Endogenous tariff formation. *American Economic Review* 74: 970–985.

Olson, Mancur. 1965. *The Logic of Collective Action*. Cambridge: Harvard University Press.

Tullock, Gordon. 1980. Efficient rent seeking. In James Buchanan, Robert Tollison, and Gordon Tullock (eds.), *Toward A Theory of the Rent Seeking Society*. College Station: Texas A and M Press, pp. 97–112.

Young, Leslie, and Stephen P. Magee. 1986. Endogenous protection, factor returns and resource allocation. *Review of Economic Studies* 53: 407–419.

# 8 Growth and Welfare in a Small Open Economy

**Gene M. Grossman and Elhanan Helpman**

The resurgence of interest in theories of economic growth stems from a simple but powerful insight. When aggregate production possibilities are characterized by increasing returns to scale, the long-run rate of growth can be determined by factors that are endogenous to the economic environment (Romer 1989). This observation stands in contrast to a central tenet from the Solowian neoclassical growth tradition, namely, that per capita income grows in the long run at the rat of exogenous technological progess.

Increasing returns arise naturally in the context of the creation and implementation of knowledge and ideas, as many forms of information display the characteristics of a public good. Recent research has focused therefore on the processes associated with the generation and dissemination of knowlege. Knowledge can be embodied in the individual worker, as in the studies of the formation of human capital (e.g., Lucas 1988) or it may be disembodied, as when new technologies are created via research and development (e.g., Romer 1990). The new models that have been developed along either of these lines enable an examination of the long-run growth effects of various goverment policies, an investigation that could not easily be carried out within the older paradigm emphasizing the accumulation of physical capital.

In our own earlier work (Grossman and Helpman 1989, 1990) we have drawn on the emerging literature on endogenous technological progess to study the determinants of long-run growth in an open world economy. We have examined the ramifications of both structural features of the international environment and policy interventions that individual trading countries might choose to undertake. We found, among other results, that trade policy can influence growth in the steady state, by altering the incentives that agents have to undertake research and development. R&D subsidies are a more direct policy instrument that can be used in many circumstances to speed growth. Suggestive as these findings may be, they fail to provide a normative basis for policy intervention because our analysis has been limited to an investigation of the positive effects of policy on long-run rates of growth.

In this chapter we study the welfare implications of growth-enhancing trade and industrial policies for a small open economy. As in our earlier work we focus on growth due to endogenous improvements in technology. Entrepreneurs devote resources to research and development whenever the present discounted value of the stream of operating profits that derive from a particular innovation justify the up-front costs of achieving that innovation. Innovation entails the development of new varieties of an intermediate input, and horizontal product differentiation of intermdiates contributes, as in Ethier (1982), to total factor productivity in the final-goods sectors. We focus on a small economy that trades two final goods at exogenously given world prices, thereby abstracting from the complex intratemporal and intertemporal terms-of-trade considerations that hinder analysis of the more general large-country case.

We find that trade policy does affect growth in our model. Protection (or promotion) of the human-capital-intensive final-goods industry draws resources out of the R&D sector and so slows growth. Protection of the labor-intensive final good has just the opposite effect on growth. Moreover "growth" is underprovided by the market equilibrium because investment in the creation of knowledge generates benefits that are not fully appropriated by the entrepreneur who bears the cost of R&D. In consequence a "small" dose of a growth-enhancing commercial policy may (but, as we shall see, need not) improve aggregate welfare.

We conduct a complete analysis of R&D subsidies. There always exists an optimal subsidy to R&D that speeds growth relative to the market-determined rate. Increasing the rate of subsidization beyond this optimum causes the growth rate to increase still further but does so at the expense of welfare. R&D subsidies alone cannot be used to achieve the first best, due to the presence of a distortion in the pricing of intermediate goods when this market is characterized by an oligopolistic structure. But we establish that the growth rate under the optimal R&D subsidy equals that in the first-best equilibrium. The optimal R&D subsidy cannot in general be welfare ranked vis-à-vis the optimal trade policy.

Our analysis of commercial policy includes a comparison of tariffs and quotas. We follow Krueger (1974) in assuming that the presence of quota rents gives rise to rent-seeking behavior. In an historical review of numerous episodes of growth or stagnation through the centuries, Baumol (1988) has emphasized the adverse consequence of the diversion of entrepreneurial efforts from innovative endeavors to rent-seeking activities. We are able to formalize this intuitive claim, and we find that trade policies that create opportunities for rent seeking may be especially onerous in a growth context. Commercial policies that would enhance growth in the absence of rent seeking (due to the relative price effects and the associated intersectoral reallocation of resources) can have just opposite effects on growth (and also welfare) when rent seeking does take place.

The chapter is organized as follows: We develop our growth model in section 8.1, and solve for the dynamic equilibrium path. In Section 8.2 we study the effects of changes in the resource stocks on the composition of output and on growth. This exercise sheds light on the structure of our model, and also facilitates discussion in the succeeding sections. In section 8.3 we derive the first-best growth path and a constrained second-best growth path, compare these to the market equilibrium, and show that a positive but finite R&D subsidy can be used to attain the second best. Sections 8.4 and 8.5 focus on commercial policies. In section 8.4 we study import tariffs and export subsidies under the assumption that revenues are raised or redistributed by lump-sum means. In section 8.5 we examine quota restrictions that generate rent-seeking behavior. The final section contains a summary of the major findings.

## 8.1   The Model

A small economy trades two final goods at exogenously given prices. The world prices of the two goods, $x$ and $y$, are $p_x$ and $p_y$, respectively. Home consumers maximize a time-separable intertemporal utility function of the form

$$U_t = \int_t^\infty e^{-\rho(r-t)} \log u[c_x(\tau), c_y(\tau)] \, d\tau, \tag{1}$$

where $\rho$ is the subjective discount rate and $c_i(\tau)$ is consumption of final good $i$ at time $\tau$. The instantaneous subutility function $u(\cdot)$ is non-decreasing, strictly quasi-concave, and homogeneous of degree one in its arguments.

A typical consumer maximizes (1) subject to an intertemporal budget constraint requiring that the present value of all expenditures after $t$ not exceed the present value of factor income after $t$ plus the value of asset holdings at $t$. In Grossman and Helpman (1990) we have shown that the solution to this problems requires an instantaneous allocation of expenditure $E(t)$ that equates the marginal rate of substitution between $x$ and $y$ to the instantaneous relative price, and a time path for expenditures that satisfies

$$\frac{\dot{E}}{E} = \dot{R} - \rho, \tag{2}$$

where $R(t)$ is the cumulative interest factor up to time $t$ and thus $\dot{R}(t)$ is the instantaneous interest rate. Savings are used to accumulate corporate bonds or ownership claims in domestic firms. There is no possibility for international borrowing or lending.

The economy is endowed with fixed stocks of two primary factors, labor and human capital. Each final good is produced locally with one of the primary factors plus an assortment of intermediate inputs. Both final-good sectors exhibit Cobb-Douglas technologies, as follows:

$$X = A_x I_x^{\beta} H_x^{1-\beta},$$
$$Y = A_y I_y^{\beta} L_y^{1-\beta}, \tag{3}$$

where $I_i$ is an index of aggregate intermediate usage in sector $i$, $H_x$ is employment of human capital in the production of $x$, and $L_y$ is employment of labor in the production of $y$.

The intermediate goods form a continuum of horizontally differentiated products. Following Ethier (1982), we assume that for a given aggregate quantity of intermediates used in final production, output is higher, the greater is the diversity in the set of inputs used. This specification captures the productivity gains from increasing degrees of *specialization* in the production of final goods. More specifically, we assume that the index of aggregate intermediate use for sector $i$, $i = x, y$, is given by

$$I_i = \left( \int_0^n z_i(\omega)^{\alpha} d\omega \right)^{1/\alpha}, \tag{4}$$

where $z_i(\omega)$ is the amount of intermediate good $\omega$ used in the production of final good $i$ and $n(t)$ is the measure (the number) of varieties available at time $t$.

Intermediate goods are not traded. There exists an unbounded set of potential varieties of these goods, but only a subset of varieties with finite measure is produced at any point in time. This is because a particular variety of the intermediate must be developed in the research lab before it can be marketed. An infinitesimal addition to the measure of varieties requires the allocation of human capital to R&D, so the activity of product development is spread over time.

At any point in time the entrepreneurs who have developed varieties of the intermediates in the past compete as oligopolists. Each one takes as given the prices set by competing producers of intermediates and also the aggregate outputs of the two final goods. Then each perceives a derived demand with constant elasticity $1/(1 - \alpha)$, and each maximizes profits by pricing at a fixed markup over marginal production cost. Let $c_z(w_H, w_L)$ represent the marginal and average cost of producing any variety of intermediate good using a common constant-returns-to-scale production technology, where $w_j$ is the wage paid to factor $j$, $j = H, L$. Then profit maximization implies that

$$\alpha p_z = c_z(w_H, w_L), \tag{5}$$

where $p_z$ is the price of any intermediate. Operating profits for the representative intermediate producer are $\pi = (1 - \alpha)p_z(z_x + z_y)$.

Since all intermediates are priced similarly, final-good producers will use equal quantities of each one. If $Z_i \equiv nz_i$ is the aggregate quantity of intermediates employed in the production of good $i$, then by (4), $I_i = n^{(1-\alpha)/\alpha}Z_i$. Now unit cost equal to (the exogenous) world price implies that

$$p_x = n^{-\gamma}c_x(w_H, p_z), \tag{6a}$$

$$p_y = n^{-\gamma}c_y(w_L, p_z), \tag{6b}$$

where $\gamma \equiv \beta(1 - \alpha)/\alpha$ and $c_i(\cdot)$ is the cost function dual (up to a constant) to the Cobb-Douglas production function in (3). We see from (6) that the introduction of new intermediate products acts like Hicks-neutral technological progress in both final-goods industries.

Equations (5) and (6) allow us to solve for the prices of the primary and produced inputs as functions of the number of intermediate products and the prices of the traded goods. If $n$ grows at rate $g(t)$, and $p_x$ and $p_y$ are taken to be constant over time, then $w_L, w_H$, and $p_z$ will all grow at rate $\gamma g(t)$. A constant relative price of the two traded goods thus implies constancy of all relative input prices.

We shall assume that new varieties are developed with two inputs, human capital and general knowledge. The greater is the stock of general knowledge among the scientific and engineering community, the smaller is the input of human capital that is needed to invent a new product. In particular, we assume that the set of available brands grows according to

$$\dot{n} = \frac{KH_n}{a_{Hn}}, \tag{7}$$

where $H_n$ is employment of human capital in the R&D sector, $K$ represents the (momentary) state of general knowledge, and $a_{Hn}$ is a productivity parameter.

General knowledge is created as a by-product of research and development. That is, each R&D project generates an appropriable output, namely, the blueprint for a new variety, but also a nonappropriable output in the form of a contribution to $K$. This specification, which we borrowed from Romer (1990) and used in our earlier work (Grossman and Helpman 1989, 1990), captures the idea that in the process of developing a particular product, the research lab may discover certain scientific properties with more widespread applicability. These discoveries may find their way into the public domain, whence future generations of researchers will draw upon them freely. For simplicity we assume that dissemination takes place immediately and that each R&D project contributes similarly to the stock of knowledge. Then $K(t)$ is proportional to cumulative R&D activity up to time $t$, and we choose units so that $K = n$.

There is free entry by entrepreneurs into R&D. Since the set of potential intermediate products is unbounded, and all such products are symmetric, an entrepreneur will never choose to develop an already existing variety. Free entry implies that whenever innovation is taking place, the present discounted value of the infinite stream of oligopoly profits that accrues to an intermdiate producer just equals the cost of introducing a new variety, or

$$\int_t^\infty e^{-[R(\tau)-R(t)]}(1 - \alpha)p_z(z_x + z_y)\,d\tau = \frac{w_H a_{Hn}}{n}.$$

Differentiating this zero-profit condition with respect to $t$, we find that

$$\dot{R} = \frac{(1 - \alpha)p_z(Z_x + Z_y)}{w_H a_{Hn}} + \left(\frac{\dot{w}_H}{w_H} - \frac{\dot{n}}{n}\right). \tag{8}$$

Equation (8) expresses a no-arbitrage condition equating the rate of interest to the sum of the instantaneous profit rate for the representative firm (first term on the right-hand side) and the capital gain on the value of the firm (second term on the right-hand side). The instantaneous value of any firm is the current cost of developing a new produt, so the capital-gain term reflects the rate of change in development costs.

The remaining equilibrium conditions reflect the clearing of factor markets. Let us define $a_{Hx}(\cdot) \equiv \partial c_x(\cdot)/\partial w_H$, $a_{Ly}(\cdot) \equiv \partial c_y(\cdot)/\partial w_L$, $a_{jz}(\cdot) \equiv \partial c_z(\cdot)/\partial w_j$ for $j = H, L$, and $a_{zi}(\cdot) \equiv \partial c_i(\cdot)/\partial p_z$ for $i = x, y$. Since relative factor prices are constant over time, so too are these input coefficients. We define as well the direct-plus-indirect coefficients $b_{Hx} \equiv a_{Hx} + a_{Hz}a_{zx}$, $b_{Lx} \equiv a_{Lz}a_{zx}$, $b_{Hy} \equiv a_{Hz}a_{zy}$, and $b_{Ly} \equiv a_{Ly} + a_{Lz}a_{zy}$. Now, using (6) and Shephard's lemma, we can write the conditions for equilibrium in the markets for labor and human capital as

$$b_{Hx}\bar{X} + b_{Hy}\bar{Y} + a_{Hn}g = H, \tag{9a}$$

$$b_{Lx}\bar{X} + b_{Ly}\bar{Y} = L, \tag{9b}$$

where $\bar{X} \equiv Xn^{-\gamma}$ and $\bar{Y} \equiv Yn^{-\gamma}$. The left-hand side of (9a), for example, gives the direct-plus-indirect demand for human capital by the two final-goods sectors, plus the demand for human capital in innovation. This must equal the exogenous supply of human capital $H$. The interpretation of (9b) is similar, except that no labor is used in R&D.

Let us assume provisionally that $g$ is constant through time (i.e., that the economy jusps immediately to a steady state); we will check later that this supposition can be consistent with all of the conditions for a dynamic equilibrium. From (9a) and (9b) the constancy of $g$ implies that $\bar{X}$ and $\bar{Y}$ are constant as well. Then $X$ and $Y$ grow at constant rate $\gamma g$. Since the current account must balance at every point in time in the absence of international trade in financial assets, nominal spending $E = p_x X + p_y Y$ also grows at rate $\gamma g$. Finally, we combine (2) and (8) to derive

$$\frac{(1 - \alpha)p_z(a_{zx}\bar{X} + a_{zy}\bar{Y})}{w_H a_{Hn}} = g + \rho. \tag{10}$$

Equations (9a), (9b), and (10) determine $\bar{X}$, $\bar{Y}$, and $g$, once (5) and (6) have been used to solve for factor prices. Provided that these equations have a solution with positive values for all three variables, our assumption of constant $g$ is justified. We proceed to use these three equations in the succeeding sections to study the welfare properties of our growth model.

## 8.2   Resources and Growth

We study in this section the effects of changes in the stocks of the two
primary factors on the rate of growth and the composition of output. These
comparative dynamics exercises shed light on the structure of our model
and also prove useful for understanding the policy analysis that follows.

As we noted in section 8.1, equations (9a), (9b), and (10) determine $\bar{X}$, $\bar{Y}$,
and $g$ once (5), (6a), and (6b) have been used to solve for input prices. We
show the equilibrium in $(\bar{X}, \bar{Y})$ space in figure 8.1. We represent (9a) by the
curve $HH$ with slope $-b_{Hx}/b_{Hy}$, and (9b) by the curve $LL$ with slope
$-b_{Lx}/b_{Ly}$. The curve $\Pi\Pi$ depicts equation (10) and has slope $-a_{zx}/a_{xy}$.
Since the locations of the $HH$ and $\Pi\Pi$ curves depend on $g$, variations in
the growth rate ensure that the three curves intersect at a single point
(labeled $E$) as shown. Our assumptions imply that production of $X$ is the
most human-capital-intensive activity in the sense of direct-plus-indirect

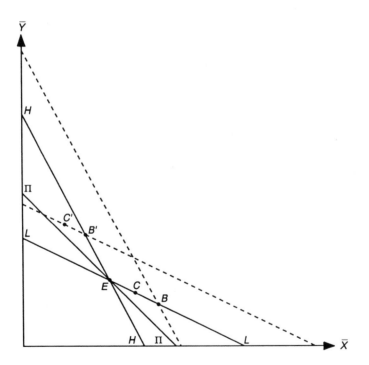

**Figure 8.1**

inputs (since human capital is used directly in this activity together with intermediates and since the share of intermediates in total cost is the same as for industry $Y$), while the production of $Y$ is the most labor-intensive activity. Hence the $HH$ curve is the steepest of the three, and the $LL$ curve is the least steep.

Now consider an increase in the stock of human capital. So long as the new equilibrium involves positive production of both final goods, this endowment change does not alter the equilibrium input prices. So techniques of production do not change. Holding $g$ constant for the moment, the $HH$ curve shifts out in a parallel fashion, as illustrated by the broken curve whose intersection with $LL$ is at point $B$. But point $B$ lies above the $\Pi\Pi$ curve, so the initial level of activity in R&D is no longer consistent with equilibrium. At point $B$ the profit rate in the intermediates sector exceeds the interest rate. Human capital is drawn into R&D, implying a higher rate of innovation and a reduction in resources available for production of final goods. The $\Pi\Pi$ curve shifts out, and the $HH$ curve shifts in, until a new equilibrium is established at a point such as $C$. We conclude that accumulation of human capital speeds growth and that, at given $n$, output of the human-capital-intensive activity expands while output of the labor-intensive activity contracts. These changes in the composition of final production reflect of course the Rybczynski forces that are present in our model.

An increase in the labor force can be analyzed similarly. The $LL$ curve shifts out, as depicted by the broken line that intersects the $HH$ curve at $B'$. Since point $B'$ lies above the $\Pi\Pi$ curve, the rate of innovation must increase. The reallocation of resources to R&D causes the $HH$ curve to shift back and the $\Pi\Pi$ curve to shift out, until they both intersect the new $LL$ curve at a point such as $C'$. Thus an increase in $L$ augments output in the labor-intensive industry (for every $n$) and shrinks output in the capital-intensive industry. The economy experinces faster growth, just as it does when the stock of human capital expands.

## 8.3  Optimal Growth and R&D Subsidies

The market equilibrium described above differs from the social optimum due to the presence of two market distortions. First, the existence of a nonappropriable benefit from research in the form of a contribution to general knowledge means that the private incentive to conduct R&D may deviate from the social incentive. Second, the monopoly power exercised by each producer of intermediates causes the consumer price of these inputs to exceed the social opportunity cost. These distortions interact of course inasmuch as the monopoly rents provide the private incentive for R&D in our economy. In general two policy instruments will be needed to achieve the first-best equilibrium. We begin, however, with an examination of a second-best problem as follows. What is the optimal growth path when the government is constrained to allow market forces to govern the determination of input prices and the allocation of inputs to intermediate and final goods producers? And what is the nature of the government intervention that attains this growth path in a decentralized equilibrium?[1]

We take as the objective of the government the maximization of utility for the representative consumer. Given the linear homogeneity of $u(\cdot)$, the associated indirect utility function has the form $v(p_x, p_y, E) = \varphi(p_x, p_y)E$. Then, using (1), the government's maximand can be written as

$$\rho U = \log \varphi(p_x, p_y) + \rho \int_0^\infty e^{-\rho t} [\log \bar{E}(t) + \gamma \log n(t)] \, dt, \tag{11}$$

where $\bar{E} = En^{-\gamma}$ and, by the definition of $g \equiv \dot{n}/n$, we have

$$\log n(t) = \log n_0 + \int_0^t g(\tau) \, d\tau. \tag{12}$$

The constraints imposed by technology and by the assumed use of the market mechanism for allocating inputs to all activities other than R&D can be expressed as follows: Input prices are determined by (5), (6a), and (6b). These fix the production techniques. Then (9a) and (9b) will determine $\bar{X}(t)$ and $\bar{Y}(t)$ as linear functions of the government's choice of $g(t)$. We can multiply (9a) by $\bar{w}_H \equiv w_H n^{-\gamma}$, multiply (9b) by $\bar{w}_L \equiv w_L n^{-\gamma}$, and add these two together to express the resource constraint as

$$[1 - (1 - \alpha)\beta]\bar{E} + \bar{w}_H a_{Hn} g = \bar{V}, \tag{13}$$

where $\bar{V} = \bar{w}_H H + \bar{w}_L L$. In writing (13), we have made use of the fact that $\beta$ is the share of middle products in the total cost of manufacturing final goods and that the current account must balance in a country lacking access to international captial markets (i.e., $E = p_x X + p_y Y$). We can interpret (13) as requiring savings to be equal to investment since $[\bar{V} + (1 - \alpha)\beta\bar{E}]n^\gamma$ represents total income (i.e., factor invome plus profits), $\bar{E}n^\gamma$ represents expenditure, and $\bar{w}_H a_{Hn} g n^\gamma$ represents outlays on R&D.

The second-best growth path maximizes (11) subject to the constraints expressed in (12) and (13). The solution to this maximization problem implies a time-invariant second-best growth rate $g^*$, where

$$g^* = \frac{\bar{V}}{\bar{w}_H a_{Hn}} - \frac{\rho}{\gamma}. \tag{14}$$

We illustrate the solution for the second-best growth rate in figure 8.2. Given the constancy of the second-best growth rate, we can substitute (12) into (11), and thereby express the objective function as

$$\rho U = \log \varphi(p_x, p_y) + \rho \log n_0 + \log \bar{E} + \left(\frac{\gamma}{\rho}\right) g. \tag{15}$$

Equation (15) defines an implicit trade-off between the initial level of spending and its rate of growth. We plot two representative "indifference" curves in $(\bar{E}, g)$ space in the figure. The government maximizes (15) subject

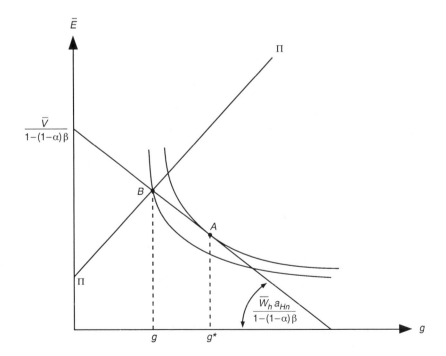

**Figure 8.2**

to the budget constraint given by (13). The optimum is found at the point
of tangency (point $A$) as usual.[2]

Figure 8.2 can also be used to locate the market equilibrium rate of
growth. Notice that the budget constraint (13) applies equally to the market
outcome. But now the no-arbitrage condition (10) also obtains. Recognizing that middle products comprise a share $\beta$ of the cost of final goods, we
can rewrite this condition as

$$\frac{(1 - \alpha)\beta\bar{E}}{\bar{w}_H a_{Hn}} = g + \rho. \tag{16}$$

The line $\Pi\Pi$ in the figure represents equation (16). The equilibrium growth
rate is found at the intersection of this line and the budget line. A simple
calculation reveals that

$$g = \frac{\alpha\gamma\bar{V}}{\bar{w}_H a_{Hn}} - \rho(1 - \alpha\gamma). \tag{17}$$

Comparing (17) with (14), we find

$$\alpha\gamma g^* - g = \rho(1 - \alpha)(1 - \beta) > 0.$$

Hence $g^* > g/\alpha\gamma = g/\beta(1 - \alpha) > g$; that is, the second-best rate of growth
exceeds the market-determined growth rate. Intuitively the market under-
provides research and development because the entrepreneur does not
capture all the social benefits from her efforts.[3]

We show now that a simple subsidy to R&D (financed by lump-sum
taxes) can be used to achieve the second-best equilibrium. Let $(S - 1)/S$,
$S \geq 1$, be the fraction of R&D expenditures borne by the government. This
policy alters only the no-arbitrage condition among all the equilibrium
relationships. With the policy in effect, we replace $a_{Hn}$ in (10) and thus (16)
by $a_{Hn}/S$. Input prices (determined by equations 5 and 6), input-output
coefficients, and the requirement of current account balance are not affected.
Hence the budget constraint (13) continues to apply.

From this discussion we see that the effect of the subsidy is to shift the
$\Pi\Pi$ line in figure 8.2 down and to rotate it in a clockwise direction. Welfare
increases monotonically as the equilibrium moves from $B$ to $A$. The optimal
subsidy achieves the second-best allocation. Note, however, that once the
subsidy brings the economy to $A$, further increases in the rate of subsidy
reduce welfare. This is true despite the fact that such subsidies continue to

speed growth. Faster growth comes at a cost in our economy, and thus growth is not desirable beyond the optimal rate.

It is easy to see that the larger is the country the larger will be the optimal subsidy to R&D. Increasing the size of the economy shifts the budget line out. The equilibrium for the larger economy falls farther out along the original ΠΠ line. But the new second-best rate obtains on a horizontal line through point $A$.[4] Thus the subsidy that rotates the ΠΠ line to pass through point $A$ no longer suffices to attain the second-best growth rate.

How does the subsidy to R&D affect the composition of final output in the economy? We answer this question with the aid of figure 8.3. There, as in figure 8.1, point $E$ represents the equilibrium with no intervention. The subsidy to R&D shifts ΠΠ inward, as represented by the broken line. Since the intersection of $HH$ with $LL$ now falls above the ΠΠ curve, resources shift to R&D, which speeds growth. The increase in $g$ causes the ΠΠ curve to shift back out, and the $HH$ curve to shift in, until they intersect along $LL$. Hence the equilibrium with the subsidy in place occurs at a point such as $S$, where output of the labor-intensive sector is greater and output of the

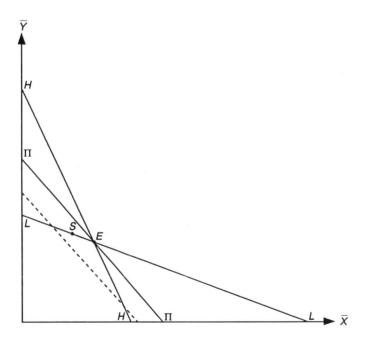

Figure 8.3

human-capital-intensive sector is smaller (for given $n$) than before the subsidy.

We conclude this section by establishing that the second-best rate of growth actually coincides with the first-best in our model. In the first-best, intermediate inputs are priced at marginal cost. Thus the $\alpha$ in (5) vanishes in the first-best, and so input prices and input-output coefficients differ from those in the second-best equilibrium. The unconstrained optimum obtains when (11) is maximized subject to (12) and (13), but with the first-best input prices and techniques of production inserted in (13). The solution to this problem takes the same form as (14), except that different values for $\bar{V}$ and $\bar{w}_H$ from those used in the calculation of the second-best now apply. But note that these variables enter (14) in ratio form and also that $\bar{V}/\bar{w}_H = H + (w_L/w_H)L$. Direct manipulation of (5) and (6) reveals that removal of the distortion caused by the markup pricing of intermediates raises the payments to labor and human capital in exactly the same proportion, and so has no effect on $\bar{V}/\bar{w}_H$. It follow that the first-best and second-best growth rates are equal. The first-best can be achieved by means of subsidies to both research and development and the production of intermediates.

## 8.4   Tariffs and Export Subsidies

We turn now to an investigation of commercial policies. We first ask how tariffs and export subsidies affect the growth rate in our economy. We then consider the welfare consequences of small policy interventions, starting from an initial equilibrium with free trade. Finally, we study small policies introduced from the point of the second-best equilibrium described in section 8.3.

Let $T_i$, $i = x, y$, represent one plus the rate of trade protection provided to sector $i$, where protection takes the form of an import tariff if good $i$ is imported or an export subsidy if that good is exported. Then domestic prices for the final goods become $q_i = T_i p_i$, and these replace the international prices on the left-hand side of equations (6a) and (6b). Differentiating (5), (6a), and (6b) with respect to the $T_i$, and letting a caret denote proportional rates of change, we find

$$\hat{\bar{w}}_H = \frac{(1 - \beta\theta_{Hz})\hat{T}_x}{1 - \beta} - \frac{\beta\theta_{Lz}\hat{T}_y}{1 - \beta}, \tag{18a}$$

$$\hat{w}_L = \frac{-\beta\theta_{Hz}\hat{T}_x}{1 - \beta} + \frac{(1 - \beta\theta_{Lz})\hat{T}_y}{1 - \beta}, \tag{18b}$$

where $\theta_{jz}$, $j = H, L$, is the share of factor $j$ in the cost of producting intermediates. Equations (18a) and (18b) imply that protection of the human-capital-intensive final good raises the reward to human capital and reduces the reward to labor, whereas protection of the labor-intensive final good has the opposite effects on these wages.

Let us define $\bar{Q} \equiv q_x\bar{X} + q_y\bar{Y}$, which represents the value of final goods (normalized to account for the number of intermediates) at domestic prices. Then we can find the equilibrium values of $\bar{Q}$ and the growth rate by proceeding in a manner analogous to that pursued in section 8.3. The resource constraint corresponding to (13) now becomes

$$[1 - (1 - \alpha)\beta]\bar{Q} + \bar{w}_H a_{Hn}g = \bar{V}, \tag{19}$$

whereas the arbitrage condition (16) becomes

$$\frac{(1 - \alpha)\beta\bar{Q}}{\bar{w}_H a_{Hn}} = g + \rho. \tag{20}$$

Of course (19) and (20) correspond exactly to (13) and (16) when $T_i = 1$ for $i = x, y$, in which case $\bar{Q} = \bar{E}$. We solve (19) and (20) for $g$ and $\bar{Q}$, which gives an equation for the growth rate that is exactly the same as in (17), and

$$\bar{Q} = \bar{V} + \bar{w}_H a_{Hn}\rho. \tag{21}$$

Differentiating (17) with respect to the $T_i$, and making use of (18), we find the following effects of trade policies on the growth rate:

$$dg = \frac{\alpha\gamma}{1 - \beta} \frac{w_L L}{w_H a_{Hn}} (\hat{T}_y - \hat{T}_x). \tag{22}$$

Protection of the human-capital-intensive final good, by raising the reward to human capital, makes R&D more costly and thus slows growth. But protection of the labor-intensive good reduces the cost of R&D and so speeds growth. In effect the $X$-sector and the R&D sector are substitutes in production since both draw on the fixed stock of human capital, whereas the $Y$ sector and R&D are complements in production. We note that these results are global in the sense that the larger the rate of protection, the greater is the effect on the growth rate—provided that the economy remains incompletely specialized.

We turn now to welfare, restricting attention to small departures from free trade. Our welfare measure again is given by (15), except that the arguments of $\varphi(\cdot)$ now are the domestic consumer prices, $q_x$ and $q_y$. Balance in the current account now requires that

$$\bar{E} = \bar{Q} + \sum_i (T_i - 1) p_1 \bar{m}_i, \tag{23}$$

where $\bar{m}_i$ denotes imports of good $i$ (negative for exports) multiplied by $n^{-\gamma}$. Equation (23) constrains the value of spending at domestic prices to be equal to the sum of the value of final output at domestic prices and tariff revenue (or subsidy outlay). We assume that the latter is redistributed to (or collected from) consumers in a lump-sum fashion.

We differentiate (15), (21), and (23) about the point where $T_i = 1$ and $\bar{Q} = \bar{E}$, and make use of Roy's identity, to obtain

$$\frac{\rho\, dU}{dT_x} = \frac{\alpha\gamma\theta_{Lz}}{1 - \beta} + \frac{(\gamma/\rho)\, dg}{dT_x}. \tag{24}$$

From (9) we derive

$$\frac{\bar{w}_H H}{\bar{Q}} = (1 - \beta)\theta_x + \alpha\beta\theta_{Hz} + \frac{\bar{w}_H a_{Hn}}{\bar{Q}},$$

$$\frac{\bar{w}_L L}{\bar{Q}} = \alpha\beta\theta_{Lz} + (1 + \beta)\theta_y,$$

were $\theta_i$, $i = x, y$, is the share of the value of output in sector $i$ in $\bar{Q}$.

Then, substituting from (22), and using (20) and the formula for $\bar{w}_L L/\bar{Q}$, we find that

$$\frac{(1 - \beta)\rho\, dU}{\alpha\gamma\, dT_x} = \theta_{Lz} - \frac{g + \rho}{\alpha\rho} [\alpha\beta\theta_{Lz} + (1 - \beta)\theta_y]. \tag{25}$$

The expression for $dU/dT_y$ is the same, except that the sign is reversed.

From (25) protection of the human-captial-intensive final good, although it always slows growth, may raise or lower aggregate welfare. To see the former possibility, recall from figure 8.1 that variations in $H$ will alter the composition of final output, causing $\theta_y$ to vary from zero to one. At the same time changes in $a_{Hn}$ will alter the growth rate. Both of these changes will not affect $\theta_{Lz}$, as factor prices are determined from (5) and (6). So there exist values for $H$ and $a_{Hn}$ such that $\theta_y$ and $g$ are both near zero.[5] In this case the right-hand side of (25) must be positive. Alternatively, the right-hand side of (25) will certainly be negative if $\theta_{Lz} = 0$ (i.e., if intermediates are produced with human capital alone). By similar reasoning, a tariff on imports of $Y$ may raise or lower welfare even though the growth rate always responds positively.

The ambiguous welfare implications of growth-enhancing (or growth-retarding) trade policies reflect the presence of two different distortions in our economy. On the one hand, the private incentives for R&D are insufficient, so any policy that stimulates growth, ceteris paribus, will boost welfare. On the other hand, the monopoly pricing of intermediates means that these inputs are under-produced in the market equilibrium. Protection of the labor-intensive good, by drawing resources into that sector and into the R&D sector may reduce the output of intermediates. If so, this effect counteracts the beneficial effect of faster growth.

We may calculate the impact of trade policy on the output of intermediates using $p_z \bar{Z} = \beta \bar{Q}$, the forumla for $\hat{\bar{Q}}$,

$$\hat{\bar{Q}} = \theta_x \hat{T}_x + \theta_y \hat{T}_y + \frac{\alpha \gamma \theta_{Lz}(\hat{T}_x - \hat{T}_y)}{1 - \beta},$$

and the expression for $\hat{\bar{p}}_z$ that comes from differentiating (5), (6a), and (6b). We find that

$$\hat{\bar{Z}} = \left[\frac{(1 - \alpha\gamma)}{(1 - \beta)}\theta_{Lz} - \theta_y\right](\hat{T}_x - \hat{T}_y). \tag{26}$$

Intermediate production is more likely to rise in response to protection of the human-captial-intensive good and fall in response to protection of the labor-intensive good, the larger is the share of labor in the cost of producing the inputs. This follows from the fact that an increase in the domestic price of $X$ causes $w_H$ to rise and $w_L$ to fall, whereas an increase in $q_y$ has the opposite effect on factor prices. For given $\theta_{Lz}$ the output of intermediates is more likely to rise the greater is the share of the protectecd sector in the value of final production. We recognize this as a demand-side effect, recalling the fact that intermediates are nontraded goods. Since protection causes one final-good sector to expand and the other to contract, it has offsetting effects at given prices on the derived demand for intermediates. The more important is the expanding sector in total derived demand, the more likely it will be that the demand curve for intermediates shifts out.

Comparing (26) and (25), it is easy to show that a decrease (increase) in output of intermecdiates is necessary but not sufficient for protection of the labor-intensive (human-capital-intensive) industry to lower (raise) welfare. A growth-enhancing policy its more likely to increase welfare despite a fall in the output of intermediates when $g/(g + \rho)$ is large, since the beneficial effect of the tariff through its indirect inducement to R&D is largest in this case. Similarly, a growth-retarding trade policy can give rise to a welfare improvement only when the initial growth rate is relatively low. Finally, (25) reveals that in general the larger the share of the protected sector in the value of the find output, the more likely is a trade policy to improve welfare.

In general, we cannot rank the optimal R&D subsidy of section 8.3 and the optimal tariff or export subsidy. This reflects the second-best nature of either form of policy intervention. The R&D subsidy most efficiently offsets the externality present in the process of knowledge generation but does nothing to correct for the undersupply of intermediate goods. Trade policy, on the other hand, has only an indirect effect on growth. But since trade policies alter domestic factor prices, they can be useful as a means to promote the production of intermediate goods.

Finally, we note that if both trade policy and R&D subsidies are available to the government as tools of intervention, then in general both will be used to augment welfare. Starting from the second-best equilibrium identified in section 8.3, we can again calculat the welfare effect of a small does of trade policy. We find that

$$\operatorname{sgn} dU = \operatorname{sgn}[(\theta_{Lz} - \theta_y)(\hat{T}_x - \hat{T}_y)].$$

When an R&D subsidy is available to spur growth, trade policy should be used to promote production of intermediates. This goal is achieved by protecting the sector that is large (a demand-side influence) or the one that competes least for primary inputs with producers of intermediates.

## 8.5   Tariffs versus Quotas

We turn now to a comparison of tariffs and quotas. We assume that the presence of quota rents gives rise to rent-seeking behavior that diverts resources from the productive sectors. We establish that the occurrence of such behavior necessarily slows growth. This finding is in keeping with the description of various historical epochs provided by Baumol (1988). We also show that the diversion of resources to rent seeking has an adverse effect on welfare, and so small tariffs are preferable to small quotas on efficiency grounds.

We specify a quantitative import restriction that fixes $\bar{m}_x$ so that the volume of imports grows at rate $\gamma g$.[6] In so doing, we are assuming that the trade authorities continually adjust the permissible level of imports to keep pace with growth in the economy. We consider a quota that slightly reduces the level of imports below the free-trade level at every moment in time.

We suppose that import licenses are distributed in proportion to the resources that an entrepreneur devotes to seeking, and that all licences are "up for grabs." We allow a general, constant-returns-to-scale technology for seeking, with unit cost function $c_R(w_H, w_L)$. Let $R$ be a measure of the intensity of seeking activity. Then in a competitive equilibrum total rents $(q_x - p_x)m_x$ must equal the total industry cost of seeking $c_R(w_H, w_L)R$. We multiply both sides by $n^{-\gamma}$ to obtain

$$(q_x - p_x)\bar{m}_x = c_R(\bar{w}_H, \bar{w}_L)R. \tag{27}$$

The use of resources in seeking import licences must now be incorporated into the factor-market-clearing coniditons. We use modified versions of (9a) and (9b), multiply the former by $\bar{w}_H$ and the latter by $\bar{w}_L$, and add, to derive

$$[1 - (1 - \alpha)\beta]\bar{Q} + \bar{w}_H a_{Hn}g = \bar{V}(\bar{w}_H, \bar{w}_L) - c_R(\bar{w}_H, \bar{w}_L)R. \tag{28}$$

This is our "resource constraint"; it takes the place of (19), which we used in the tariff case. The no-arbitrage condition (20), derived for the tariff case using domestic prices in the calculation of profits, continues to apply.

Now consider the introduction of a small restriction to imports from an initial position of free trade. From (27) and the fact that initially $R = 0$, we have

$$\bar{m}_x dq_x = c_R(\bar{w}_H, \bar{w}_L)\,dR.$$

The quota generates an increase in the domestic price of the importable good and draws some resources into rent seeking. These two effects of the quota can be distinguished for purposes of analyzing the implications for resource allocation and growth.

The implications of the rise in the domestic price of the importable are identical to those for a tariff. From (6a) and (6b), $\bar{w}_H$ rises and $\bar{w}_L$ falls. Then, ignoring the last term in (28) for the moment, this change in factor prices alters the allocation of resources given by (20) and (28) in the same way that the tariff affected the allocation given by (19) and (20).

The diversion of resources to rent seeking acts like a shrinkage of the resource endowment of the economy. The partial effect of this (for given $\bar{w}_H$ and $\bar{w}_L$) can be seen in figure 8.4. There we have plotted (20) and (28) in $(g, \bar{Q})$ space. From (28) an increase in $R$, holding $\bar{w}_H$ and $\bar{w}_L$ constant, causes the resource constraint to shift in while leaving the no-arbitrage condition unaffected. The resource contraction reduces both the growth rate and the value of the output of final goods as the equilibrium shifts from $E$ to $E'$.

We conclude that whatever is the effect of a small tariff on the growth rate, a quota-cum-rent-seeking that similarly protects the domestic importables industry will be more deleterious. The same can be said with regard to welfare. The welfare consequences of a small departure from free trade continue to be a function of the effects of policy on the rate of growth and the (normlized) level of spending as they were for the tariff. Under the quota trade balance again requires $\bar{E} = \bar{Q} + (q_x - p_x)\bar{m}_x$. So a quota must be

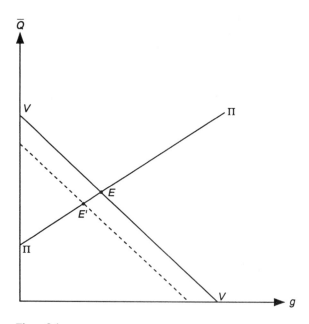

Figure 8.4

inferior to a price-equivalent tariff since the former has both smaller $g$ and smaller $\bar{E}$.

## 8.6   Conclusions

In this chapter we have examined the welfare properties of a dynamic model of trade and growth in a small open economy. Growth stems from endogenous technological progress, as farsighted entrepreneurs introduce innovative (intermediate) products whenever the present value of the stream of operating profits covers the cost of product development. Diversity of intermediate inputs contributes to total factor productivity in two consumer-good sectors, and a balanced growth path generally exists. In the dynamic equilibrium the small country trades the two final goods at exogenously given terms of trade.

Two market distortions featured prominently in our analysis. First, we posited an externality in the process of knowledge generation. We assumed that when entrepreneurs invest in research and development, they fail to appropriate all of the social benefits from the scientific and engineering discoveries they make. This captures, we feel, an important aspect of knowledge creation that relates to the public-good nature of most information. Second, the producers of innovative products must capture some private rewards in the form of monopoly profits it they are to have an incentive to bear the cose of R&D. But the exercise of monopoly power means that the supply of innovative products generally will not be statically efficient.

We identified the first-best growth path and a constrained second-best path. The first-best can be attained with subsidies to both R&D and the production of intermediates, with each policy instrument set so as to correct one of the two distortions noted above. The second-best problem involves maximization of welfare of the representative consumer when the government is constrained to allow market forces to determine factor prices and the allocation of resources to all manufacturers of tangible products. We showed that the first- and second-best rates of growth are the same and that the second-best can be achieved with a subsidy to R&D alone. Subsidies to R&D beyond the rate that we have shown to be optimal accelerate growth even further but at the expense of welfare.

We have examined the growth and welfare implications of commercial policy. We have shown that promotion of the human-capital-intensive final-goods sectors by means of an import tariff or an export subsidy speeds growth, whereas promotion of the labor-intensive final-goods sector slows growth. But acceleration of growth is neither necessary nor sufficient for trade policy to improve welfare. A trade policy that spurs growth may nevertheless reduce welfare if it causes a fall in the output of (undersupplied) intermediates. And similarly a trade policy that encourages production of intermediates by means of the induced reallocation of resources can raise welfare even if expansion of the intermediates sector comes partly at the expense of R&D and hence growth. We have derived an exact expression for the welfare effects of small import tariffs and export subsidies in either sector.

Finally, we have compared tariffs and quotas as tools of trade protection under the assumption that the distribution of quota licences can be influenced by rent-seeking behavior. As in the static models of Krueger (1974) and others, the diversion of resources to rent seeking reduces the production possibilities for the economy. In our growth model some of the resources that engage in rent seeking come at the expense of the R&D sector, and so the occurrence of rent seeking reduces the rate of growth. We have shown that a small restriction of trade achieved via a quota-cum-rent-seeking leads to a lower level of welfare than a similar restriction achieved by means of a tariff.

## Notes

We are grateful to the National Science Foundation and the Institute for Advanced Studies at the Hebrew University of Jerusalem for providing financial support and to Avinash Dixit for commenting on an earlier draft.

1. A command economy interpretation of our second-best problem is as follows: Suppose the government performs all R&D but then must grant exclusive rights to each blueprint to single private producer. What path of R&D expenditures by the government maximizes social welfare?

2. The constraint (13) becomes nonlinear for high values of $g$, because the economy is lead to specialize in the labor-intensive good $y$; see Grossman and Helpman (1991, ch. 6). In the following analysis we assume that the relevant outcomes are on the linear position of this curve.

3. The entrepreneur fails to appropriate the social gain from her contribution to general knowledge, as well as part of the contribution she makes to consumer surplus. Against this, the entrepreneur sees as a private benefit the profit that she realizes at the expense of other producers, whereas the social benefit from this profit capture is nil. With our constant elasticity specification the last two effects just offset, and the R&D spillovers turn out to be decisive.

4. From (13) and (14) we see that the level of $\bar{E}$ at the second-best outcome is independent of $\bar{V}$.

5. When $\theta_y$ is near zero, good $Y$ must be imported. Then the trade policy under discussion (i.e., protection of the human-capital-intensive industry) involves a subsidy to exportes of good $X$.

6. The analysis of a quota on imports of good $Y$, if that happens to be the import good, is analogous. The conclusions regarding the comparison of the tariff and quota are identical.

## References

Baumol, William J. 1988. Entrepreneurship: Productive unproductive and imitative; or the rule of the rules of the game. Unpublished manuscript.

Ethier, Wilfred J. 1982. National and international returns to scale in the modern theory of international trade. *American Economic Review* 72: 389–405.

Grossman, Gene M., and Helpman, Elhanan. 1989. Endogenous product Cycles. Discussion Paper in Economics No. 144. Princeton, NJ: Woodrow Wilson School of Public and International Affairs.

Grossman, Gene M., and Helpman, Elhanan. 1990. Comparative advantage and long-run growth. *American Economic Review* 80: 796–815.

Grossman, Gene M., and Helpman, Elhanen. 1991. *Innovation and Growth.* Cambridge: MIT Press.

Krueger, Anne O. 1974. The politicial economy of the rent-seeking society. *American Economic Review* 64: 291–303.

Lucas, Robert E., Jr. 1988. On the mechanics of economic development. *Journal of Monetary Economics* 22: 3–42.

Romer, Paul M. 1990. Endogenous technological change. *Journal of Political Economy* 90: S71–S102.

Romer, Paul M. 1989. Capital accumulation in the theory of long run growth. In R. Barro (ed.), *Modern Macroeconomics.* Cambridge: Harvard University Press.

# II TRADE POLICY: EVIDENCE

# 9 Quality Upgrading and Its Welfare Cost in U.S. Steel Imports, 1969–74

Randi Boorstein and Robert C. Feenstra

During the past two decades the U.S. government, prompted by the faltering steel industry, has made numerous attempts to restrict the flow of imported steel. The U.S. industry was once the leading steel producer of the postwar period, but by the late 1950s that position was challenged by foreign producers, particularly Japan, whose newer industries were more efficient and reliable. A crippling strike by steel workers caused the United States to become a net importer of steel for the first time in 1959. As countries such as Brazil and Korea began to increase their steel production, and as the U.S. industry failed to remain competitive, imports continued to erode the domestic producers market share.

In 1950 imported steel accounted for only 1.4% of total U.S. steel consumption. In 1968, when the import share had reached 17%, the United States negotiated a voluntary restraint agreement (VRA) with Japan and the European Community (EC). The agreement limited the total tonnage of steel imports but not their total value. Existing theoretical work, such as Falvey (1979), Rodriquez (1979), Das and Donnenfeld (1987, 1989), and Krishna (1987, 1989), shows that the imposition of a quantitative restriction, as opposed to an ad valorem tariff, will likely lead countries to upgrade the quality of their imports within quota categories. This has been demonstrated to have occurred in the automobile industry by Feenstra (1984, 1985, 1988), in the footwear industry by Aw and Roberts (1986, 1988), and in the cheese industry by Anderson (1985, 1988).

In this chapter we measure the quality change which has occurred in U.S. steel imports during the 1969–74 VRA, using the same method as Aw and Roberts (1986, 1988).[1] Under this method the yearly changes in unit values is broken into three components: a quality-adjusted or pure price index; a quality index, which measures changes in the product mix; and a supplier index, which measures changes in the source of supply. In section 9.1 we theoretically justify this technique as a valid way to measure "quality."[2] In section 9.2 we go beyond existing literature by showing how the welfare cost of the quality change in imports can be evaluated.[3] In particular, we derive a measure of welfare cost that depends only on some easily calculated index numbers: The welfare cost equals the inverse of a Paashe price index minus the inverse of an exact price index. So long as producers are minimizing costs, this welfare cost is nonnegative.

In section 9.3 we outline our data and the method of calculating the index numbers, and results are presented in section 9.4. Over the 1969–74 period of the VRA, we find quality upgrading of 7.4% in U.S. steel imports, which occurs most strongly in the first year. This compares with a 1.4% quality decline in the following years. The welfare cost of the quality change varies around one percent of import expenditure during 1970–73. We argue that this cost is at least as large as the conventional deadweight loss triangle but smaller than the transfer of quota rents. Conclusions are given in section 9.5.

## 9.1   Model of Trade Restrictions and Quality Change

Let us assume that inputs into an economy's production function may be separated into $M$ discrete varieties of an imported good, which we shall call steel and denote by the column vector $x$, and all other inputs (including domestically produced steel) denoted by the column vector $z$. Let us further assume that imported steel is weakly separable from all other inputs in production.[4] This means that the economy's production function can be written as

$$y = f[g(x), z], \tag{1}$$

where $y$ denotes output, and $g$ is increasing, concave, and homogeneous of degree one in $x$. The function $g(x)$ can be interpreted as an aggregate of imported steel.

Let $p$ denote the $M$-dimensional price vector of imported steel, and $q$ the price vector of all other inputs. These are treated as columns unless transposed with a prime. Then since the production function in (1) is separable, the corresponding cost function can be written as (see Blackorby, Primont, and Russell 1978, thm. 3.8):

$$C[\pi(p), q, y], \tag{2}$$

where

$$\pi(p) \equiv \min_{x} \{p'x \mid g(x) = 1, x \geq 0\}. \tag{3}$$

That is, the prices of imported steel are separable from $q$ and $y$ in the economy's cost function. From (3), $\pi(p)$ is interpreted as a unit-cost function for imported steel and is increasing, concave, and homogeneous of degree one in $p$.

Separability of the prices of imported steel means that the relative demand for import varieties depends only on the import prices, and not on $q$ or $y$. This can be demonstrated by differentiating the cost function with respect to some $p_i$ and $p_j$ to derive the demand functions for two varieties of imported steel and then by examining their ratio:

$$\frac{x_i}{x_j} = \frac{C_{p_i}}{C_{p_j}} = \frac{C_\pi \pi_i}{C_\pi \pi_j} = \frac{\pi_i(p)}{\pi_j(p)},$$

where $\pi_i \equiv \partial\pi/\partial p_i$. One can see that although the absolute demand for an individual variety of imported steel is a function of the prices of all goods and the level of output, the relative demand for any two varieties is a function only of imported steel prices.

Before examining the effects of trade policy on the type of steel products imported, we need to have a suitable definition of "quality." Let $n$ denote a column vector of one's with dimension $M$, and let $X \equiv x'n$ denote the summed quantity of steel imports. We are supposing that the varieties of steel imports are measured in some common unit (i.e., tons), but the summation is still objectionable since we are adding rods, sheets, stainless steel, and so on. The purpose of our "quality" measure is to turn the objectionable magnitude $X$ (tons of imported steel) into a meaningful aggregate. To this end we use the following:

DEFINITION 1    The quality of steel imports is $Q \equiv g(x)/X$.

Thus, given data on $X$, the researcher would multiply it by quality $Q$ to obtain the aggregate imports $g(x)$. However, this definition of quality is only useful if it can be computed relatively easily. The following result shows that this is the case:

PROPOSITION 1    Let $x^0 \neq 0$ denote the cost-minimizing choice of imports given $(p, q, y)$, with $X^0 = n'x^0$. Then $Q = (p'x^0/X^0)/\pi(p)$.

*Proof*    Let $\lambda = g(x^0) > 0$. Then using a slight change of notation in (3), we can write

$$\pi(p) = \min_x \left\{ p'\left(\frac{x}{\lambda}\right) \,\middle|\, g\left(\frac{x}{\lambda}\right) = 1, \left(\frac{x}{\lambda}\right) \geq 0 \right\}$$

$$= \min_x \left\{ p'\left(\frac{x}{\lambda}\right) \,\middle|\, g(x) = \lambda, x \geq 0 \right\}$$

(since $g$ is homogeneous of degree one),

$$= \left(\frac{1}{\lambda}\right) \min_{x} \{p'x | g(x) = \lambda, x \geq 0\}$$

$$= \left(\frac{1}{\lambda}\right) p'x^0 = p'x^0/g(x^0) \qquad \text{(by definition of } x^0 \text{ and } \lambda^0\text{).}$$

Thus we have $g(x^0) = p'x^0/\pi(p)$ and so the proposition follows directly from the definition of $Q$. □

Proposition 1 states that the quality of imported steel can be obtained as a ratio of the unit value $(p'x^0/X^0)$ and the unit cost $\pi(p)$. Let us denote the former by $UV$. Now consider evaluating the change in quality between two time periods, labeled 0 and 1. We have

$$\ln Q^1 - \ln Q^0 = \ln\left(\frac{UV^1}{UV^0}\right) - \ln\left[\frac{\pi(p^1)}{\pi(p^0)}\right]. \qquad (4)$$

In this formula $\pi(p^1)/\pi(p^0)$ can be measured by an exact price index (see Diewert 1976, and section 9.3). Thus (4) states that the change in quality can be measured by the difference of the growth in the unit value and an exact price index between two periods. This is precisely the method used by Waldorff (1979), Chinloy (1980), Aw and Roberts (1986, 1988), and others.[5]

Our next step is to determine how the quality of imports is affected by trade restrictions. A quota (or VRA) limits the total amount imported as measured by $X$ (i.e., tons of steel). As argued by Falvey (1979), we expect this restriction to cause the same specific or dollar increase in all varieties of the import since, if the specific markups on two varieties differed, there could be profits earned by lowering (raising) imports with the low (high) markup, keeping total imports constant.[6] Letting $\sigma > 0$ denote the specific increase in the price of imported steel due to a quota and $p$ denote the exogenous international prices, the import prices after the quota are $p + \sigma n$. In contrast, an ad valorem tariff of $\tau$ leads to the same percentage increase in all import prices, resulting in a price vector of $p(1 + \tau)$.

The effect of the quota or ad valorem tariff on the quality of imports is given by the following:

PROPOSITION 2

a. A quota leads to an increase in import quality whenever $p_i \neq p_j$ for some $i$ and $j$ and $\pi_{pp}$ is of rank $(M - 1)$.
b. An ad valorem tariff leads to no change in import quality.

*Proof*

a. We evaluate the change in quality using (4), with $p^0 = p$ and $p^1 = p + \sigma n$. Note that $UV = p'x/X = p'C_\pi \pi_p/C_\pi \pi'_p n = \pi'_p p/\pi'_p n = \pi(p)/\pi'_p n$ since $\pi$ is homogeneous of degree one. Substituting the expressions for $p^0$, $p^1$, and $UV$ into (4) and canceling terms, we obtain

$$\ln Q^1 - \ln Q^0 = \ln[\pi'_p(p)n] - \ln[\pi'_p(p + \sigma n)n].$$

Since the natural log is an increasing function, the sign of this expression is identical to the sign of $[\pi'_p(p)n - \pi'_p(p + \sigma n)n]$. Define $\psi(\lambda) = \pi'_p[\lambda p + (1 - \lambda)(p + \sigma n)]n$. Then from the mean value theorem we have

$$\pi'_p(p)n - \pi'_p(p + \sigma n)n = \psi(1) - \psi(0)$$

$$= \psi'(\lambda^0) \quad \text{for some } \lambda^0 \in [0, 1]$$

$$= -\sigma n' \pi_{pp}[\lambda^0 p + (1 - \lambda^0)(p + \sigma n)]n$$

$$\geq 0, \tag{5}$$

where the last inequality follows since $\pi$ is concave so that $\pi_{pp}$ is negative semidefinite. We know in general that $\pi_{pp}(p)p = 0$, and given our rank assumption, there is no vector other than $kp$ that can be multiplied with $\pi_{pp}(p)$ to yield zero. Thus (5) is zero if and only if $[\lambda^0 p + (1 - \lambda^0)(p + \sigma n)] = kn$ for some $k > 0$, which implies that $p = [k - (1 - \lambda^0)\sigma]n$ so $p_i = p_j$ for all $i$ and $j$.
b. We follow the same procedure as in part a, where now $p^0 = p$ and $p^1 = p(1 + \tau)$. Then expression (4) becomes

$$\ln Q^1 - \ln Q^0 = \ln[\pi'_p(p)n] - \ln[\pi'_p(p(1 + \tau))n].$$

Since $\pi$ is homogeneous of degree one in $p$, $\pi_p$ is homogeneous of degree zero. It follows that $\pi_p(p) = \pi_p(p(1 + \tau))$, and so the above expression equals zero. □

The assumption that $p_i \neq p_j$ in proposition 2a simply means that some varieties of imported steel have different prices; otherwise, the specific price increase from a quota would be equivalent to an ad valorem tariff. The assumption that $\pi_{pp}$ is of rank $(M - 1)$ rules out a Leontief production function $g(x)$, for example, since the corresponding cost function $\pi(p)$ is linear and $\pi_{pp} = 0$. In the Leontief case the varieties of steel would be imported in fixed proportions $x_i/x_j$, and a quota has no effect on import composition. But aside from this case we expect the specific price increase to shift import demand toward the varieties with higher initial prices since those varieties experience a lower relative price increase. It is this shift in the composition of imports which is captured by our measure of "quality." Since the ad valorem tariff leaves relative import prices unchanged, it leads to no shift in the composition of imports.

Proposition 2 should be regarded as a generalization of the results in Falvey (1979), and certainly depends on our assumption of separability of steel imports.[7] New results are obtained when we consider the welfare effect of quality change, which we turn to next.

## 9.2   Welfare Cost of Quality Change

To evaluate the welfare cost of a quota or ad valorem tariff, we shall use the conventional deadweight loss definition (Diamond and McFadden 1974): The difference between the rise in production costs due to the trade restriction, and the revenue or rents generated from it.[8] Letting $L_\sigma$ and $L_\tau$ denote the deadweight loss due to the quota and ad valorem tariff, respectively, we have

$$L_\sigma = C[\pi(p + \sigma n), q, y] - C[\pi(p), q, y] - C_\pi \pi_p'(p + \sigma n)\sigma n, \tag{6a}$$

$$L_\tau = C[\pi(p(1 + \tau)), q, y] - C[\pi(p), q, y] - C_\pi \pi_p'(p(1 + \tau))\tau p. \tag{6b}$$

The first two terms in (6a) and (6b) are production costs with and without the trade restriction, and the third terms are quota rents or tariff revenue, respectively, where $C_\pi \pi_p(\cdot)$ is the vector of import purchases.[9] If the quota rents are obtained by foreigners, then the third term in (6a) should be omitted when calculating the social cost of the quota.

In this study we wish to focus on the excess cost of the quota due to the quality upgrading. Our analysis is complementary to Crandall (1981), Congressional Budget Office (1984), Tarr and Morkre (1984), Hufbauer, Berliner, and Elliot (1986), and other studies that estimate the price increase due to the steel quota, the corresponding reduction in aggregate imports, and then calculate the deadweight loss triangle. We will provide an additional welfare cost due to the quality change itself, which can be added to the conventional deadweight loss triangle and to the rectangle of quota rents (see section 9.4).

To isolate the welfare effect of the quality change, let us consider an ad valorem tariff that has the same effect on the aggregate import price as the quota, namely, that satisfies

$$\pi(p(1 + \tau)) = \pi(p + \sigma n). \tag{7}$$

If the quota led to no change in the composition of imports (e.g., if the production technology was Leontief), then the tariff and quota satisfying (7) would have the same deadweight loss. Then a natural way to isolate the welfare effect of the quality change is to consider the difference between $L_\sigma$ and $L_\tau$ when (7) holds. Formally, we state this as follows:

DEFINITION 2   The welfare cost of quality upgrading due to the quota is $W \equiv (L_\sigma - L_\tau)/C_\pi \pi(p + \sigma n)$, where (7) holds.

Several points should be noted. First, in this definition the term $C_\pi \pi(p + \sigma n)$ is the total expenditure on imports with the quota, and we measure the welfare cost relative to this expenditure. Second, we have referred to $W$ as a "cost" without yet proving it is positive; this is the point of our next proposition. Third, the ad valorem tariff and quota satisfying (7) can be thought of as price equivalent. The welfare cost of the quota is equal to the welfare cost of the price-equivalent tariff ($L_\tau$) plus $W$ (before dividing by import expenditure). An alternative comparison of tariffs and quotas can be made by considering those that are quantity equivalent as defined by $X$, that is, leading to the same tonnage of steel imports. This approach is taken by Krishna (1987), and the two approaches are compared by Anderson (1988).

The next result shows that $W$ can be measured by a comparison of index numbers.[10] We suppose that import prices and quantity before and after the quota are available to the researcher. The Paasche price index measures the change in import expenditure using the post-quota quantities:

$$P_a(p, p + \sigma n) \equiv \frac{C_\pi \pi'_p(p + \sigma n)(p + \sigma n)}{C_\pi \pi'_p(p + \sigma n)p}$$

$$= \frac{\pi'_p(p + \sigma n)(p + \sigma n)}{\pi'_p(p + \sigma n)p}. \tag{8}$$

In contrast, an exact price index (see Diewert 1976, and section 9.3) uses the price and quantity data to measure the true change in the aggregate import price:

$$P_e(p, p + \sigma n) \equiv \frac{\pi(p + \sigma n)}{\pi(p)}. \tag{9}$$

We then have the following proposition:

PROPOSITION 3    $W = [1/P_a(p, p + \sigma n)] - [1/P_e(p, p + \sigma n)] \geq 0.$

*Proof*    Since $\pi$ is homogeneous of degree one, we have $\pi'_p(p)p = \pi(p)$ and $\pi_p(p(1 + \tau)) = \pi_p(p)$. Then substituting (7) into (6) and canceling terms, we obtain

$$L_\sigma - L_\tau = C_\pi[\pi'_p(p(1 + \tau))\tau p - \pi'_p(p + \sigma n)\sigma n]$$

$$= C_\pi[\pi'_p(p + \sigma n)p - \pi'_p(p(1 + \tau))p]$$

$$\text{since } \pi'_p(p(1 + \tau))p(1 + \tau) = \pi'_p(p + \sigma n)(p + \sigma n) \text{ from (7)}$$

$$= C_\pi[\pi'_p(p + \sigma n)p - \pi(p)]. \tag{10}$$

From (3) this expression must be nonnegative since the quantities $x = \pi_p(p + \sigma n)$ are feasible to produce $g(x) = 1$ but not cost minimizing with prices $p$. Dividing this expression by $C_\pi\pi(p + \sigma n) = C_\pi\pi'_p(p + \sigma n)(p + \sigma n)$ and using (8) and (9), we obtain the proposition. ∎

The result that $W \geq 0$ in proposition 3 means that the quota has greater deadweight loss than a price-equivalent tariff, as defined by (7). Note that this quota and tariff also lead to equivalent aggregate imports, given by $g(x) = C_\pi(\pi(p(1 + \tau)), q, y) = C_\pi(\pi(p + \sigma n), q, y)$. However, the quantity of imports as measured by $X$ (tonnage of steel) certainly differ between the quota and ad valorem tariff since the former leads to quality upgrading. Indeed from definition 1 we have that $X = g(x)/Q$, and since $Q$ rises with the quota but not the tariff, we see that imports $X$ are lower with the quota than with a price-equivalent ad valorem tariff.

## 9.3    Calculation of Index Numbers

We obtained annual seven-digit TSUSA data on the quantity $X$ and value $V$ of steel imports by country of origin from the U.S. Bureau of the Census for 1968 through 1978. The countries used accounted for virtually all the steel imported into the United States. One hundred sixteen product categories are included; all steel products other than pipe and tube. Overall, this group of products represents about 95% of U.S. steel imports in 1968. Denoting varieties of steel by $m$ and countries by $c$, the rate of growth of a unit value $(\Delta UV)$ of steel imports can be measured as follows:

$$\Delta UV^t = \ln UV^t - \ln UV^{t-1}, \tag{11}$$

where

$$UV^t = \frac{\sum_m \sum_c V_{mc}^t}{\sum_m \sum_c X_{mc}^t}.$$

Superscripts denote time periods, and subscripts identify the particular product-country combination.

The rate of growth of a discrete Divisia price index $(\Delta P_d)$ of imported steel may be written as

$$\Delta P_d^t = \sum_m \sum_c S_{mc}^t \left[ \ln \left( \frac{V_{mc}^t}{X_{mc}^t} \right) - \ln \left( \frac{V_{mc}^{t-1}}{X_{mc}^{t-1}} \right) \right], \tag{12}$$

where

$$S_{mc}^t = \frac{1}{2} \left[ \frac{V_{mc}^t}{\sum_m \sum_c V_{mc}^t} + \frac{V_{mc}^{t-1}}{\sum_m \sum_c V_{mc}^{t-1}} \right].$$

As shown above, the Divisia price index weights the individual price change of each type of steel, from each country, by its average share in the total value of steel imports over the two periods. It will not change simply because of a change in the product or country mix. This index is an exact price index if the import expenditure function is translog (Diewert 1976), and as such is a good choice as the true price index.

The difference between $\Delta UV$ and $\Delta P_d$ is an index of the change in product and supplier mix. It captures the rate of growth of steel import prices which is not due to the price increase of any particular product from a particular country. It may be written as

$$\Delta Q_d^t = \Delta UV^t - \Delta P_d^t. \tag{13}$$

Partial Divsia indexes may also be constructed to measure changes in product and country mix individually. This is done by aggregating over one factor, either by treating products as homogeneous to measure changes in the source of supply or by treating suppliers as homogeneous to measure changes in the product mix. A partial Divisia index is not a pure index because it contains one source of aggregation bias. However, the difference between the rate of growth of a unit value index and the rate of growth of a partial Divisia index may be interpreted as a product quality index only $(Q_m)$ or a supplier index only $(Q_c)$. To create a product quality index, we first create a partial Divisia index treating countries as homogeneous. The rate of growth of this index $\Delta P_m$ is

$$\Delta P_m^t = \sum_m S_m^t \left[ \ln\left[\frac{\sum_c V_{mc}^t}{\sum_c X_{mc}^t}\right] - \ln\left[\frac{\sum_c V_{mc}^{t-1}}{\sum_c X_{mc}^{t-1}}\right] \right], \tag{14}$$

where

$$S_m^t = \frac{1}{2}\left[ \frac{\sum_c V_{mc}^t}{\sum_m \sum_c V_{mc}^t} + \frac{\sum_c V_{mc}^{t-1}}{\sum_m \sum_c V_{mc}^{t-1}} \right].$$

If this index is then subtracted from $\Delta UV$ constructed previously, we get a measure of product quality change, or quality index, corresponding to proposition 1 and to (4):

$$\Delta Q_m^t = \Delta UV^t - \Delta P_m^t. \tag{15}$$

If a partial Divisia index treating goods rather than countries as homogeneous is constructed, then the difference between $\Delta UV$ and the rate of growth of that partial Divisia index $(\Delta P_c)$ is a supplier index, measuring the change in import prices due to different foreign suppliers:

$$\Delta Q_c^t = \Delta UV^t - \Delta P_c^t. \tag{16}$$

The composite quality and supplier index in (13) is not necessarily equal to the sum of (15) and (16) because substitution may take place toward more expensive products from more expensive countries (see Aw and Robert 1986).

Finally, we need to calculate the cumulative Paasche and exact indexes to measure the welfare cost $W$. Using 1968 as the base year, the cumulative Paasche price index is calculated as

$$P_a^t = \left[ \frac{\sum_m \sum_c V_{mc}^t}{\sum_m \left(\sum_c V_{mc}^{68} / \sum_c X_{mc}^{68}\right) \sum_c X_{mc}^t} \right]. \tag{17}$$

Note that in this index we are treating countries as homogeneous and are therefore measuring the change in product prices only. This corresponds to our treatment of countries in the quality index. The cumulative Divisia index treating countries as homogeneous is calculated from (14) as

$$P_m^t = \exp\left( \sum_{\tau=69}^{t} \Delta P_m^\tau \right). \tag{18}$$

The welfare cost corresponding to proposition 3 is given by

$$W_d^t = \left( \frac{1}{P_a^t} \right) - \left( \frac{1}{P_m^t} \right), \tag{19}$$

where the subscript $d$ is used to emphasize that a (partial) Divisia index has been used as the exact index.

Since it will be apparent that the welfare cost is sensitive to the choice of the exact index, we shall also report results using the Fisher (1922) Ideal price index, which is exact for a linear, Leontief, and quadratic production function (Diewert 1976). The cumulative Ideal index ($P_i^t$) is obtained by first calculating the Laspeyres price index ($P_l^t$) with 1968 as the base year and then taking the geometric mean of the Paasche and Laspeyres indexes:

$$P_l^t = \left[ \frac{\sum_m \left( \sum_c V_{mc}^t / \sum_c X_{mc}^t \right) \sum_c X_{mc}^{68}}{\sum_m \sum_c V_{mc}^{68}} \right], \tag{20}$$

$$P_i^t = (P_a^t P_l^t)^{1/2}. \tag{21}$$

In these formulae we are again treating countries as homogeneous. The welfare cost $W$ using the Ideal index is given by

$$W_i^t = \left( \frac{1}{P_a^t} \right) - \left( \frac{1}{P_i^t} \right). \tag{22}$$

## 9.4   Effects of the 1969–74 VRA in Steel

### Estimates of Quality and Supplier Changes

When the VRA was first negotiated by the Johnson administration in 1968, the decision was made to limit overall steel imports to 12.7 million tons (including pipe and tube). Forty-one percent was allocated to each of Japan and the European Community (EC) and 18% was allocated to the rest of

**Table 9.1**
U.S. steel imports

|      | Quantity (million tons) | Unit value (dollars/ton) |
|------|-------------------------|--------------------------|
| 1968 | 15.68 | 104.7 |
| 1969 | 11.71 | 121.3 |
| 1970 | 10.78 | 142.5 |
| 1971 | 15.46 | 139.1 |
| 1972 | 14.69 | 151.9 |
| 1973 | 12.50 | 178.1 |
| 1974 | 13.33 | 304.6 |
| 1975 |  9.56 | 301.2 |
| 1976 | 11.41 | 263.5 |
| 1977 | 15.76 | 269.5 |
| 1978 | 16.91 | 305.5 |

the world. The VRA was agreed to formally, however, only by Japan and the EC. It was to begin in 1969 and last three years, with a 5% growth rate in imports allowed each year.

As seen in table 9.1, from 1968 to 1970 the quantity of steel imports fell from 15.7 million tons, with a unit value of $105 per ton, to 10.8 million tons, with a unit value of $143 per ton. In table 9.2 the aggregate unit value change is decomposed into a Divisia index and, using partial Divisia indexes, into quality and supplier indexes.

During the first year of the VRA the unit value of steel imports rose 14.7%, with about half of that increase due to product quality upgrading. In the second year of the VRA the unit value rose 16.1%, with about two percentage points of that increase due to importing higher quality products. The agreement broke down in 1971 when the Nixon administration placed a 10% surcharge on all imported products. The Europeans and the Japanese claimed that this violated the quota agreement. They responded by increasing steel exports to a level that exceeded their alloted quotas. As a result, the quantity of imports rose by about 50% in 1971, reaching 15.5 million tons. The unit value of steel imports fell to $139 per ton that year. However, since the exact price (Divisia) index actually rose by 2.3%, the entire decline in the unit value index can be attributed to changes in the product and country mix to include more low quality steel products, imported from Japan and the EC.

**Table 9.2**
U.S. steel import indexes

|  | Unit value index ($\Delta UV$) | Divisia index ($\Delta P_d$) | Quality index ($\Delta Q_m$) | Supplier index ($\Delta Q_c$) |
|------|------|------|------|------|
| 1969 | 14.7 | 8.0 | 6.9 | −0.1 |
| 1970 | 16.1 | 13.4 | 1.9 | 0.7 |
| 1971 | −2.4 | 2.3 | −4.1 | −1.7 |
| 1972 | 8.8 | 7.6 | 1.2 | 0.7 |
| 1973 | 15.9 | 13.3 | 1.5 | 0.3 |
| 1974 | 53.7 | 52.1 | 0.0 | −1.0 |
| 1975 | −1.1 | −1.3 | 0.8 | −0.3 |
| 1976 | −13.4 | −11.5 | −0.9 | 0.1 |
| 1977 | 2.3 | 5.4 | −1.8 | −1.2 |
| 1978 | 12.5 | 12.4 | 0.5 | −2.1 |

Note: All indexes are expressed as percentage yearly changes, i.e., equations (11), (12), (15), and (16) multiplied by 100.

In May 1972, after over a year of negotiation, the agreement was renewed, with more specific restrictions placed on high valued products, specifically stainless steel and alloy tool steel (so-called specialty steel). There was a renewed pledge by countries to maintain the product mix of imports, and annual import growth rates were reduced from 5% to 2.5%. In 1973 there was a dramatic increase in world steel demand, which caused the agreement to become superfluous. It lapsed in 1974. During the time the renegotiated VRA was in place, from mid-1972 to 1974, there was some additional quality upgrading. However, because the agreement was binding with the EC only in 1973, and was not binding with Japan in either 1973 or 1974, it is not surprising that further quality upgrading was small.

Over the entire five-year period of the VRA, the unit value of steel imports rose by 53%, an average increase of 10% per year. About one-seventh or 7.4 percentage points of that increase was due to product quality upgrading. Since 1971 is included, this is a conservative estimate. The upgrading is most apparent in the first year of the VRA. There was virtually no movement, however, toward importing steel from higher priced producers. Since the VRA was based on historic market shares, this result follows naturally.

To see how instrumental the VRA was in the occurrence of this quality upgrading, we compare the VRA period 1969 to 1973 (this is the last year the agreement was binding) to a period when there were relatively few restrictions, 1975 to 1978. In the latter years there were no formal quantitative restrictions on carbon steel imports, although there were quantitative restrictions on specialty steel imports between 1976 and 1980.

The industry went through a period of strong demand worldwide in 1973 and 1974. In 1974, 13.3 million tons of steel with a unit value of $305 were imported into the United States. Although imports increased dramatically, the share of imports in total domestic steel consumption fell from about 17% to about 13%. Therefore import penetration was not a major concern. In 1975 and 1976 the situation reversed. Steel prices fell, and producers, who had expanded in the previous two years, were left with enormous levels of excess capacity. In addition, because the decline in demand was viewed as temporary, the industry was relectant to retire its older facilities, exacerbating the problem. Steel imports fell by 30% in 1975, reaching their lowest level of 9.6 million tons. However, the import share rose slightly.

To maintain employment levels in their domestic steel industries, many countries subsidized steel production and/or dumped imports into the United States. This led to a disintegration in the price structure and added to the crisis already facing the domestic steel industry. Increased imports of low priced foreign steel once again spurred action by the domestic industry, in the form of antidumping and countervailing duty lawsuits. By 1978, when the quantity of steel imports has risen to 17 million tons, a new method of curbing steel imports—the trigger price mechanism—was introduced.

From 1975 to 1978 the Divisia price index of imported steel rose erratically by about 5%, but the unit value rose by less than 1%. That is because the product quality index fell by 1.4%, and the supplier index fell by 3.5%. This is a reversal of the previous period, with lower quality products being imported from lower pricing countries.

In summation, product quality seemed to be affected by the imposition of the VRA. Quality upgrading was most pronounced during the first year of the VRA, when it accounted for one-half of the unit value increase. Product quality increased by 7.4% when the VRA was in effect. This compares to a 1.4% quality decline in the following years.

Although supplier changes seemed less dramatic, this may be explained by the smaller differential in the prices among suppliers ($70 to $375 per ton) as compared to the differential in product prices ($41 to $2,387 per ton). The supplier index indicates that there was a greater movement

**Table 9.3**
Welfare cost of quality upgrading

|      | Paasche index $(P_a)$ | Laspeyres index $(P_l)$ | Welfare cost (using Divisia) $(W_d)$ | Welfare cost (using Ideal) $(W_i)$ |
| --- | --- | --- | --- | --- |
| 1969 | 1.076 | 1.081 | 0.42 | 0.21 |
| 1970 | 1.229 | 1.262 | 1.10 | 1.08 |
| 1971 | 1.255 | 1.285 | 0.71 | 0.92 |
| 1972 | 1.352 | 1.391 | 0.82 | 1.05 |
| 1973 | 1.557 | 1.621 | 0.86 | 1.27 |
| 1974 | 2.698 | 2.799 | 0.04 | 0.68 |

Note: The Paasche and Laspeyres indexes are cumulative as in (17) and (20). The deadweight losses are expressed as a percentage of import expenditure, i.e., equations (19) and (22) multiplied by 100.

toward buying products from lower pricing countries when the VRA was removed ($-0.1\%$ during 1969–73 compared to $-3.5\%$ after the VRA). Therefore, even if the agreement did not cause an increase in import purchases from high priced suppliers because it preserved historic market shares, the agreement may have prevented the increase in purchases from lower priced suppliers.

**Welfare Cost of Quality Upgrading**

In table 9.3 we report the welfare cost of quality change, focusing on the 1969–74 period of the VRA. We first show the cumulative Paasche and Laspeyres price indexes with 1968 as the base year. The Ideal index is calculated as the geometric mean of these, and the cumulative (partial) Divisia can be computed from table 9.2 using (15) and (18). Then the welfare costs using the Divisia and Ideal indexes are obtained from (19) and (22), and are shown in the last two columns of table 9.3.

In 1969, the first year of the VRA, the welfare cost was 0.42% and 0.21% of import expenditure, using the Divisia and Ideal indexes, respectively. From table 9.1 import expenditure was $1.64 billion, so the deadweight loss of the quality change is $6.9 and 3.4 million using the two indexes. The welfare cost rises to exceed 1% of import expenditure in 1970, or about $15.5 million. After this the welfare cost using the Divisia index falls below 1% of import expenditure, while the welfare cost from the Ideal index fluctuates around 1%. Although the magnitude of these welfare costs differs somewhat, the yearly directions of change are the same.

It is useful to compare the welfare cost due to upgrading with the other welfare costs arising from the VRA: the conventional deadweight loss triangle from increased domestic production and reduced consumption, and the transfer of quota rents to foreigners. From Hufbauer, Berliner, and Elliot (1986, case M-12), the VRA is estimated to have increased the price of imported steel by 7.3%, which is also a median estimate from Crandall (1981, 105–106). Expressed as a percentage of import expenditure after the quota, the conventional deadweight loss triangle is approximately (1/2) $\eta(0.073/1.073)^2$, where $\eta$ is the elasticity of import demand.[11] Hufbauer et al. use an import demand elasticity of 2.5, whereas Crandall reports a range of estimates for various products ranging from 2.1 to 5. If we use $\eta = 2.5$, then we obtain a conventional deadweight loss of 0.58% of import expenditure, which is below the welfare costs of upgrading reported in table 9.3 for 1970–73. Even with a high value of $\eta = 4.5$, as used by Crandall, we obtain a deadweight loss of 1.04%, which lies between the welfare costs in table 9.3 for 1970–73. Thus, for the VRA in steel, the cost of quality upgrading is at least as large as the conventional deadweight loss.

Considering the transfer of quota rents to foreigners, the 7.3% increase in the import price induced by the VRA corresponds to quota rents of $(0.073/1.073)100 = 6.8\%$ of import expenditure after the quota. Since the welfare cost of upgrading fluctuates around 1% during 1970–73, we can see that it is considerably smaller than the transfer of quota rents.

## 9.5   Conclusions

In this study we have examined the quality upgrading that occurred in U.S. steel imports during the 1969–74 VRA. Quality change is measured by a comparison of unit values with exact price indexes as was theoretically justified in section 9.1. We also derived a measure of the welfare cost of quality change, which equals the inverse of the Paasche price index minus the inverse of an exact price index. So long as producers are minimizing costs, this welfare cost will be nonnegative.

Empirically, we found quality upgrading of 7.4% in U.S. steel imports during the VRA, with most of the upgrading occurring during 1969. This compares with a 1.4% quality decline in the following years. The welfare cost of the quality change varies around 1% of import expenditure during 1970–73. The measured cost is somewhat sensitive to the choice of exact index number, with the Ideal index giving a higher welfare cost in several years than the Divisia index.

We should stress that it is valid to take our measure of the cost of quality upgrading and simply add it on to the conventional deadweight loss and transfer of quota rents obtained from other studies, such as Crandall (1981) and Hufbauer, Berliner, and Elliott (1986). This procedure gives the total welfare cost of the VRA. The reason it is valid is that the earlier studies convert the quota into price-equivalent tariff, as in (7), before calculating the deadweight loss. This means that the earlier studies are really calculating the loss $L_\tau$ rather than $L_\sigma$. From definition 2 we have that $L_\sigma = L_\tau + WC_\pi \pi(p + \sigma n)$, and so given the deadweight loss $L_\tau$, we can simply add on the additional welfare cost of upgrading to obtain $L_\sigma$. Applying this procedure to the 1969–74 VRA, we have argued that the cost due to upgrading is at least as large as the conventional deadweight loss, so $L_\sigma$ is twice as large as $L_\tau$. However, the transfer of quota rents is considerably larger than either of these welfare costs.

Finally, it is useful to compare our results with those that could be obtained for later time periods. American steel producers and the government certainly became aware that quality upgrading was a response of foreign producers to the 1969–74 VRA, and later protection attempted to limit upgrading by specifying quotas on very detailed product categories. Boorstein (1987) finds that these programs were partially effective in limiting upgrading: The magnitude of upgrading during the 1976–80 specialty steel quota, or the 1982–85 EC agreement covering specific carbon and alloy products, is less than we have found for the 1969–74 VRA. This means that the welfare cost of quality change is also smaller. However, even in cases where the United States has imposed very detailed restrictions, some amount of upgrading is often observed, so the economic forces we have identified in this study are still operative.

## Notes

The authors thank Gene Grossman and participants at Tel Aviv University for helpful comments. Financial support from the U.S. Department of Labor is gratefully acknowledged. The views expressed are solely those of the authors and do not represent the views of the International Trade Commission.

1. This method has also been used to measure changes in labor quality by Waldorff (1973) and Chinloy (1980) and, more generally, is related to the literature on technological change such as Jorgenson and Griliches (1967) and Christensen and Jorgenson (1969, 1970).

2. Note that the concept of "quality" used here refers only to the composition of imports across products. An alternative concept arises when firms change the content of products, as with Japanese exporters sending larger, more powerful cars to the United States. In that case "quality" can be measured using hedonic regressions, as in Feenstra (1984, 1985, 1988).

3. Anderson (1985, 1988) measures the welfare cost of inefficient allocation of quotas to U.S. cheese imports. We contrast our approach to his in note 10.

4. The concept of weak separability we use is from Blackorby, Primont, and Russell (1978, lemma 3.3a). Crandall (1981, 46–69) discusses why domestic and imported steel should not be considered perfect substitutes; see also Tarr and Morkre (1984). Note that separability is an assumption in Falvey's (1979) model.

5. Note that these authors simply define quality change according to an equation like (4). In contrast, we have used the more primitive definition 1, and then related it to existing techniques using proposition 1. We hope this clarifies what is meant by "quality."

6. This statement does not hold if there are limits on the ability to arbitrage between sources of suply, as when the quota specifies the maximum amount exported from various countries. The effect of the VRA in steel on sources of supply is captured by our supplier index, which is discussed in sections 9.3 and 9.4.

7. A generalization that allows for nonseparability of imports, leading to ambiguous effects of a quota, is in Dinopoulos and Koo (1986).

8. Recent analyses of deadweight loss in an open economy are provided by Diewert (1983, 1985).

9. Note that in all expressions of the form $C_\pi \pi_p(\cdot)$ the arguments of $C_\pi$ are $C_\pi[\pi(\cdot), q, y]$.

10. If a researcher actually had estimates of the cost functions $C$ and $\pi$, then the deadweight loss of the quota could be evaluated directly from (6a). This is the approach taken by Anderson (1985, 1988), who estimates a translog expenditure function over nine imported (and six domestic) cheese varieties. In our study we have over one hundred categories of imported steel, necessitating the use of index numbers.

11. To derive this formula, we define the ad valorem tariff which is price equivalent to the quota by (7). Then (6b) is the conventional deadweight loss. Dividing (6b) by $C_\pi \pi(p(1 + \tau))$, and using the approximation $C[\pi(p), q, y] \doteq C[\pi(p(1 + \tau)), q, y] - C_\pi \pi(p)\tau + (\frac{1}{2})C_{\pi\pi}\pi(p)^2\tau^2$, we obtain $L_\tau / C_\pi \pi(p(1 + \tau)) \doteq (\frac{1}{2})\eta[\tau/(1 + \tau)]^2$, where $\eta = -C_{\pi\pi}\pi(p(1 + \tau))/C_\pi$.

# References

Anderson, James E. 1985. The relative inefficiency of quotas. *American Economic Review* 75(1): 178–90.

Anderson, James E. 1988. *The Relative Inefficiency of Quotas.* Cambridge: MIT Press.

Aw, Ben Yan, and Mark J. Roberts. 1986. Measuring quality changes in quota constrained import markets: The case of U.S. footwear. *Journal of International Economics* 21: 45–60.

Aw, Ben Yan, and Mark J. Roberts. 1988. Price and quality comparisons for U.S. footwear imports: An application of multilateral index numbers. In Robert C. Feenstra (ed.), *Empirical Methods for International Trade.* Cambridge: MIT Press, pp. 257–275.

Blackorby, Charles, Daniel Primont, and Robert Russell. 1978. *Duality, Separability, and Functional Structure.* Amsterdam: North Holland.

Boorstein, Randi. 1987. The effect of trade restrictions on the quality and composition of imported products: An empirical analysis of the steel industry. Ph.D. dissertation. Columbia University.

Chinloy, Peter. 1980. Sources of quality change in labor input. *American Economic Review* 70 (March): 108–119.

Christensen, L. R., and D. W. Jorgenson. 1969. The measurement of U.S. real capital input, 1929–1962. *Review of Income and Wealth* 15: 293–320.

Christensen, L. R., and D. W. Jorgenson. 1970. U.S. real product and real factor input (1927–67). *Review of Income and Wealth* 16 (March): 19–50.

Congressional Budget Office. 1984. *The Effects of Import Quotas on the Steel Industry.* U.S. Congress. Washington, DC: Government Printing Office.

Crandall, Robert. 1981. *The U.S. Steel Industry in Recurrent Crisis.* Washington, DC: Brookings Institution.

Das, Satya P., and Shabtai Donnenfeld. 1989. Oligopolistic competition and international trade: Quantity and quality restrictions. *Journal of International Economics* 27: 299–318.

Das, Satya P., and Shabtai Donnenfeld. 1987. "Trade policy and its impact on the quality of imports: A welfare analysis. *Journal of International Economics* 23: 77–96.

Diamond, Peter A., and Daniel L. McFadden. 1974. Some uses of the expenditure function in public finance. *Journal of Public Economics* 3: 3–21.

Diewert, W. Erwin. 1976. Exact and superlative index numbers. *Journal of Econometrics* 4 (May): 115–145.

Diewert, W. Erwin. 1983. The measurement of waste within the production sector of an open economy. *Scandanavian Journal of Economics* 85: 159–177.

Diewert, W. Erwin. 1985. A dynamic approach to the measurement of waste in an open economy. *Journal of International Economics* 19: 213–240.

Dinopoulos, Elias, and A. Koo. 1986. On the product mix within import-restricted product categories. Mimeo. Michigan State University. October.

Falvey, Rodney E. 1979. The composition of trade within import-restricted product categories. *Journal of Political Economy* 90(6): 1142–1165.

Feenstra, Robert C. 1984. Voluntary export restraints in U.S. autos, 1980–1981: Quality, employment, and welfare effects. In R. E. Baldwin and A. O. Krueger (eds.), *The Structure and Evolution of Recent U.S. Trade Policy.* Chicago: University of Chicago Press, pp. 35–59.

Feenstra, Robert C. 1985. Automobile prices and protection: The U.S.-Japan trade restraint. *Journal of Policy Modelling* 7: 49–68.

Feenstra, Robert C. 1988. Quality change under trade restraints in Japanese autos. *Quarterly Journal of Economics* 103(1): 131–146.

Fisher, Irving. 1922. *The Making of Index Numbers.* Boston: Houghton Mifflin.

Hufbauer, Gary C., Diane T. Berliner, and Kimberly Ann Elliott. 1986. *Trade Protection in the U.S.: 31 Case Studies.* Washington, DC: Institute for International Economics.

Jorgenson, Dale W., and Z. Griliches. 1967. The explanation of productivity change. *Review of Economic Studies* 34 (July): 249–283.

Krishna, Kala. 1989. Protection and the product line: Monopoly and product quality. *International Economic Review.* 31: 87–102.

Krishna, Kala. 1987. Tariffs vs. quotas with endogenous quality. *Journal of International Economics* 23: 97–117.

Rodriguez, Carlos Alfredo. 1979. The quality of imports and the differential welfare effects of tariffs, quotas, and quality controls as protective devices. *Canadian Journal of Economics* 12: 439–449.

Tarr, David, and Morris Morkre. 1984. *Aggregate Costs of Tariffs and Quotas: General Tariff Cuts and Removal of Quotas on Automobiles, Sugar and Textiles.* Bureau of Economics Staff Report to the Federal Trade Commission. Washington, DC: Government Printing Office.

United States Bureau of the Census. 1968–78. *U.S. Imports for Consumption and General Imports: TSUSA Commodity by Country of Origin.* FT246. U.S. Department of Commerce. Washington, DC: Government Printing Office.

Waldorf, William. 1973. Quality of labor in manufacturing. *Review of Economics and Statistics* 35: 284–291.

# 10 Counting the Cost of Voluntary Export Restraints in the European Car Market

**Alasdair Smith and Anthony J. Venables**

The objective of this chapter is to study the effects of quantitative restrictions on trade in imperfectly competitive markets. We set up a formal model that describes the interaction between quantitative restrictions and market power, calibrate the model to data on the European car market in 1988, and illustrate the possible size of the effects of quantitative restrictions by numerically simulating the effects of policy changes in that market.

This work derives from earlier partial equilibrium modeling of trade policy in imperfectly competitive industries (Venables and Smith 1986; Smith and Venables 1988). The detailed implications of the present model for the effects on likely policy changes in the European car market are discussed in a related paper (Smith 1990), and more general issues concerning the model, notably its sensitivity to changes in the level of aggregation and in the values of key parameters, are addressed in Smith (1989). In this chapter we focus on the ranking of policy instruments in an imperfectly competitive industry as a means of illustrating the interaction between quantitative restrictions and imperfect competition.

The standard analysis of a voluntary export restraint (VER) in the context of perfectly competitive markets identifies two effects. First, by restricting imports, it raises prices to consumers in the same way as any other import restriction like a tariff. Second, by letting the exporters do the restricting, it allows the exporters to obtain the rents associated with the artificially high prices rather than have them go to the government of the importing country as tariff revenue.

In an imperfectly competitive market, however, there is a third effect: Quantitative import restrictions may increase some firms' market power, as was illustrated first by Bhagwati (1965) in a simple model of an import-competing monopolist. The Bhagwati argument is presented and extended in Helpman and Krugman (1989, ch. 3). The anticompetitive role of quantitative restrictions in oligopolistic markets is discussed by Harris (1985) and Krishna (1989). These, however, are models in which restrictions on the level of imports are imposed in markets with Bertrand competition, whereas the model presented below has restrictions on the market share of imports with Cournot competition.

Previous work on formal modeling of the motor industry in an imperfectly competitive setting includes Dixit (1987) and Laussel et al. (1988), but the present study differs in that it incorporates an explicit treatment of VERs.

## 10.1  The Model

The formal model is fully presented in the appendix at the end of this chapter. It follows Smith and Venables (1988) in treating the industry under study as an imperfectly competitive industry producing differentiated products. Firms that produce several different "models" of cars see the demand for their products as depending on the price of the individual model as well as on the overall price of cars. The Dixit-Stiglitz (1977) representation of consumer choice in markets with differentiated products allows us to write the demand per model in market $j$ for cars produced by firm $i$ as

$$x_{ij} = (a_{ij}b_j)\left(\frac{p_{ij}}{q_j}\right)^{-\varepsilon}(q_j)^{-\eta} \tag{1}$$

(equation A4 in the appendix), where $a_{ij}$ and $b_j$ are shift parameters describing the size of the market, $p_{ij}$ is the price of this model of car, $q_j$ is an aggregate price index for cars in market $j$ (and is a constant elasticity function of the prices $p_{ij}$ of all models sold). Then $\varepsilon$ is the elasticity of demand with respect to the relative price of the individual model of car, reflecting the extent to which there is substitutability in demand between different product varieties, while $\eta$ is the aggregate elasticity of demand for cars.

The Dixit-Stiglitz formulation is convenient as it gives rise to this demand function in which demand is a constant elasticity function of two prices. It is based on the assumption that each individual consumer chooses to buy some of each of the products on the market, and this is not as appealing a description of consumer choice of cars as the Lancaster (1979) approach in which the consumer chooses one product whose price and characteristics come closest to the consumer's needs. Anderson et al. (1989) have presented conditions under which the Dixit-Stiglitz model describes the behavior of the aggregate market, even if individual consumer's behavior is described by the Lancaster approach.

Firms maximize profits, taking account of the impact of scale economies on marginal costs, of the effect of taxes, tariffs and transport costs on the wedge between producer and consumer prices, and of the elasticity of demand in different markets on their marginal revenues. We make the Cournot assumption that in equilibrium firms maximize profits, taking their rivals' outputs as given (modified in the presence of sales restrictions in a way described below). National markets are assumed to be segmented, so firms can set different prices in different markets. A producer with a large market share in a particular national market sees its own behavior as having a strong influence on the overall price of cars in that market and thus perceives a relatively inelastic demand for its product; and this leads such firms to have higher price-cost margins. Specifically the model described fully in the appendix derives the first-order condition for a firm selling in a market in which there are no quantitative restrictions on sales as the standard equation of marginal revenue and marginal cost

$$p_{ij}t_{ij}\left(1 - \frac{1}{e_{ij}}\right) = mc_i \tag{2}$$

(equation A7 in the appendix), where $p_{ij}t_{ij}$ is the producer price, $mc_i$ is the firm's marginal cost, and $1/e_{ij}$, the firm's perceived inverse demand elasticity, is a weighted average of the inverses of the two demand elasticities that appear in the demand function

$$\frac{1}{e_{ij}} = \left(\frac{1}{\varepsilon}\right)(1 - s_{ij}) + \left(\frac{1}{\eta}\right)s_{ij} \tag{3}$$

(appendix equation A8), where $s_{ij}$ is firm $i$'s share in value terms of market $j$ (described in A5). This relation has the appealing feature of making firms perceive a less elastic demand for their product the larger is their market share. A firm with a small market share takes almost no account of the elasticity of the aggregate market demand, whereas a monopoly perceives only the aggregate demand elasticity.

The model takes account of two particular kinds of sales restrictions, both taking the form of a voluntary export restraint (VER) that limits the *share* that firms from a particular country may have in a market. The first kind of VER we consider restricts these firms to fixed shares of particular national markets (as Japanese firms are currently restricted in several European national markets). We alternatively allow there to be a restriction on the firms' overall market share in a group of national markets as a whole (as Japanese firms may in the near future be restricted to a fixed share of the aggregate European Community market).

When a firm is subject to either type of sales restriction, it maximizes profits subject to the restriction, and this modifies the relation between its marginal cost and marginal revenues, in a way spelled out in the appendix.

Firms in markets that are not subject to sales restrictions are assumed to behave as Cournot competitors. This assumption is also made about the behavior of the restricted firms in markets with sales restrictions. It would, however, be an unreasonable assumption to make of unrestricted firms in markets where other firms are subject to restrictions on their market shares. In this case an unrestricted firm is assumed to take account of the effect that a change in its sales will have on the sales of restricted firms.

To give a concrete example, in the U.K. market Japanese firms are presently restricted to an 11% market share. A non-Japanese firm planning to sell 1,000 more cars in the U.K. market should therefore take into account not only the impact on prices of its own sales but also the fact that Japanese firms would thereby be enabled to sell 124 more cars as a result (as $124/1,124 = 0.11$). The implication is that firms will behave less competitively in the presence of a VER than they would in the presence of, say, a tariff "equivalent" to the VER.

Thus the anticompetitive effect of quantitative restrictions is here treated in a rather specific way to include the effect of market share restrictions in a model of Cournot competition. The formal argument is presented in the appendix. The effect of the share restriction on firms' behavior is most clearly seen in equation (A8a), which describes the perceived demand elasticity of an unrestricted firm in a market with share restrictions. In equation (3) the unrestricted firm's actual value market share $s_{ij}$ is replaced with the larger expression

$$\tilde{s}_{ij} = s_{ij} + n_r s_{rj} \frac{m_i x_{ij}}{\sum_{l \notin R} m_l x_{l_j}}, \tag{4}$$

where $n_r$ is the number of (equal-sized) firms subject to sales restraint in market $j$ and $s_{rj}$ the value market share of each, $m_i$ the number of models produced by firm $i$, and $R$ the set of restricted firms. Thus the second term in (4) is the product of the value market share of the restricted firms and the volume share taken by firm $i$ of the sales of all the unrestricted firms. Clearly firm $i$ behaves as if its market share were larger than it actually is and perceives a more inelastic demand than it would in the absence of the VER. One particularly interesting, if extreme, case is where all firms but

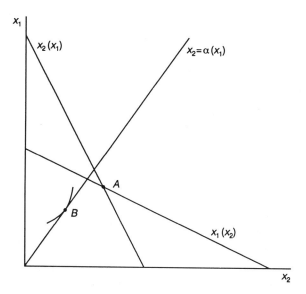

**Figure 10.1**
Duopoly with VER

one are subject to VERs, when (4) reduces to $s_{ij} = 1$. The firm takes into account the fact that all other firms are constrained to fixed market shares, and it behaves as a monopolist. In the general case the anticompetitive effect of the VER is less strong but still leads firms to set higher price-cost margins than they would in the absence of the VER.

The essential point can be illustrated in a simple Cournot duopoly model. Figure 10.1 displays the usual reaction curves, and $A$ is the Cournot equilibrium. The line $x_2 = \alpha x_1$ shows the restriction in firm 2's sales, which must lie on or to the left of this line. At the point $B$ firm 1 maximizes profits subject to firm 2 satisfying the restriction $x_2 = \alpha x_1$; while at this level of $x_1$ firm 2 can raise its profits only by raising its output, so the constraint does indeed bite. The point $B$ is the new equilibrium.

## 10.2 Data and Model Calibration

The model is calibrated to data for the world car market in 1988. The world is divided into eight markets: France, West Germany, Italy, the United Kingdom, Iberia (Spain and Portugal), the rest of the European Community (ROEC) (an aggregation of Benelux, Ireland, Greece and Denmark), the European Free Trade Association (EFTA), and the rest of the world (ROW). This level of country disaggregation is needed in order to model the differences in trade policy in 1988 between different members of the European Community and to deal with the fact that the Iberian countries are still in the process of harmonizing their trade policy with the common external tariff of the EC.

The producers are divided into eight groups: French (two producers, Peugeot and Renault), Volkswagen (VAG), Fiat, Rover, the U.S. multinationals in Europe (Ford and GM in Europe, who are treated as entirely independent of their American parents), the "specialist" producers (Mercedes, BMW, Volvo, Saab, Jaguar, and Porsche), the Japanese, and the rest of the world (who are mainly the North American producers). This level of producer disaggregation is necessary in order to capture in the model the strong differences in national sales patterns. Within each group firms are assumed to be identical. In the case of the French and the Americans in Europe, this is very close to reality: In each pair the firms are of roughly equal size and have similar sales patterns. The specialists and the Japanese are more heterogeneous, and calculations of Herfindahl indexes suggests it is appropriate to assume the existence of three equal-sized specialist manufacturers and five equal-sized Japanese firms.

Table 10.1 summarizes the shape of the European car market in 1988. The top panel of the table shows sales in the eight markets and the distribution of those sales by producer group, based on registration data in the *Automotive Industry Data 1989 Car Yearbook*. Both the rest of the world market and the sales by "other" producers in Europe are included only to close the model, and no attention has been given to accurate modeling of the non-European markets. Thus, in reporting the effects of policy changes, both the effects on "other" producers and in the rest of the world market are ignored.

The shares of Japanese producers in the different markets display the effects of trade restrictions. In our base year of 1988 there were restrictions on imports from Japan to France, Italy, the United Kingdom, Portugal, and Spain. Since 1977 Japanese imports have been restricted to 3% of the French market and 11% of the U.K. market. (The 11.4% Japanese share of the U.K. market shown in table 10.1 includes a small number of U.K.-produced cars, but in the model all "Japanese" cars are treated as being imports.) Italy, Spain, and Portugal have long-standing and tight limits on

**Table 10.1**
The European car market, 1988

|  | France | Germany | Italy | UK | RoEC | Iberia | EFTA | ROW |
|---|---|---|---|---|---|---|---|---|
| **Market sales total (million cars)** | | | | | | | | |
|  | 2.2 | 2.8 | 2.2 | 2.2 | 1.1 | 1.3 | 1.2 | 17.2 |
| **Market shares** | | | | | | | | |
| French | 63.2 | 6.7 | 14.8 | 12.6 | 18.3 | 38.0 | 9.3 | 2.6 |
| VAG | 8.6 | 29.4 | 11.7 | 5.9 | 13.0 | 17.5 | 14.2 | 1.6 |
| Fiat group | 7.2 | 4.7 | 59.9 | 3.7 | 5.3 | 9.7 | 5.2 | 0.0 |
| Rover | 1.9 | 0.3 | 1.1 | 15.0 | 1.2 | 1.9 | 0.2 | 0.2 |
| Ford/GM | 11.3 | 25.4 | 6.9 | 40.1 | 22.5 | 26.9 | 19.2 | 0.6 |
| Specialists | 3.6 | 17.7 | 3.4 | 7.9 | 8.4 | 3.3 | 17.5 | 2.6 |
| Japanese | 3.0 | 15.2 | 0.9 | 11.4 | 26.6 | 2.1 | 31.9 | 39.0 |
| Others | 1.3 | 0.8 | 1.2 | 3.4 | 4.6 | 0.6 | 2.5 | 53.4 |
|  | 100.0 | 100.0 | 100.0 | 100.0 | 100.0 | 100.0 | 100.0 | 100.0 |
| **Estimated sales value (billion ecu)** | | | | | | | | EC total |
|  | 26.2 | 28.9 | 25.2 | 25.3 | 17.1 | 16.1 | | 138.9 |
| **Sales tax rates (%)** | | | | | | | | |
|  | 28 | 14 | 20 | 25 | 55 | 39 | 20 | 20 |

|  | Sales (millions) | Models per firm | Firm numbers | Sales/model (thousands) |
|---|---|---|---|---|
| French | 3.443 | 7 | 2 | 246 |
| VAG | 2.205 | 7 | 1 | 315 |
| Fiat group | 1.929 | 6 | 1 | 322 |
| Rover | 0.475 | 6 | 1 | 79 |
| Ford/GM | 2.935 | 5 | 2 | 293 |
| Specialists | 1.622 | 3 | 3 | 180 |
| Japanese | 8.190 | 6 | 5 | 273 |
| Others | 9.442 | 12 | 2 | 393 |

Japanese imports. Both the Italian and Iberian restrictions are modeled, like the French and U.K. restrictions, as limiting Japanese market shares. This is not strictly accurate, but the levels to which Japanese imports are restricted in these markets is so low that the distinction between levels and shares is of little significance. In the German market there is no explicit restraint on Japanese sales, and we have assumed that the German market has no VER.

Calibration of the model to these data requires assumptions about the form of the cost function, about demand elasticities, and about taxes, tariffs, and transport costs.

In earlier work (Venables and Smith 1986; Smith and Venables 1988), variation in numbers of models per firms was used as a device to account for the difference in the scale of different firms. In the case of the car industry, however, it is possible to give the device a concrete interpretation. The Ludvigsen study for the European Commission (Ludvigsen Associates Limited 1988) centered its description of scale economies on the concept of a "platform," essentially a floorplan on which a family of cars can be based. The Ludvigsen information on the numbers of platforms per producer is used to give the model numbers shown in table 10.1 (where, however, the model numbers for Japanese and rest of the world producers are simply assumed).

Ludvigsen provides a great deal of information about the relation between variable costs and scale of output per platform, and rather sketchier information about fixed costs. On the basis of that information, we chose a cost function to satisfy the properties (1) average variable cost declines by 5% for every doubling of output per platform, (2) fixed costs are 20% of total costs for a firm producing five platforms and 200,000 cars of each platform, and (3) a proportion of fixed costs is independent of the number of platforms, while the rest of fixed costs rise linearly with the number of platforms, and for a producer of five platforms, the proportion of fixed costs independent of the number of platforms is half. The function chosen to satisfy these properties was

$$C(x, m) = c[5 + m + 0.0001x^{0.925} m], \tag{5}$$

where $x$ is output per platform, $m$ is the number of platforms, and the level of $c$, which is permitted to vary between firms, is calibrated.

Ludvigsen also provides some information on the prices of cars of different types in different markets. We chose the German market prices as a base on the ground that this is the market least distorted by taxes and protection of the markets on which Ludvigsen provides data. Assuming that the distribution of cars of different types (utility, small, lower medium, etc.) in each firm's output is the same as in the firm's German sale gives a price for each producer group's "typical" car in Germany; from the model is then derived a price in each of the other markets. (An interesting test of the descriptive accuracy of the model would be to compare these derived prices with independent information on actual prices, but this test has not been undertaken.)

On the demand side there have been many econometric estimates of the aggregate industry elasticity of demand for different countries in different time periods. OECD (1983) reports a range from 1 to 3. Hess (1977) surveys many previous studies and reestimates demand equations to obtain a value of 1.63. More or less arbitrarily, we use the value 1.5. For the elasticity of demand for an individual model of car, estimates in Cowling and Cubbin (1971) (see also Maxcy and Silberston 1959) suggest a value of around 7; a value in this area is consistent with the calibration of our data to a long-run equilibrium in which the average of profits across firms is zero. However, the work of Bresnahan (1981) suggests a value of 2.3. Feenstra and Levinsohn (1989) obtain a much smaller elasticity of 0.467 from estimated demand functions but a very much larger value from the pricing equation in their model. Levinsohn (1988) and Feenstra and Levinsohn (1989) argue that it is not very sensible to apply a single elasticity value at a rather aggregate level. It would be desirable to disaggregate the present model, which at present treats the car market as a single market, and to treat separately five or six submarkets. In the absence of such disaggregation, we have chosen to use the value of 4 for the elasticity of demand for individual car models.

The calibration of the model then consists of the choice of firm-specific cost levels to reproduce the German prices and, in the absence of VERs, choice of parameters to scale the demand functions to observed sales, that is to say, to explain the pattern of sales displayed in table 10.1. However, this procedure cannot be adopted where sales by Japanese firms are affected by a VER. In such cases we would simply "observe" a very low demand for Japanese cars. In markets where VERs are in operation, we have no observations on Japanese market shares in the absence of constraints and are therefore unable to use these to infer the demand parameters. These parameters are therefore obtained by assuming first that consumers in

France and Italy have the same preference for Japanese cars relative to German cars as do consumers in the rest of the EC. This particular assumption was chosen as being the comparison least contaminated by the relatively large market shares of domestically produced cars in all markets. However, it produces unrealistic numbers for the United Kingdom and Iberia, so for the United Kingdom it was the ratio of French to Japanese sales and for Iberia the ratio of Ford/GM to Japanese sales in the rest of the EC that were used as benchmarks.

In the calibration we assume that cars imported across national borders both within Europe and between Europe and the rest of the world incur transport costs. We also allow for the 10.3% tariff that Japanese cars face in the EC. In the base year of 1988 Spanish and Portugese trade policy had not been fully aligned with that of the European Community, and we have assumed that the Spanish 1988 tariff levels of 35% on Japanese cars and 23% on EC cars apply to the whole Iberian market. We also assume the existence of sales taxes at the levels shown in table 10.1. However, all of the trade policy changes reported below are supposed to take place in a "post-1992" European Community, in the sense that they are changes not from the 1988 base data used in the calibration but from a base that is derived by simulating a 5% reduction in intra-EC cross-border transport costs, and a full alignment of Iberian tariffs with the EC's trade policy. For further details both on these assumptions and on the simulations that produce the base for the simulations described below, see Smith (1990).

The second panel of table 10.1 reports the estimated value of car sales in each of the EC markets and in the EC market as a whole. These estimates are based on the prices calibrated in the model. They are useful in translating into proportions of consumption the welfare changes reported in later tables.

It should be noted that although firms produce several varieties of car, we do not in this chapter model the choice of the number of varieties produced, nor do we model entry and exit of firms. The policy simulations presented below should therefore be interpreted as short-run simulations. It should also be noted that one disadvantage of the level of aggregation of the model is that it does not allow for the possibility of quality upgrading by the constrained producers in response to VERs. Jones (1987) suggests that there is little evidence of upgrading in the U.K. market, though Messerlin and Becuwe (1987) argue that upgrading has occurred in France.

## 10.3    The Costs of VERs

Table 10.2 through 10.9 look at a range of policy changes from which some lessons may be learned both about the model and about the effects of policy changes in the European car market. At this level of product aggregation and in the absence of sensitivity analysis, the numbers presented should be interpreted as plausible illustrative calculations rather than detailed predictions.

Table 10.2 presents the results of simple removal of the 3% restriction on the Japanese share of the French market. The Japanese share rises to 13.2% as a result of a 363.5% increase in the number of Japanese cars sold in France. Japanese car prices fall by 34.3%. The prices of non-Japanese cars fall also, although by less than 1% in the case of all producers except the French whose prices fall by 2.7%. The non-Japanese price reductions are quite small. They are the result largely of changes in the price-cost margins derived in equations (3) and (4). The fact that the French producers

**Table 10.2**
Removal of French VER

| | French market: percent changes | | |
| --- | --- | --- | --- |
| | Sales quantities | | Consumer prices |
| French | −3.5 | | −2.7 |
| VAG | −10.7 | | −0.8 |
| Fiat | −11.2 | | −0.7 |
| Rover | −13.2 | | −0.1 |
| Ford/GM | −11.7 | | −0.6 |
| Specialis | −13.2 | | −0.1 |
| Japanese | 363.5 | | −34.3 |

| | Welfare: changes in million ecu per year | | | | |
| --- | --- | --- | --- | --- | --- |
| | Profits | | | Consumer surplus | Tax revenue | CET revenue |
| French | −499.0 | France | | 1,574.3 | 172.2 | 171.0 |
| VAG | −58.7 | | | | | |
| Fiat | −41.4 | | | | | |
| Rover | −11.0 | | | | | |
| Ford/GM | −76.4 | | | | | |
| Specialis | −37.1 | | | | | |
| Japanese | 216.4 | | | | | |

cut their prices more than the other non-Japanese producers reflects the two effects that removal of the VER has on the market power of the French producers: The anticompetitive effect, shown in (4), on their "effective" market share is removed, and their actual market shares fall. The former effect is, in this example, the smaller one: In the base equilibrium, marginal cost is 61.65% of price; removing the effect of the VER on the calculation of price elasticity would have raised this to 62.33%, but the reduction in market share, when the VER is removed, raises it to 63.51%.

The gains to French consumers at 1,574 million ecu per year are 6% of the value of consumers expenditure on cars in the calibrated base. There are also small effects on tax and tariff revenue. The biggest effects on profits are a profit reduction of 500 million ecu per year to French producers and a gain of 216 million for the Japanese, but the losses even to all European producers are much less than the gains to French consumers.

Table 10.3 shows the effects of removing all the import restrictions. The top panel reports the predicted sales changes by each producer (row) in each market (column), and on the right the total sales change of each producer. The second panel reports the associated price changes. The Japanese shares of each of the EC markets and of the EC market as a whole before and after the change are reported in the third panel. Finally the fourth panel reports (in million ecu) the impact of the policy change on producers' profits, consumer welfare, and government revenue. The multinationality of much of the European industry means that it is impossible to attribute profit changes to individual countries. It would also be inappropriate to attribute changes in common external tariff revenue to individual countries, as this goes to the EC budget. Therefore a welfare total is calculated only for the EC as a whole. The EC total includes half of the profit changes of Ford and GM on the assumption that part of their economic profits will be reflected in workers' and managers' incomes. (Such changes in employees' incomes would affect marginal cost, and the effects of this are not allowed for in the simulations.) It is questionable whether changes in tax revenue should be counted as a welfare gain: Insofar as taxes on cars are at the same rate as on other goods or reflect the social costs of pollution and congestion, tax revenue changes should not be counted as welfare gains. Therefore the EC welfare total is reported both with and without tax revenue included. In contemplating the total welfare changes reported in this and subsequent tables, one can use as a standard of

**Table 10.3**
Removal of all VERs

| | France | Germany | Italy | UK | ROEC | Iberia | EFTA | Total (including ROW) |
|---|---|---|---|---|---|---|---|---|
| **Quantity changes (%)** | | | | | | | | |
| French | -4.4 | -1.7 | -21.0 | -5.4 | -1.8 | -12.2 | -2.1 | -6.6 |
| VAG | -11.6 | -1.1 | -19.3 | -5.6 | -1.6 | -13.1 | -1.7 | -6.0 |
| Fiat | -11.4 | -0.6 | -0.4 | -5.9 | -0.9 | -11.6 | -1.0 | -2.9 |
| Rover | -14.1 | -1.6 | -23.8 | -1.9 | -1.8 | -17.5 | -1.7 | -5.8 |
| Ford/GM | -12.2 | -0.9 | -22.3 | 0.6 | -1.2 | -13.8 | -1.3 | -4.3 |
| Specialis | -14.0 | -1.1 | -23.3 | -6.9 | -1.5 | -17.5 | -1.4 | -4.8 |
| Japanese | 378.6 | 4.3 | 1,816.6 | 47.3 | 3.9 | 758.0 | 3.7 | 15.2 |
| **Consumer price changes** | | | | | | | | |
| French | -2.4 | 0.5 | -0.6 | -0.4 | 0.4 | -1.6 | 0.5 | |
| VAG | -0.5 | 0.3 | -1.1 | -0.4 | 0.4 | -1.6 | 0.5 | |
| Fiat | -0.5 | 0.2 | -6.2 | -0.3 | 0.2 | -1.8 | 0.2 | |
| Rover | 0.2 | 0.4 | 0.3 | -1.4 | 0.4 | -0.0 | 0.4 | |
| Ford/GM | -0.3 | 0.3 | -0.2 | -2.0 | 0.3 | -1.1 | 0.3 | |
| Specialis | 0.2 | 0.3 | 0.1 | -0.1 | 0.3 | -0.0 | 0.3 | |
| Japanese | -34.8 | -1.0 | -55.2 | -10.9 | -1.0 | -44.3 | -1.0 | |
| **Market shares of Japanese** | | | | | | | | *EC total* |
| Initial | 3.0 | 14.6 | 0.9 | 11.4 | 23.5 | 2.1 | | 8.8 |
| Final | 13.7 | 15.3 | 16.2 | 16.3 | 24.5 | 17.6 | | 16.5 |

**Table 10.3** (continued)

| Welfare changes (in million ecu per year) | | | | | | |
|---|---|---|---|---|---|---|
| | | Profits | Consumer surplus | Tax revenue | CET revenue | EC totals |
| French | France | −940.3 | 1,543.4 | 168.8 | 177.6 | 6,349.1 (con surp) |
| VAG | Germany | −305.6 | −27.2 | −1.6 | 11.3 | 659.0 (tax rev) |
| Fiat | Italy | −966.0 | 2,736.4 | 228.0 | 283.1 | 713.3 (CET rev) |
| Rover | UK | −90.7 | 756.9 | 75.7 | 69.7 | −2,701.8 (profits) |
| Ford/GM | ROEC | −416.7 | 7.1 | 1.2 | 6.7 | |
| Specialis | Iberia | −190.8 | 1,332.5 | 186.9 | 164.9 | 5,019.6 |
| Japanese | EFTA | 1,050.0 | 10.7 | 0.9 | 0.0 | 4,360.6 (excluding taxes) |

comparison the 135.22 billion ecu shown in table 10.1 as the estimated value at consumer prices of sales of cars in the EC market.

The effects in all the freed markets are comparable to the effects that we saw in the previous table for the French market alone. (There are small spillover effects on other markets resulting from changes in producers' marginal costs, effects that were present but not reported in the previous case.) The overall welfare benefit to the European Community is of the order of 3% of base consumption.

Table 10.4 shows the effects in the model of simulation of replacement of the national VERs with a European VER holding the Japanese producers to their existing market share of the whole EC market. In France, Italy, and Iberia the effects on sales follow the same pattern as in table 10.3, though with all effects reduced, but there is a significant difference in the effects on prices, with only the market leaders now cutting their prices in response to Japanese entry and other firms actually raising prices. In the United Kingdom the model finds that the EC-wide VER would be more restrictive than the existing national VER, and Japanese sales fall and prices rise. The EC-wide VER also, of course, has effects in the two markets that formerly had no VER, with reductions in Japanese sales and rises in prices of non-Japanese as well as Japanese cars. Thus there are substantial consumer surplus losses in these markets and increases in the profits of those producers for whom the European VER provides more protection than the national VERs. There is also a substantial increase in Japanese producers' profits, as the removal of national constraints allows them to redistribute their sales between markets. To emphasise the point that the major effect of this policy change is on the distribution of welfare within Europe, the change in overall EC welfare is very small. The effects of the VER, both the direct effects and the anticompetitive effects are being spread more evenly across all the EC markets.

The effects of removing the European VER can be found by subtracting the effects shown in table 10.4 from the effects shown in table 10.3. Removal of the European VER leads to a more or less uniform Japanese expansion in European markets which is bad for all European producers and good for all European consumers. The gain to Japanese producers is modest, but the overall gain to EC welfare of not having a VER is substantial.

Smith and Venables (1988) find the biggest effects of completing the EC's internal market arise if firms are induced to treat the European market as a single integrated market rather than a set of separate national markets.

**Table 10.4**
Replacement of national VERs with European VER

|  | France | Germany | Italy | UK | ROEC | Iberia | EFTA | Total (including ROW) |
|---|---|---|---|---|---|---|---|---|
| **Quantity changes (%)** | | | | | | | | |
| French | -2.0 | 4.5 | -13.5 | 0.2 | 6.5 | -7.2 | -0.7 | -2.5 |
| VAG | -7.7 | 0.6 | -13.3 | -1.0 | 4.8 | -8.7 | -0.7 | -2.8 |
| Fiat | -9.5 | 1.6 | -1.9 | -3.4 | 4.9 | -9.4 | -0.9 | -3.0 |
| Rover | -4.8 | 9.3 | -12.1 | 6.0 | 13.1 | -7.4 | 0.9 | 2.6 |
| Ford/GM | -6.3 | 4.3 | -13.8 | 4.9 | 7.1 | -7.7 | 0.3 | 1.0 |
| Specialis | -4.6 | 7.8 | -11.7 | 2.8 | 12.2 | -7.4 | 0.6 | 2.3 |
| Japanese | 139.0 | -47.8 | 895.8 | -26.0 | -45.2 | 338.8 | -0.0 | -0.2 |
| **Consumer price changes** | | | | | | | | |
| French | -0.7 | 1.3 | 0.4 | 0.5 | 1.7 | -0.2 | 0.2 | |
| VAG | 0.8 | 2.3 | 0.3 | 0.8 | 2.1 | 0.2 | 0.2 | |
| Fiat | 1.3 | 2.0 | -2.7 | 1.4 | 2.1 | 0.4 | 0.2 | |
| Rover | 0.0 | 0.1 | 0.0 | -0.9 | 0.2 | -0.1 | -0.2 | |
| Ford/GM | 0.4 | 1.3 | 0.5 | -0.7 | 1.6 | -0.1 | -0.1 | |
| Specialis | -0.0 | 0.5 | -0.1 | -0.1 | 0.4 | -0.2 | -0.2 | |
| Japanese | -20.6 | 20.5 | -45.5 | 8.4 | 20.1 | -32.3 | 0.0 | |
| **Market shares of Japanese** | | | | | | | | *EC total* |
| Initial | 3.0 | 14.6 | 0.9 | 11.4 | 23.5 | 2.1 | | 8.8 |
| Final | 7.1 | 8.0 | 8.9 | 8.5 | 13.6 | 9.3 | | 8.8 |

Welfare changes (in million ecu per year)

| | | Profits | Consumer surplus | Tax revenue | CET revenue | EC totals |
|---|---|---|---|---|---|---|
| French | France | −251.3 | 520.2 | 56.9 | 75.5 | 197.8 (con surp) |
| VAG | Germany | 77.6 | −1,098.4 | −67.4 | −125.6 | −1.7 (tax rev) |
| Fiat | Italy | −481.4 | 1,327.9 | 110.7 | 165.7 | 81.4 (CET rev) |
| Rover | UK | 10.7 | 220.0 | −22.0 | −45.5 | −405.6 (profits) |
| Ford/GM | ROEC | 176.0 | −897.4 | −159.2 | −74.8 | |
| Specialis | Iberia | 150.8 | 565.5 | 79.3 | 86.1 | −128.1 |
| Japanese | EFTA | 814.1 | −0.1 | 0.0 | 0.0 | −126.4 (excluding taxes) |

In the Cournot model the modeling of the integration of a set of national markets is a little complicated, but if we make the simplifying, if incorrect, assumption that the sum of the national market constant elasticity demand functions will give rise to an integrated demand function that also has constant elasticity, then the set of integrated markets can be described by the same equations used to describe a single national market.

Table 10.5 shows the effects of market integration on the market in the presence of a European VER. As each firm sets one price for the whole market, there are substantial price reductions, especially by national market leaders who lose market power. There are large consequent welfare gains.

Table 10.6 displays the effect of the removal of a common European VER in the case of market integration. The results have the same shape as the results of removing a common European VER but are consistently smaller, reflecting the fact that the VER has less strongly anticompetitive effects in the more competitive market structure. (Or, to put the same point another way, the shift from segmented markets to integrated markets is a little less procompetitive in the absence of the VER.)

## 10.4   The Nonequivalence of Tariffs and VERs

The motivation for import protection is the maintenance of the level of domestic activity in the protected industry. The fact that the VER has an anticompetitive effect, in addition to the effects of a tariff in which the tariff revenue is given away to foreigners, suggests that it will be a more costly instrument of protection than a tariff.

This issue is investigated in table 10.7, which shows the effects of replacing the French VER with a tariff on Japanese car imports into France. Such a policy change is, of course, infeasible since GATT rules do not permit discriminatory tariffs and the Treaty of Rome bars the setting of national external tariffs. The point of the experiment is to provide a measure of the "excess" cost of the tariff. Here we have chosen the tariff "equivalent" to the VER as the one that keeps the production level of the French producers constant, and this requires an increase in the French tariff on Japanese cars from the 10.3% level of the EC's common external tariff on all non-EC (and non-EFTA) cars to the level of 34.9%. (Because the "French" producers have some production facilities outside France, keeping their production

**Table 10.5**
Market integration with European VER

| | France | Germany | Italy | UK | ROEC | Iberia | EFTA | Total (including ROW) |
|---|---|---|---|---|---|---|---|---|
| **Quantity changes (%)** | | | | | | | | |
| French | 33.0 | −22.9 | −44.8 | −16.3 | −6.3 | 5.5 | 1.4 | 6.3 |
| VAG | −24.3 | 33.7 | −42.1 | −19.7 | −1.3 | −2.9 | 0.7 | 4.2 |
| Fiat | −31.5 | −27.7 | 97.8 | −28.5 | −23.0 | −5.6 | 12.4 | 53.9 |
| Rover | −18.1 | −13.9 | −40.6 | 18.3 | −6.9 | −2.9 | 1.7 | 8.0 |
| Ford/GM | −24.1 | −4.0 | −46.9 | 15.8 | 2.1 | −3.0 | −0.5 | −0.7 |
| Specialis | −21.0 | −0.5 | −42.0 | −8.7 | −3.2 | −6.9 | −1.7 | −5.1 |
| Japanese | 7.8 | 17.4 | −19.5 | 20.2 | 28.8 | 26.0 | 0.2 | 1.9 |
| **Consumer price changes** | | | | | | | | |
| French | −11.1 | 4.0 | 2.7 | 2.4 | 0.5 | −2.4 | −0.4 | |
| VAG | 2.4 | −9.4 | 1.5 | 3.4 | −0.8 | −0.3 | −0.3 | |
| Fiat | 5.0 | 5.7 | −25.3 | 6.5 | 5.6 | 0.3 | −3.0 | |
| Rover | 0.4 | 1.2 | 0.9 | −6.1 | 0.7 | −0.3 | −0.6 | |
| Ford/GM | 2.3 | −1.6 | 3.8 | −5.6 | −1.6 | −0.3 | 0.0 | |
| Specialis | 1.3 | −2.4 | 1.5 | 0.2 | −0.3 | 0.7 | 0.3 | |
| Japanese | −6.3 | −6.4 | −6.5 | −6.5 | −7.2 | −6.7 | −0.1 | |
| **Market shares of Japanese** | | | | | | | | *EC total* |
| Initial | 7.1 | 8.0 | 8.9 | 8.5 | 13.6 | 9.3 | | 8.8 |
| Final | 6.9 | 8.8 | 5.2 | 9.7 | 17.3 | 11.6 | | 8.8 |

**Table 10.5** (continued)

| | | Welfare changes (in million ecu per year) | | | |
|---|---|---|---|---|---|
| | | Profits | Consumer surplus | Tax revenue | CET revenue | EC totals |
| French | France | −722.6 | 2,005.0 | 219.3 | −3.1 | 10,009.4 (con surp) |
| VAG | Germany | −348.5 | 1,190.1 | 73.1 | 18.8 | 919.8 (tax rev) |
| Fiat | Italy | −307.5 | 5,353.7 | 446.1 | −59.9 | 27.8 (CET rev) |
| Rover | UK | −81.3 | 860.9 | 86.1 | 19.1 | −2,082.7 (profits) |
| Ford/GM | ROEC | −524.0 | 298.0 | 52.9 | 30.3 | |
| Specialis | Iberia | −360.8 | 301.7 | 42.3 | 22.6 | 8,874.3 |
| Japanese | EFTA | −285.8 | 21.3 | 1.8 | 0.0 | 7,954.5 (excluding taxes) |

**Table 10.6**
Removal of European VER, integrated markets

| | France | Germany | Italy | UK | ROEC | Iberia | EFTA | Total (including ROW) |
|---|---|---|---|---|---|---|---|---|
| **Quantity changes (%)** | | | | | | | | |
| French | −1.6 | −2.0 | −3.4 | −2.0 | −5.2 | −3.8 | −0.8 | −2.2 |
| VAG | −0.7 | −1.0 | −2.5 | −1.1 | −4.2 | −2.8 | −0.5 | −1.4 |
| Fiat | 3.4 | 3.1 | 1.6 | 3.0 | −0.3 | 1.2 | 0.3 | 1.7 |
| Rover | −6.0 | −6.3 | −7.7 | −6.4 | −9.4 | −8.1 | −1.7 | −6.4 |
| Ford/GM | −2.6 | −3.0 | −4.4 | −3.0 | −6.1 | −4.8 | −1.0 | −3.3 |
| Specialis | −6.0 | −6.3 | −7.7 | −6.3 | −9.4 | −8.0 | −1.4 | −4.9 |
| Japanese | 57.8 | 57.3 | 55.0 | 57.2 | 52.1 | 54.4 | 2.4 | 9.8 |
| **Consumer price changes (all EC markets)** | | | | | | | | |
| French | −1.1 | | | | | | 0.2 | |
| VAG | −1.3 | | | | | | 0.1 | |
| Fiat | −2.3 | | | | | | −0.1 | |
| Rover | 0.0 | | | | | | 0.5 | |
| Ford/GM | −0.8 | | | | | | 0.2 | |
| Specialis | 0.0 | | | | | | 0.3 | |
| Japanese | −12.1 | | | | | | −0.6 | |
| **Market shares of Japanese** | | | | | | | | *EC total* |
| Initial | 6.9 | 8.8 | 5.2 | 9.7 | 17.3 | 11.6 | | 8.8 |
| Final | 10.6 | 13.4 | 7.8 | 14.8 | 25.2 | 17.3 | | 13.2 |

**Table 10.6** (continued)

| Welfare changes (in million ecu per year) | | | | | |
|---|---|---|---|---|---|
| | Profits | Consumer surplus | Tax revenue | CET revenue | EC totals |
| French | France | −452.4 | 677.8 | 74.1 | 62.2 | 4,264.7 (con surp) |
| VAG | Germany | −254.1 | 749.9 | 73.1 | 89.5 | 463.5 (tax rev) |
| Fiat | Italy | −397.5 | 917.7 | 446.1 | 55.3 | 396.7 (CET rev) |
| Rover | UK | −67.7 | 674.4 | 86.1 | 77.6 | −1,580.1 (profits) |
| Ford/GM | ROEC | −389.9 | 668.0 | 118.5 | 57.8 | |
| Specialis | Iberia | −213.5 | 576.9 | 81.0 | 54.3 | 3,544.8 |
| Japanese | EFTA | 25.8 | 8.6 | 0.7 | 0.0 | 3,081.3 (excluding taxes) |

**Table 10.7**
Replacement of French VER with 35% tariff

| | French market: percent changes | |
| --- | --- | --- |
| | Sales quantities | Consumer prices |
| French | −0.0 | −1.7 |
| VAG | −4.6 | −0.5 |
| Fiat | −5.0 | −0.5 |
| Rover | −6.3 | −0.1 |
| Ford/GM | −5.3 | −0.4 |
| Specialis | −6.4 | −0.1 |
| Japanese | 128.2 | −20.0 |

| | Welfare changes in million ecu per year | | | | |
| --- | --- | --- | --- | --- | --- |
| | Profits | | Consumer surplus | Tax revenue | CET revenue |
| French | −215.1 | France | 738.8 | 80.8 | 345.0 |
| VAG | −28.7 | | | | |
| Fiat | −21.5 | | | | |
| Rover | −5.7 | | | | |
| Ford/GM | −38.2 | | | | |
| Specialis | −18.1 | | | | |
| Japanese | −114.8 | | | | |

constant does not actually guarantee unchanged production in the car industry in France.)

Table 10.7 shows that this policy change reduces consumer prices in France (though by less, of course, than the simple removal of the VER shown in table 10.2). Japanese sales more than double, but at the expense of non-French producers. Including tariff revenue changes as a gain to France, there is a net gain to French consumer surplus, tax and tariff revenue, and profits of about 950 million ecu per year, compared with the gain of 1418 million ecu associated with the simple abandonment of the VER. Thus about two-thirds of the cost of the VER (70% if tax revenue is excluded from the calculation) is an excess cost, in the sense that the same protective effect could be obtained at one-third of the cost to aggregate French welfare. It is well-known in the context of perfectly competitive markets that VERs have higher welfare costs than tariffs because they give the tariff revenue away to the exporters. However, the profits that the Japanese producers gain as a result of the switch from the tariff to the VER

**Table 10.8**
French VER at "nonbinding" level

| | French market: percent changes | |
| | Sales quantities | Consumer prices |
|---|---|---|
| French | −6.3 | 3.0 |
| VAG | 1.4 | 1.0 |
| Fiat | 2.0 | 0.9 |
| Rover | 4.7 | 0.2 |
| Ford/GM | 2.8 | 0.7 |
| Specialis | 4.9 | 0.1 |
| Japanese | −3.1 | 2.2 |

| | Welfare changes in million ecu per year | | | | |
| | Profits | | Consumer surplus | Tax revenue | CET revenue |
|---|---|---|---|---|---|
| French | 61.7 | France | −587.5 | −64.3 | −1.2 |
| VAG | 21.6 | | | | |
| Fiat | 20.0 | | | | |
| Rover | 5.1 | | | | |
| Ford/GM | 31.2 | | | | |
| Specialis | 14.5 | | | | |
| Japanese | 35.4 | | | | |

is 115 million ecu, and the fact that this is much less than the gain to the French of replacing the VER with a tariff implies that the VER is still a very inefficient means of compensating the Japanese for the effects on them of protecting the French car industry.

An alternative way to see the anticompetitive effect of VERs is to look at the effect of setting a VER at an apparently "nonbinding" level. Table 10.2 shows Japanese imports to France rising to a market share of 13.2% in the absence of a French VER. Table 10.8 shows the effect of restricting Japanese sales to 13.2% of the French market. This policy change does have effects. The effect of the VER on the price-cost margins of non-Japanese firms leads to price rises, and the VER does actually constrain Japanese sales. There is a redistribution of welfare from consumers to producers, and a substantial net cost to the French economy.

Finally, table 10.9 presents the nonequivalence of tariffs and VERs at the European level, by illustrating the effects of replacing a European VER that holds the Japanese share of the EC market to 8.8% with an increase in the

**Table 10.9**
Replacement of European VER with 25% tariff

| | France | Germany | Italy | UK | ROEC | Iberia | EFTA | Total (including ROW) |
|---|---|---|---|---|---|---|---|---|
| **Quantity changes (%)** | | | | | | | | |
| French | 0.6 | -0.2 | -1.6 | 0.0 | -0.8 | -0.3 | -0.1 | -0.1 |
| VAG | 0.9 | 1.5 | -0.3 | 1.2 | 0.5 | 0.7 | 0.1 | 0.8 |
| Fiat | 2.9 | 3.2 | 2.6 | 3.3 | 2.2 | 2.5 | 0.6 | 2.6 |
| Rover | -3.7 | -3.5 | -5.3 | -2.4 | -4.5 | -4.0 | -0.9 | -2.8 |
| Ford/GM | -0.6 | -0.1 | -2.2 | 0.2 | -0.9 | -0.8 | -0.2 | -0.3 |
| Specialis | -4.0 | -3.1 | -5.5 | -3.5 | -4.4 | -4.3 | -0.8 | -2.6 |
| Japanese | 25.7 | 25.9 | 23.7 | 25.9 | 24.0 | 24.8 | 1.0 | 4.1 |
| **Consumer price changes** | | | | | | | | |
| French | -1.2 | -1.0 | -1.1 | -1.0 | -1.1 | -1.1 | 0.0 | |
| VAG | -1.3 | -1.4 | -1.4 | -1.3 | -1.4 | -1.4 | -0.1 | |
| Fiat | -1.8 | -1.8 | -2.1 | -1.8 | -1.8 | -1.8 | -0.2 | |
| Rover | -0.2 | -0.1 | -0.1 | -0.4 | -0.1 | -0.2 | 0.2 | |
| Ford/GM | -0.9 | -1.0 | -0.9 | -1.1 | -1.1 | -1.0 | 0.0 | |
| Specialis | -0.1 | -0.2 | -0.1 | -0.1 | -0.2 | -0.1 | 0.2 | |
| Japanese | -6.6 | -6.6 | -6.6 | -6.5 | -6.5 | -6.5 | -0.3 | |
| **Market shares of Japanese** | | | | | | | | *EC total* |
| Initial | 7.1 | 8.0 | 8.9 | 8.5 | 13.6 | 9.3 | | 8.8 |
| Final | 8.7 | 9.8 | 10.7 | 10.5 | 16.4 | 11.4 | | 10.7 |

**Table 10.9** (continued)

Welfare changes (in million ecu per year)

| | | Profits | Consumer surplus | Tax revenue | CET revenue | EC totals |
|---|---|---|---|---|---|---|
| French | France | −277.7 | 472.1 | 51.6 | 246.8 | 2,668.1 (con surp) |
| VAG | Germany | −144.8 | 469.1 | 28.8 | 330.7 | 283.4 (tax rev) |
| Fiat | Italy | −157.1 | 627.3 | 52.2 | 306.5 | 1,604.6 (CET rev) |
| Rover | UK | −43.5 | 410.1 | 41.0 | 290.7 | −891.0 (profits) |
| Ford/GM | ROEC | −236.8 | 353.5 | 62.7 | 231.7 | |
| Specialis | Iberia | −149.5 | 336.0 | 47.1 | 198.2 | 3,665.1 |
| Japanese | EFTA | −1,289.1 | 7.1 | 0.6 | 0.0 | 3,381.7 (excluding taxes) |

common external tariff from 10.3% to 25.2%, the tariff that holds total output of European producers at the same level as the European VER. The results are as in the French case, writ large. Prices and profits fall, and the gains to European consumers outweigh the losses to European producers. The net gain to Europe of replacing the VER with a tariff is much greater than the loss of Japanese profits, so again in this case the VER is inefficient even as a means of transferring revenue to the Japanese.

## 10.5  Conclusions

The analysis of economic policy changes using calibrated models is not uncontroversial. It is a procedure that gives rather more weight to the structure of the underlying theoretical model than to the modest amount of data used to calibrate the model numerically, and the results have to be interpreted in this light. Both the theoretical structure and the data impose discipline on the calculation of the likely welfare effects of policy changes, so the results are surely more reliable than back-of-the-envelope calculations based on informal modeling, though less reliable than the results one might obtain from an econometric model estimated on a run of reliable and consistent data if the production of such a model were feasible. The numerical results presented in this chapter are to be taken as illustrations of possible order of magnitude associated with the effects discussed in the theoretical model rather than as precise numerical predictions.

This caveat notwithstanding, the message is a clear one. The effects of quantitative import restrictions on the behavior of firms in a market as imperfectly competitive as the car market seem likely to be of sufficient magnitude to make such restrictions an expensive and inefficient form of policy intervention.

## Appendix:  The Model

### The Basic Model

The formal model follows Smith and Venables (1988) in treating the industry as an imperfectly competitive industry producing differentiated products. The world is divided into $J$ countries, indexed $j$, and production is undertaken by $I$ firms, indexed $i$. (In the empirical implementation of the model, some firms are grouped together, and all of the firms in the same group are assumed to be identical—but for the purposes of theoretical exposition, it is clearer to treat all firms as distinct.) Each firm produces $m_i$ different varieties of the product. The quantity of a single product variety produced by a firm in producer group $i$ and sold in country $j$ is denoted $x_{ij}$. In addition to the industry under study, each economy contains a perfectly competitive sector producing a single tradable output under constant returns to scale, and this output is taken as the numeraire.

Demand for the differentiated product is represented by a two-stage budgeting process, following Dixit and Stiglitz (1977). Welfare is separable between the differentiated product and the numeraire good, with the sub-utility function representing welfare in country $j$ obtained from consumption of the differentiated product represented by the constant elasticity of substitution function

$$y_j = \left( \sum_{i=1}^{I} m_i a_{ij}^{1/\varepsilon} x_{ij}^{(\varepsilon-1)/\varepsilon} \right)^{\varepsilon/(\varepsilon-1)}, \tag{A1}$$

where $\varepsilon > 1$ and $j = 1, \ldots, J$. The function $y_j$ can be regarded as a quantity index of aggregate consumption of the good, with the parameters $a_{ij}$ describing consumer preferences between products of different origin. Dual to the quantity index is a price index $q_j$, which takes the form

$$q_j = \left( \sum_{i=1}^{I} m_i a_{ij} p_{ij}^{1-\varepsilon} \right)^{1/(1-\varepsilon)} \tag{A2}$$

and represents the price of the aggregate product, where the $p_{ij}$ are the prices of the individual varieties.

We ignore income effects so that demand for the aggregate product is a function only of the price index $q_j$. We assume that this function is isoelastic, so

$$y_j = b_j q_j^{-\mu} \tag{A3}$$

for $j = 1, \ldots, J$, where the $b_j$ reflect the size of the respective country markets. Utility maximization implies that demand for individual product varieties depends both on the price of the individual variety and on the aggregate price index:

$$x_{ij} = a_{ij} \left( \frac{p_{ij}}{q_j} \right)^{-\varepsilon} y_j = a_{ij} b_j p_{ij}^{-\varepsilon} q_j^{\varepsilon-\mu}, \tag{A4}$$

where $i = 1,\ldots, I, j = 1,\ldots, J$; and the corresponding inverse demand functions are

$$p_{ij} = a_{ij}^{1/\varepsilon}\left(\frac{x_{ij}}{y_j}\right)^{-1/\varepsilon} \quad q_j = a_{ij}^{1/\varepsilon}b_j^{1/\mu}x_{ij}^{-1/\varepsilon}y_j^{(1/\varepsilon)-(1/\mu)}. \tag{A4a}$$

The market share, in value terms, in country $j$ of a firm from producer group $i$ is

$$s_{ij} = \frac{m_i p_{ij} x_{ij}}{q_j y_j} = \frac{m_i a_{ij} p_{ij}^{1-\varepsilon}}{\sum_k m_k a_{kj} p_{kj}^{1-\varepsilon}} = \frac{m_i a_{ij}^{1/\varepsilon} x_{ij}^{(\varepsilon-1)/\varepsilon}}{\sum_k m_k a_{kj}^{1/\varepsilon} x_{kj}^{(\varepsilon-1)/\varepsilon}} \tag{A5}$$

The profit of a typical firm in producer group $i$ is

$$\pi_i = \sum_{j=1}^{J} m_i x_{ij} p_{ij} \tau_{ij} - C_i(x_i, m_i), \tag{A6}$$

where the factor $\tau_{ij}$ represents the *ad valorem* costs of selling in market $j$, including transport costs, nontariff barriers, import taxes, and sales taxes. (For notational convenience the factor $\tau$ measures the inverse wedge so $\tau_{ij} < 1$, where such costs are positive). The function $C_i$ is the firm's cost function, assumed to depend positively on the output per variety, $x_i = \sum x_{ij}$, and on the number of varieties $m_i$.

Firms choose sales $x_{ij}$ to each of their markets independently. Where sales are not restricted, the first-order condition for profit-maximizing choice of $x_{ij}$ is the equality of marginal revenue to marginal cost:

$$p_{ij}\tau_{ij}\left(1 - \frac{1}{e_{ij}}\right) = \frac{1}{m_i}\frac{\partial C_i}{\partial x_i}, \tag{A7}$$

this equality holding for all $j$ if $i \notin R$, and for $j \notin E$ if $i \in R$, where $E$ is the set of markets in which there are sales restrictions, $R$ is the group of firms subject to sales restrictions in the markets $E$, and where $e_{ij}$ is the perceived elasticity of demand.

### Trade Restrictions

We model two types of sales restrictions; both of them taking the form of a voluntary export restraint (VER) that limits the *share* that a firm from the set $R$ (assumed to be foreign firms) may have in a market. In the first we suppose that each firm in the set $R$ is restricted to fixed shares of each of a subset $E$ of world markets so that, if $j \in E$, the market share $\sigma_{rj}$ is constrained not to exceed some fixed level. However, we alternatively want to allow there to be a restriction on the firm's *overall* market share in a set of markets $E$, $\sigma_r$. Note that these shares are volume shares as opposed to the value shares $s_{ij}$ defined earlier.

When a firm $r$ is subject to a restriction on its share of each of a set of markets $E$, the Lagrangean for its profit maximization problem is

$$\mathscr{L}_r = \sum_{j=1}^{J} m_r x_{rj} p_{rj} \tau_{rj} - C_r(x_r, m_r) - \sum_{k \in E} \lambda_k \left( m_r x_{rk} - \sigma_{rk} \sum_{i=1}^{I} m_i x_{ik} \right),$$

with first-order conditions in each restricted market $j$

$$p_{rj} \tau_{rj} \left( 1 - \frac{1}{e_{rj}} \right) = \frac{1}{m_r} \frac{\partial C_r}{\partial x_r} + \lambda_j (1 - \sigma_{rj}), \tag{A7a}$$

while for a restriction on the overall share of a set of markets $E$, the Lagrangean is

$$\mathscr{L}_r = \sum_{j=1}^{J} m_r x_{rj} p_{rj} \tau_{rj} - C_r(x_r, m_r) - \lambda \sum_{k \in E} \left( m_r x_{rk} - \sigma_r \sum_{i=1}^{I} m_i x_{ik} \right),$$

giving first-order conditions for each market $j$ in the set $E$:

$$p_{rj} \tau_{rj} \left( 1 - \frac{1}{e_{rj}} \right) = \frac{1}{m_r} \frac{\partial C_r}{\partial x_r} + \lambda (1 - \sigma_r). \tag{A7b}$$

The perceived elasticity of demand $e_{ij}$ is derived by assuming that firms are Cournot competitors, except in the case where firms that are not themselves subject to restrictions perceive that the behavior of rivals from producer group $R$ is constrained. Cournot behavior therefore applies to all firms in markets without restrictions and to all firms from the constrained group of producers. The perceived elasticity of demand is then derived from equations (A4a) and (A1), holding sales of competitors constant, as

$$\frac{1}{e_{ij}} = \frac{1}{\varepsilon} + \left( \frac{1}{\mu} - \frac{1}{\varepsilon} \right) s_{ij} \tag{A8}$$

for all $j$ if $i \in R$, and for all $i$ if $j \notin E$.

Consider now the behavior of unconstrained firms in the presence of a VER limiting the overall market share of a group $R$ of firms in the set $E$ of national markets. An unconstrained firm $i$ maximizes (A6), taking account of effects of changes in $x_{ij}$ on $x_{rk}$ in all $k \in E$, so

$$x_{ij}\frac{\partial C}{\partial x_i} = m_i p_{ij} x_{ij}\tau_{ij} + \sum_{k\in E} m_i p_{ik} x_{ik}\tau_{ik}\frac{x_{ij}}{p_{ik}}\frac{dp_{ik}}{dx_{ij}}.$$

From (A4a) it follows that

$$\frac{x_{ij}}{p_{ij}}\frac{dp_{ij}}{dx_{ij}} = -\frac{1}{\varepsilon} - \left(\frac{1}{\mu} - \frac{1}{\varepsilon}\right)\frac{x_{ij}}{y_j}\frac{dy_j}{dx_{ij}},$$

and for $k \neq j$,

$$\frac{x_{ik}}{p_{ik}}\frac{dp_{ik}}{dx_{ij}} = -\left(\frac{1}{\mu} - \frac{1}{\varepsilon}\right)\frac{x_{ik}}{y_k}\frac{dy_k}{dx_{ij}}.$$

Therefore the first-order condition for an unconstrained firm is

$$x_{ij}\frac{\partial C}{\partial x_i} = m_i p_{ij} x_{ij}\tau_{ij}\left(1 - \frac{1}{\varepsilon}\right)$$

$$-\left(\frac{1}{\mu} - \frac{1}{\varepsilon}\right)\sum_{k\in E} m_i p_{ik} x_{ik}\tau_{ik}\frac{x_{ik}}{y_k}\frac{dy_k}{dx_{ik}}.$$

However, from the fact that

$$y_k = \left(\sum_{i\in F} m_i a_{ik}^{1/\varepsilon} x_{ik}^{(\varepsilon-1)/\varepsilon}\right)^{\varepsilon/(\varepsilon-1)},$$

it follows that

$$\frac{x_{ik}}{y_k}\frac{\partial y_k}{\partial x_{ik}} = \frac{m_i a_{ik}^{1/\varepsilon} x_{ik}^{(\varepsilon-1)/\varepsilon}}{\sum_{i\in F} m_i a_{ik}^{1/\varepsilon} x_{ik}^{(\varepsilon-1)/\varepsilon}} = s_{ik},$$

so

$$\frac{x_{ij}}{y_k}\frac{dy_k}{dx_{ij}} = s_{ij}\delta_{jk} + n_r s_{rk}\frac{x_{ij}}{x_{rk}}\frac{dx_{rk}}{dx_{ij}},$$

where $n_r$ is the number of (identical) restricted firms. The first-order condition becomes

$$x_{ij}\frac{\partial C}{\partial x_i} = m_i p_{ij} x_{ij}\tau_{ij}\left[1 - \frac{1}{\varepsilon} - \left(\frac{1}{\mu} - \frac{1}{\varepsilon}\right)s_{ij}\right]$$

$$-\left(\frac{1}{\mu} - \frac{1}{\varepsilon}\right)\sum_{k\in E} m_i p_{ik} x_{ik}\tau_{ik} n_r s_{rk}\frac{x_{ik}}{x_{rk}}\frac{dx_{rk}}{dx_{ik}}. \tag{A9}$$

The constrained firms' behavior enters the unconstrained firms' first-order condition. The constraint that must be met is that

$$\sum_{k \in E} m_r x_{rk} = \sigma_r \sum_{k \in E} \sum_{i \in F} m_i x_{ik},$$

where $F$ is the set of all firms, and $\sigma_r$ is the fixed share of the aggregate market in $E$ to which each of the firms $r$ is constrained. Differentiating with respect to $x_{ij}$ gives

$$\sum_{k \in E} m_r \frac{dx_{rk}}{dx_{ij}} = \sigma_r \left( m_i + \sum_{k \in E} n_r m_r \frac{dx_{rk}}{dx_{ij}} \right)$$

so

$$(1 - \sigma_r n_r) \sum_{k \in E} m_r x_{rk} \frac{x_{ij}}{x_{rk}} \frac{dx_{rk}}{dx_{ij}} = \sigma_r m_i x_{ij}. \tag{A10}$$

We assume that firm $i$ conjectures that restrained firms will, in equilibrium, change their sales in each of their markets equiproportionately in response to the change in their constrained output resulting from a change in $x_{ij}$, and let

$$\xi = \frac{x_{ij}}{x_{rk}} \frac{dx_{rk}}{dx_{ij}} \qquad \text{for all } k,$$

which implies that (A10) can be written as

$$\xi = \frac{\sigma_r m_i x_{ij}}{(1 - \sigma_r n_r) \sum_{k \in E} m_r x_{rk}},$$

and the first-order condition (A9) now becomes

$$p_{ij} \tau_{ij} \left( 1 - \frac{1}{\varepsilon} - \left( \frac{1}{\mu} - \frac{1}{\varepsilon} \right) s_{ij} \right) - \frac{\sum_{k \in E} m_i x_{ik} p_{ik} \tau_{ik} n_r s_{rk}}{\sum_{k \in E} \sum_{i \notin R} m_i x_{ik}} \left( \frac{1}{\mu} - \frac{1}{\varepsilon} \right)$$

$$= \frac{1}{m_i} \frac{\partial C_i}{\partial x_i}. \tag{A8b}$$

In the case of there being a share quota in each of a group of markets $j$, the above argument can be applied to the market $j$ individually, and (A8b) then implies that the unrestricted firm's optimum choice in market $j$ is given by (A7) but with inverse elasticity:

$$\frac{1}{e_{ij}} = \frac{1}{\varepsilon} + \left(\frac{1}{\mu} - \frac{1}{\varepsilon}\right)\left\{s_{ij} + n_r s_{rj}\frac{m_i x_{ij}}{\sum_{i \notin R} m_i x_{ij}}\right\}. \tag{A8a}$$

The case of a market with no share quotas, which we have already seen in (A7) and (A8), can be derived from (A8b) by letting $n_r = 0$, in which case (A8b) does indeed reduce to (A7) and (A8).

## Notes

This is a radically revised version of a paper with the same title by Caroline Digby, Alasdair Smith, and Anthony J. Venables, circulated as CEPR Discussion Paper No. 249. We are grateful for funding from the Economic and Social Research Council (grants no. B00232149 and R000231763), for the research assistance of Caroline Digby and Michael Gasiorek, and for the comments of Avinash Dixit, Rob Feenstra, Morris Goldstein, and Jim Levinsohn.

## References

Anderson, Simon P., André de Palma, and Jacques-François Thisse. 1989. Demand for differentiated products, discrete choice models, and the characteristics approach. *Review of Economic Studies* **56**: 21–35.

Bhagwati, Jagdish. 1965. On the equivalence of tariffs and quotas. In Robert E. Baldwin et al. (eds.), *Trade, Growth and the Balance of Payments: Essays in Honor of Gottfried Haberler.* Chicago: Rand McNally.

Bresnahan, Timothy. 1981. Departures from marginal-cost pricing in the American automobile industry. *Journal of Econometrics* **17**: 201–227.

Cowling, Keith and John Cubbin. 1971. Price, quality and advertising competition: an econometric investigation of the United Kingdom car market. *Economica* **38**(152): 378–394.

Dixit, Avinash 1987. Optimal trade and industrial policies for the US automobile industry. In Robert Feenstra (ed.), *Empirical Methods for International Trade* Cambridge: MIT Press.

Dixit, Avinash, and Joseph Stiglitz. 1977. Monopolistic competition and optimum product diversity. *American Economic Review* **67** (3): 297–308.

Feenstra, Robert, and James Levinsohn. 1989. Estimating demand and oligopoly pricing for differentiated products with multiple characteristics. Unpublished manuscript.

Harris, Richard. 1985. Why voluntary export restraints are "voluntary." *Canadian Journal of Economics* **18**: 799–801.

Helpman, Elhanan, and Paul Krugman. 1989. *Trade Policy and Market Structure.* Cambridge: MIT Press.

Hess, Alan C. 1977. A comparison of automobile demand equations. *Econometrica* **45** (3): 683–701.

Jones, Daniel. 1987. Prudent marketing and price differentials in the UK car market: a case study. In *The Costs of Restricting Imports: The Automobile Industry.* Paris: OECD.

Krishna, Kala. 1989. Trade restrictions as facilitating practices. *Journal of International Economic* **26** (3–4): 251–270.

Lancaster, Kelvin. 1979. *Variety, Equity and Efficiency*. New York: Columbia University Press.

Laussel, Didier, Christian Montet, and Anne Peguin-Feissolle. 1988. Optimal trade policy under oligopoly: A calibrated model of the Europe-Japan rivalry in the EEC car market. *European Economic Review* **32** (7): 1547–1565.

Levinsohn, James. 1988. Empirics of taxes on differentiated products: The case of tariffs in the U.S. automobile industry. In Robert E. Baldwin (ed.), *Trade Policy Issues and Empirical Analysis*. Chicago: University of Chicago Press.

Ludvigsen Associates Limited. 1988. *The EC92 Automobile Sector*. Commission of the European Communities. Research on the "Cost of Non-Europe," Basic Findings, vol. 11. Luxembourg: European Communities Publications Office.

Maxcy, George, and Z. Aubrey Silberston. 1959. *The Motor Industry*. London: George Allen and Unwin.

Messerlin, Patrick, and S. Becuwe. 1987. French trade and competition policies in the car industry. In *The Costs of Restricting Imports: The Automobile Industry*. Paris: OECD.

Organization for Economic Cooperation and Development. 1983. *Long Term Outlook for the World Automobile Industry*. Paris: OECD.

Organization for Economic Cooperation and Development. 1987. *The Costs of Restricting Imports: The automobile industry*. Paris: OECD.

Smith, Alasdair. 1989. Alternative models of trade policy in the European car market. Paper presented to the NBER/CEPR conference on Empirical Studies of Strategic Trade Policy. Cambridge, MA, October 1989.

Smith, Alasdair 1990. The market for cars in the enlarged European Community. In Christopher Bliss and Jorge Braga de Macedo (eds), *Unity with Diversity in the European Economy: The Community's Southern Frontier*. Cambridge: Cambridge University Press for CEPR.

Smith, Alasdair, and Anthony J. Venables. 1988. Completing the internal market in the European Community: Some industry simulations. *European Economic Review* **32** (7): 1501–1525.

Venables, Anthony J., and Alasdair Smith. 1986. Trade and industrial policy under imperfect competition. *Economic Policy* **1** (3): 622–672.

# III STRUCTURAL ISSUES

# 11 Services in International Trade

**Wilfred J. Ethier and Henrik Horn**

Services are prominent in world trade. Exactly how prominent is hard to say, as data are scanty and unreliable. But in most industrial countries services now contribute more to the national product than do goods. There is at present no international legal framework for trade in services comparable to the GATT framework for trade in goods. Accordingly the role of services in international trade is prominent in current policy debate. For instance, a major source of controversy preceding the Uruguay Round was whether trade in services should be on the agenda. Trade theorists have reacted by asking whether trade in services is really different from trade in goods and, if so, what the major differences are. If no systematic difference can be uncovered, there is no economic reason to treat services differently from goods in trade policy. These queries have not led to any clear conclusions. While Hindley and Smith (1984, 388–389) argue that "... from a *conceptual* point of view there is no difficulty about applying the standard toolkit of the international economist to the problems of trade and investment in services," others have expressed less confidence in standard theory. For instance, it is argued that theories based on the assumption that factors of production are internationally immobile are inadequate as explanations of trade in certain types of services (see, e.g., Sampson and Snape 1984).

The literature contains a bewildering variety of suggested differences between goods and services. A common distinction is that the producer and the consumer must meet physically for the service to be provided, while this is atypical for goods. Other emphasized differences are that services are nonstorable and/or nontangible, require a small proportion of intermediate inputs of goods, or require international direct investment when traded. More abstractly, a service has been defined as a transaction that leads to a change in the condition of a person or a good. Sometimes services are simply taken to be those commodities that are classified as services in trade statistics.[1]

To answer the question "is there a good economic reason to treat goods and services differently in trade policy?" one must first systematically model perceived differences between the two commodities and analyze the consequences of these differences. This chapter is an attempt to do so. Its starting point is the (admittedly casual) observation that many services share certain characteristics that are less typical for goods:[2]

1. Services are often specialized to the requirements of the buyer.
2. Service firms typically provide several varieties of services since they tend to supply several buyers.
3. There are overhead costs that are fixed (at least within certain ranges of output) that give rise to economies of scope. However, increasing the variety of services is more costly than increasing the level at which a single service variety is provided, so there are also *marginal* diseconomies of scope.
4. Service markets often seem highly competitive.

Many examples seem to fit this description: A typing firm types documents for several different customers. The firm has fixed costs for its office and office machinery, etc. While the firm can type different types of documents, such as legal or medical documents, and use different kinds of word-processing programs, its productivity will be the highest if it specializes in one particular type. Similarly a firm that writes computer software can create specialized programs for several clients. But it will be the most productive if it concentrates on the requirements of a single customer, using a particular programming language, etc. Other examples are financial-services firms that can handle the needs of electronics manufacturers or of toy manufacturers, management consultants who can advise different firms, retailers that deal in different goods, etc. Typical for all of these examples is that the firms mostly provide specialized services, have fixed costs, and suffer productivity losses from servicing several customers. What is less clear perhaps is whether these firms in general operate in competitive markets.[3] However, many of them clearly do so, and in this chapter we take this to be the typical case.

We develop a general equilibrium model of world trade in which a commodity with these features ("services") plays a distinctive role. We then analyze different arrangements for trade in such services. One factor—labor—produces services and differentiated intermediate goods manufactures. The latter are produced under increasing returns to scale by monopolistically competitive firms and thus differ from services in both production technology and market structure. Services and manufactures are then combined to produce final differentiated outputs. The world economy consists of two countries both of which are capable of producing manufactures and services in this manner. These countries can also engage in international trade.

Of particular interest is whether restriction on trade in services can be motivated from a welfare point of view. To examine this, we compare autarky and three regimes that differ in the extent to which services are tradable: In *service autarky* locally produced services are combined with possibly imported manufactures. With *embodied service trade* there is still no direct trade in services, but they may be embodied in traded manufactures. Finally, *free trade in services* allows both services and manufactures to be traded directly. Does welfare increase as the economy replaces one regime by another with fewer restrictions on service trade? The answer is not as self-evident as it may first appear. There are several distortions in this economy: fixed costs, monopolistic competition, economies, and diseconomies of scope. A comparison of regimes is a second-best exercise, and it could in principle yield any result.

To isolate the consequences of trade in such services from conventional trade, we first investigate international trade between identical countries. Section 11.3 shows that in this case trade in services, either directly or embodied in goods, confers gains relative to service autarky, which in turns yields higher welfare than complete autarky.

Although this welfare ranking is by no means self-evident, one suspects that it is partly due to the total symmetry between the two countries. Section 11.4 therefore considers consequences of trade in services in situations where the countries differ. There are obviously a large number of possible asymmetries that could be considered. The particular difference examined here is a technological asymmetry, which implies that in autarky service firms are smaller in one of the two countries. In this case there are richer possibilities with regard to patterns of trade. Unfortunately, this comes at a price: analytical complexity. The analysis is therefore not as complete as in the case of identical countries. But the embodied service trade regime and the free service trade regime are both characterized in detail. For instance, it is shown that embodied service trade yields higher welfare for both countries than does complete autarky. Service autarky is substantailly more involved, and we make no welfare comparisons of this regime with other trading arrangements.

## 11.1   The Model

There are two countries, each inelastically supplied with a single internationally immobile factor of production, labor $L$. There are two productive sectors: services $S$ and manufacturing $M$. Home labor is the numéraire.

The manufacturing sector produces a set of $n$ endogenously determined differentiated consumer goods. All goods use the same technology, available to both countries, and enter symmetrically into demand. We shall consider only symmetric equilibria, and our notation will accordingly not distinguish between produced varieties. Define one unit of foreign labor to be the quantity that can perform the same tasks in the manufacturing sector as can one unit of home labor. The production process for each variety is two stage. First, labor is used to produce a rudimentary good, with $a + bx$ units of labor required to produce the quantity $x$ of some variety. Next, a specialized service must be applied to the rudimentary good to produce the finished consumer good. The quantity $x$ of the rudimentary good will produce $M = x$ of the finished good, provided the specialized service is applied in the amount $M$ (i.e., we define one unit of each specialized service to be that quantity required to finish one unit of the manufactured variety which that service serves). Each variety of manufacture requires a unique specialized service. The manufacturing sector has a monopolistically competitive market structure.

The service sector consists of an endogenously determined number $\Gamma$ of service firms, each of which supplies an endogenously determined number $N$ of different specialized services, $0 \leq N \leq N^0$. Again, we shall consider only symmetric equilibria and so shall not distinguish among provided services or among existing service firms. A services firm can supply related specialized services, but increasing the variety of services is more costly than increasing the level at which a single service is provided. More precisely, we assume that each service firm's requirement of labor is determined by the following (labor) cost function:

$$L_S = \left[ \sum_{j=1}^{N} (S_j)^{1/\alpha} \right]^{\alpha \delta} + \phi = (N^\alpha S)^\delta + \phi \qquad \text{for } \alpha, \delta > 1, \phi > 0.$$

$S_j$ denotes the level at which specialized service $j$ is provided and $S$ denotes their common value in a symmetric equilibrium. The parameter $\alpha$ measures the degree of marginal diseconomies of scope in the provision of services, $\delta$ measures diseconomies of scale, and $\phi$ measures fixed costs. Let $s$ denote the total service effort provided by a firm, $s = N^\alpha S$. Our cost function implies that a firm's choice of total service effort is separable from its choice of how to divide that effort between $N$ and $S$. Then $[s^\delta + \phi]/s$ is a U-shaped average cost curve (in labor) with a minimum at the level $[\phi/(\alpha\delta - 1)]^{1/\delta} \equiv s^0$, and at this level the average labor cost is $\alpha\delta[\phi/(\alpha\delta - 1)]^{(\delta-1)/\delta} \equiv c$.

In the service sector each individual firm determines the number of services to provide and their price $q$. Because of the marginal diseconomies of scope, each service firm will wish to minimize the number of services it produces and, instead, provide larger volumes of a fewer number of services. But the firm is constrained in its ability to sell large volumes by the individual manufacturer's demand $S_D(q)$ and by the threat that a competitor takes over its customers if the price is too high. The fact that each service firm wants to limit the number of services produced implies that each service will be provided by only one firm. Nevertheless, potential competition is introduced by firms' ability to supply alternative services. We assume that this competition is sufficiently pronounced to make all demand vanish when $q$ exceeds the equilibrium market price $q^c$ for other service firms. At a price below $q^c$, one the other hand, the service firm faces the individual manufacturer's demand $S_D(q)$. We can hence write the profit of the service firm as

$$y_s(N, S, q) = qNS - N^{\alpha\delta}S^\delta - \phi,$$

where $S = S_D(q)$ when $q$ does not exceed the price $q^c$ of competing services, and where $S = 0$ if $q > q^c$.

Consumption baskets consist of the $n$ produced finished manufactures. We suppose that in each country the demands for these goods are generated by a utility function of the following (now standard) form:

$$u = \left[ \sum_{i=1}^{n} M_i^\beta \right]^{1/\beta} = n^{1/\beta} M,$$

where $M_i$ denotes consumption of the $i$th finished manufacture and $M$ that of each manufacture in a symmetric equilibrium.

We now describe an equilibrium in the service sector. First, each service firm provides a profit-maximizing number of services $N(S_D(q), q)$. Second, the equilibrium price ensures zero profits: $y_s(N(S_D(q), q), S_D(q), q) = 0$. These two conditions imply that each service firm will operate at the level $s^0$, and thus that $c\Gamma s^0$ units of labor are allocated to the service sector.

The third property we want the equilibrium to fulfill is that individual service firms cannot increase their respective profits by charging a different price than the hypothesized equilibrium price. It is clear that a price higher than that of competitors cannot be profit maximizing. Hence all firms must charge the same price $q = q^c$. However, the conditions specified so far do not ensure that at this common price it doesn't pay the firm to reduce its price in order to get larger volumes and possibly also limit the number of services provided. We thus require that in equilibrium $dy_S/dq > 0$ for $dq < 0$, that is, that $\alpha b(1 - \beta) + (1 - \alpha\beta)q > 0$.

## 11.2 Autarky Equilibrium

We now examine autarky equilibrium in the home country. Labor is the numéraire; let $P$ and $q$ respectively denote the prices of representative finished manufactures and specialized services.

The utility function implies that the marginal revenue of an additional unit of a finished manufacture is $\beta P$. Thus the marginal revenue confronting a producer of raw manufactures is $\beta P - q$. (We assume that the producers of raw manufactures are imperfectly competitive. However, it does not matter whether they also finish the goods themselves or whether they sell them to other [competitive] firms for this purpose). Marginal cost is $b$. The service sector prices at average cost. Since it supplies the total quantity $SN\Gamma$ of services at aggregate cost $c\Gamma s^0$, $q = c\Gamma s^0/s^0 N^{1-\alpha}\Gamma = cN^{\alpha-1}$. Thus the condition of profit maximization by each manufacturer, that marginal revenue equal marginal cost, is

$$\beta P - cN^{\alpha-1} = b. \tag{1}$$

Free entry into manufacturing will drive profit to zero in equilibrium:

$$Px - cN^{\alpha-1}x - (a + bx) = 0. \tag{2}$$

The labor market will clear when the supply of labor equals the total demand of the two sectors:

$$L = c\Gamma s^0 + n(a + bx). \tag{3}$$

Finally, the market for services will clear when $n$ specialized services are provided, each in the amount $x$:

$$N\Gamma = n, \tag{4}$$

$$s^0 = N^\alpha x. \tag{5}$$

These five equilibrium conditions determine the values of the five variables $P$, $N$, $x$, $\Gamma$, and $n$. However, a subsystem corresponding to the equilibrium of individual manufacturing and service firms can be separated out. Equation (1) can be substituted into (2), eliminating $P$ and yielding the condition

[M] for a manufacturing firm to be in equilibrium. The analogous expression [S] for a service firm is simply equation (5) rewritten.

[M]     $x[b + cN^{\alpha-1}] = \dfrac{\alpha\beta}{1-\beta},$

[S]     $N^{\alpha}x - s^0 = 0.$

Together, [M] and [S] determine $x$ and $N$ independently of the rest of the system:

$$\left.\frac{dx}{dN}\right|_M = -x\left[\frac{cN^{\alpha-1}}{b + cN^{\alpha-1}}\right]\frac{\alpha-1}{N} < 0,$$

$$\left.\frac{dx}{dN}\right|_S = -x\frac{\alpha}{N} < \left.\frac{x}{dN}\right|_M < 0.$$

The situation is depicted in figure 11.1.

If there were no services sector, [M] would have determined $x$ independently of the rest of the system by the parameters $a$, $b$, and $\beta$. This is familiar from differentiated-product models with Dixit-Stiglitz preferences. But with services, $x$ is determined jointly with $N$ and both depend also on the parameters $c$, $\alpha$, and $s^0$:

$$x = x(\overset{+}{a}, \overset{-}{b}, \overset{+}{\beta}, \overset{-}{c}, \overset{?}{\alpha}, \overset{-}{s^0}),$$
$$N = N(\overset{-}{a}, \overset{+}{b}, \overset{-}{\beta}, \overset{+}{c}, \overset{?}{\alpha}, \overset{+}{s^0}).$$

The relation [M] has a negative slope because an increase in the diversity of services provided by a single-service firm increases their cost, thus raising

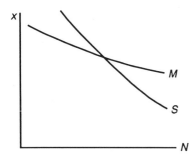

**Figure 11.1**

the marginal cost of providing finished manufactures and so inducing a fall
in quantity of the latter. **[S]** has a negative slope because an increase in the
diversity of services provided must itself reduce the amount of each service,
with the overall size of the service firm fixed.

From (1), $P$ is positively related to $N$, as is $q$:

$$\frac{dP}{dN} = (\alpha - 1)\frac{c}{\beta}N^{\alpha-2} > \frac{dq}{dN} = (\alpha - 1)cN^{\alpha-2} > 0.$$

Equations (3) and (4) can be substituted together to give a composite
market clearing condition:

$$\textbf{[MC]} \qquad L = n\left[\left(\frac{cs^0}{N}\right) + a + bx\right].$$

This determines $n$, given the solutions of $x$ and $N$ from the firm-equilibrium
subsystem. Clearly changes in $L$ result in equiproportional changes in $n$
and $\Gamma$; all other variables are independent of market size:

$$\left.\frac{dx}{dN}\right|_{n^0} = \frac{cs^0}{bN^2}.$$

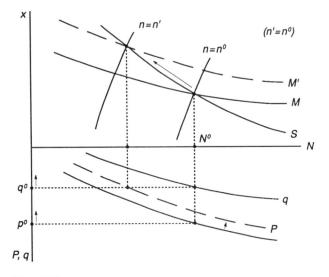

**Figure 11.2**

Figure 11.2, complete autarky equilibrium, shows the effect of a rise in $\beta$, namely, an increase in the substitutability of finished manufactures for each other and consequent reduction in the degree of product differentiation. The output of each manufacture rises, their number falls, each service firm serves fewer clients, and both manufactures and services become cheaper in terms of labor.

## 11.3 International Trade between Identical Countries

We now introduce international trade in services. In order to focus solely upon the implications of such trade, we initially suppose that the home country is identical to the rest of the world in every way. Thus there will be no comparative advantage basis for trade, for example. We shall study and compare three distinct international trade equilibria.

[SA] *Service autarky.* There is free trade only in unfinished manufactures $x$. Thus each country must provide the specialized services for all produced varieties of manufactures, and each such service is provided by each country.

[ES] *Embodied service trade.* There is free trade in all types of manufactures, both finished and unfinished. Thus services are not traded directly but may be embodied in traded goods. Then each country need provide only the services required by the manufactures that it finishes.

[FST] *Free trade in services.* All manufactures and services may be traded directly.

The distinction between an *SA* equilibrium and an *ES* one is probably a matter of the nature of services more than policy, but the difference between *FTS* and the other two is clearly one of policy. Thus it is probably best to compare a movement from *SA* to *FTS* with one from *ES* to *FTS*, though we can also fictionally decompose the movement from *SA* to *FTS* into one from *SA* to *ES* plus one from *ES* to *FTS*. We start with an analysis of service autarky.

### Service Autarky

Suppose that the home country can trade freely in unfinished manufactures with (a part of) the rest of the world, but that there is no trade in finished manufactures or in services. Let $\tau$ denote the ratio of the home labor force to that of the free trade area of which the home country is a part. Thus $\tau = 1$ corresponds to autarky, and reductions in $\tau$ below unity reflect opening of trade (in $F$ and $x$ only) with larger parts of the world.

The conditions for profit maximization and for equilibrium zero profit for home producers of unfinished manufactures are the same as before since the home country is identical to the rest of the world. Thus equations (1) and (2) continue to hold, and the **[M]** schedule is accordingly unchanged. However, services must now be provided to finish only that part of manufacturing production that is not exported, so (5), and thus **[S]**, become

**[S']**     $s^0 = \tau N^\alpha x.$

Furthermore services are also required to finish imports of manufactures, so the labor market-clearing relation becomes

**[MC']**     $L = c\Gamma s^0 + \tau n(a + bx) = n\left[\left(\dfrac{cs^0}{N}\right) + \tau(a + bx)\right].$

Other equations are unchanged.

It is evident from the above equations that a movement to free trade—that is, a reduction in $\tau$ below unity—shifts the **[S]** schedule out, with equilibrium moving down and to the right along **[M]**. Thus $x$ falls and $N$, $P$, and $q$ rise. Differentiating the conditions of equilibrium implies the following.

$$\frac{\tau}{x}\frac{dx}{d\tau} = \frac{(\alpha - 1)cN^{\alpha-1}}{\alpha b + cN^{\alpha-1}} > 0,$$

$$0 > \frac{\tau}{N}\frac{dN}{d\tau} = -\frac{b + cN^{\alpha-1}}{\alpha b + cN^{\alpha-1}} > -1 = \frac{\tau}{n}\frac{dn}{d\tau}.$$

It follows from this analysis that international trade produces two distinct effects, working through economies of scale, that have different implications for welfare. On the one hand, trade makes possible the consumption of a greater variety of finished manufacture, each produced under conditions of increasing returns to scale. This beneficial effect is familiar from the literature on trade in differentiated goods. But this greater variety of finished goods requires the provision of a greater variety of services, each at a lower level since only that portion of manufactures not exported requires servicing (and since $x$ also falls). Here scale economies work in a detrimental way. With the size $s^0$ of each services firm determined by its

U-shaped cost curve, the firm produces an increased number $N$ of services at a lower level for each. The marginal diseconomies of scope faced by service firms imply that the service sector requires more resources than before, and these resources must come from manufacturing. Thus $x$ falls. The bottom line is that trade causes the economy to consume a smaller quantity of finished manufactures, but with more variety.

Because of the distortions that are present, it is not clear whether we should expect a move to free trade to raise home welfare on balance or not. Differentiate the welfare function to obtain

$$\frac{\tau}{n}\frac{du}{d\tau} = \frac{1}{\beta}\left(\frac{\tau}{n}\frac{dn}{d\tau}\right) + \left(\frac{\tau}{x}\frac{dx}{d\tau}\right).$$

This expression decomposes the total welfare change into a (positive) variety effect and a (negative) quantity effect. The relative importance of those two effects is determined by $\beta$, which measures the degree of complementarity among finished manufactures in consumption. The variety effect is relatively more important for small values of $\beta$, that is, if varieties are not easily substituted for each other, or if consumers have a desire for variety. Substituting into this expression and rearranging gives the following:

$$-\left(\frac{\tau}{u}\frac{du}{d\tau}\right) = \frac{1}{\beta} + 1 - \frac{\alpha\beta P}{(\alpha - 1)b + \beta P}.$$

According to the above expression, the detrimental effect of trade will dominate the beneficial one if $\alpha b + (1 - \alpha\beta + \beta)q < 0$. For a positive $q$ this requires $1 - \alpha\beta + \beta < 0$, and hence that $q > \alpha b/(\alpha\beta - 1 - \beta)$. On the other hand, the equilibrium condition—that the price of services must be such that it doesn't pay for service firms to lower the price—requires, as noted above, that $q < \alpha b(1 - \beta)/(\alpha\beta - 1)$, where we have taken into account the fact that $1 - \alpha\beta < 0$ when $1 - \alpha\beta + \beta < 0$. Hence, since these two inequalities are incompatible with each other, complete autarky cannot be better than service autarky.

### Embodied Service Trade

Suppose now that free trade in final manufactures is also possible so that services can be traded when embodied in goods, but not directly. As we argued above, the relevance of this case compared to service autarky is more likely to depend on the nature of services than on the nature of policy. No doubt both types of services coexist in the world. We proceed by contrasting the two "pure" cases in order to find out what difference the nature of services makes.

The embodied service trade equilibrium is easy to describe, given the last section's description of complete autarky. Equations (1), (2), and (5) are unaffected by free trade in finished manufactures, so the [M] and [S] schedules are as in autarky. Thus embobied service trade between identical economies features $x$, $N$, $P$, and $q$ at their autarky levels. But equation (5) becomes

$$N\Gamma = n\tau, \tag{4'}$$

where $n$ denotes the number of varieties of finished manufactures actually *consumed* at home. It follows from this that the home labor market-clearing condition now becomes

$$[\mathbf{MC'}] \qquad L = c\Gamma s^0 + \tau n(a + bx) = \tau n\left(\frac{cs^0}{N} + a + bx\right).$$

Then [MC'] at once implies that

$$\frac{\tau}{n}\frac{dn}{d\tau} = -1.$$

The only effect of trade, relative to total autarky, is to increase the total number of varieties consumed in full proportion to the increased extent of the market. In effect, embodied service trade does not disturb the usual conclusions regarding trade in differentiated goods. One expects an un-ambiguous welfare improvement, and indeed we now have

$$-\frac{1}{u}\frac{du}{d\tau} = -\frac{1}{\beta}\frac{\tau}{n}\frac{dn}{d\tau} = \frac{1}{\beta}.$$

The negative quantity effect present with service autarky simply drops out, leaving only the positive variety effect. The latter effect remains of the same magnitude, so embodied service trade must be preferable to service autarky, even when the latter provides gains relative to total autarky.

### Free Trade in Services

We now say a few words about free trade in services, in addition to trade in all goods. Only a few words are necessary because a little thought quickly

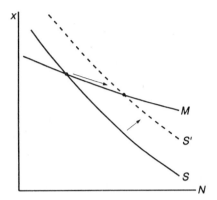

**Figure 11.3**

reveals that all the equations of the previous subsection continue to hold. Thus, with embodied service trade, allowing the services themselves to be traded directly has no effect.

In summary, the following conclusions apply to trade in services between identical economies.

1. Service autarky yields higher utility than complete autarky, to a degree depending upon the relative strength of variety and quantity effects.
2. Trade in services, either directly or embodied in traded goods, confers gains relative to both service autarky and total autarky.
3. With free trade in goods, embodied service trade is a perfect substitute for the direct trade of services.

## 11.4   International Trade between Dissimilar Countries

Now that we have seen the implications of services in a "pure" environment unencumbered by differences across countries it is time to investigate how services interact with such differences when they are present. In this model countries might differ in size, in tastes, and in technology in any of the three sectors. Allowing differences in all these parameters at once seems a sure bet for confusion, so we prefer to continue to advance a step at a time.

Differences in size are straightforward and uninteresting in this model, and we think of manufacturing as employing a standardized technology available worldwide (though this assumption could be abandoned, of course). This leaves tastes, labor productivities, and the service parameters as candidates for international differences. Tastes and labor productivities are the standard determinants of comparative advantage, so let us leave them internationally identical to focus on technological differences in the service sector, the distinctive focus of the present chapter.

The service technology might differ across countries in $\alpha$ (measuring the degree of marginal diseconomies of scope), in $\phi$ (fixed cost), or in $\delta$ (diseconomies of scale). Equivalently they might differ in $\alpha$, in $c$ (equilibrium average labor cost), or in $s^0$ (optimal firm size). Again, it seems best to proceed a step at a time and to isolate the effects of differences in a single variable. So suppose that $\alpha$ and $c$ are identical across countries, but that $s^0$ is smaller at home than abroad: $s^{0*} > s^0$. That is, the optimal size of an individual home service firm is smaller. This will be the case (with $\alpha$ and $c$ identical at home and abroad) if $\phi^* > \phi$ and $\delta^* < \delta$ in the right proportions, that is, if the foreign service sector has greater fixed costs but more moderate diseconomies of scale than the home service sector. In sum, we study in this section the nature of economic transactions of the home economy with another country identical in every way except that $s^{0*} > s^0$.

### Autarky

To get some idea of the role of the size of service firms, first compare equilibria in the two countries when there is no economic intercourse between them. From equations (1) through (5) it is clear that an increase in $s^0$ causes the **[S]** schedule in figure 11.1 to shift out, so equilibrium moves down and to the right along the **[M]** schedule. Also, from **[M]**, **[S]**, and **[MC]**, $dn/ds^0 = 0$. Thus, comparing autarky in the two countries, $x > x^*$, $N < N^*$, $q < q^*$, $P < P^*$, $P - q < P^* - q^*$, $n = n^*$, $\Gamma > \Gamma^*$, and $F = F^*$. The two economies consume equal numbers of finished manufactures, but the foreign economy consumes a smaller quantity of each manufacture because its service sector is less efficient in operation. This efficiency difference is due to diseconomies of scope: We have assumed that the greater foreign fixed costs and smaller diseconomies of scale cancel in terms of average labor cost $c$ but result in larger-sized service firms; in autarky equilibrium this causes foreign service firms to provide a larger number $N^*$ of distinct services, exacerbating the effects of diseconomies of scope.

### Embodied Service Trade

We now introduce international trade. It will prove convenient to focus first on the case of embodied service trade, so suppose that the home and foreign countries can exchange finished manufactures.

The embodied service trade equilibrium is again easy to describe, given the description of complete autarky. Equations (1), (2), and (5) for each country are unaffected by free trade in finished manufactures, so the [M] and [S] schedules for both the home and foreign economies are as in autarky. Thus embodied service trade features $x$, $N$, $P$, and $q$, and also $x^*$, $N^*$, $P^*$, and $q^*$, at their autarky levels. Trade consists only of the intra-industry exchange of similar finished manufactures. The international markets for these latter goods will clear, consistently with the demand conditions in this model, when the home country consumes the fraction $h \equiv L/(L = L^*)$ of the world production of each variety and when the foreign country consumes the fraction $1 - h$. The home trade surplus will then equal $Pxn(1 - h) - P^*x^*n^*h$, which equals $Pxn - [1/(L + L^*)](Pxn + P^*x^*n^*)$. Now $(Pxn + P^*x^*n^*) = L + L^*$ because in the international equilibrium the aggregate value of world demand for finished manufactures must equal world income, and $Pxn = L$ because in the home autarky equilibrium the aggregate value of home demand for finished manufactures must have equaled home income. Thus trade balances.

In sum, the only effect of trade, relative to total autarky, is to increase the total number of varieties consumed in each country in full proportion to the increased extent of the market so that both countries gain. In effect, just as when the two countries were completely identical, embodied service trade does not disturb the usual conclusions regarding trade in differential goods. But now the international equilibrium is an *asymmetric* one. This is because in markets for finished manufactures the contribution of services is on the cost side. In equilibrium services cost more abroad than at home, so marginal costs are higher for foreign firms than for domestic ones. Thus in the (Cournot) monopolistically competitive equilibrium foreign firms sell less at a higher price than do domestic firms. This does not invite additional domestic entry because the latter has already progressed to the point where a potential domestic entrant would lose by offering a completely new product, and it cannot be more advantageous to offer instead a product already provided by another firm, even a high cost one.

## Free Trade in Services

With completely identical economies embodied service trade was a perfect substitute for the direct trade of services. This is not true now because the embodied service trade equilibrium is an asymmetric one, and in particular, $q < q^*$. In the previous subsection a similar price asymmetry in manufacturing was consistent with a trading equilibrium because of the monopolistically competitive market structure. But the perfectly contestable nature of service markets makes it incompatible with service trade: A home service firm would always find it profitable to make a hit-and-run switch to a foreign-supplied service.

It is now easy to describe international equilibrium. The home economy will export services. Two cases (and their boundary) are possible depending upon whether $L/(L + L^*)$ is sufficiently large for the home market to supply all services by itself. If it is, all services are produced at home, and both home and foreign wages equal unity. Both countries can produce manufactures on equal terms, so the allocation of production of commodities is indeterminate but inconsequential. Trade is all interindustry, with the home economy exporting all services for some mix of goods. In all significant respects the equilibrium is the same as when the two countries were completely identical since trading services allows the world to avoid completely the inefficient foreign technology.

If instead $L/(L + L^*)$ is too small for the home economy to supply all services, no commodities are produced at home and some services are produced abroad. This requires the foreign wage to be less than unity by just enough so that $q^* = q$. Thus further gains could be achieved if labor were able to move to the home country to produce services there.

### Service Autarky

Now allow the two countries to trade only unfinished manufactures. As with embodied service trade, equilibrium is likely to be characterized by services provided in both countries at different prices. When finished manufactures were traded, this price difference implied an international difference in marginal cost between the manufacturing sectors, resulting in an asymmetric equilibrium, as we have seen. But when unfinished manufactures are instead traded, a difference in service prices instead implies a difference on the *demand* side, leading manufacturing firms to price discriminate, assuming that they are able to segment markets. With all this in mind, we proceed to describe an international service autarky equilibrium in a case where relative endowments permit both countries to produce traded goods (so that both wages equal unity).

First, each manufacturer of unfinished goods, regardless of which country it is located in, will price its product so that the marginal revenue in each market equals marginal cost.

$$\beta P - cN^{\alpha-1} = b, \tag{6}$$

$$\beta P^* - cN^{*\alpha-1} = b. \tag{6'}$$

Entry into manufacturing proceeds until profit is zero:

$$(P - cN^{\alpha-1})x_h + (P^* - cN^{*\alpha-1})x_f = a + b(x_h + x_f), \tag{7}$$

where $x_h$ and $x_f$ denote the amount of total production of each variety sold in the home and foreign markets, respectively. (Home and foreign producers face identical problems and so make identical decisions.) The net (intraindustry) trade balance in unfinished manufactures must be zero:

$$(P - cN^{\alpha-1})x_h n_h = (P^* - cN^{*\alpha-1})x_f n_f, \tag{8}$$

where $n_h$ and $n_f$ denote the number of unfinished manufactures produced at home and abroad, respectively. The services market must also be in equilibrium in each country:

$$s^0 = N^\alpha x_h, \tag{9}$$

$$s^{0*} = N^{*\alpha} x_f, \tag{9'}$$

$$N\Gamma = n_h + n_f, \tag{10}$$

$$N^*\Gamma^* = n_h + n_f. \tag{10'}$$

Finally, each country's labor market must clear:

$$L = c\Gamma s^0 + n_h[a + b(x_n + x_f)], \tag{11}$$

$$L^* = c\Gamma^* s^{0*} + n_f[a + b(x_h + x_f)]. \tag{11'}$$

We wish to expose some of the more interesting responses involved in a change of trade regime, in particular, a movement from total autarky to service autarky. The present equilibrium is sufficiently complicated so that the comparative statics employed in the discussion of service autarky in section 11.3, though still feasible, is not very efficient. Instead, we examine two special cases involving specific relative endowments $L^*/L$, explicitly describe the service autarky equilibrium for each case, and compare it with total autarky, treated in the first subsection of this section.

CASE 1: $L^*/L = s^{0*}/s^0 \equiv \gamma.$

We assume first that the foreign labor supply exceeds the home labor supply in exactly the same proportion as the sizes of the respective least-cost

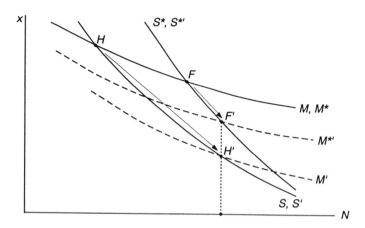

**Figure 11.4**

service firms. Total autarky is as in the previous subsection, and points $H$ and $F$ in figure 11.4 show the respective home and foreign equilibria. The foreign economy consumes a smaller quantity of each manufacture than does the home economy because in equilibrium its service sector is less efficient, with $N^* > N$. However, the larger size of the foreign economy is pronounced enough so that a larger variety of goods is consumed there in autarky equilibrium $(n^* > n)$.

When the foreign labor force stands in the proportion $\gamma$ to the home labor force, a service autarky equilibrium is possible in which each foreign sector operates at that same scale relative to its home counterpart. With wages identical across countries, all manufacturing firms face the same problem and make the same decision, so the foreign manufacturing sector will be $\gamma$ times the home sector in aggregate size when it produces that many more varieties: $n_f = \gamma n_h$. Each country must supply the same number of distinct services (i.e., a number equal to the total number of varieties), so the foreign economy will provide exactly $\gamma$ as many total service units as the home economy if it consumes exactly $\gamma$ as much of each variety: $x_f = \gamma x_h$. In this case it follows from (9) and (9') that home and foreign service firms each provide the same number of distinct services, $N^* = N$. Then the price of services will be the same across countries, as will the prices of finished manufactures, and equation (8) will hold, implying balanced trade. Evidently $L^*/L = \gamma$ is the boundary case allowing a service autarky equilibrium in which manufacturers just choose not to discriminate across countries. Equations (6) through (11'), and the assumed relative endowments, imply that in service autarky equilibrium

$$[M'] \qquad x_h[b + cN^{\alpha-1}] = \frac{a\beta}{1-\beta} \frac{1}{1+\gamma},$$

$$[S'] \qquad N^{\alpha}x_h - s^0 = 0,$$

and

$$[M^{*\prime}] \qquad x_f[b + cN^{\alpha-1}] = \frac{a\beta}{1-\beta} \frac{\gamma}{1+\gamma},$$

$$[S^{*\prime}] \qquad N^{*\alpha}x_f - \gamma s^0 = 0.$$

A comparison of expressions reveals that [M'] and [M*'] can be depicted as downward vertical shifts of [M], with [M'] shifting more. This is shown in figure 11.4, where $H'$ and $F'$ depict service autarky equilibrium positions for the two countries. The home manufacturing equilibrium schedule shifts by just enough more than the foreign to put $H'$ directly below $F'$. Each country moves down and to the right along its service equilibrium schedule, experiencing the negative quantity effect we discovered in the previous section's discussion of service autarky: Both countries are led to provide a wider spectrum of services at lower volumes, inducing diseconomies of scope and reducing the amount of each final good available. But note that now this effect is much more pronounced for the home country. Since both countries adjust in the same direction, the home economy must adjust more to "overtake" the foreign.

Both countries again experience the favorable variety effect, as each consumes a greater number of distinct final goods than in total autarky. This effect is also more pronounced for the home country, since both countries consume the same number of goods in service autarky, whereas the home country consumes fewer than the foreign in total autarky.

CASE 2: $L^*/L$ is such that $x_h = x_f \equiv x$ in service autarky.

This case will require $L^*$ to exceed $L$ but not by as much as above. If $x_h$ does equal $x_f \equiv x$ in service autarky, (9) and (9') imply that $(N^*/N)^{\alpha-1} = \gamma^{(\alpha-1)/\alpha} \equiv \eta$ in equilibrium so that $\gamma > \eta > 1$. Then the price of services abroad will exceed that at home in the proportion $\eta$, so producers of unfinished manufactures will discriminate between the markets in equilibrium, charging a higher price abroad than at home.

Equations (6) through (11′), and the assumed relative endowments, imply that in service autarky equilibrium

[M″]     $x\left[b + cN^{\alpha-1}\dfrac{1+\eta}{2}\right] = \dfrac{a\beta}{2(1-\beta)},$

[S″]     $N^{\alpha}x - s^0 = 0,$

and

[M*″]     $x\left[b + cN^{*\alpha-1}\dfrac{1+\eta}{2\eta}\right] = \dfrac{a\beta}{2(1-\beta)},$

[S*″]     $N^{*\alpha}x - \gamma s^0 = 0.$

A comparison of expressions reveals that [M″] and [M*″] can be depicted as downward vertical shifts of [M], combined with a leftward horizontal shift for [M″] and a rightward horizontal shift for [M*″]. This is shown in figure 11.5, where $H″$ and $F″$ depict service autarky equilibrium positions for the two countries. The home manufacturing equilibrium schedule shifts by just enough more than the foreign to put $H″$ directly to the left of $F″$. Each country once again moves down and to the right along its service equilibrium schedule, again experiencing the negative quantity effect: Both countries are led to provide a wider spectrum of services at lower volumes, inducing diseconomies of scope and reducing the amount

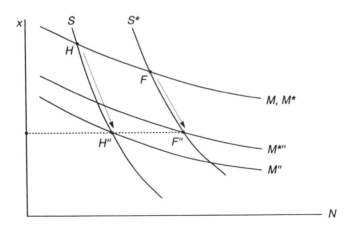

Figure 11.5

of each final good available. Although both countries are once again affected in the same direction by a movement to service autarky, there is no longer the dramatic difference in degree that we observed in the previous example. It is true that the consumption of each variety must fall by more at home than abroad since the home economy was consuming more in total autarky. But the disparity in adjustment is less than before, and that in adjustment of $N$ and $N^*$ even less pronounced.

## 11.5 Concluding Remark

This chapter has examined a model in which a commodity with features similar to those of many real-world services plays a distinctive role. The model is very special and should be viewed as a small initial step in the direction of incorporating services in models of international integration. But this seems to us to be the direction in which we have to go, to be able to illuminate one of today's central trade policy issues.

### Notes

The research for this chapter was supported by a grant from the Bank of Sweden Tercentenary Foundation. Robert Feenstra, Elhanan Helpman, Kala Krishna, James Markusen, and Robert Staiger supplied constructive comments.

1. See, for example, Hill (1977), Sapir and Lutz (1981), Kravis (1983), Bhagwati (1984a,b) Grubel (1984), Sapir (1985), Djajic and Kierzkowski (1986), Stern and Hoekman (1987), and Jones and Kierzkowski (1988). See GATT (1989) for a comprehensive overview of developments in service trade during the last two decades.

2. These differences are obviously largely a matter of degree. We do not believe that there is a fundamental qualitative difference between goods and services in this respect, perhaps with the exception of point 1.

3. The fact that many services require irreversible investments in human capital may complicate this issue.

### References

Bhagwati, Jagdish. 1984a. Splintering and disembodiment of services and developing nations. *The World Economy* 7 (June): 133–144.

Bhagwati, Jagdish. 1984b. Why are services cheaper in poor countries? *Economic Journal* 94 (June): 279–286.

Djajic, Slobodan, and Henryk Kierzkowski. 1986. Goods, services and trade. Mimeo.

GATT. 1989. *International Trade 1988–89*, vol. 1. Geneva: The Secretariat of the General Agreement on Tariffs and Trade.

Hill, Peter. 1977. On goods and services. *Review of Income and Wealth* 23 (December): 315–338.

Hindley, Brian, and Alasdair Smith. 1984. Comparative advantage and trade in services. *The World Economy* 7 (December): 369–390.

Jones, Ronald and Henryk Kierzkowski 1988. The role of services in production and international trade: A theoretical framework. Mimeo.

Kravis, Irving. 1983. Services in the domestic economy and in world transactions. National Bureau of Economic Research Working Paper No. 1124. Cambridge, MA.

Melvin, James. 1989. Trade in producer services: A Heckscher-Ohlin approach. *Journal of Political Economy* 97 (October): 1180–1196.

Sampson, Gary, and Richard Snape. 1985. Identifying the issues in trade in services. *The World Economy* 8 (June): 171–182.

Sapir, André. 1985. North–South issues in trade in services. *The World Economy* 8 (March): 27–42.

Sapir, André, and Ernst Lutz. 1981. Trade in services: Economic determinants and development related issues. World Bank Staff Working Paper No. 480. Washington, DC.

Stern, Robert, and Bernard Hoekman. 1987. Issues and data needs for GATT negotiations on services. *The World Economy* 10 (March): 39–60.

# 12 First Mover Advantages, Blockaded Entry, and the Economics of Uneven Development

James R. Markusen

It is probably reasonable to suggest that increasing returns to scale are now believed to be an important cause of international trade along with, if not as important as, more traditional determinants of trade such as differences in factor endowments. More recently economists have incorporated elements of increasing returns into models designed to explain long-run sustained growth in per capita incomes without having to appeal to ad hoc factors such as exogenous technical change. Little work has been done, however, on investigating the possibility of divergent growth between two economies due to dynamic increasing returns.

The setting of this chapter is two countries that are initially identical in all respects, so that there is no comparative advantage basis for trade. One of the two sectors has an increasing-returns-to-scale technology. The approach follows Ethier (1982) and later Romer (1987), Grossman and Helpman (1988), and Markusen (1988, 1989, 1990) in that the final good is produced from specialized intermediate inputs. There are increasing returns to the number of inputs, incorporating the Smithian notion of increased division of labor. But the specialized inputs themselves require a fixed cost plus a constant marginal cost, indicating that the division of labor is limited by the extent of the market. The fixed cost is once and for all, paid by a firm only in the period of entry, and thus it conforms to the notion of nondepreciating knowledge capital that has been introduced in a number of recent papers. The specialized inputs are nontraded and are produced by a monopolistically competitive industry with free entry. The inputs can be thought of as knowledge-based consulting services that are costly to trade internationally or, as is often the case, face high trade barriers.

The issues I wish to address with this model are suggested by the chapter's title. I am interested in whether "accidents of history," whereby one country is able to enter the increasing returns sector one period earlier than the other country, translate into permanent advantages for the first entrant. This question is perhaps of considerable importance to our understanding of the dynamics of uneven development. The discussion thus relates to issues addressed by Krugman (1981, 1989), Grossman and Helpman (1988, 1989), and Murphy, Shleifer, and Vishny (1988) but has a somewhat different focus.

The first entrant, referred to as the home country, builds knowledge capital in the first period, and because specialized inputs are complementary in final production, the incentives for the entry of additional firms in the second period are strengthened by the first period entry. This effect is the key to understanding why the present model behaves quite differentily from a traditional model with diminishing returns to factor accumulation.

Because of this *complementarity effect* the disadvantaged country (referred to as the foreign country) may fall further behind in the second period for either of two reasons, despite being allowed to enter the increasing-returns sector. First, its firms may be unable to enter at all due to the inherited productivity advantage in the home country. This is referred to as *blockaded entry*. Second, some firms may be able to enter, but the level of entry may be well below the level of additional entry in the home country such that the foreign country falls further behind.

Section 12.1 examines the role of various parameters in determining whether firms from country $f$ can enter in the second period. Suppose that parameters are chosen so that the solution to the model is that country $f$ is "marginally" blockaded in the second period. Any of the following changes will switch the model solution to one in which country $f$ enters in the second period: (1) the length of the second period increases, (2) the consumer's rate of time preference increases, (3) the complementarity of specialized inputs (degree of scale economies) increases, (4) the elasticity of the wage rate with respect to labor demand in the increasing-returns sector increases, (5) the fixed cost of producing a new specialized input decreases. A theoretical analysis of whether $f$ catches up when it does enter is not presented. It turns out that the qualitative roles of key parameters depend on the numerical values of other parameters and on the convexity of the wage function in particular. This will be confirmed in numerical analysis.

Section 12.3 employs numerical analysis to solve for parameter regimes in which entry by the foreign country is and is not blocked, examine the welfare consequences of these two alternative outcomes, and examine whether or not the foreign country "catches up" in the second period when it is able to enter. Results concerning the roles of the various parameters confirm those derived analytically.

Several results emerge with respect to welfare issues. First, the foreign country suffers a large welfare loss and the home country a smaller welfare gain when the foreign firms are blockaded from entering relative to a situation where firms from both countries can enter in the first period. Second, arbitrarily small parameter changes that shift the equilibrium from one in which foreign firms are blockaded in the second period to one in which

which they may enter result in large changes in world production and trade flows and, in some cases, a significant discrete jump in welfare. This discrete jump resulting from an infinitesimal parameter change is due to the non-convex technology (when firms enter they enter in large numbers) and to the fact that the social marginal product of an additional input exceeds the private marginal product. With respect to the issue of catching up in the second period when foreign firms do enter, simulation results produce both outcomes in which the foreign country does catch up and in which it falls further behind.

## 12.1 Production

In this section we examine the production side of the general equilibrium model. There are two countries, home $h$ and foreign $f$, and two time periods $T = 0, 1$. There are two traded final goods $X$ and $Y$, which have identical production functions in the two countries. $Y$ is produced by a competitive industry with constant returns to scale from labor $L$ and sector specific capital $K$:

$$Y = G(L_y, K), \qquad G_L > 0, G_{LL} < 0. \tag{1}$$

Countries $h$ and $f$ have identical endowments of $L$ and $K$ in each time period, but their (common) second-period endowment of capital and labor may be larger than the first-period endowment by some multiple, indicating that the second period is perhaps longer. Further discussion of this point is postponed until section 12.2. The assumption of identical endowments and technologies is quite deliberately made to ensure that there is no ex ante comparative advantage basis for trade.

Good $X$ is assembled from produced intermediate inputs $S$, as in Ethier (1982) followed by Markusen (1989, 1990). The $S_i$ are nontraded and can be thought of as the services of specialized consulting firms that do not deal internationally. A simple CES function is used as in those papers in order to exploit symmetry to solve the model:

$$X = \left[ \sum_{i=1}^{n} S_i^\beta \right]^{1/\beta}, \qquad 0 < \beta < 1. \tag{2}$$

The number $n$ and level of the $S_i$ are endogenous. It is assumed that production of an $S_i$ requires only labor and that units are chosen such that the marginal cost of $S$ in terms of labor is 1. There is a fixed cost in terms of labor $F$. Let $Y$ be numéraire, and let $w$ denote the wage rate in terms of $Y$ ($w = G_L$). The cost of producing in $S_i$ in terms of $Y$ are then given by

$$C_i = wS_i + wF. \tag{3}$$

The fixed cost need only be incurred once, in the initial period of entry. $F$ could be thought of as the learning costs of acquiring knowledge capital, which does not depreciate. $p$ will denote the price of $X$ in terms of $Y$, and $r$ will denote the price of an $S$ in terms of $Y$. Because of the symmetry in (2) and identical cost functions in (3), any $S_i$ that is produced will be produced in the same amount as any other $S_j$ and sell for the same price $r$. $p$ is equalized across countries be free trade while $r$ is not. The demand for the $S_i$ is a derived demand and the demand price $r$ is the value of the marginal produce (VMP) of $S_i$ in $X$. Multiplying (2) by $p$ and differentiating, this VMP is given by

$$r = \left(\frac{p}{\beta}\right)\left[\sum S_j^\beta\right]^\alpha \beta S_i^{\beta-1} = [p(\sum S_j^\beta)^\alpha] S_i^{\beta-1}, \tag{4}$$

$$\alpha \equiv \frac{1}{\beta} - 1.$$

There is a simple assumption about $S$ producers' conjectures that gives a markup pricing rule familiar from the final-goods literature. Assume that each $S_i$ producer views $n$ and the total input demand in the $X$ sector as fixed, $d(\sum S_j)/dS_i = 0$: An increase by producer $i$ of $dS_i$ leads each other $S_j$ producer to decrease output by $dS_j = -dS_i/(n-1)$. A conjecture that $(\sum S_j)$ is constant also implies that $(\sum S_j^\beta)^{1/\beta}$ and $(\sum S_j^\beta)^\alpha$ are locally constant due to the initial symmetry of the $S_i$. This conjecture in turn implies that $p$ is constant and that the term in brackets in (4) is constant. Note from (4) that $r$ is nevertheless not constant and is decreasing in producer $i$'s own output (there is a diminishing marginal product to substituting one's own output for the output of other firms). Multiplying $r$ in (4) by $S_i$ to get producer $i$'s revenue ($rS_i$), we then see that marginal revenue is given by

$$MR_i = \frac{d(rS_i)}{dS_i} = \beta[p(\sum S_j^\beta)^\alpha] S_i^{\beta-1} = \beta r. \tag{5}$$

Since the marginal cost of an $S_i$ is just $w$, the marginal-revenue-equals-marginal-cost conditions thus have the simple markup form $\beta r = w$.

Let subscripts 0 and 1 denote the first and second periods, respectively (subscripts denoting individual $S$ producers are henceforth dropped so $S_j$ denotes the output level of a representative $S$ at $T = j$). Let $i$ denote the interest rate at which producers are allowed to borrow and lend in terms of $Y_0$, the numéraire. Superscripts $h$ and $f$ will denote the home and foreign countries. For firms entering in the first period in $h$, three equations determine the equilibrium values of $S_0$, $S_1$, $n_0$. These are the two $MR = MC$ conditions for each period and the zero-profit, free-entry constraint that the present value of profits is zero. These are given by

$$\beta r_0^h - w_0^h = 0, \tag{6}$$

$$\beta r_1^h - w_1^h = 0, \tag{7}$$

$$(r_0^h - w_0^h)S_0^h + (1 + i)^{-1}(r_1^h - w_1^h)S_1^h - w_0^h F = 0. \tag{8}$$

Now consider firms entering in the second period (if any) in the home country. The intuition as to why additional firms might enter despite the shorter time horizon to recover $F$ can be seen by considering the possibility that they do not enter. If the output of $S$ was the same across periods (it generally is not), then the labor previously devoted to financing $F$ returns to the $Y$ sector, the world production and consumption ratio $Y/X$ must rise, and $p$ rises. $r_1 = p_1 n_0^z$ (from equation 4) therefore exceeds $r_0 = p_0 n_0^z$. Similarly $w_1 < w_0$ as labor returns to $Y$ production. With a higher $r$ and lower $w$, second-period entry may be possible. The first-order condition ($MR = MC$) and the free-entry condition are given by

$$\beta r_1^h - w_1^h \leq 0, \tag{9}$$

$$(r_1^h - w_1^h)S_1^h - w_1^h F \leq 0. \tag{10}$$

The first of these inequalities is identical to (7), implying that it holds with equality. The zero-profit condition in (10) need not hold with equality, in which case there is no entry at $T = 1$. Substituting for $w_1^h$ from (7), this zero-profit condition becomes

$$(1 - \beta)r_1^h S_1^h - \beta r_1^h F \leq 0. \tag{11}$$

Equation (11) gives a result that will be heavily exploited in what follows. If there is entry at $T = 1$, then the equilibrium level of $S_1$ is necessarily given by

$$S_1 = \beta F/(1 - \beta) \quad \text{(if entry at } T = 1\text{)}, \tag{12}$$

which is independent of the values of all other endogenous variables. This applies of course to firms that entered at $T = 0$ as well, since all firms have the same marginal cost and marginal revenue functions at $T = 1$.

Foreign firms, which can only enter at $T = 1$ by assumption, have the same first-order condition and free-entry condition as firms entering in $h$ at $T = 1$:

$$\beta r_1^f - w_1^f \leq 0, \tag{13}$$

$$r_1^f S_1^f - w_1^f S_1^f - w_1^f F \leq 0. \tag{14}$$

If entry occurs, then both equations hold with equality, and we again have the equilibrium level of $S_1$ given by $S_1 = \beta F/(1 - \beta)$ as in (12).

The production side of the model is summarized by six equations and inequalities (6, 7, 8, 10, 13, and 14) in six unknowns ($n_0^h$, $n_1^h$, $S_0^h$, $S_1^h$, $n_1^f$, and $S_1^f$). We noted that $S_1^h = S_1^f = \beta F/(1 - \beta)$ if there is second-period entry in both countries. Two questions are of interest. The first is whether or not entry into $X$ by $f$ at $T = 1$ is blockaded equations (13 and 14 are slack). The second is whether $f$ catches up in the second period when it does enter. The first question will occupy the remainder of this section, and the second will be addressed numerically.

The question of whether $f$ can enter at $T = 1$ is a difficult question due to the nonconvex technology. In particular, we note below that we cannot simply check whether or not a single firm can enter in $f$. Because of the complementarity of the $S_i$, a large number may be able to enter, whereas a single firm cannot. But the entry of a large number of firms disturbs the initial prices at which we are evaluating the possibility of entry. Nevertheless, a good deal of progress can be made.

For the remainder of this section, all variables will be taken to refer to country $f$ in period $T = 1$, so, unless otherwise noted, the superscript $f$ and the subscript 1 will be dropped to avoid clutter. We will also assume a Cobb-Douglas technology in $Y$ in order to obtain explicit results and to be consistent with the later numerical analysis. $Y$ and $w$ are given by

$$Y = L_y^\gamma K^{1-\gamma},$$
$$w = \gamma L_y^{\gamma-1} K^{1-\gamma}. \tag{15}$$

The wage function can be rearranged to give us a labor demand function for $L_y$:

$$L_y = \left(\frac{w}{\gamma}\right)^{1/(\gamma-1)} K = \left(\frac{w}{\gamma}\right)^{\varepsilon} K,$$

(16)

$$\varepsilon \equiv \frac{1}{\gamma - 1} < -1.$$

From (4) we have that $r = pn^{\alpha}$, and from (13) that $w = \beta r$. We can thus replace $w$ in (16) with $p\beta n^{\alpha}$:

$$L_y = \left(\frac{p\beta n^{\alpha}}{\gamma}\right)^{\varepsilon} K = \left(\frac{p\beta}{\gamma}\right)^{\varepsilon} n^{\sigma} K,$$

(17)

$$\sigma \equiv \alpha\varepsilon < 0.$$

We noted in (12) that $S$ has a constant value if firms do enter. Since the labor demand in $X$ is $n(S + F)$, we have

$$L_x = n\left(\frac{\beta F}{1 - \beta} + F\right) = \frac{nF}{1 - \beta}.$$

(18)

The sum of (17) and (18) gives us the total demand for labor as a function of $p$ and $n$:

$$L_d = L_y + L_x = \left(\frac{p\beta}{\gamma}\right)^{\varepsilon} n^{\sigma} K + \frac{nF}{1 - \beta}.$$

(19)

The derivative of labor demand with respect to $n$ at constant $p$ is given by

$$\frac{d(L_d)}{dn} = \sigma\left(\frac{p\beta}{\gamma}\right)^{\varepsilon} n^{\sigma-1} K + \frac{F}{1 - \beta}.$$

(20)

The first term is negative ($\sigma < 0$), and the second term is positive. Since the exponent of $n$ is negative, the first term obviously dominates for small $n$ and (20) is negative, whereas the second term must dominate for a sufficiently large $n$. Labor demand as a function of $n$ at constant $p$ is thus given by the U-shaped curves shown in figure 12.1.

The minimum point on this $L_d$ curve is at the level of $n$ that sets (20) to zero. For firms in $f$ to be able to enter the $X$ industry, the $L_d$ curve must touch or pass below the labor supply curve $L_s$ in figure 12.1. Strictly speaking, the $L_d$ curve evaluated at the (lower) postentry $p$ must have this property, but the postentry price is itself a function of the level of entry. In what follows, we shall ignore this interdependency and focus on factors

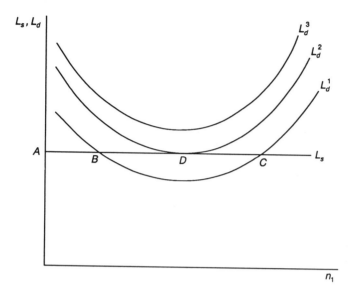

**Figure 12.1**

that shift $L_d$ relative to $L_s$ at no-entry prices. But we should keep in mind that it is not in general sufficient to just touch $L_s$ as is the case with $L_d^2$ in figure 12.1.

Figure 12.1 emphasizes two important points. The first is that a small number of firms may not be able to enter, but a large number may. Second, there may be three equilibria as illustrated with demand curve $L_d^1$ in figure 12.1. One is at $A$ (no entry into $X$), and the other two are at $B$ and $C$. Equilibrium $B$ is presumably unstable under some reasonable adjustment mechanism and can be thrown out. The subsequent analysis will not focus on getting stuck at $A$, although that is an interesting and important research topic. Rather, we will be concerned with whether an equilibrium like $C$ (or $D$) in figure 12.1 exists and will assume that country $f$ reaches that equilibrium when it does exist.

The U-shaped labor demand curve in figure 12.1 is closely related to the shape of the production frontier shown in figure 12.2. I have derived the properties of the production frontier elsewhere (Markusen 1988, 1989, 1990), so I will simply repeat the results here. Given the constant output of any $S$ that is produced at $T = 1$, the marginal rate of transformation along the production frontier is given by the ratio of the marginal product of labor in $Y$ ($MP_{ly}$) to the (social) marginal product of labor in $X$ ($MP_{lx}$).

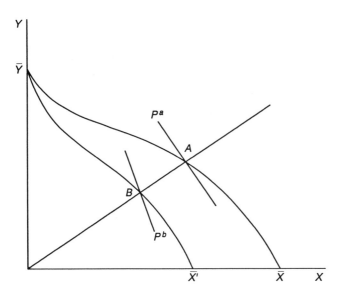

**Figure 12.2**

$$MRT = \frac{w}{n^\alpha} = \frac{MP_{ly}}{MP_{lx}}. \tag{21}$$

The production frontier is locally concave if and only if

$$\theta > \alpha, \tag{22}$$

$$\theta \equiv \frac{dw/w}{dn/n} = \frac{(1-\gamma)(S+F)n}{L_y},$$

where $\theta$ is the elasticity of $w$ (or of $MP_{ly}$) with respect to $n$, given in the Cobb-Douglas case by the right-hand equation of (22). The production frontier is locally concave if and only if the elasticity of $MP_{ly}$ with respect to $n$ exceeds the elasticity of $MP_{lx}$ with respect to $n$, the latter simply being $\alpha$. The right-hand equation of (22) shows that in the Cobb-Douglas case $\theta$ runs from zero to infinity as we move down the production frontier, thus the frontier must be convex in the neighborhood of $X = 0$ and concave in the neighborhood of $Y = 0$ with a single inflection point as shown in figure 12.2.

My earlier papers also show that the relationship between $p$ and the $MRT$ is given by $p\beta = MRT < p$ (the private $MP_{lx} = \beta n^\alpha$), so the price ratio cuts the production frontier as shown in figure 12.2.

The supply price ratio $MRT/\beta$ at first falls and then rises due to the nonconvexity. The analysis of figure 12.1 is equivalent to asking in figure 12.2 if the (U-shaped) supply price ever falls below the prevailing world (home country) price. Country $h$ inherits a productivity advantage at the beginning of $T = 1$ in the form of $n_0^h$, so we could think of the inner and outer frontiers of figure 12.2 as representing countries $f$ and $h$, respectively, at $T = 1$. It seems intuitive that depending on the gap between $\bar{X}'$ and $\bar{X}$, there may exist an equilibrium with $f$ producing $X$.

To analyze the possibility of entry by $f$, consider a change in $L_d$ in response to a change in $p$, the second-period price (recall that all variables are second-period values unless otherwise indicated). Assume that $f$ cannot enter at the initial $p$. We can focus only on whether the minimum point on $L_d$ moves up or down. By differentiating (19) and evaluating it at the minimum value of $n$ (equation 20 equal to zero), we get

$$\frac{dL_d}{dp} = \varepsilon \left(\frac{\beta}{\gamma}\right)^{\varepsilon} p^{\varepsilon-1} n^{\sigma} K + \frac{(0)dn}{dp} < 0 \tag{23}$$

since $\varepsilon < 0$ (the second term emphasizes that equation 23 is evaluated at the minimum value of $L_d$). Equation (23) states that an increase in $p$ shifts $L_d$ down, and thus a sufficient increase makes entry by $f$ feasible.

Since $p$ is endogenous, the question is, What can change $p$ independently of second-period parameters? A principal determinant of $p$ is $n_0^h$, which is in turn influenced by certain independent first-period parameters. Suppose that $n_0^h$ falls due to a change in a first-period parameter. The second-period effect is described in figure 12.2. The decrease in $n_0^h$ reduces the output of $X_1^h$ from any given $L_{x1}^h$ and shifts country $h$'s second-period production frontier from $\overline{YX}$ to $\overline{YX}'$. Compare points $A$ and $B$, which have the same production ratio $(Y/X)$ in figure 12.2. The $MRT$ along the production frontier is as noted above.

$$MRT_1^h = \frac{w_1^h}{(n_1^h)^{\alpha}},$$

$$n_1^h = n_0^h + (n_1^h - n_0^h), \tag{24}$$

where $n_1$ denotes total $n$ at $T = 1$ (not new entry), the latter given by $(n_1^h - n_0^h)$.

In moving from $A$ to $B$ in figure 12.2, labor is withdrawn from $Y$ (the decrease in $n_0^h$ will be partly offset by additional second-period entry), so the $(K/L_y)$ ratio rises and $w$ rises. Since $S_1^h$ is constant and $X_1^h$ decreases, $n_1^h$ must decrease implying in turn that $(n_1^h)^a$ falls. The $MRT$ at $B$ is unambiguously higher than at $A$, and $p^b > p^a$.

Considering $A$ and $B$ in figure 12.2 further, world supply of $X$ has decreased more than $Y$ (country $f$ remains specialized in $Y$), so the demand–price ratio rises (preferences are assumed to be homothetic). The latter may rise more or less than the supply price rise $(p^b - p^a)$ shown in figure 12.2, but using a simple proof by contradiction, we can show that the new equilibrium price ratio must be higher than the initial price ratio $p^a$.

Suppose that the new equilibrium price ratio did fall back to $p^a$. Beginning at $B$ in figure 12.1, this would require an increase in $X_1^h$ and a decrease in $Y_1^h$ relative to $B$ in order to restore the world output ratio to its original level. But this raises the supply price ratio further (assuming production on the concave portion of the production frontier) in $h$ above $p^b$. Thus clearly the decrease in $n_0^h$ cannot leave the equilibrium price ratio at or below its initial level $p^a$.

What factors can reduces $n_0^h$ and therefore increase $p_1$ for given values of second-period parameters? Two factors are obvious, and their effects are presented without formal proof. The first is to lower both countries' first-period factor endowments $(K_0, L_0)$ (remember that we wish to keep the countries identical). With reference to equations (7) and (8), this raises the wage rate for a given $L_{x0}^h$ and $n_0^h$ and lowers the demand price for that given level of $X$ (the output of $Y$ is falling). Thus fewer firms can be supported at $T = 0$. The second factor is to raise the consumer's discount rate $\rho$, which leads to a higher $i$, ceteris paribus. The heavier discounting of future profits leaves the present value negative and forces some firms to exit at $T = 0$.

Changes in other parameters of the model have complicated effects due to changing first-period entry and second-period prices. An obvious example is that an increase in $F$ might make it harder for $f$ to enter at $T = 1$ at constant $p_1$. But such a change in $F$ might raise $p_1$ for two reasons. First, the increase in $F$ will reduce intial entry $(n_0^h)$ at $T = 0$ and, second, reduce additional entry by firms in $h$ at $T = 1$. Although there is no reason to expect the intuitive effect to be reversed by the effect on $p_1$, unambiguous results are difficult to obtain from the algebra because of the large number of equations and unknowns.

In order to obtain some results and intuition, let us therefore introduce the notion of compensated changes. By a compensated change in parameter $z$, I will mean a change in $z$ accompanied by a change in the first-period endowment (thereby changing $n_0^h$) such that $p_1$ is left unchanged $(dp_1/dz = 0)$.

Thus, if an increase in $z$ raises $p_1$, other things equal, the first-period endowment is increased to return $p_1$ to its initial level. Referring back to equation (19), $p_1$ but not $(K_0, L_0)$ appears in this equation. Thus in performing comparative statics with (19), it is assumed that "background" changes are affected for $(K_0, L_0)$ to hold $p_1$ constant.

Consider an increase in $\gamma$, which is a reduction in the elasticity of $w$ with respect to $n$ as shown in (22). An increase in $\gamma$ does not necessarily increase $w$ for a given labor demand in $X$ and therefore does not necessarily have the intuitive effect of shifting the labor demand curve up at constant $p$. $w$ can be written as

$$w = \gamma \left(\frac{K}{L_y}\right)^{1-\gamma},$$

$$\ln w = \ln \gamma + (1 - \gamma) \ln \left(\frac{K}{L_y}\right),$$

$$(25)$$

$$d \ln \frac{w}{d\gamma} = \frac{1}{\gamma} - \ln \left(\frac{K}{L_y}\right) \gtrless 0. \tag{26}$$

In our simulations of section 12.3, capital and labor endowments are assumed equal, so (26) is positive for small sizes of the $X$ sector ($K/L_y < e$) and negative for large sizes of the $X$ sector. When firms in $f$ do enter, figure 12.2 emphasizes that they enter in large numbers. Thus we cannot be sure of the sign of (26) at the minimum of $L_d$.

Despite this ambiguity, it is easy to show that an increase in $\gamma$ shifts up the minimum point of $L_d$ at constant $p$ by reducing $L_y$. The first term of (19), the demand for labor in $Y$, written in full becomes

$$\left(\frac{p\beta}{\gamma}\right)^{\varepsilon} n^{\sigma} K = \left(\frac{p\beta n^{\alpha}}{\gamma}\right)^{\varepsilon} K = K \left[\frac{\gamma}{(p\beta n^{\alpha})}\right]^{1/(1-\gamma)}. \tag{27}$$

$\gamma$ appears in the bracketed term and in the exponent, and (27) is increasing in $\gamma$ with both cases. Thus the derivative of (19) with respect to $\gamma$ at minimum $L_d$ ($dL_d/dn = 0$) must be positive. $d\gamma > 0$ shifts up the minimum point of the labor demand curve. Conversely, a sufficiently large $d\gamma < 0$ (increasing the elasticity of $w$ with respect to $n$) makes entry by $f$ possible by reducing $L_y$.

Now consider the effects of an increase in $F$, which at constant $p_1$ has the intuitive effect of shifting $L_d$ up. The first term of (19) is independent of $F$, but the second term is positive and increasing in $F$. Holding $p$ constant, the effect of an increase in $F$ on the minimum point of $L_d$ is

$$\frac{dL_d}{dF} = \frac{n}{1-\beta} + \frac{(0)\,dn}{dF} > 0. \tag{28}$$

A (compensated) decrease in $F$ thus prmits $f$ to enter.

Finally, consider the effects of an increase $\beta$ (decrease in the complementarity of the $S_i$, decrease in returns to scale to $n$). Differentiating (19) at the minimum value of $L_d$, we have

$$dL_d = \left[ \varepsilon K \left( \frac{p\beta}{\gamma} \right)^{\varepsilon-1} n^\sigma \left( \frac{p}{\gamma} \right) + K \left( \frac{p\beta}{\gamma} \right)^\varepsilon n^\sigma (\varepsilon \ln n) \frac{d\alpha}{d\beta} + \frac{nF}{(1-\beta)^2} \right] d\beta$$

$$+ (0)\,dn_1. \tag{29}$$

The first term of (29) is negative ($\varepsilon < 0$), and the third term is positive. The second term, which derives from the fact that $\alpha$ (or $\beta$) appears in the exponent $\sigma$, is positive ($\varepsilon < 0$, $d\alpha/d\beta < 0$).

A sufficient condition for (29) to be positive is that the first term is less in absolute value than the third term. Multiplying (29) through by $\alpha\beta/n$, the first and third terms are

$$\left\{ \sigma K \left( \frac{p\beta}{\gamma} \right)^\varepsilon n^{\sigma-1} + \frac{F[\alpha\beta/(1-\beta)]}{(1-\beta)} \right\} \frac{n}{\alpha\beta}. \tag{30}$$

But $\alpha\beta(1-\beta) = 1$ since $\alpha = (1-\beta)/\beta$. Thus (30) is the same as (20) set equal to zero: The minimum value of $L_d$. At this value the first and third terms of (29) cancel, and we are left with

$$dL_d = \frac{K \left( \dfrac{p\beta}{\gamma} \right)^\varepsilon n^\sigma (\varepsilon \ln n)\, d\alpha}{d\beta} d\beta > 0. \tag{32}$$

At constant $p$, an increase in $\beta$ shifts the labor demand curve up. Conversely, a decrease in $\beta$ can permit $f$ to enter. This may seem paradoxical insofar as a decrease in $\beta$ is in a sense an increase in the returns to scale to $n(X = n^{1/\beta}S)$. I think that the intuition lies in the fact that a decrease in $\beta$ supports a smaller firm size ($S = F\beta/(1-\beta)$). Thus for a given $w$ (given amount of labor drawn into the $X$ sector), a smaller $\beta$ permits a greater measure of differentiation $n$ and an unambiguously greater value of marginal product in $X$, $pn^\alpha$ ($\alpha$ increases with a decrease in $\beta$). Thus at a constant $p$, entry by $f$ becomes more likely as $\beta$ decreases.

**Results**

Assume that entry by $f$ is marginally blockaded in the second period. The equilibrium shifts toward permitting entry if any of the following changes occur:

1. The first-period endowment shrinks (the second period becomes relatively "longer").
2. Time preferences increase ($\rho$ increases).
3. There is a (compensated) fall in $F$.
4. There is a (compensated) fall in $\beta$.
5. There is a (compensated) fall in $\gamma$.

Before turning to the simulations, we now specify a demand side to the model, which is assumed identical in the two countries.

## 12.2  Demand

Consumers have a two-period Cobb-Doublas utility function given by

$$U(Y_0, X_0, Y_1, X_1) = (Y_0^{\delta_0} X_0^{\delta_0})(Y_1^{\delta_1} X_1^{\delta_1}). \tag{33}$$

Consumer's may borrow and lend at interest rate $i$ (endogenous in general equilibrium) in terms of $Y_0$. $p_0$ continues to denote the price of $X_0$ in terms of $Y_0$ and $p_1$, and the price of $X_1$ in terms of $Y_1$. $p_1(1 + i)^{-1}$ is thus the price of $X_1$ in terms of $Y_0$. Let $I_0$ and $I_1$ denoe first- and second-period factor income. The intertemporal budget constraint is given by

$$I_0 + (1 + i)^{-1} I_1 - Y_0 - (1 + i)^{-1} Y_1 - p_0 X_0 - p_1(1 + i)^{-1} X_1 = 0. \tag{34}$$

Maximizing (33) subject to (34) gives us marginal-rate-of-substitution conditions familiar for Cobb-Douglas functions:

$$p_0 = \left(\frac{Y_0}{X_0}\right),$$

$$p_1 = \left(\frac{Y_1}{X_1}\right), \tag{35}$$

$$(1 + i) = \left(\frac{\delta_0}{\delta_1}\right)\left(\frac{Y_1}{Y_0}\right). \tag{36}$$

In order to interpret (36), suppose that $Y$ was the only good in the economy and that consumer's had an indentical endowment of it in each period: $Y_1 = Y_0$. From (36) the rate of interest that would induce consumer's to just hold their endowment is given by

$$i = \left(\frac{M}{D}\right) - 1,$$

$$M \equiv \frac{Y_1}{Y_0}, \tag{37}$$

$$D \equiv \frac{\delta_1}{\delta_0}.$$

The term $(M/D) - 1$ is a natural measure of time preference, and we shall denote it by $\rho \equiv (M/D) - 1$. The reason for this is that numerical analysis shows that entry by $f$ is always blockaded when the second-period endowment is the same as the first, even at $D \to 0$ ($\rho$ approaching infinity). Rather than add additional periods, which greatly increases the dimensionality, I will assume that the second period can be longer than the first. $M$ will now be defined as the ratio of the second period's factor endowment to that of the first, factor proportions being the same.

$$M \equiv \frac{L_1}{L_0} = \frac{K_1}{K_0},$$

$$\rho \equiv \left(\frac{M}{D}\right) - 1. \tag{38}$$

A value of $M = 2$ suggests a situation of no growth with a second period twice as long. Equation (37) gives the value of $i$ necessary to induce consumers to consume twice as much in the second period as the first. The definition of $\rho$ in (38) implies that the utility weighting of second-period consumption must increase in proportion to the length of that period if the rate of time preference is to be constant. Thus in the simulations an adjustment of $M$ at constant $\rho$ means that $D$ is adjusted in proportion to $M$.

## 12.3  Numerical Analysis

In order to quantify the theory, I created a seven-equation model in the seven unknowns: $n_0^h$, $n_1^h$, $n_1^f$, $S_0$, $L_{y0}^h$, $L_{y1}^h$, and $L_{y1}^f$. Using the assumption that equilibria involve second-period entry by firms in country $f$ (we do not need the additional equation for $S_1$ since it equals $\beta F/(1 - \beta)$ if entry occurs in either country), the model is solved by a Newton method of successive approximation. A solution is found for a certain set of parameters, and then one parameter is adjusted in the direction that, as the theory suggests, will lead to blockaded entry (i.e., the nonexistence of a solution to the seven-equation model). I chose values of $M$ and $\beta$ ex ante, and then successively decreased $\rho$ until no solution to the model existed.

Two values of $\beta$ were chosen: 0.5 and 0.6. In the former case scale economies are very strong with $X$ homogeneous of degree 2 in $n$, whereas $X$ is homogeneous of degree 1.67 in $n$ in the latter case. I then solved for the integer value of $M$ below which entry cannot occur at any rate of time preference and for the integer value of $M$ above which entry can occur even at a zero rate of time preference (for the two values of $\beta$ indicated). These values are, respectively, $M = 2$ and $M = 4$.

Tables 12.1 through 12.4 present results for four sets of critical values of $M$, $\beta$, and $\rho$, where the latter is solved for from the other two. In each table three sets of results are presented. The first (solution $A$) results are for entry by $f$ at time $T = 1$. The second (solution $B$) results assume that country $f$ does not enter in either period. Rather than adjust parameters slightly so that the latter are the only equilibria in each case (leaving confusion about what is the effect of the parameter change and what is the effect of blocking), solution $B$ is computed at the same set of parameter values as solution $A$ so that the effect of blocking is presented. Solution $C$ in each case presents the equilibrium with both countries entering at $T = 0$. $I_0$ and $I_1$ give the value of production in periods 0 and 1, respectively (at current period prices in terms of $Y$), and $E_0^f$ is country $f$'s excess demand (current account deficit) at $T = 0$.

Several results are apparent from these four tables. Note first the results for the number of foreign firms entering at $T = 1$ in solution $A$ $(n_1^f)$. This is clearly a discrete number of firms not close to zero. Remembering that these are equilibria that are arbitrarily close to no entry by $f$, we see the problem that I noted in figure 12.1. We have entry possible only with a unique large number of foreign firms. Slight decreases in $M$ or $\rho$, or slight increases in $\beta$, $F$, or $\gamma$ drop this number to zero (solution $B$).

Second, note that entry in country $f$ is always less than the additional

**Table 12.1**
Case 1: parameter values $M = 2$, $\beta = 0.5$, $\rho = 2.704$

| | Solution $A$: $f$ enters at $T = 1$ | Solution $B$: $f$ does not enter | Solution $C$: $f$ enters at $T = 0$ |
|---|---|---|---|
| $n_0^h$ | 201.4 | 204.3 | 175.7 |
| $n_1^h$ | 435.8 | 455.1 | 375.3 |
| $n_0^f$ | 0 | 0 | 175.7 |
| $n_1^f$ | 194.3 | 0 | 375.3 |
| $S_0$ | 8.27 | 8.05 | 7.98 |
| $S_1$ | 10.0 | 10.0 | 10.0 |
| $i$ | 2.528 | 2.856 | 3.042 |
| $p_0$ | 0.437 | 0.437 | 0.254 |
| $p_1$ | 0.123 | 0.147 | 0.097 |
| $E_0^f$ | 3,622.0 | $-1,388.0$ | 0 |
| $I_0^f/I_0^h$ | 0.516 | 0.518 | 1.0 |
| $I_1^f/I_1^h$ | 0.602 | 0.487 | 1.0 |
| $U^f/U^h$ | 0.545 | 0.507 | 1.0 |
| $U^f$ | 122,793.0 | 116,751.0 | 193,351.0 |
| $U^h$ | 225,019.0 | 230,345.0 | 193,351.0 |
| Income ratios in terms of $X$ | | $(I_{1a}^f/I_{1b}^f)_x = 1.260$ $(I_{1a}^f/I_{1c}^f)_x = 0.690$ | $(I_{1a}^h/I_{1b}^h)_x = 1.020$ $(I_{1a}^h/I_{1c}^h)_x = 1.008$ |
| Income ratios in terms of $Y$ | | $(I_{1a}^f/I_{1b}^f)_y = 1.051$ $(I_{1a}^f/I_{1c}^f)_y = 0.769$ | $(I_{1a}^h/I_{1b}^h)_y = 0.851$ $(I_{1a}^h/I_{1c}^h)_y = 1.227$ |

Notes: Parameters are $L_0 = K_0 = 4{,}000$, $F = 10$, $\gamma = 0.3$, and $c = 25$ ($c$ is a scaling parameter on $Y = cL_y^\gamma K^{1-\gamma}$). $I_k^j$ is the value of production in country $j$ in period $k$. $E_0^f$ (equal to $-E_0^h$) is country $f$'s current account deficit at $T = 0$.

**Table 12.2**
Case 2: parameter values $M = 4$, $\beta = 0.5$, $\rho = 0.023$

|  | Solution $A$:<br>$f$ enters at $T = 1$ | Solution $B$:<br>$f$ does not enter | Solution $C$:<br>$f$ enters at $T = 0$ |
|---|---|---|---|
| $n_0^h$ | 256.7 | 261.1 | 236.2 |
| $n_1^h$ | 825.7 | 844.8 | 706.2 |
| $n_0^f$ | 0 | 0 | 236.2 |
| $n_1^f$ | 257.9 | 0 | 706.2 |
| $S_0$ | 4.74 | 4.53 | 4.33 |
| $S_1$ | 10.0 | 10.0 | 10.0 |
| $i$ | 0.033 | 0.096 | 0.204 |
| $p_0$ | 0.453 | 0.457 | 0.236 |
| $p_1$ | 0.076 | 0.085 | 0.054 |
| $E_0^f$ | 543.0 | $-5304.0$ | 0 |
| $I_0^f/I_0^h$ | 0.546 | 0.549 | 1.0 |
| $I_1^f/I_1^h$ | 0.552 | 0.494 | 1.0 |
| $U^f/U^h$ | 0.551 | 0.501 | 1.0 |
| $U^f$ | 461,175.0 | 436,518.0 | 726,161.0 |
| $U^h$ | 837,642.0 | 864,445.0 | 726,161.0 |
| Income ratios in terms of $X$ | | $(I_{1a}^f/I_{1b}^f)_x = 1.137$<br>$(I_{1a}^f/I_{1c}^f)_x = 0.537$ | $(I_{1a}^h/I_{1b}^h)_x = 1.012$<br>$(I_{1a}^h/I_{1c}^h)_x = 0.970$ |
| Income ratios in terms of $Y$ | | $(I_{1a}^f/I_{1b}^f)_y = 1.017$<br>$(I_{1a}^f/I_{1c}^f)_y = 0.757$ | $(I_{1a}^h/I_{1b}^h)_y = 0.912$<br>$(I_{1a}^h/I_{1c}^h)_y = 1.373$ |

Notes: Parameters are $L_0 = K_0 = 4{,}000$, $F = 10$, $\gamma = 0.3$, and $c = 25$ ($c$ is a scaling parameter on $Y = cL_y^\gamma K^{1-\gamma}$). $I_k^j$ is the value of production in country $j$ in period $k$. $E_0^f$ (equal to $-E_0^h$) is country $f$'s current account deficit at $T = 0$.

**Table 12.3**
Case 3: parameter values $M = 2$, $\beta = 0.6$, $\rho = 5.667$

| | Solution $A$: $f$ enters at $T = 1$ | Solution $B$: $f$ does not enter | Solution $C$: $f$ enters at $T = 0$ |
|---|---|---|---|
| $n_0^h$ | 157.6 | 157.9 | 134.5 |
| $n_1^h$ | 345.2 | 347.6 | 287.6 |
| $n_0^f$ | 0 | 0 | 134.5 |
| $n_1^f$ | 42.7 | 0 | 287.6 |
| $S_0$ | 13.2 | 13.2 | 13.2 |
| $S_1$ | 15.0 | 15.0 | 15.0 |
| $i$ | 5.709 | 5.855 | 6.704 |
| $p_0$ | 2.423 | 2.423 | 1.369 |
| $p_1$ | 1.131 | 1.177 | 0.718 |
| $E_0^f$ | $-96.0$ | $-633.0$ | 0 |
| $I_0^f/I_0^h$ | 0.512 | 0.512 | 1.0 |
| $I_1^f/I_1^h$ | 0.509 | 0.492 | 1.0 |
| $U^f/U^h$ | 0.512 | 0.508 | 1.0 |
| $U^f$ | 41,176.0 | 40,972.0 | 69,665.0 |
| $U^h$ | 80,478.0 | 80,719.0 | 69,665.0 |
| Income ratios in terms of $X$ | | $(I_{1a}^f/I_{1b}^f)_x = 1.043$ | $(I_{1a}^h/I_{1b}^h)_x = 1.007$ |
| | | $(I_{1a}^f/I_{1c}^f)_x = 0.471$ | $(I_{1a}^h/I_{1c}^h)_x = 0.926$ |
| Income ratios in terms of $Y$ | | $(I_{1a}^f/I_{1b}^f)_y = 1.002$ | $(I_{1a}^h/I_{1b}^h)_y = 0.967$ |
| | | $(I_{1a}^f/I_{1c}^f)_y = 0.743$ | $(I_{1a}^h/I_{1c}^h)_y = 1.458$ |

Notes: Parameters are $L_0 = K_0 = 4{,}000$, $F = 10$, $\gamma = 0.3$, and $c = 25$ ($c$ is a scaling parameter on $Y = cL_y^\gamma K^{1-\gamma}$). $I_k^j$ is the value of production in country $j$ in period $k$. $E_0^f$ (equal to $-E_0^h$) is country $f$'s current account deficit at $T = 0$.

**Table 12.4**
Case 4: parameter values $M = 4$, $\beta = 0.6$, $\rho = 0.081$

|  | Solution $A$: $f$ enters at $T = 1$ | Solution $B$: $f$ does not enter | Solution $C$: $f$ enters at $T = 0$ |
|---|---|---|---|
| $n_0^h$ | 225.9 | 227.3 | 205.0 |
| $n_1^h$ | 659.5 | 663.8 | 555.4 |
| $n_0^f$ | 0 | 0 | 205.0 |
| $n_1^f$ | 74.4 | 0 | 555.4 |
| $S_0$ | 6.71 | 6.16 | 6.34 |
| $S_1$ | 15.0 | 15.0 | 15.0 |
| $i$ | 0.125 | 0.148 | 0.245 |
| $p_0$ | 2.528 | 2.535 | 1.283 |
| $p_1$ | 0.770 | 0.796 | 0.475 |
| $E_0^f$ | $-3,002.0$ | $-4,595.0$ | 0 |
| $I_0^f/I_0^h$ | 0.543 | 0.543 | 1.0 |
| $I_1^f/I_1^h$ | 0.511 | 0.496 | 1.0 |
| $U^f/U^h$ | 0.518 | 0.506 | 1.0 |
| $U^f$ | 149,766.0 | 147,579.0 | 252,038.0 |
| $U^h$ | 289,240.0 | 291,840.0 | 252,038.0 |
| Income ratios in terms of $X$ | | $(I_{1a}^f/I_{1b}^f)_x = 1.035$ | $(I_{1a}^h/I_{1b}^h)_x = 1.050$ |
|  | | $(I_{1a}^f/I_{1c}^f)_x = 0.462$ | $(I_{1a}^h/I_{1c}^h)_x = 0.905$ |
| Income ratios in terms of $Y$ | | $(I_{1a}^f/I_{1b}^f)_y = 1.002$ | $(I_{1a}^h/I_{1b}^h)_y = 0.971$ |
|  | | $(I_{1a}^f/I_{1c}^f)_y = 0.750$ | $(I_{1a}^h/I_{1c}^h)_y = 1.467$ |

Notes: Parameters are $L_0 = K_0 = 4,000$, $F = 10$, $\gamma = 0.3$, and $c = 25$ ($c$ is a scaling parameter on $Y = cL_y^\gamma K^{1-\gamma}$). $I_k^j$ is the value of production in country $j$ in period $k$. $E_0^f$ (equal to $-E_0^h$) is country $f$'s current account deficit at $T = 0$.

entry in country $h$ at $T = 1$. In three of the four cases the number of firms entering in $f$ is less than the number that entered in $h$ in the first period. If we were to define "catching up" in terms of the number of specialized inputs in the $X$ sector, and hence the marginal productivity of labor in the $X$ sector, the foreign country always falls further behind in the sense that $n_1^f < (n_1^h - n_0^h)$.

Note that solution $A$ has substantially more total firms in the market at $T = 1$ than solution $B$ but fewer than solution $C$. This is due to the increased costs in a single country of drawing labor from the $Y$ sector and is reflected in the differences in the equilibrium relative price of $X$ at $T = 1$.

The current account statistic $E_0^f$ in tables 12.1 through 12.4 is of some interest. In solution $B$ this value is always negative, indicating that the foreign country is making consumption loans to the home country in the first period in order to help the latter either finance capital formation or smooth its consumption stream. There is naturally no intertemporal or temporal trade in solution $C$ when the countries are in the same situation. The interesting results occur in solution $A$, where we see that country $f$ is the first-period borrower in cases 1 and 2 but a first-period lender in cases 3 and 4. The reason for this, as we shall see shortly, is that country $f$ catches up a bit in terms of production income in cases 1 and 2, and thus it borrows in the first period to smooth consumption.

Now we turn to overall welfare measures (utility). Here the results in all four cases suggest that whether country $f$ is just able to enter or is blockaded in period 2 is of much less welfare significance than the fact that it is not allowed to enter at $T = 0$ in the first place. Nevertheless, there clearly is a discrete jump in welfare moving from the blockaded solution $B$ to the entry solution $A$. The biggest difference is in table 12.2 (case 2), where utility at solution $A$ is 5.6% higher than at solution $B$. In this table the ratio of $U^f/U^h$ is 0.551 in solution $A$ versus 0.501 in solution $B$, about 10% higher.

One limitation of the welfare measure is that it smooths the second-period effect over two periods. We also wish to focus on the second-period situation, particularly with respect to the catch-up issue. These four tables thus present levels and ratios of the value of production ($I$) at $T = 0, 1$ for the two countries and three equilibria. In cases 1 and 2 the ratio of $f$'s to $h$'s second-period income is higher at $T = 1$ than at $T = 0$. This seems to be a sensible measure of catch-up. By this measure country $f$ falls further behind in cases 3 and 4 and falls further behind in solution $B$ for all cases.

These very limited results thus suggest that catching up is more likely to occur at strong scale economies (low values of $\beta$).

One interesting aspect of the catch-up question in that an important component of it is a strong terms-of-trade effect in which the price of $X$ falls significantly in the second period, as we can see by comparing $p_0$ and $p_1$ in these table. It is not of course possible to separate the terms-of-trade effect from the dynamic scale economies effect because the former is simply the general equilibrium consequence of the great productivity increase afforded by the latter. Nevertheless, the terms-of-trade effect is of conceptual importance, especially in understanding (1) why $f$ may catch up measured in income while falling behind measured in specialized inputs, and (2) why the degree to which $f$ falls further behind in solution $B$ is not much worse than it is. Country $f$ catches up or falls less further behind due to the strong appreciation in its terms of trade at $T = 1$.

There is an important limitation to using production income measures, which relates to comparing the income of a single country across the different equilibria. We are interested in such comparisons in order to assess the discrete difference to $f$ and $h$ of reaching solution $A$ versus $B$. $p_1$ is significantly different in solutions $A$, $B$, and $C$ as is clear from the tables. With $p_1$ at solution $A$ less than $p_1$ at $B$, country $f$ will gain more at $A$ over $B$ when income is measured in $X$ than in $Y$. Conversely, country $h$ will lose less at $A$ versus $B$ when income is measured in terms of $X$ than in $Y$. At bottom of the tables I have therefore presented income ratios both in terms of $X$ and $Y$. For example, $(I_{1a}^{f}/I_{1b}^{f})_x$ is the ratio of $f$'s second-period income in solution $A$ to solution $B$ measured in terms of $X$.

Case 1 involves the largest difference between solution $A$ and solution $B$ for country $f$, with the former increasing output by 26% in terms of $X$ (5% in terms of $Y$) over its value in the blockaded case. The smallest such difference for country $f$ is in case 4, where solution $A$ increases the value of production by only 3.5% in terms of $X$ (0.2% in terms of $Y$) over solution $B$. These discrete changes resulting from an infinitesimal parameter change are due to the nonconvex technology (if firms in $f$ enter, they enter in large numbers), and to the fact that the social marginal cost of an additional input is less than the private marginal cost, the ratio of the two being given by $\beta$ (Markusen 1988, 1989, 1990).

Recall also in this context that country $f$ can get stuck at the $n_1 = 0$ solution due to the lack of coordination among firms. Case 1 then gives a situation where the gains from a policy that kicks the economy over to the other equilibrium results in a significant welfare gain. I should emphasize again in this connection that these welfare gains for country $f$ in solution $A$ over solution $B$ are in a sense minimum, in that they are calculated for cases in which the $A$ equilibrium marginally exists.

As a final point, the results for the home country presented in tables 12.1 through 12.4 are also worth examining. They indicate that the home country makes significant welfare gains from being able to prevent entry by the foreign country in the first period, with additional gains from being able to prevent second-period entry as well. In cases 3 and 4 (the low scale economies cases), the additional gains from preventing second-period entry are very small relative to the gains from preventing first-period entry.

## 12.4  Summary and Conclusions

This chapter has considered the consequences of first-mover advantage in a trade model with dynamic scale economies. The model follows Ethier (1982) in that one (traded) final good is assembled from specialized inter-mediate inputs. There are increasing returns to the number of specialized inputs (the division of labor), but fixed costs limit the number of such inputs. The fixed costs need only be incurred in the initial period of entry, corresponding to the notion of nondepreciating knowledge capital. The fact that the specialized inputs are complementary in production means that the country that enters in the first period inherits a productivity advantage at the beginning of the second period. The disadvantaged coun-try either may not be able to enter the increasing-returns sector at the beginning of the second period or may enter but fall further behind.

The chapter focused on situations in which the late entrant (the foreign country) is marginally able to enter in the sense that small parameter changes flip the solution from one equilibrium to the other. Parameter regimes that support one equilibrium or the other were analyzed theoreti-cally and numerically. Numerical analysis permits us to quantify the effects of blockaded entry on both countries. For the parameters chosen, the welfare costs of being blockaded in the first period are large, with the costs of being blockaded in the second period being smaller. Of course the latter result is partly due to the focus on cases where second-period entry is only marginally possible. Even so, one case was found (case 1) in which the ability to enter in the second period increases the value of second-period production by 26% to 5% (depending on choice of numéraire) over its value when no entry occurred. This discrete difference due to a small parameter change is due to the nonconvex technology (if entry occurs, it occurs with a large number of firms) and to the fact that the social marginal productivity of an additional input is greater than its private marginal productivity.

The first entrant (the home country) clearly benefits from the fact that the foreign country is blockaded in the first period and receives a much smaller additional benefit if the latter is blockaded in the second period as well. There are two effects at work. First, if both countries enter at $T = 0$, there is no trade and no gains from trade. Second, the first entrant produces more of the increasing-returns good when the foreign country is blockaded, and this is a good in which the (social) marginal cost of an additional unit is less than its price, so expansion in its production generates an additional welfare gain of price minus marginal cost times the change in output. We also noted that the gains to country $h$ and the losses to country $f$ from blockaded entry are in large part offset by a large deterioration in the home country's terms of trade in the second period.

The model can serve as a simple model of uneven development. Using this simple framework, we are not forced into the constraints of steady states and constant growth rates and, indeed a principal contribution of the chapter is to show how growth rates may diverge due to some arbitrary accident of history. In addition the results suggest further normative and policy work that is beyond the scope of this chapter. Almost all of the trade/industrial organization literature has focused on marginal price/output effects in discussing strategic trade policy (Horstmann and Markusen 1991 is an exception). This chapter focuses on the discrete question of entry versus no entry. In our marginal cases 1 through 4, for example, the foreign country can possibly get a large benefit from a very small subsidy that shifts the equilibrium from solution $B$ (no entry) to solution $A$ (second-period entry). Conversely, the home country can potentially get a very large welfare benefit from a very small subsidy that blockades the foreign country from entering in one or both periods.

### References

Ethier, Wilfred. 1982. National and international returns to scale in the modern theory of international trade. *American Economic Review* 72: 389–405.

Grossman, Gene M., and Elhanan Helpman. 1988. Comparative advantage and long-run growth. Working paper 2809. NBER.

Grossman, Gene M., and Elhanan Helpman. 1989. Endogenous product cycles. Working paper 2913. NBER.

Helpman, Elhanan, and Paul R. Krugman. 1985. *Market Structure and Foreign Trade: Increasing Returns, Imperfect Markets, and the International Trade.* Cambridge: MIT Press.

Horstmann, Ignatius, and James R. Markusen. 1991. Endogenous market structures in the theory of international trade. *Journal of International Economics,* forthcoming.

Krugman, Paul R. 1981. Trade, accumulation, and uneven development. *Journal of Development Economics* 8: 149–161.

Krugman, Paul R. 1989. History versus expectations. Working paper.

Lucas, Robert E., Jr. 1988. On the mechanics of economic development. *Journal of Monetary Economics* 22: 3–42.

Markusen, James R. 1988. Production, trade, and migration with differentiated, skilled workers. *Canadian Journal of Economics* 21: 492–506.

Markusen, James R. 1989. Trade in producer services and in other specialized intermediate inputs. *American Economic Review* 79: 85–95.

Markusen, James R. 1990. Derationalizing tariffs with specialized intermediate inputs and differentiated final goods. *Journal of International Economics* 28: 375–383.

Markusen, James R., and Randall Wigle. 1989. Nash equilibrium tariffs for the U.S. and Canada: The roles of country size, scale economies, and capital mobility. *Journal of Political Economy* 97: 368–386.

Murphy, Kevin M., Andrei Shleifer, and Robert Vishny. 1987. The big push stage of industrial development. Working paper.

Nobohiro, Kiyotaki. 1988. Multiple expectational equilibria under monopolistic competition. *Quarterly Journal of Economics* 103: 695–714.

Romer, Paul M. 1987. Growth based on increasing returns due to specialization. *American Economic Review* 77: 56–62.

# 13 Wage Sensitivity Rankings and Temporal Convergence

## Ronald W. Jones and Peter Neary

Attempts by governments and private groups to influence the distribution of income often introduce distortions into factor markets. In appraising these attempts, a distinction must be drawn between the immediate short-term consequences of such policies and longer-term effects that incorporate the induced relocation of productive factors. These factor reallocations over time may serve dramatically to frustrate the intended objectives of such policies.

This contrast between the short-run and long-run effects of labor market interventions has been noted in a number of different models. The transition from short- to long-run equilibrium has been studied in the context of wage policies following a devaluation by Jones and Corden (1976), of proportional factor-price differentials by Neary (1978), and of the Harris-Todaro model of unemployment in developing countries by Neary (1981). Without explicitly considering the adjustment process, the possibility that a diversified long-run equilibrium may not exist or may not be approached has been noted in the minimum-wage context, whether economywide as in Brecher (1974) or sector specific as in McCulloch (1974) and Carruth and Oswald (1982). However, the general principles that underlie these different results have so far defied elucidation.

In this chapter we introduce a new concept—the wage sensitivity ranking of two sectors—that serves to synthesise these and other existing results and to suggest many new ones. We define a sector as *wage sensitive* if the short-run return to capital there is more vulnerable to a tightening of labor market pressures than that in the other sector. In the absence of labor market distortions, the wage-sensitive sector is necessarily the labor-intensive one. A major finding of our chapter is that problems of convergence to long-run equilibrium are likely to arise when the rankings of sectors by these two criteria diverge.

Section 13.1 introduces the model and develops the key result for local stability of equilibrium. The subsequent three sections then examine the global as well as local responses of the economy to the introduction of three alternative labor market distortions: sector-specific or economywide minimum wages in a completely open economy and sector-specific real wage ceilings in a dependent economy producing nontraded as well as traded goods. In all three cases we demonstrate that the wage-sensitivity ranking of the sectors reveals the incentives for medium-run capital reallocation generated by the distortion in question. By contrast, it is the physical factor intensity ranking that determines the implications of such reallocation. Finally, section 13.5 summarizes our results and draws some general lessons for the efficacy of labor market interventions.

## 13.1   Local Stability of the Capital Reallocation Process

In this section we describe the process of adjustment when a disturbance to factor markets from an initial long-run equilibrium position causes returns to sector-specific capitals to differ, thus providing a signal for a subsequent reallocation of capital (and labor) between sectors. Such a re-allocation itself puts pressure on factor prices to change, and the question raised is whether these subsequent alterations serve to restore factor prices to their initial long-run values. If so, the capital reallocation process is locally stable.

The setting is general in the specification of the wage relationships in the two sectors as a consequence of labor market distortions and/or policies built in to guide wage behavior. Think of a free wage rate $w$ typically associated with the wage rate in at least one sector of the economy; this wage rate is sensitive to pressures in the labor market. Then let the wage rate in each sector be linked to the free wage rate:

$$w_1 = f^1(w) \quad \text{and} \quad w_2 = f^2(w). \tag{1}$$

If pressures in the labor market cause the free wage $w$ to change, this change is transmitted to each sector in the form of an elasticity:

$$\hat{w}_1 = \alpha_1 \hat{w} \quad \text{and} \quad \hat{w}_2 = \alpha_2 \hat{w}, \tag{2}$$

where a caret over a variable indicates relative changes ($\hat{x} = dx/x$). Major cases of labor market distortions that have been considered in the literature can be related to these elasticities. Thus a sector-specific minimum wage in sector $j$ implies that $\alpha_j = 0$, with the $\alpha$ in the free sector set equal to unity. A constant *proportional* wage differential, extensively treated in the literature, can be captured by setting each $\alpha_j$ equal to unity. (This of course does not imply that wages are equal in the two sectors, only that their proportional gap is kept constant.) A constant absolute wage differential would imply that $\alpha_1$ equals $1/w_1$ and $\alpha_2$ equals $1/w_2$. We return to these cases later.

The competitive profit equations of change when capital is temporarily tied to each sector, thus allowing rental rates $r_1$ and $r_2$ to differ, are shown in equations (3):

$$\theta_{L1}\hat{w}_1 + \theta_{K1}\hat{r}_1 = \hat{p}_1,$$
$$\theta_{L2}\hat{w}_2 + \theta_{K2}\hat{r}_2 = \hat{p}_2. \tag{3}$$

The $\theta_{ij}$ refer to factor $i$'s distributive share in the $j$th sector. To analyze the local stability of the capital reallocation process, we assume that initially rates of return to capital are equal and that throughout the process commodity prices are kept constant. Making use of the link between wage rates in each sector described in (2), the competitive profit equations of change can be rewritten as

$$\tilde{\theta}_{L1}\hat{w} + \tilde{\theta}_{K1}\hat{r}_1 = 0,$$
$$\tilde{\theta}_{L2}\hat{w} + \tilde{\theta}_{K2}\hat{r}_2 = 0, \tag{4}$$

where $\tilde{\theta}_{Lj}$ is defined as $\alpha_j\theta_{Lj}$ divided by $(\alpha_j\theta_{Lj} + \theta_{Kj})$ and $\tilde{\theta}_{Kj}$ is $\theta_{Kj}$ deflated by this same term. (These deflations allow the sum of the $\tilde{\theta}$'s in each sector to add to unity.) Such a revision of the competitive profit conditions shows how, at given commodity prices, an increase in the free market level of wages is transmitted into a fall in returns to capital in each sector. This restatement encourages a new concept—that of *wage sensitivity*:

DEFINITION    Sector $j$ is relatively *wage sensitive* if and only if at constant commodity prices upward pressure on wages in the labor market squeezes rentals relatively more in sector $j$ than in the other sector.

Given this definition of wage sensitivity, sector 1 is clearly the wage-sensitive sector for a small increase in the wage if the *distributive share* for the free wage in that sector, $\tilde{\theta}_{L1}$, exceeds that in sector 2, $\tilde{\theta}_{L2}$. This may be expressed in terms of the determinant of coefficients in equations (4), $|\tilde{\theta}|$; the fact that the sum of the $\tilde{\theta}$'s in each industry is unity implies that $\tilde{\theta}_{L1}$ exceeds $\tilde{\theta}_{L2}$ if and only if $|\tilde{\theta}|$ is positive. Straightforward calculations of this determinant reveal that sector 1 is the wage-sensitive sector if and only if

$$\alpha_1 w_1 l_1 > \alpha_2 w_2 l_2, \tag{5}$$

where $l_j$ indicates the physical labor–capital ratio employed in sector $j$. In completely undistorted markets this reduces to a comparison of physical labor–capital ratios. The case of proportional wage distortions, with the $\alpha$'s unity, allows sector 1 to be the wage-sensitive sector even if sector 2 is physically labor intensive. This requires of course that labor receive a wage premium in the first sector. In such a case we refer to a reversal of the factor intensity ranking between the *physical* and *value* versions of factor proportions. Sector 1 is labor intensive in a value sense if $|\theta|$, the determinant of distributive factor shares, is positive (or if $w_1 l_1$ exceeds $w_2 l_2$), whereas sector 2 is labor intensive in a physical sense if $l_2$ exceeds $l_1$.

The concept of wage sensitivity applies as well to cases in which distortions and/or policies in labor markets dictate that wage rates intersectorally do not even maintain a proportional relationship to each other. For example, even if sector 1 is physically labor intensive, and even if labor employed in that sector receives a premium, sector 2 is the wage-sensitive sector if sector 1 is bound by minimum wage regulations. Upward pressure on labor markets would not disturb the return to capital in sector 1 but would depress it in wage-sensitive sector 2.

To pursue the question of local stability or convergence of the capital reallocation process, suppose that the free wage rate is dislodged by a small downward movement relative to its long-run equilibrium value. In the short run, before capital can reallocate between sectors, returns to capital are driven up in each sector, but more so in the wage-sensitive sector. Assume that $|\tilde{\theta}| > 0$ so that this is sector 1 and thus $r_1 > r_2$. With factor prices temporarily frozen at these new levels, examine the pressures on factor markets once capital begins to relocate, with the rental discrepancies ensuring that $\hat{K}_1 > \hat{K}_2$.

Two relationships bind the changes in capital employed in each sector. On the one hand, we assume that no new capital is created and that the capital leaving one sector is employed in the other sector. This implies that

$$\lambda_{K1}\hat{K}_1 + \lambda_{K2}\hat{K}_2 = 0, \tag{6}$$

with $\lambda_{ij}$ denoting the fraction of the economy's supply of factor $i$ employed in sector $j$. On the other hand, consider the overall demand for labor, which is made up of the demand in each industry. With factor prices temporarily frozen, the relative change in each sector's demand for labor is tied one for one to its demand for capital (i.e., $\hat{L}_j = \hat{K}_j$). It follows that

$$\lambda_{L1}\hat{K}_1 + \lambda_{L2}\hat{K}_2 = \hat{L}^D, \tag{7}$$

where $L^D$ indicates the economy's total demand for labor. Subtracting (6) from (7),

$$\hat{L}^D = |\lambda|(\hat{K}_1 - \hat{K}_2), \tag{8}$$

where $|\lambda|$ equals $\lambda_{L1} - \lambda_{K1}$ and is positive if and only if sector 1 is the physically labor-intensive sector. If so, the flow of capital toward physically labor-intensive sector 1 must put upward pressure on wages in the labor market. The capital reallocation process would in this case tend to restore the wage rate to its long-run equilibrium value as well as to restore the equality in returns to capital. Thus we have proved the following:

THEOREM   The capital reallocation process is locally stable if and only if the physically labor-intensive sector is the wage-sensitive sector. That is, stability requires that $|\lambda||\tilde{\theta}|$ be positive.

The wage sensitivity ranking indicated by $|\tilde{\theta}|$ shows which rental is driven up relatively more when the free wage falls. This provides the signal for the direction of capital (and labor) reallocation. The physical factor intensity ranking, indicated by the sign of $|\lambda|$, reveals the consequence of such a reallocation for aggregate labor demand and thus the direction of subsequent changes in wage rates and rentals. Stability requires $|\tilde{\theta}|$ and $|\lambda|$ to have the same sign.[1]

To see the usefulness of this result, consider its implications for three particular forms of labor market distortion:

1. *Proportional wage differentials.* This form of distortion, which implies that $\alpha_1$ and $\alpha_2$ are both unity, has been extensively studied in writings on tax incidence, stemming from Harberger (1962), on the effects of unionization by Johnson and Mieszkowski (1970) and on international trade issues (e.g., see Jones 1971 and Magee 1973, 1976). In this special case the ranking of sectors by wage sensitivity reduces to the value factor intensity ranking provided by $|\theta|$, the determinants of the coefficient matrix in (3). Hence we have the result of Neary (1978) that a necessary and sufficient condition for local stability of an equilibrium is that the determinants $|\lambda|$ and $|\theta|$ have the same sign; in other words, that the rankings of the two sectors by physical and value factor intensities coincide. More generally, we should not expect the sign of $|\theta|$, which measures the relative importance of wages in each sector in an average sense, to play any role in the adjustment process. It matters only with proportional (or zero) wage differentials when it coincides with the sign of $|\tilde{\theta}|$, which measures the relative vulnerability of each sector to wage changes at the margin.

2. *Absolute wage differentials.* The case of a specific rather than an ad

valorem wage differential has not been studied extensively in the literature, with the exceptions of Dixit and Norman (1980, ch. 5) and Schweinberger (1979). This is ironic since it turns out always to be consistent with stability and thus to be much simpler than any of the other forms of labor market distortions that have been considered. Recall that when $w_1$ equals $w_2$ plus a constant, $\alpha_j$ equals $1/w_j$. Substitution into (5) reveals that the measure of relative wage sensitivities, $|\tilde{\theta}|$, has the same sign as $|\lambda|$. It therefore follows from the proposition that an equilibrium with this form of labor market distortion is always locally stable.

3. *Sector-specific minimum wages.* In this case the wages in the two sectors are not directly related at all. As previously noted, if one sector is bound by a minimum wage, the other sector must be the wage-sensitive sector. Thus, as the relevant corollary of the theorem, a necessary and sufficient condition for local stability is that the minimum-wage sector must be capital-intensive in physical terms. For example, if the minimum wage is imposed in sector 1, $|\tilde{\theta}|$ is negative and, for stability of the capital reallocation process, $|\lambda|$ must be negative as well.

This concludes our consideration of the issue of local stability. A different issue of considerable import ance concerns the price-output responsiveness of the economy in the presence of a general labor market distortion of the form of (1). By manipulating the equations of the two-sector model in the manner developed in Jones (1965, 1971), it is straightforward to show that output response with respect to own price in either sector is positive if and only if the wage-sensitive sector is physically labor intensive.[2] Hence, as in Neary (1978), local stability of equilibrium implies a normal price-output response whatever form the labor market distortion takes.

## 13.2  Sector-Specific Minimum Wages

We turn next to examine in more detail the global as well as local implications of particular special cases of the general wage distortion shown by equation (1). The first case we consider is where a minimum wage is imposed in only one of the two sectors.[3] This does not lead to unemployment. Instead, the wage in the undistorted sector adjusts to equate that sector's demand for labor with the residual supply.

Suppose first that the minimum wage is imposed in the relatively capital-intensive sector. The economy's response is shown in figure 13.1, which

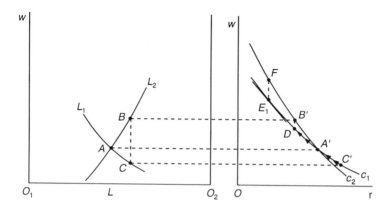

**Figure 13.1**
Effects of a minimum wage in the capital-intensive sector

combines the standard labor market diagram in the left-hand panel with
the unit cost curve diagram in the right-hand panel.[4] Initial equilibrium in
the absence of any minimum wage distortion is represented by points $A$
and $A'$. We assume that sector 1 is relatively labor intensive, so the $c_1$ curve
is flatter at $A'$ than the $c_2$ curve. Suppose now that a minimum wage that
is not too far above the competitive level is imposed in sector 2. In the short
run employment in that sector is reduced as its production point moves to
$B$ and the laid-off workers are rehired in sector 1 at a wage rate lower than
the initial equilibrium level, as shown by point $C$. With one sector paying
a higher wage and the other a lower one, a rental differential must have
emerged in favor of sector 1, and this is shown by the points $B'$ and $C'$ in
the right-hand panel. Capital therefore begins to leave the high-wage sector
2. As it does so, the expansion of the relatively labor-intensive sector 1 leads
to a tightening of the labor market. Only the wage in sector 1 is free to
adjust, and so it rises during the adjustment process, reducing the intersectoral rental differential and so tending to restore the capital market to
equilibrium. The adjustment process is shown by the arrows in the right-
hand panel of figure 13.1 and ends when sector 1 reaches point $D$. Note
that the wage in that sector initially overshoots its new long-run equilibrium
level, and note also that there is no obstacle preventing stable convergence
toward a new long-run equilibrium at which both goods are produced.
    The only difficulty that may emerge when a minimum wage is imposed
in the relatively capital-intensive sector is when the wage is sufficiently high

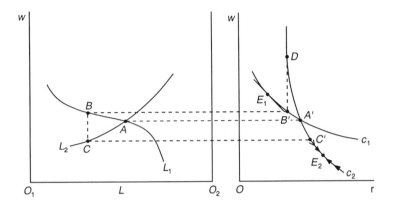

**Figure 13.2**
Effects of a minimum wage in the labor-intensive sector

to force that sector to cease production. In figure 13.1 this occurs if the wage is at or above the level indicated by the point $F$. This point lies vertically above $E_1$, which we assume is the point on sector 1's unit cost curve where the capital–labor ratio in that sector equals the endowment ratio in the economy as a whole. If the minimum wage is set above point $F$, the short-run response of outputs and rentals to the imposition of the minimum wage will be as already indicated, and the resulting capital reallocation moves the economy closer to capital market equilibrium. However, before that can be attained, sector 1 absorbs all the factors of production in the economy and so specialisation in production takes place, with factor returns denoted by point $E_1$.

A very different outcome ensues when the minimum wage is imposed in the relatively labor-intensive sector.[5] As shown by points $B$ and $C$ in figure 13.2, the labor-intensive sector 1 contracts in the short run, and the residual labor is rehired by sector 2 at a wage below the initial equilibrium level. At the corresponding points $B'$ and $C'$ in the right-hand panel, the rental differential is again in the expected direction, and it encourages a reallocation of capital out of the high wage sector 1 into sector 2. In this case, however, by contrast with the last, the expanding sector is physically capital intensive, which tends to reduce the demand for labor in the economy as a whole. As a result the only wage rate that is free to adjust, that in sector 2, falls during the adjustment process. But this tends to raise the rental in that sector and so to *widen* the intersectoral rental differential. As shown by the arrows in figure 13.2, this process continues until point $E_2$ is reached; sector 2 has now absorbed all the economy's factor endowment and production of good 1 has ceased.

This outcome illustrates the result of section 13.1—that an equilibrium with a minimum wage imposed in the relatively labor-intensive sector is necessarily unstable and so will not be approached; the minimum wage has made the labor-intensive sector completely wage insensitive. However, an even more striking feature of this case may be noted from figure 13.2: The only long-run outcome consistent with capital market equilibrium and with sector 1 paying the new minimum wage is represented by points $D$ and $B'$. But this is not a feasible outcome in the labor market since there exists no barrier to an increase in the wage in sector 1 or a decrease in the wage in sector 2.

Crucial in the analysis thus far is the comparison between physical factor intensity and wage sensitivity rankings. However, the physical factor intensity ranking itself is not independent of the minimum wage. In figure 13.2 a minimum wage at or above the level indicated by the point $E_1$ (where the slope of $c_1$ at point $E_1$ indicates the economy's endowment proportions) reverses the physical factor intensity ranking of the two sectors. In the short run the capital–labor ratio in sector 1 exceeds that in the economy as a whole, and since both factors are fully employed throughout, the capital–labor ratio in the other sector must be below the endowment ratio. The minimum wage (and thus wage-insensitive) sector has now become capital intensive, but this does not mean that an unspecialized equilibrium can be attained. In the short-run equilibrium sector 2 lies below point $E_2$ on its unit cost curve, and as capital flows into it over time, the wage rate there rises. The rental differential is therefore narrowed by the reallocation, but before it is eliminated sector 2 absorbs all the economy's endowment and sector 1 is eliminated. Thus the only difference that a physical factor intensity reversal makes in this case is that the new long-run equilibrium $E_2$ is approached from below rather than from above, as the arrows in figure 13.2 indicate.

## 13.3   Sector-Specific Real Wage Ceilings

The cases discussed above have involved distortions that yield intersectoral differentials in nominal wages in economies where all commodities are traded at fixed world prices. We turn now to a case of government interference in factor markets in which the nominal wages in the two sectors of the economy are kept fixed and equal to each other but with one of the commodities nontraded. As a consequence the real wage in one sector is flexible, making the concept of wage sensitivity and its relationship with that of physical labor intensity again useful in exploring the transition from a short-run equilibrium as capital becomes intersectorally mobile.

Suppose that the government responds to a rise in price in the traded goods sector $(p_T)$ by taxation and expenditure policy whose aim is to affect the price of goods in the nontraded sector $(p_N)$ in whatever manner required to keep the (uniform) wage rate from rising. In an analysis by Jones and Corden (1976) of various policies designed to accompany exchange rate changes for a small open economy, the rise in the price of tradables was identified with a devaluation of the currency. Here we dispense with the interpretation in terms of exchange markets and consider only an exogenous rise in the price of tradables. The government is assumed to interfere in the private market with tax or spending policies in order to determine the price of nontradables. As opposed to our treatment in the next section of an economywide minimum wage that produces unemployment, in our present scenario the wage rate clears the labor market.

A simpler type of government policy examined by Jones and Corden— one that stabilizes the price of nontradables instead of the wage rate in the face of a given rise in the price of tradables—provides a useful background to our analysis. With such a policy the transition from short- to long-run equilibrium is stable regardless of factor intensity rankings. To see why, note that with no wage distortions the rankings of industries by wage sensitivity and by labor intensity coincide. In the short-run equilibrium in which capital is specific to each sector, a policy of pegging the price of nontradables when $p_T$ rises causes the wage rate to rise and the return to capital in nontradables $(r_N)$ to fall. The rental in tradables $(r_T)$ has of course gone up by more than the price of tradables so that the signal clearly implies a reallocation of capital (and labor) toward tradables. If tradables are labor intensive, the extra demand for labor which is thus created exerts upward pressure on wages and, at constant commodity prices, squeezes rentals in both sectors. The rental is driven down by more in the wage-sensitive tradables sector. Thus both rentals eventually fall toward each other, and the wage rate approaches its long-run equilibrium value (with $\hat{w} > \hat{p}_T > \hat{p}_N = 0 > \hat{r}$).[6]

The difficulty emerges if the government targets the nominal wage rate instead of the price of nontradables. In the case in which tradables are labor intensive, such a ceiling on wages in effect converts the capital-intensive nontradable good into the wage-sensitive commodity, and during the capital reallocation process the policy drives the return to capital in nontradables ever downward and further from the return to capital in tradables. As before, the initial rise in $p_T$ puts upward pressure on the labor market, and the authorities now are presumed to counter this by an appropriate tax policy that causes the price of nontradables to fall sufficiently to keep a lid on wage rates. During the adjustment process as capital (and labor) flow from nontradables toward labor-intensive tradables, upward pressure is created in the labor market. To avoid a wage increase, the government now must drive down the price of nontradables so that the labor market clears at the initial wage. Such a fall in $p_N$ drives down $r_N$ (just as did the alternative policy of allowing an increase in the wage rate). But $r_T$ is now insulated. The upward pressure in the labor market has been syphoned off completely by the policy-prescribed fall in $p_N$ that serves to keep a ceiling on wage rates. Since the capital-intensive nontradables sector is now the wage-sensitive sector, the upward pressure in the labor market has pushed $r_N$ down by relatively more than (unchanged) $r_T$.[7] This scenario reveals that certain policies that interfere with factor markets are inappropriate because they run afoul of the adjustment process whereby capital and labor reallocations exert pressure on factor markets.

The setting described in this section is closely analogous to the case considered in the preceding section in which a minimum wage is imposed in the labor-intensive sector. In that analysis the labor market is cleared by a fall in the real wage faced by employers in the capital-intensive sector—such a fall taking the form of a lowering of the wage rate in that sector with commodity prices fixed. In the present setting the excess demand created in the labor market when the price of tradables rises is eliminated by an increase in the real wage faced by employers in the capital-intensive nontradables sector—but with such an increase taking the form of a lowering of the commodity price for nontradables with the nominal wage fixed. In each case the rates of return to capital are driven further apart during the capital reallocation process; the policy (minimum wage imposed in the labor-intensive sector or an imposed overall wage ceiling supported by continued falls in the price of the capital-intensive good) serves to convert the physically labor-intensive sector into the wage-insensitive sector.

## 13.4   An Economywide Minimum Wage

The final case we consider—an economywide minimum wage set above the free-market level—shares with the preceding section a setting in which nominal wage rates are uniform throughout the economy, and policy is directed toward targeting the level of wages. It differs, however, in that both commodities are traded so that no flexibility is allowed in factor returns. As a consequence the labor market does not clear.[8] In analyzing this case, we focus on the difference that may be made by the level at which the minimum wage is imposed. Once again, a variation on the interplay between wage sensitivity rankings and physical labor intensity rankings proves crucial in highlighting the effects of the capital reallocation process from a position of short-run equilibrium.

The situation in this two-sector, price-taking economy is pictured in figure 13.3. We assume that the economy starts in competitive full employment equilibrium, as indicated by point $A$, with sector 1 relatively labor intensive (as shown by the fact that its unit cost curve is less steeply sloped than that of sector 2 at $A$). The response to the imposition of a minimum wage that is not "too far" above the competitive level is now easily illustrated. Assuming that the wage rises to a level denoted by a point such as $D$, the rentals in both sectors are squeezed in the short run. However, that in sector 1 falls by more: Since the first sector is relatively wage sensitive, its rental is more vulnerable to a wage increase. With capital sector-specific in the short run, both goods are still being produced in this economy, but now an incentive has emerged to reallocate capital out of sector 1 into sector 2. The striking feature of the economywide minimum wage case is that this reallocation of itself does not alter the rentals in either sector.[9] They continue to encourage a reallocation of capital out of sector 1, and this process can end only when that sector loses all capital and ceases production.

The same sequence of events is illustrated from the perspective of the goods markets in figure 13.4. Initial equilibrium is at point $A'$, where the world price line is tangential to the full employment production possibilities frontier $TT$, along which capital is mobile between sectors. In the short run,

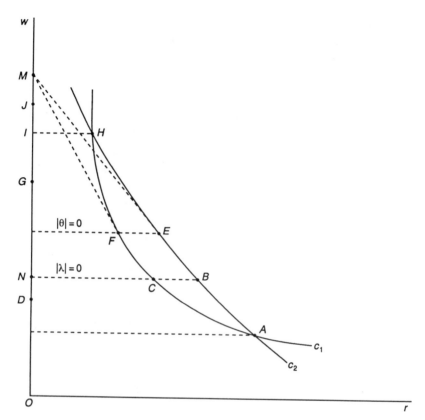

**Figure 13.3**
Factor price effects of an economywide minimum wage

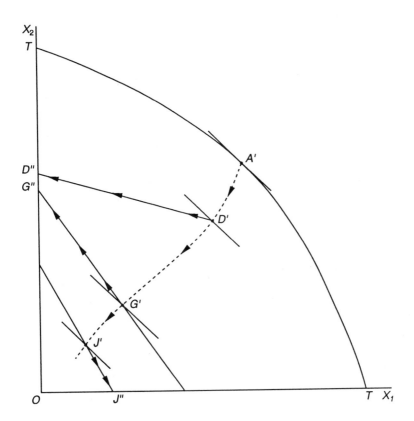

**Figure 13.4**
Output effects of an economywide minimum wage

with capital fixed in each sector, the minimum wage creates unemployment and reduces the output of both goods as production moves to point $D'$. The subsequent capital reallocation then moves the production point along the Rybczynski line $D'D''$ until the economy specializes in the production of good 2 at point $D''$. Note that the output of the capital-intensive good $X_2$ overshoots its new long-run equilibrium value during the adjustment period, first falling from point $A'$ to $D'$ and then rising to the level indicated by point $D''$, which may lie above or below the initial level at $A'$. By contrast, the level of unemployment rises monotonically, initially because both sectors shed labor when required to pay a higher wage and, during the transition period, because the expansion of the relatively capital-intensive sector cannot absorb all the labor laid off by the declining labor-intensive sector.

It is intuitively plausible that the introduction of a minimum wage should drive the labor-intensive sector out of existence, and this outcome is implied by the discussion in Brecher (1974). However, figure 13.3 has deliberately been drawn to show that this outcome is by no means inevitable. Sector 1 has a higher elasticity of substitution between labor and capital than sector 2. Thus, although an increase in the wage rate induces both sectors to become more capital intensive, this effect is more pronounced in sector 1. As a result a sufficiently high minimum wage may lead to a physical factor intensity reversal: In figure 13.3 the critical wage rate is that which leads the two sectors to points $B$ and $C$, where their capital–labor ratios are equal to each other.[10] If, from the initial equilibrium at $A$, a minimum wage is imposed at a higher level, say, that represented by point $G$, then the incentive to reallocate capital is the same as before, and sector 1 will eventually be eliminated. However, that sector has now become relatively capital intensive, so its decline leads to a fall in unemployment during the transition period. This corresponds to the move from $G'$ to $G''$ in figure 13.4.

If the minimum wage is set above the level $OI$ at a point such as $J$, the path of adjustment is significantly altered. The rental differential now favors sector 1, so capital leaves sector 2 until that sector ceases production. In this case the economy again specializes in the production of the relatively capital-intensive good, and unemployment rises during the adjustment process. The adjustment path is shown by the line $J'J''$ in figure 13.4.

In conclusion, note that the concept of wage sensitivity and its potential lack of correspondence with physical labor intensity can be applied to the cases we have just described. However, a global interpretation of wage sensitivity rankings is required. The definition given in section 13.1 continues to apply, but now the wage-sensitive sector is the sector whose rental is squeezed more by the imposition of the minimum wage rather than by a small change in wages. Figure 13.3, which incorporates the reversal of the physical labor intensity ranking (at $N$), also shows the possibility of a reversal of the wage sensitivity ranking, but at a different minimum wage rate (at $I$). If these two rankings coincide, unemployment rises during the capital reallocation process; otherwise (for minimum wages set between $ON$ and $OI$), unemployment falls.

## 13.5   Concluding Remarks

Disturbances in labor markets have differential effects on the returns to cooperating capital. In international trade models a physical factor intensity ranking between sectors serves to indicate these differences when factor markets are undistorted. However, the existence of policies aimed at affecting wage rates in one or both sectors may introduce distortions that require a new concept—that of a wage sensitivity ranking—to indicate the sector in which capital's return is more severely depressed by upward pressure in the labor market. This concept allows not only for a premium to be paid to workers in one sector but also for differences in the allowable response of wages in each sector to disturbances in the labor market. For given commodity prices excess supply in the labor market would benefit capital especially in the wage-sensitive sector of the economy. Thus a wage sensitivity ranking indicates the direction in which capital gets reallocated during the transition period, and the physical labor intensity ranking reveals the consequences of such reallocations on excess demand or supply of labor. Our basic result is that the transition from short-run equilibrium converges to the corresponding long-run equilibrium only if these two rankings correspond.

In this chapter we have considered a variety of labor market distortions, ranging from proportional or absolute wage differentials between sectors to sector-specific minimum wages and to policies aimed at preventing the real wage in some sector from rising. In all of these cases the wage rate in at least one sector is free to vary, thus guaranteeing full employment. In section 13.4 we considered an economy facing given world prices and imposing a uniform minimum wage that precluded an adjustment of factor

prices during the transition period. The concept of wage sensitivity nonetheless proved of value—this time to indicate that the unemployment
created by the minimum wage was rendered more acute by the capital
reallocation during the transition phase if the wage sensitivity ranking of
sectors corresponded to that of labor intensity.

That the intention of a policy designed to improve the welfare of certain
groups can be thwarted by the resulting transitional reallocations is well
illustrated by the case of a sector-specific minimum wage. If the sector in
which this wage floor is imposed is capital intensive, the policy succeeds
not only in raising the wages of those in the target sector but also wages
in the other sector (although not by as much). By contrast, if the minimum-
wage sector is labor intensive, workers there may benefit in the short run
but not in the long run. Once capital gets reallocated, this sector gets wiped
out, and the wage rate in the other sector falls below its initial level. The
intentions behind such a policy are completely frustrated by the transitional
capital reallocations in this case because the wage-sensitive sector (which
cannot be the minimum-wage sector) is capital intensive.

## Notes

Jones wishes to thank the National Science Foundation for research support in Grant
#SES-8510697.

1. Formally, the expression linking the change in the ratio of returns to capital and the capital
stocks is shown by

$$\hat{r}_1 - \hat{r}_2 = -\frac{|\lambda||\tilde{\theta}|}{\Delta \theta_{K1} \theta_{K2}}(\hat{K}_1 - \hat{K}_2),$$

where $\Delta$, the aggregate economywide elasticity of demand for labor (as of fixed capital stocks)
with respect to the free wage rate, is

$$\Delta \equiv \alpha_1 \lambda_{L1} \frac{\sigma_1}{\theta_{K1}} + \alpha_2 \lambda_{L2} \frac{\sigma_2}{\theta_{K2}}.$$

In this expression $\sigma_j$ is the elasticity of substitution in sector $j$, and therefore $(\sigma_j/\theta_{Kj})$ is the
elasticity of demand for labor in sector $j$ with respect to the wage rate in that sector. The term
$\alpha_j$ links sector $j$'s wage rate to the free wage.

2. The formal solution for the change in relative outputs when $p_1$ rises and $p_2$ is constant is
shown by

$$|\lambda||\tilde{\theta}|(\hat{X}_1 - \hat{X}_2) = \phi_1 \phi_2 [(\alpha_1 \theta_{K2} + \alpha_2 \theta_{L2})\delta_1 + \alpha_2 \delta_2]\hat{p}_1,$$

where $\phi_j = (\theta_{Lj}\alpha_j + \theta_{Kj})^{-1}$ and $\delta_j = (\theta_{Lj}\lambda_{Kj} + \theta_{Kj}\lambda_{Lj})\sigma_j$, the elasticity of aggregate demand for
capital relative to labor with respect to the wage–rental ratio in sector $j$. Except for the
presence of some additional terms in $\alpha_1$ and $\alpha_2$, the coefficient of $\hat{p}_1$ is identical to that in the
absence of labor market distortions; in any case it is clearly positive.

3. Previous studies of this case include Johnson (1969) and McCulloch (1974). The literature on urban unemployment in developing countries is also relevant; see Harris and Todaro (1970), Corden and Findlay (1975), Khan (1980), and Neary (1981). Although unemployment emerges as an equilibrium phenomenon in these models, they are best understood as applications of the sector-specific minimum wage model. With a minimum wage in manufacturing (so that it is the wage-insensitive sector) stability requires the urban sector to be capital intensive (as indicated by the ratio of its capital stock to the manufacturing work force plus the urban unemployed).

4. This diagrammatic technique was used by Jones and Neary (1984).

5. Some of the difficulties which emerge in this case have been noted by McCulloch (1974) and Carruth and Oswald (1982).

6. The case in which tradables are capital intensive is also stable, with the long-run equilibrium such that $\hat{r} > \hat{p}_T > \hat{p}_N = 0 > \hat{w}$.

7. Jones and Corden (1976) point out that a policy of devaluation when tradables are labor intensive and the wage rate is fixed is associated with a long-run equilibrium in which rates of return to capital are equated at a higher level than originally and in which the price of nontradables rises by relatively more than the initiating rise in tradables. Thus in the long run $\hat{r} > \hat{p}_N > \hat{p}_T > \hat{w} = 0$. Such a devaluation is unsuccessful in two different senses: Since tradables are relatively cheaper, at the new long-run equilibrium the nominal devaluation represents a real appreciation and the adjustment process from the initial short-run equilibrium drives the economy ever further from the long-run equilibrium.

8. Previous treatments of this case include Haberler (1950), Johnson (1969), Lefeber (1971), and Brecher (1974).

9. In this respect an economywide minimum wage has the same effects as the availability of internationally mobile capital at a given world rental, as pointed out by Neary (1985).

10. We have also indicated in figure 13.3 that the value factor intensity ranking gets reversed at a wage rate higher than that required to reverse physical factor intensities. The critical value of the wage rate at which the value shares in the two sectors are equalized is shown in figure 13.3 by the points $E$ and $F$, since tangents from the two unit cost curves at these points intersect the vertical axis at the same point $M$. (See Jones and Neary 1979 and Mussa 1979 for details of this geometric construction.) However, it should be stressed that this reversal has no substantive implications for the behavior of the model.

## References

Brecher, R. A. 1974. Minimum wage rates and the pure theory of international trade. *Quarterly Journal of Economics* 88: 98–116.

Carruth, A. A., and A. J. Oswald. 1982. The determination of union and non-union wages. *European Economic Review* 16: 285–302.

Corden, W. M., and R. Findlay. 1975. Urban unemployment, intersectoral capital mobility and development policy. *Economica* 42: 59–78.

Dixit, A. K., and V. Norman. 1980. *Theory of International Trade: A Dual General Equilibrium Approach*. Cambridge: Cambridge University Press.

Haberler, G. 1950. Some problems in the pure theory of international trade. *Economic Journal* 60: 223–240.

Harberger, A. C. 1962. The incidence of the corporation income tax. *Journal of Political Economy* 70: 215–240.

Harris, J. R., and M. P. Todaro. 1970. Migration, unemployment and development: A two-sector analysis. *American Economic Review* 60: 126–142.

Johnson, H. G. 1969. Minimum wage laws: A general equilibrium analysis. *Canadian Journal of Economics* 2: 599–604.

Johnson, H. G., and P. M., Mieszkowski. 1970. The effects of unionization on the distribution of income: A general equilibrium approach. *Quarterly Journal of Economics* 84: 539–561.

Jones, R. W. 1965. The structure of simple general equilibrium models. *Journal of Political Economy* 73: 557–572.

Jones, R. W. 1971. Distortions in factor markets and the general equilibrium model of production. *Journal of Political Economy* 79: 437–459.

Jones, R. W., and W. M. Corden. 1976. Devaluation, non-flexible prices, and the trade balance for a small country. *Canadian Journal of Economics* 9: 150–161.

Jones, R. W., and J. P. Neary. 1979. Temporal convergence and factor intensities. *Economics Letters* 3: 311–314.

Jones, R. W., and J. P. Neary. 1984. The positive theory of international trade. In R. W. Jones and P. B. Kenen (eds.), *Handbook of International Economics*, vol. 1. Amsterdam: North Holland, pp. 1–62.

Khan, M. A. 1980. The Harris-Todaro hypothesis and the Heckscher-Ohlin-Samuelson trade model: A synthesis. *Journal of International Economics* 10: 527–548.

Lefeber, L. 1971. Trade and minimum wage rates. In J. N. Bhagwati, R. W. Jones, R. A. Mundell, and J. Vanek (eds.), *Trade, Balance of Payments and Growth: Essays in Honour of C. P. Kindleberger*. Amsterdam: North Holland, pp. 91–114.

Magee, S. P. 1973. Factor market distortions, production and trade: A survey. *Oxford Economic Papers* 25: 1–43.

Magee, S. P. 1976. *International Trade and Distortions in Factor Markets*. New York: Marcel Dekker.

McCulloch, J. H. 1974. The effect of a minimum wage law in the labour-intensive sector. *Canadian Journal of Economics* 7: 316–319.

Mussa, M. 1979. The two-sector model in terms of its dual: A geometric exposition. *Journal of International Economics* 9: 513–526.

Neary, J. P. 1978. Dynamic stability and the theory of factor-market distortions. *American Economic Review* 68: 671–683.

Neary, J. P. 1981. On the Harris-Todaro model with intersectoral capital mobility. *Economica* 48: 219–234.

Neary, J. P. 1985. International factor mobility, minimum wage rates and factor price equalization: A synthesis. *Quarterly Journal of Economics* 100: 551–570.

Schweinberger, A. G. 1979. The theory of factor price differentials: The case of constant absolute differentials. *Journal of International Economics* 9: 95–115.

# Index